OUT OF NOWHERE

Something intruded into her dream world, something frightening. She jumped back, but not quite fast enough. She was running and screaming even before she felt the pain in her chest, but she didn't slow down to examine her wound.

Her cry awakened Cerberus. The dog barked as he ran, and he ran as if he were racing to catch up to his hateful baying. He announced death, but when he came to her side there was only air at which to snap.

The presence of the dog gave her the courage to stop running and look around. There was nothing to be seen. From around the corner she thought she heard an engine start, and a car drive away, but she couldn't be sure. She was in shock and her chest hurt. She reached for her heart, felt to see if it was broken anew, and came away with blood on her fingers....

MULTIPLE WOUNDS

ALAN RUSSELL

LEISURE BOOKS NEW YORK CITY

This one is for the sibs.
In chronological order from oldest to youngest:
Joan Roxane (aka "J.R."), Bret (who pushed
his way forward thirteen minutes ahead of his
twin sister), and Ronni.

A LEISURE BOOK®

September 2005

Published by

Dorchester Publishing Co., Inc.
200 Madison Avenue
New York, NY 10016

Copyright © 1996 by Alan Russell

ISBN 0-8439-5579-1

Printed in the United States of America.

Visit us on the web at www.dorchesterpub.com.

ACKNOWLEDGMENTS

I would like to thank Sergeant Bill Holmes and all the detectives on San Diego Police Department's Homicide Team IV for allowing me the opportunity to work with them and gain a better understanding of the painstaking work that surrounds homicide investigations, as well as letting me get a feel for their jobs and workplace. SDPD's allowing me to go behind the scenes helped immeasurably with this book.

I would also like to thank Faith Niles, head librarian of the Cardiff by the Sea Library (small, but mighty!), as well as librarian Mary Lou Kammerer, for always cheerfully assisting me in the gathering of all the eclectic materials that eventually go into the making of my novels. My gratitude also to other San Diego city and county librarians who have always been very kind with their time and efforts (and have somehow refrained from asking, "You want what?").

My thanks to Linda Ashmore, who was gracious enough to open up to me about her own struggles with DID, and offered insights to those afflicted with this disorder.

This novel was a "transition" book for me. It was a work that needed my full attention, and I went from writing part time and working a full-time job, to writing full time (otherwise known as "fool-time"). I would like to thank my father, Mark Russell, for his support and encouragement in helping me achieve this lifelong goal. My family (Laura, Luke, and Hart) also deserves credit for putting up with a "stay-at-home dad." Kudos also to my in-laws Ann and Mike, who have always been there to keep the Russell menagerie going.

And thanks to Rainbow, for warming my lap during the year and a half I worked on this book, and warming my heart for the ten years she graced the Russell household. Rainbow was the only good thing to come out of a very terrible situation (her first family was murdered). I cribbed from that tragedy in this book. I miss your purrs, cat.

"What is your name?" Jesus asked.
"My name is legion," he answered,
"for there are many of us."
—Mark 5:9

Do I contradict myself?
Very well then I contradict myself
(I am large, I contain multitudes).
—Walt Whitman

For he that lives more lives than one,
More deaths than one must die.
—Oscar Wilde

One

She thought of Chaos, and the original confusion, and felt as if she were a part of that tumult. Earth and sea and heaven and hell were mixed up, and everything inside of her was a whirligig. The Greek Chorus was screaming in her head, all of them wanting out.

Cube state. She tried to hold on to the phrase. That's how the doctor described her states of flux. Everything was multiplied, squared, cubed, a Picasso painting.

The yellow tape stopped her: POLICE LINE DO NOT CROSS. The words repeated themselves throughout the tape, runes for rumination.

"Gordian Knot," she said, talking over all the vying voices.

What was the oracle telling her? She decided the words on the tape had to be an anagram, but there were so many possibilities.

She looked at the words and deciphered a welcome among the letters. PROCEED IN. She didn't bother with the remaining letters, just slipped under the yellow banner, dragging her bag behind her. As she walked into the

1

gallery, she thought, What if the words are a warning? They could be saying, *Sirens Plot*, or *Cronos Inside*.

Sometimes a cigar is just a smoke, Freud had said. Her analyst had once told her that.

She was at the art gallery because one of the voices had clamored louder than the others, had insisted that she change the statues's clothing, show her respects that way. She avoided the display area, walking down the corridor toward the garden. Not for the first time she wished for blinders to help her when she was like this. She remembered watching a program on insects and being given a bee's-eye view of the world. Bees perceive scores of images and look out into a different universe than humans. In cube state, so did she.

There was a buzzing in her head and a sting in her heart as she entered the garden.

Cheever was thinking about death. That's what homicide detectives do, but in this instance there was a merging of mortalities. The all-nighter had taken its toll on him. The echoes were getting assertive, were shouting back from the caves. You're too old for this. And you're bucking the odds. Cops who retire at fifty have the same mortality stats as butchers and bakers and candlestick makers, but those that stay on the job until they are fifty-five or older usually die within two years of leaving the force. Cheever contemplated his fifty-four years. Then he thought about Bonnie Gill. She hadn't done very well by the actuary tables herself, dying at the age of thirty-seven. That was how they had been introduced.

Bonnie Gill had been murdered in her own art gallery, Sandy Ego Expressions, a one-story structure on 10th and J near the old Carnation building. She had died in a garden out back, an area full of wind chimes, flowers (especially carnations), crafted pottery, and ornamental fountains that expanded on the usual motif of little boys peeing. Her

2

throat had been slashed adjacent to an exhibition that a placard announced as "The Garden of Stone." Daylight hadn't improved Cheever's opinion of the display, but it had been worse the night before when everyone had kept being confronted by the statues. Most of the damn things were clothed. That had made it worse, especially in the semi-darkness. He had kept mistaking them for human beings.

The statues weren't the kind found in public squares or the park, the men on horses and the women saints. These were statues with faces of pain and fear and anger. He had almost pulled his gun on one of them. The piece looked real enough, and threatening enough—a man holding a knife with both hands over his head. That's how Bonnie Gill had died, or close enough. She had been killed with two knife wounds—had been stabbed in the back, then had had her throat slashed.

He sought out the offensive statue with his eyes, wasn't sure whether it was the morning light, or the softer stone around the knife wielder's face that gave the head such a glow. Maybe both. Cheever supposed the man with the knife was some kind of priest. That didn't seem to matter to the woman being sacrificed. Her expression was one of terror.

Cheever decided he had indulged himself too long at the crime scene. He liked to take his own impressions without the jostling of the evidence tech, and the M.E., and the rest of his homicide team. He wrote down a few notes, not for himself, but for the opposing lawyers in case he ever got called to the stand. Around the department Cheever's memory was legendary. The other detectives knew he didn't need to write anything down once it was in his head. He liked to go out on a call, spot somebody he had popped ten, even twenty years back, and yell out a first name greeting. Many didn't like to be remembered. They felt uneasy, marked, like Big Brother was watching them, monitoring everything they did.

He turned and was startled to find a woman standing at the entrance to the garden. This time he was the one under observation. Shaken, it took him a moment to get his breath back, but when he did, he put his wind to good use. "What the hell are you doing in here?"

His yelling helped her. It was louder than her chorus. The cacophony submerged into the background. She closed her eyes for a moment, and when she opened them her world had changed again.

She had big eyes, he noticed. They were alert and blue and aware. She was like one of those Keane paintings where the kids' eyes take up half the picture. He had started angrily toward her, but stopped now that he saw her terrified look. He was afraid she would bolt if he breathed hard. She looked like she was ready to drop her athletic bag and run.

"I'm Detective Cheever," he said. His words didn't put her at ease.

"I'll show you identification," he said. From a distance, he offered up his brass shield. She relaxed, but just a little.

"You're trespassing," he advised her, "on a police investigation scene."

She considered his words and finally spoke: "I am the sculptor."

Cheever motioned with his head. "You did these?"

The smallest of nods claimed credit. Cheever took his time examining the artist, could tell by her body language that it was still not the right time to approach her. He figured she was in her mid-twenties. She stood around five-eight, and was quite thin—weighed maybe one-fifteen. The woman liked jewelry. Her ears had been pierced more than Custer's body, with at least six earrings hanging from each lobe. She went for the shiny metallic look, jewelry that could have been mistaken for fishing lures or perhaps was. Bracelets ran up her arms, and baubles and bangles had

4

found their way to most parts of her body. She wore plenty of rings, but no apparent wedding ring. The only nonornamental piece among her trimmings was a Medic-Alert bracelet, but she might have been wearing it as another misplaced fashion statement. She had done a yin-yang kind of thing on her mane so that it was half black and half white. Cheever was surprised. It detracted from her natural beauty.

"What are you doing here?"

Her words came a little faster now: "Checking on my pieces."

"The 'Garden of Stone,'" he said, the slightest hint of sarcasm in his words.

"That wasn't the name I wanted for the exhibition."

"Oh? What name did you want?"

She mumbled her answer: "'What the Gorgon Saw.'"

"'What the Gorgonzola?'"

"Forget it."

Words invariably uttered when there was something that should be remembered. In his mind Cheever made sense of what she had said. What he couldn't make sense of was why she was here.

"I wouldn't worry about anyone trying to make off with your rocks," he said. "They're too heavy."

"They're not as heavy as you'd think," she said. "They're faux marble."

Cheever didn't like her answer. It sounded too goddamn superior to him. He knew lack of sleep was coloring his mood, but he still didn't like her statues. He wanted to tell her that they were pieces of crap, and not even faux pieces of crap. Her stuff disturbed. To his thinking, the best art showed a way out of the cesspool, didn't offer a wallow in it.

"You know about the murder?" he asked.

She could hear the anger in his voice even if she didn't know the source. "Yes," she said.

He closed the distance between them. "How well did you know Bonnie Gill?"

"She's represented me for several years."

Cheever let the silence build. People usually started talking about the dead, saying all kinds of things, but not this one. "That's all you have to say about her?"

She didn't immediately respond. Her expression was sad, despondent, then, to his surprise, he thought he saw a momentary smile, a glee. Her posture shifted, her face went slack, and she straightened. Her chin tilted up and her manner became imperious.

So, she thought. Cop wants a confrontation. I can play that game. "I'm not good at eulogies," she said.

They had a little stare down. She was acting tough now. Yeah, she was a rock, he thought. Faux rock. What was that children's game? Scissors, paper, rock. It was time for paper to wrap rock. "What's your name?"

The smallest hesitation: "Holly Troy."

"Got some I.D.?"

"Not on me."

He flipped open his pad. "What's your address and phone number?"

Monotone, she gave him both.

"Any reason for Ms. Gill to be dead?" he asked.

"I wouldn't know," she said.

The words were offered without any feeling. Holly Troy was young to be that uncaring, he thought. Usually you have to live for a while to earn the right.

"And you don't give a damn, do you?"

Holly ignored his question. "It's going to be a bother," she said, "finding a new gallery. Not many take on statuary, or at least pieces of any size."

She was avoiding the issue of a body, playing scissors now on his paper, cutting out lines of inquiry she didn't like. It was time to rock her. Smash her scissors.

"When we discovered Bonnie Gill's body last night," he

6

said, "she was already cool. Not cold, not in San Diego. When the dead are described as being cold that's sort of a myth. After the heart stops pumping the body loses heat. Gradually it becomes the temperature of its surroundings. Of the air, of the ground . . ."

Cheever walked over to a small statue of a little girl crying. One of Holly Troy's horrors. The statue had been clothed in a yellow dress with red polka dots. The girl's mouth was open. She was scared. She was terrified. Cheever wished he could tell her everything was all right.

". . . of the stone," he said.

The anger rose in him unexpectedly. "By the time we got here she was the temperature of your fucking faux-marble," he said. "But your stone doesn't bleed, lady. She did. But then you don't care, do you?"

The same question again, and another silence. Her shifting of posture was the only indicator that she had heard.

Bonnie Gill didn't fit the profile of most San Diego homicides. She didn't use or abuse, didn't have a record, was a business owner and community leader. She was an attractive woman whose death would make the taxpayers uneasy. San Diegans weren't going to like seeing Bonnie Gill's smiling, freckled face staring at them from their morning newspaper.

Cheever didn't have one of the smiling pictures. He had the other kind. The crime scene shots had been processed that morning. When Cheever had first started in homicide the pictures had all been black and white. Now they were color, the better to see with, and the better to sicken juries. To make an impact even on the jaded.

"Two wounds," he said, holding up one of the pictures to Holly's face. She looked different now, diffident even, but Cheever didn't care. "One in the back here." Cheever slapped the spot hard, did it so she could hear the impact, and feel it. "And one here, across the throat." He pushed the second picture almost to her nose, tapped on it to show the wound, then demonstrated on his own throat with particular savagery, leaving an angry red line across his neck.

In the pictures, Bonnie looked small. Only her wounds looked large. She had red hair, and looked like a fallen Raggedy Ann doll.

For some reason Cheever had lost it with this woman, something he rarely did. He prided himself on his control. It made the job possible, but something had kicked in.

"You'll have to excuse me," Cheever told her as he shoved the pictures into his coat pocket, "for mistaking you for someone who cared."

Two

"Lady crazy about flowers. Car-nations."

Flamingo had two legs, but preferred standing on one. He was a familiar character, doing his one-legged sentry duty at corners around the downtown area. Flamingo was a tall black man of indeterminate years, but probably around sixty, and his pose had delivered him his nickname. He liked to talk, enjoyed having an audience, but was known to chatter amiably to himself for hours on end when no one else was around.

"While back there she sent out artists, pretty girls they was, to paint car-nations everywhere. You can't miss them, Captain. They be on sidewalks, and stores and fences. Flower power."

Cheever had seen them. The carnations were Bonnie Gill's trademark, her metaphor for the area. Near her gallery was the old and decrepit Carnation building. Its ruins had inspired Bonnie to establish the ReinCarnation Foundation, a group dedicated to the rebirth of her downtown neighborhood. As part of a beautification program, she had installed planter boxes around the area. The planters had not only managed to remain standing but had somehow sprouted carnations hearty enough to survive a too steady diet of urine and cigarette butts.

"Where have all the flowers gone," Flamingo sang, but forgot the rest of the words. He remembered part of the tune, and continued to hum it.

"You know Bonnie Gill?" asked Cheever.

"Sure. Nice lady. We talked. I'd see her and say, 'Hey, pretty flower mama, let's see that green thumb of yours.'"

"Know anyone who had a beef with her?"

"No one I know. Hurtful world out there, though. Some people just like to hurt."

"Anyone in the neighborhood like that?"

"Must be, Captain. But those the kinds of people I try not to know."

That was how Cheever's day was going. No one was even offering up the usual bogeyman, the drunk who always made a nuisance of himself, or the hairy, crazy street person who started fights, or the kid that liked to set fires. For once, it would have been nice to have had one of those.

The night before, Homicide Team IV had canvassed the neighborhood talking mostly to the homeless. Cheever and the other detectives had gone from one bedroll to another. The way the homeless had been laid out along the sidewalks, cocooned and unmoving, had reminded Cheever of body bags put out to be collected. The team had spoken to at least a hundred homeless people in a five-block radius, but none remembered seeing anything out of the usual. In the light of day the remembering hadn't gotten any better.

"You ever go inside of her gallery?"

"Nuh-uh. I look from the outside in. Like to do my viewing from the garden. Always something going on in there. Parties and such. People working at their pots and the ovens always cooking. Times you'd think the place was a bakery. Or a flower shop. All those pretty flowers."

Flamingo smiled, remembering them. "Red flowers, pink flowers, white flowers."

Cheever had walked through the gallery's outdoor garden at least half a dozen times, but he didn't remember it as fondly as Flamingo. It was rectangularly shaped, about 250 by 200 feet. Flamingo was right about there being plenty of flowers, but there was also an eight-foot-high chain-link fence topped by concertina wire. Bonnie's killer had caught up with her in that garden. She was already wounded, was probably running when she was grabbed from behind by the hair and her throat slashed. The crime scene told them that, if little else. Maybe Bonnie had thought she could hide in the garden, or maybe there hadn't been any other place to run. Perhaps she chose to die among her flowers.

"Who's going to water them flowers, Captain?"

Cheever shrugged. "Maybe it will rain."

Flamingo looked up to the sky briefly, doubtfully.

"I'll check on the flowers," said Cheever.

"Thank you, Captain."

Cheever wondered whether Flamingo had served in the military. The Navy had brought millions of men through San Diego; Cheever was one of many who had stayed. He reached into his wallet, found a five-dollar bill, and handed it to Flamingo along with his card. "If you hear anything, anything at all, I'd like you to call me."

Flamingo offered something that resembled a salute, and Cheever returned the gesture.

Team IV was scheduled to meet at headquarters at five o'clock. For most of the day the four detectives and one sergeant had worked the field alone to get in as many interviews as possible. Cheever's last scheduled appointment was with Reuben Martinez at his auto repair shop. He had talked with him the night before, but only briefly. Martinez was the block captain for the Neighborhood Watch, and was in the habit of driving around the area each night. He had noticed Bonnie's car on the street, and the too dark gallery. From experience, Martinez knew Bonnie liked to spotlight her business. He had called the police at ten-thirty, and they had responded before eleven. Early indications were that she had already been dead for several hours.

Martinez was on the phone at a metal desk shoved off in a corner of the shop. He was short, no more than five and a half feet tall, but stocky, with large, strong hands. There were tattoos on his arms, mostly military in nature. He was in his forties, his hair salt-and-pepper, though his thick mustache was still a dark black.

"So, I can put you down for a thousand bucks?" he asked, tapping the desk with his fingers.

There seemed to be some resistance to that amount. "Listen," said Martinez, "it's not like there's any guarantee you're going to have to cough up that money. But we got to show we're serious. Adams said he'd match whatever we came up with up to twenty-five grand."

He listened to the reply, rolled his eyes to show the detective what he thought about it. "Yeah, I know it's easier for him to come up with the scratch, but we're the ones doing business here. It's our turf. So I can count on you for a grand? Good."

Martinez finished the conversation, wrote down some numbers, then wondered aloud how he'd become the "damned community chest."

"That's the term, isn't it?" he asked Cheever. "Community chest? Sounds like a strip club, but I remember it from Monopoly. It's that card where the guy's happily giving away money. Two hundred bucks, I think. Ever notice how people are a lot freer with Monopoly money?"

"What's the fund-raiser?"

"Bonnie Gill's the fund-raiser," Martinez said. "We've

started the Carnation Fund. You know what they say: money talks and bullshit walks. We're looking for any information that nails the fucker, you know. That's the kind of thing Bonnie would have organized, but since she's not around anymore the rest of us are trying to do it."

"How's it going?"

"Nobody doing business around here has said 'no' yet. That tells you something. We're going to be dangling a carrot that's got fifty grand written on it. That ought to make people remember, if anything will."

And probably generate more false leads than there were Lindbergh baby sightings, thought Cheever.

"How's your work goin'?" asked Martinez.

"So far no one's given me a good reason for Bonnie Gill to be dead."

"Reason?" Martinez laughed. "A crazy man don't need no reason to do somethin'. The zoo's not in Balboa Park, man. It's right here."

"How long did you know Bonnie?"

"Since she opened the gallery. Almost five years. I thought it was a joke when I heard an art gallery was moving in. I said the only gallery that belonged in this neighborhood was a shooting gallery. But she made it work. How the hell Bonnie did it, I'll never know. She even got me to buy a couple of paintings."

Martinez shook his head, looked like he had half a mind to beat up on the smashed Camaro he was working on. The garage was small, couldn't accommodate more than three wrecks at a time, which was two more than were there.

"Last night you said you'd served on some groups with Bonnie."

"Yeah. You didn't say no to her."

"What kind of projects did she involve you in?"

"Business outreach, help the neighborhood bums, stuff like that. ReinCarnation Foundation do-gooding."

"Did anyone around here have reason to dislike Bonnie? To want to hurt her?"

He shook his head without having to think: "No."

"Sometimes there's resentment against activists."

"Hey, it's not like some people didn't think Bonnie's ideas weren't a little out there, but who'd be dumb enough to kill the fucking golden goose?"

"What do you mean?"

"Bonnie was trying to make things happen. She wasn't just prettying up the neighborhood. The foundation, and her arts and crafts classes, kept bringing in outsiders with money. She had us talking together, trying to do stuff, and she kept coming up with these ideas of what could be. Lotta dreams died with Bonnie."

His tone was angry, but his hands reached out for a cleaned-up oil can that held a bunch of cut carnations. It was the first time Cheever had ever seen flowers in a garage. The carnations were starting to wilt, and Cheever wondered if they would ever be replaced.

Cheever looked out from his fourth-floor window down to the Edutek Professional Colleges on 15th Street. The industrial building didn't offer much of a view. Or maybe, Cheever realized, he brought his own gray landscapes to whatever he looked at. Over the years the names had changed on the building, though it had remained one kind of vocational school or another. Cheever had seen the students filing in and had wondered what kind of careers they were being trained for. Sometimes he pictured himself joining one of the new classes and learning another vocation. It was a pleasant fantasy.

Except for Team IV, the homicide division was deserted. Most homicide detectives went home by four o'clock, but in the early stages of a case detectives were expected to work round the clock, if necessary for days without a break. Circadian rhythms went to hell and stayed that way. The cycles could be debilitating. Cheever knew some detectives who no longer knew how to fall asleep, only how to pass out.

From appearances, no one on Team IV looked like they would have any trouble falling asleep. The detectives sat at their desks yawning. They were tired, weren't even sustained by the adrenaline of a lead. Cheever had the feeling this wasn't going to be an easy one. The Kid must have been thinking the same thing.

"Gotta believe in that needle, right, Cheever?"

Cheever didn't say anything at first, just looked at the Kid, made him sweat a little. The Kid's real name was Cory Lincoln. He offered his question while styling his short dark hair with an Afro comb. The Kid was good-looking, but not as good-looking as he thought he was. The Kid spent most of his spare time working at weights. He had been with the team for a year, was the new guy on the block, at age thirty-four the youngest of all the homicide detectives, which meant that most of the time Cheever treated him like a puppy not quite housebroken.

"Faith," said Cheever in a monotone that suggested he was lacking in the same.

Jacoba Diaz and Will Hayes, the other two detectives on Team IV, turned their heads to Cheever in the expectation of his continuing. Cheever met their eyes, but didn't immediately say anything. Not for the first time he thought the other detectives could have come out of Hollywood casting, with skin colors of black, and brown, and white. Cheever had made that observation aloud before: What's black, and brown, and white and red? Homicide Team IV working a murder. And where did he fit into the equation? The token old guy, he supposed.

They were still looking his way. The hell with all of them, he thought. It was his own fault, though. It served him right for having tried to explain something to the Kid.

In a tired voice Cheever said, "A needle in the haystack

doesn't mean the impossible. It just means something's waiting to be discovered."

Cheever hadn't told the Kid that's why most detectives didn't last in homicide. The Kid would probably understand better when he put in for his own transfer in two or three years. Most detectives didn't last more than five years in homicide, about the time Cheever figured it took them to get half decent in their work. To be a good homicide detective required unnatural patience. That's what the Kid still needed to learn. A good homicide detective never rushed a case. You had to learn to be methodical, to almost work a case in slow motion. As if you were looking for that needle.

"You becoming one of those mystics, Cheever?" Will Hayes asked the question with a sneer. Hayes looked like a walrus, and that's what they called him. He had a mustache that was long and brown and drooped southward. His face was meaty and red, making him look older than his forty-odd years.

Cheever didn't answer. He went back to gazing out the window, looking at the vocational school and thinking about that different career, wondering how his life would have turned out if he had been a plumber or an electrician. Probably not too different, he thought. It wasn't that he needed a new job so much as a course on being a new person.

The room became quiet again. In the days preceding their current case everyone on the team had been antsy, the result of having been "up" on the rotation for a week. Their call had been overdue and the anticipation had gotten to them. They weren't ghoulish, no more than a firefighter who scans the horizon looking for a wisp of smoke. They were trained to do a unique job. In a department with close to two thousand sworn officers, less than forty worked homicide. They had wanted the case, God help them.

Sergeant Falconi walked into the work area and sat down in his chair with a loud sigh. Everyone was eighteen hours tired, him included. SDPD homicide sergeants work the case with their team. It was the sergeant's turn to be the "crime scene guy," which meant he was in charge of all the paperwork and had to work with the evidence tech documenting and collecting evidence. The scene guy also had to attend the autopsy, which was scheduled for the next morning.

Falconi stretched out, and the motion threatened to break his chair. He was a big man. A few people had made the mistake of thinking he was a fat man. He reminded Cheever of a forty-five-year-old Jackie Gleason. The extra pounds were a part of him. He had the coordination and grace of a slim man, but the heft of someone who knew how to throw around his more than two hundred pounds whenever the situation called for it.

"Lots of phone calls going on today," Falconi said. "Rollo Adams called the mayor, who called the chief, who called the captain, who called the lieutenant, who called me into his office."

"Enter Rollo," said the Kid, "and the brass follow."

Everybody knew the name. It was hard not to with as many buildings as it had been splashed on. Adams was a developer who had seemingly been involved with every major downtown building project in the last ten years.

"Rollo was friends with Bonnie Gill," Falconi said. "Lots of people were. No one likes it when a saint dies."

"Church doesn't mind," said the Walrus.

"Takes the church a long time to figure out who's a saint, and who isn't," Jacoba said. If anyone knew what was entailed in canonization proceedings, she would. Jacoba wasn't a stereotypical detective. She was in her late thirties, had thick glasses, put her dark hair up in a bun, and was soft-spoken. The glitter-crusted prayer card and family pictures that decorated her workstation reflected her concern for God and family first—but murder was a close second.

"We got an easier job," Cheever said. "We just have to figure out who the devil is."

Their talk sounded flat, even to them, but that didn't stop Jacoba from crossing herself at his comment.

"Show and tell time, kiddies," Falconi said. "Show and tell."

Falconi looked to the Kid, a cue for him to talk. "Like you say, Bonnie Gill's got lots of friends, and a few of them are rich."

"Best kind to have," the Walrus said.

"They're mad and they're organized," the Kid said. "They've already put together something called the Carnation Fund. Rollo Adams has gone public telling everyone that the fund's offering at least fifty thousand for any information leading to the conviction of Bonnie Gill's murderer."

If justice couldn't be bought, you could at least grease the skids. Cheever listened to the tired voices, and when his turn came he covered his day. Though everyone was exhausted, it was clear that this one mattered. When Cheever had first started working homicide there had been a term for lowlife murders: N.H.I.—no humans involved. No one got too worked up over the death of a gang-banger, or a hooker, or a dealer. They worked the case— their way of doing justice to the dead or at least the system—but they really didn't care because they knew the victim had chosen to live out there on the edge and had just paid the consequences.

The death of a Bonnie Gill struck closer to home. She could have been a wife, or a friend, or a lover, or a sister.

"Midnight," Falconi said, interrupting Cheever's musing. He studied the detectives. "Hayes and Diaz, you got the call tonight. Start at the gallery and work the interviews four hours out."

"Shit," said the Walrus, "I better wear a body condom."

Jacoba didn't say anything. It made sense for her to be out there, but she got stuck with more than her share of neighborhood interviews because of her bilingual abilities. They called her the "Cómo se llama mama." Because San Diego's a border town, almost half of its homicide cases called for someone fluent in Spanish.

The assignments and areas of concentration for the next day were discussed and divvied. Tomorrow they'd work some more angles, and pound some more pavement. And hope. For a phone call, for a break. Maybe Cal I.D. would match one of the fingerprints on the scene with some notorious felon. Or maybe, thought Cheever, pigs would fly.

Falconi made it a short show and tell. Hayes and Diaz needed to get some sleep before they went out that night. The team had turned the stones and looked under them, and were going to turn some more, but not today. Falconi dismissed everyone by saying, "Get some sleep." It wasn't something he had to tell them.

Cheever's phone rang. He looked at it suspiciously before picking it up. Phone calls at the end of a long day were usually best avoided. "Detective Cheever."

"This is O'Brien." He was the officer working the desk. "You got a visitor. Name of Holly Troy. You want me to let her up?"

Cheever's eyes dropped to an athletic bag on the floor. Holly Troy's. She'd left it at the gallery, had up and disappeared right after he'd yelled at her. Cheever had turned away for a moment and she'd been gone. He'd thought about leaving the bag at the gallery, but had decided to take it with him for safekeeping. And because he was curious about what was inside. The bag was filled with black clothing, men and women's. There also were several black wigs. Color seemed to be the only thing the items had in common.

Officer O'Brien cleared his throat. He was still waiting for his answer. Civilians couldn't gain entrance to headquarters, or homicide's fourth floor, without clearing their visit with a uniform in the lobby. For some reason, Cheever didn't feel like letting the sculptor see his domain.

"No," Cheever said. "I'll come downstairs."

He took his time putting some paperwork in order, and was the last detective to leave the office. Bag in hand, Cheever hummed the line from "Amazing Grace" about being lost and then found, and took the elevator downstairs. The words were for the bag, not him.

She had her back turned to him, was looking out the glass doors toward the fountain. Besides the uniform behind the desk, there were only two other people in the lobby. When Holly turned and faced him, Cheever was surprised, although he tried not to show it. She had a shawl over her two-tone hair that tempered her look, made her appear almost nunlike. Her face was freshly scrubbed, pink. He had seen her in jeans and a T-shirt that morning, but now she was wearing a white dress with a high collar. Her earrings were gone, and so was all of her jewelry, save for her Medic-Alert bracelet. She looked naked without her trinkets, and must have felt it. Her arms were held tightly over her breasts, shielding them as if they were exposed.

"Detective Cheever," she said.

Even her voice was different. It was higher. And beseeching. That wasn't the kind of tone he had figured was in Holly Troy's repertoire.

When she dropped to her knees Cheever was even more surprised. She reached her hands up and said, "Detective Cheever, I do care."

Everything going on in the lobby stopped. All was quiet. Everyone was watching them.

"I care," she said, bowing her head and resting it against his legs. "I care."

Her hunched-over pose revealed a bloody stain on her upper back. She tilted her neck back and looked up at him. There was a second red stain, this one under her collar. Cheever carefully reached down, loosened two buttons, and gently pulled her collar back. There was a slight wound on her neck, what looked to be a laceration. The injury was bleeding, beginning to redden the front of her dress.

"I care," she said, then shed a tear.

It wasn't the kind of tear that Cheever had ever seen. The red drop rolled down her cheek. It was followed by another. He reached for her cheek, and wiped away a tear of blood.

"Jesus," he said.

THREE

Cheever snuck another glance at Holly Troy. She sat in the passenger seat of his Taurus looking very serene and self-contained. At least she wasn't crying anymore. He had looked for an eye injury but hadn't been able to find one. Her tears had somehow been intermixed with blood. Cheever suspected some trick, but damned if he knew how it had been accomplished.

He returned his eyes back to the road. Cheever still wasn't sure whether Holly was a mental case, or reacting to some drug, or both. Cheever had seen diabetics with insulin imbalance acting like rock monsters. Holly's Medic-Alert bracelet hadn't clued him in to her condition. No disease was identified, or caveat offered. There was only her patient number and an inscription that read: *Before beginning any treatment, call Dr. R. Stern.* That's what Cheever had done, calling Dr. Stern at the pager number engraved on the bracelet. Holly's close-mouthed doctor hadn't deigned to clarify the situation for him, had just treated him like a delivery boy, asking whether he couldn't "drop Helen off at my office." The doctor had interchanged the names Holly and Helen several times during their short conversation. Cheever had wanted to ask her about that, and other matters, but Dr. Stern had sidestepped any inquiries.

"I think it would be better, Detective," she had said, "if you waited to ask your questions at my office."

The doctor had hung up before he could respond, an effective way of deferring his questions. And of pissing Cheever off.

He turned onto Fifth Avenue, tires lightly squealing, and headed east. Cheever didn't need a doctor to tell him that Holly Troy was a strange one. She ran hot and cold. Over the course of a day he'd seen her go from being totally uncaring to displaying an almost desperate solicitude.

Holly turned toward him. "Where are we going?" she asked.

Cheever had explained their destination at the beginning of their drive, but did so again. "I am taking you to your doctor," he said. "She can treat your wounds."

"Wounds?" asked Holly.

Cheever motioned to her bloody shirt. "Your cuts," he said.

"They're not mine," she said.

"Whose are they?"

She didn't answer the question, saying instead, "I would like to cure Antiope, but she won't let me. She is afraid."

"Who is Antiope?"

Holly changed the subject again. "If I accept their pain," she said, "she won't hurt anymore."

"Whose pain?"

"You're right," she said. "It is not only the dead I should be thinking about. There is the matter of your own pain."

Her pronouncement surprised Cheever. "I am not the one who is hurting," he said.

He tried not to be too dismissive, tried to keep his expression neutral. He knew how to deal with crazy people.

But Holly wasn't as adept at masking her expressions or hiding her feelings. She looked at him with great sympathy, as if he were a victim of some terrible accident, as if he were the one who had taken leave of his senses.

"I wish to help you," she said. "Will you let me take on your pain?"

"I am not sick," he said.

Holly shook her head sadly. "You are barely alive," she said. "You are carrying deep wounds."

"Let's worry about your own," Cheever said, his voice sharper than he wanted it to be. "Mind telling me how you hurt yourself?"

"I was playing with Graciela," she said.

"Graciela?"

"Graciela Fernandez."

Little Grace. Cheever took a deep breath, and wondered if it was the same Graciela Fernandez. His Graciela. Two years ago Team IV had taken on her case. Little Grace was a seven-year-old who had disappeared. During the three months she was missing there were purported sightings of her around the country, but those proved to be cases of mistaken identity. Graciela was ultimately found under a pile of junk in an abandoned lot less than a mile from where she had been abducted. They still hadn't caught her murderer.

"What do you mean you were playing with her?"

Holly didn't answer the question, just gave him a beatific smile. "Graciela is fine," she said. "Her spirit is lovely. She came back and told me that everything was all right."

"When was this?"

She didn't answer, except to smile a little more.

"Where did you see her?"

"On the billboard," she finally answered, her voice as far away as the clouds.

24

Holly wasn't alone in saying she had seen Grace after the little girl died. Many San Diegans had claimed to see little Grace's reflection on a South Bay billboard not long after her body was discovered. For a short time the billboard had become a San Diego shrine, with thousands of San Diegans flocking to see the so-called miracle. The skeptical said the "miracle" was a result of the lighting, and that when the illumination was turned off, Graciela's reflection couldn't be seen. Cheever hadn't joined the crowds looking for a miracle. He had been too busy looking for a murderer. Futilely looking.

Two more tears of blood dropped from Holly's eyes. Her neck and back began bleeding again, making her dress more red than white.

"Don't," Cheever said. For a second time he reached out to her cheek, gathering in one of her red tears. What he held wasn't crimson mascara, or tears colored by some reflection, or tinted lights. It was blood. Even Doubting Thomas would have been convinced.

"I would like to help you with your pain," she said. "That is my purpose."

Early in his career with SDPD Cheever had been assigned to vice. He knew about scams, had been in on the arrest of a group of gypsies that were peddling everything from fountain of youth water to the baby Jesus's foreskin. But if Holly was pulling an act, where was the profit in an old cop? They looked at one another until Cheever broke off their eye contact. He wasn't used to her kind of intense searching. It was his job to do the looking. Who was she to stare at him with such pity?

"If it will make you feel any better," he said, "go ahead and take on my pain."

"Thank you," she said, as if he was the one bestowing the boon.

Her bloody waterworks let up, and she smiled at him.

Damned if she didn't look like one of those martyred saints, he thought. Even supermarkets were getting into the icon business. Whenever he wheeled his cart around his local market he always paused at the large candles with idealized portraits of Jesus and Mary and the Virgin of Guadalupe and a few of the better-known saints. The Mexicans were big on those candles. Lights for inspiration. He could probably use one or two of them himself.

Holly's eyes were closed again. She didn't speak for almost a minute. When she awoke from her meditation she said, "Trouble always occurs when statues come to life. It's all so confusing, isn't it? It would have been better had Galatea just slept and never awakened."

The name was familiar to Cheever, but he couldn't immediately place it. "Galatea?"

She sat there without moving, without blinking, not responding to his question. Then, shaking her head as if awakening, she turned to Cheever and asked, "Did you know my father?"

"What was his name?"

"He was a great healer who was killed because of his powers. He brought the dead to life, and some couldn't abide that. It has always been so, hasn't it?"

Cheever kept the skepticism, and the certain knowledge that he was dealing with someone not in her right mind, out of his voice. "Raising the dead," he agreed, "has always seemed to get people in trouble."

"I am my father's daughter," she said, sounding not altogether happy at the pronouncement. "Within me are his powers. I have to accept that mantle. But you don't raise the dead without paying a great price, and making yourself a target for mighty enemies."

The car in front of them slowed and Cheever had to brake. Cheever thought the traffic on Fifth was heavier than usual, or maybe it just seemed that way because of Holly's strange sermonizing.

"My destiny is to help others," she said, "to see to their needs, to cure them of their ailments."

Cheever wondered whether it was his imagination, or whether the faster she preached the more she bled. He was looking at her reddening shirt when the Taurus hit a large pothole that bounced both of them around in their seats. Cheever swore, then quickly glanced over to see if his words had shocked Sister Holly. The eyes that looked back at him didn't want to save his soul. They regarded him coolly, speculatively.

"You want to try it one more time?" she asked. "I might have a couple of teeth left."

"Sorry."

"Damn," she said. "I'm bleeding."

Cheever wondered at her apparent surprise. The bleeding sounded like a revelation to her. "We're almost there," he said. "Dr. Stern will help you."

"By doing what? Yammering until my blood beats a bored retreat?"

He tried to suppress a smile, but wasn't totally successful. "She's a psychologist?"

"Worse. A psychiatrist. License to pill."

Was this the same woman? So concerned before, so righteous, and now so glib and insouciant? He sneaked another look at her. "You seem better," he said.

She played with her bloody garb. "I'm obviously over my PMS," she said.

He didn't let her humor distract him. "You were . . . out of it . . . earlier."

"I must have been."

"Is there anyone I should contact to say you'll be late?"

"You might tell my dog his bowl of Purina is going to be delayed."

"What kind of dog?"

"Rottweiler. He was bartered as a puppy for one of my pieces."

"Nice breed."

"You got a dog waiting for you?"

Cheever shook his head.

"A wife?" she asked.

"No."

"Kids?"

How had she become the questioner? Cheever hesitated a moment before saying, "None."

"Where do you live?"

Usually he was purposely vague with people he didn't know, answering "north county." They never knew whether he was referring to inland or along the coast. He could be talking anywhere from Poway to Oceanside. But for once he was specific. "Leucadia. The area where I live used to be one big avocado grove."

Cheever had gone bird hunting a few times as a kid. Holly's sudden stillness reminded him of the way his father's setter used to freeze when he saw a bird. Out loud, she whispered, "Leucadia." He figured she was surprised at his long work commute. "It's a haul, but . . ."

"It was from the promontory of Leucadia," Holly said, "that Sappho threw herself into the sea."

She was looking different again, he thought, smaller and sadder, more contemplative. "Sappho," she said again, offering the name like you would a friend's. Then Holly told the story as if it meant something to her, as if she knew all there was to know about lost love.

"Sappho was one of the great Greek poets. She was in love with Phaon, who didn't return that love. From atop a ridge Sappho threw herself into the sea. It was believed if you survived such a leap you would lose your love and get over your heartache."

"A cure worse than the disease," Cheever said.

"Not necessarily," she said.

She looked at him, watched as he began to change. She

28

was used to that happening, knew that he wasn't the one really changing, but that she was.

Was this the one, she wondered? Messengers of the gods assumed many forms. He was tall and of medium build. His hair was mostly white. He had blue eyes, but they were clouded over, and in order to truly see them, you had to travel past his layers of hard, the cataracts to his being. If he was the one, he hid his passport of divinity well. As she tried to see more clearly, she switched again.

Damn daylight savings, thought Cheever. It got dark too early these days. The time change had occurred the week before. From the shadows he could see that Holly was moving her hands around. He turned his head and watched as her fingers pantomimed stretching something out.

"Like Sappho, you threw yourself from a promontory to try and get over a lost love," she declared. Her voice had changed again, had become raspy and unpleasant.

She was nuts, Cheever thought. Just ignore her. Anyone could talk about a lost love and hit the mark. It was a universal soft spot. But he was still annoyed. Her hands were snapping or cutting something. They looked like a crab having spasms.

"Since you're well enough to make speeches," he said, "I'd say you're well enough to answer some questions. Let's begin with your telling me about the last time you saw Bonnie Gill."

Holly's dramatics suddenly ceased. She was completely silent, though her eyes remained watchful.

"Did you see Bonnie yesterday?" he asked.

She didn't say anything, clammed up completely. Cheever asked his question again. Holly again said nothing. She wasn't talking, unless you took her eyes into account. They looked afraid.

Four

Holly's mute act didn't stop in the car. Her silence continued for the rest of the drive, and didn't help improve Cheever's mood. But Holly was able to communicate when it suited her. She pointed out where Cheever should park, and signed which elevator to take. The medical building was mostly deserted. No doubt all the doctors were making house calls, thought Cheever.

Dr. Stern's office was on the third floor. Holly pressed a button, and they were buzzed inside. The operation was like a prison, thought Cheever. The first opened door only got them as far as an anteroom where there were several chairs and a desk for a receptionist who wasn't there. They weren't alone for long. Another door opened and a woman walked into the waiting room. She looked to be in her early forties, and wore her caduceus in her expression: concerned, professional, and supercilious. Her hair, more pepper than salt, was medium length and wavy, and her eyes a dark brown. She had on a gray suit with a white blouse that was either a size too small or her bust was a size too large. She was about five and a half feet tall, but her high heels and erect posture made her look taller.

The doctor acknowledged Holly with a nod and slight smile of welcome. She took note of her bloodied garments with the professionalism of an admitting nurse, but made no comment about them. Then she turned to Cheever, stuck out her hand, and said, "I am Dr. Rachel Stern."

"Detective Cheever."

"Detective, I need you to wait here while I talk with Helen inside."

The doctor was used to being in control. So was Cheever. "Is her name Holly," Cheever asked, "or is it Helen?"

"That is a matter we will discuss shortly."

That wasn't a timetable of Cheever's choosing, and he wanted her to know it. "Doctor, for the last eighteen hours I've been investigating the murder of Bonnie Gill, the owner of an art gallery that Holly was professionally, if not personally, associated with. Holly's reaction to Bonnie Gill's death has been . . . unusual."

"What do you mean by *unusual*, Detective?"

"Look at her," he said, as if that should have been explanation enough. "This morning she acted like she couldn't care less about the murder. Then eight hours later she comes to me doing a sackcloth and ashes routine and then some. And for the last fifteen minutes she's been playing the mute and not saying anything at all."

"I will talk with her, Detective."

"I'd like to know where she was last night from six o'clock until midnight. I also want to hear about the last time she saw Bonnie Gill."

"I will talk with her," the doctor said again, then motioned to her patient. "Please come inside, Helen."

Cheever watched as the door closed on him. He wasn't pleased about being shut out of their conversation, and paced the room for a minute before stopping to examine a few of the doctor's too many diplomas. When Cheever tired of counting her *magna cum laudes*, he stepped over to the window and took in the view. The street below was lined with mostly whitewashed ancillary medical buildings. To the south was the Hillcrest business district. Cheever knew San Diego Bay was several miles to the west, but the darkness only allowed him to catch a hint of it, more mirage than not.

Holly or Helen? When the connection came to him, Cheever almost laughed aloud. Helen Troy, he realized. Here he was waiting outside of a psychiatrist's office to talk with Helen of Troy. The shrink probably treated Napoleon too. And Joan of Arc.

Cheever was tempted to leave, but instead he went and sat in a chair. How many chances do you get to talk with Helen of Troy anyway? As far as Cheever could determine, the only thing the modern Helen had in common with her namesake was a natural beauty that even her punk and monk outfits couldn't hide. Settling into the chair, Cheever contemplated the legendary Helen and the furious war waged over one beautiful woman . . .

"Detective Cheever. Detective Cheever."

Dr. Stern didn't touch him, just repeated his name incrementally louder until he woke up. Cheever opened his eyes, blinked hard a few times, then got up, albeit unsteadily. He looked at his watch, saw that he had slept for almost an hour.

"I almost didn't want to wake you," she said.

"For my sake or yours?"

The doctor's goodwill vanished. She motioned for Cheever to follow her into the office. Tired though he was, her shrink's couch wasn't tempting. One wall of her office was lined with books, thick-looking tomes, while another had paintings, mostly modern. There weren't many homey touches in the room, nothing soft, nothing revealing, no pictures or mementos to be seen.

"Where's Holly?" Cheever asked.

"She'll return in half an hour."

Had he slept that deeply that she had been able to walk by him? No. There was another door leading out to the hallway. The way the office was designed gave it an almost confessional air, the separate entrances and exits adding to the feel of byzantine intrigue.

They sat down at the same time, each measuring the other's movements and acting accordingly. Cheever flipped open his pad; the doctor picked up a pen to make her own notes. She also motioned to a tape recorder. "Do you mind?" she asked.

Cheever had the feeling it was a moot question. He shrugged, and she turned the machine on.

"Where was Holly last night?" he asked.

"I am afraid she was unable to answer that."

Unable to answer, thought Cheever. Screw that. He opened his mouth, but the shrink spoke before he did.

"Helen wasn't being uncooperative. She was in a fugue state from the early evening until this morning. In layman's terms a fugue state translates to a blackout."

"In layman's terms that strikes me as being damn convenient," Cheever said.

The doctor met the challenge in his eyes and tone. "Helen has a history of fugue states. Sometimes she forgets days. Other times years."

Unbelievingly: "Years?"

"That happened when she was much younger. Helen still has no memories from age five to seven."

"How do you explain that?"

"The explanation is very complicated."

Cheever was tired of being patronized. "If you speak real slowly, then maybe I'll be able to understand it."

"I can modify my speech," she said, not responding to his barb, "but I can't simplify Helen's condition. She has been in therapy with me for four years, a journey which

33

doesn't allow for check-the-box answers. Though she has given me permission to speak with you about her, I must also consider our doctor-client relationship."

"In that case, why don't I just bypass the middleman and go directly to the source?"

"Because you need a translator. Because I'm the only one who can call the Greek Chorus."

"What do you mean?"

She made forceful eye contact: "Helen has a dissociative identity disorder."

"She has what?"

"Helen is a multiple personality."

Cheever shook his head, leaned back in the chair, put his thumbs in his pockets, and then looked at the ceiling. Holly wasn't just nuts. She was nuts several times over.

"What are you thinking?" asked Dr. Stern.

"I'm thinking that I'm wasting my time."

"What else are you thinking?"

"I'm thinking you shouldn't be treating me like one of your goddamn patients. I'm not one of your Hollys—or should I say Helens?"

The doctor nodded noncommittally, then answered his question. "She was born Helen Olympia Troy. When she was seven she started calling herself Holly. That's one of her personalities. She has approximately a dozen more."

"So I was taken in by a certifiable who's into self-mutilation and parlor tricks?"

"I object to the word *certifiable*, and Helen does not practice self-mutilation."

"You're saying her wounds weren't self-inflicted?"

"Yes—and no."

"Can you be a little more ambiguous?"

"If, by your question, you are asking whether Helen took a knife and cut herself, or used any other implement to injure herself, then no, she didn't."

Dr. Stern opened a drawer, and took out a packet of

photos. She flipped through the pictures, selecting a handful for Cheever. Some were Polaroids she had snapped that night; most had been taken at other times.

"This is not the first time stigmata have appeared on Helen," she said. "You can see that I've photographed them on other occasions. One of Helen's personalities is extremely empathic. I am glad this particular personality doesn't emerge very often because she cares entirely too much. She wants to take on the pain of the world."

Cheever thumbed through the Polaroids. The shots were mostly close-ups of wounds on different parts of Holly's anatomy. "If she didn't mutilate herself, how'd these cuts occur?"

The doctor tapped her head. "They came out of her mind."

"What do you mean?"

"Most of the stigmatics throughout the ages have been extremely devout Christians. They assumed the same wounds as Jesus, with their own flesh reflecting his torture. Romans weren't needed to do the physical rending. Their minds produced the wounds."

She walked over to her library, picked out several books, and brought them back with her. "There are accounts of stigmata appearing more than a thousand years ago," she said. "In the last century photographic evidence has been collected." She opened one of the books, found the section she was looking for, and then handed it to Cheever. He flipped through the pages and saw pictures of stigmata ranging from small sores to flesh that was completely eaten through. Cheever put the book aside.

"Maybe these people just mutilated themselves," he said.

"And maybe Helen did the same?"

"That's right."

Rachel changed her tone, became less dogmatic. "I can understand your skepticism," she said. "I went through it myself. What you are looking at seemingly defies logic, but multiples have their own rules. Or they break what rules there are. Many of my patients have ulcers caused by stress. Is it so hard to imagine external manifestations instead of internal ones?"

"It's certainly not the norm."

"And neither is dissociative identity disorder."

"This morning I showed Helen crime scene photos," Cheever said, "pictures of the wounds inflicted upon Bonnie Gill. What you're telling me is that through the power of Helen's mind her stigmata manifested themselves over the course of eight hours or so?"

"I suppose so," Rachel said, but she sounded unsure.

"There seems to be some doubt in your mind, Doctor. In the past, did Helen's wounds appear so quickly?"

"No," she admitted, "but I expect this murder was particularly traumatic for Helen."

"In the past, how long did it take for her stigmata to form?"

"A day. Several days."

"Do tears of blood," he asked, "always accompany her stigmata?"

"You witnessed that?" Rachel was excited, and for a moment lost her reserve.

Cheever nodded. He could tell the shrink had seen the same thing, and was glad of it. Seeing was supposed to be believing, but Cheever still found it hard to believe in Helen's bloody tears. Or her stigmata. He was reminded of a cop he knew who claimed to have seen a UFO, but who never sounded very sure in his telling. What the cop always kept coming back to was that his friend had seen the same thing. Only with the corroboration of other eyes do most people believe. It's a rare person who has complete trust in himself.

The doctor started to ask him questions, but Cheever held up his hand: "I want to hear your sob stories first," he said.

"I only saw her tears of blood the one time," Rachel said. "It happened two years ago in this office. Helen had the late appointment that night. She came in acting more excited than I had ever seen her. She told me that she had just witnessed a miracle, just seen the spirit of a little girl materialize . . ."

"Graciela Fernandez?"

Surprised: "Yes."

"Did Helen know her?"

The doctor shook her head. "No."

"You're sure?"

"Yes."

Cheever tried to keep the disappointment off his features, and motioned for her to continue.

"Helen talked about seeing this vision of Graciela materialize on a billboard. She told me she wasn't the only one who saw Graciela. She said that hundreds of other people saw her, maybe thousands. But Helen said she felt special because she could sense that both God and Graciela were sending a message directly to her."

"Why would she care so much about a stranger?"

"Graciela was in the news so often she wasn't a stranger to Helen, just as I don't think she was a stranger to most San Diegans."

That was true enough. There had been prayer vigils and public entreaties from the little girl's parents. The abduction of Graciela had been played up locally and nationally. She was everybody's missing daughter.

"What do you think moved Helen to cry those tears that first time?" he asked.

"I can only speculate. It might have been a validation for Helen of something greater, something better. But what I sensed most was her relief. She knew Graciela was at peace and that meant so much to her."

It was Cheever's turn. He recounted the story of Helen's bloody tears dispassionately, as if he hadn't been moved by the spectacle, and then told about their drive over. When he finished, the detective and the doctor looked at one another. Neither blinked much. They both knew how to play verbal poker. Show a few cards, hold a few.

"Did Helen say anything to you about Bonnie Gill?" he asked.

The doctor shook her head. "No. Pandora is maintaining her silence on that subject."

"Pandora?"

"One of Helen's personalities."

"She chose the name?"

"Or it chose her."

Next stop the Twilight Zone, he thought. How much stranger could this case get? "Is Pan-dor-a," he said, stretching out the name as well as his sarcasm, "always so reluctant to speak?"

"No. Pandora is what is called an ISH, an internal or inner self-helper. All multiples have one. She is the memory link to all of Helen's personalities."

"And she's not saying anything?"

The doctor nodded.

"So why is Pandora clamming up?" he asked.

"I don't know."

"But she knows what happened last night?"

Rachel reluctantly nodded her head.

"How frequently does Helen have these fugue states?"

"Two or three times a year. In the past Pandora has always been able to tell me what occurred."

"But not this time?"

"That's right."

Cheever looked dubious. "Tell me about Helen's two-year fugue state as a child," he said.

"I wish I could, but I can't."

"Can Pandora?"

"I believe so."

"But let me guess," said Cheever, "she's not talking."

Dr. Stern didn't respond.

"Why her veil of secrecy then and now?" Cheever asked.

"It would only be conjecture on my part . . ."

"Speculate away."

"She might be trying to protect Helen and the other alters."

"From what Pandora saw, or what they did?"

"I would imagine the former."

"But you don't know?"

"How could I?"

"It's been almost twenty years between Pandora's Quaker meetings. What does that suggest?"

"I'm not certain."

"What are the names of her other personalities?"

"Alphabetically, they're Caitlin, Cronos, Eris, Eurydice, Helen, Holly, Hygeia, the Maenads, the Moirae, Nemesis, and Pandora."

Cheever surprised Rachel by not asking her to repeat the names, by apparently assimilating the information in his mind with her solitary recitation. He surprised her even more with his apparent familiarity with mythology.

"Cronos is a male," he observed.

"Yes. Multiples often have alters of the other gender."

"Who is Caitlin?"

"A five-year-old little girl. Most multiples have an inner child."

"She's the only one besides Helen and Holly who's not a mythological character."

"That's right."

"The Moirae are the Fates, aren't they?"

"Yes. Clotho is the Fate who spins the thread of life, Lachesis the one who measures it, and Atropos the Fate who cuts it." After a small pause Rachel added, "When they emerge, they tend to be unsettling."

"The Fates," mused Cheever. "I think those lovely ladies made a brief appearance during the drive."

Dr. Stern didn't bother to tell him she already knew that. She also didn't inform Cheever that he had met at least four of Helen's other personalities on the drive over.

"Nemesis," Cheever said, as if making a point, "is the goddess of vengeance. I imagine that alter would also be *unsettling.*"

He used Rachel's word, but gave it a sinister intonation.

"Some personalities are more expressive than others," she said.

"What do you mean by that?"

"Cronos, in particular, is angry."

"Enough to be a danger to others?"

"Enough to be careful around."

Rachel didn't tell the detective about the time Cronos had emerged in her office. She had called for Pandora, but it was Cronos that popped out. He had screamed at her, had said no one controlled him, and had swept everything off her desk. Then he had grabbed her. There was incredible strength in those arms; there was something there that was definitely not Helen. Talking Cronos out of his rage had been difficult. Since that day, Rachel had made sure there were no paperweights or letter openers on her desk. She had discarded anything that could be used to injure her, had gone so far as to get both a stun gun *and* pepper oil spray. They were sitting in her top drawer, ready in case Cronos came at her again.

As Cheever continued to probe Helen's other alters, the doctor found herself offering mostly monosyllabic answers. She was concerned for her patient. This man didn't care about Helen; she was only a stepping stone to his grisly end of finding a murderer. The detective said that this was a case that needed "clearance," as if he was talking about a sale. She viewed Cheever as a potential bull in a china shop. No, worse. He was a potential Minotaur in a china shop mind.

"At what age did Helen's personalities emerge?"

"Between four and eight."

"Between four and eight," he said. "Most little girls are playing with Barbie then. What kind of a girl was Helen that she even knew about such mythological characters?"

"Helen's father is a professor of classics, professor *emeritus* now. He raised her on the myths. They were the stories of her youth."

"Still, isn't it unusual that Helen's personalities are mostly derived from mythological characters?"

"Exotic personalities are not uncommon among multiples."

"Did her father name her Helen?"

"Yes."

"Cruel man."

Dr. Stern didn't rise to his bait.

"So which came first, the gods or her personalities?"

"What do you mean?" she asked.

"Cronos is angry. Eurydice is sad. Hygeia feels for others. And so on. Instead of feelings, Helen has personalities. Is her behavior predicated on which god she is, or is it the other way around?"

"Cause and effect are difficult to separate."

"Are the personalities antagonistic to one another?"

"At times."

"To what degree?"

"It's analogous to sibling rivalry."

Actually, it was often more pronounced than that, but Rachel decided that was something else Cheever didn't need to know. There was jealousy among the personalities, running battles over conduct, and who should be allowed "out," and the pecking order in general. Rachel had heard of more extreme cases where the alters detested one another, hurting and sabotaging each other whenever they could. She had been told about one personality who loved her kitten more than anything in the world, and how another personality, to get back at her, had strangled it. Although there was antipathy between some of Helen's alters, it wasn't as extreme as that, or at least Rachel didn't think so.

"As I see it then," said Cheever, "if I want to know what Helen was up to last night, I need to pry open Pandora's box."

"I can't recommend that course of action, Detective. It could be extremely deleterious to Helen's mental health."

"I'd think it would be hard to screw her up any more than she already is."

"Then you'd be very wrong about that," she said. "Helen and I are working toward a positive resolution of her disorder. I would hope you could respect those efforts."

Cheever let his long workday get the better of him. "Your job is to listen to people, isn't it?"

"That's part of my job."

"Well, just in case you missed something, Doctor, this is a murder investigation."

FIVE

As Helen and Cheever drove out of the parking garage, he couldn't help but wonder, Who the hell is sitting next to me?

Helen had undergone another metamorphosis, had returned to the shrink's office looking like a different woman. She had replaced her bloody garments with a black top and shorts pulled from her athletic bag, but her transformation transcended a change of clothing. Helen had stopped bleeding, and was no longer pale and drawn. Her posture was different, as was her demeanor. The doctor had noticed Cheever's amazement, and had commented on the amazing recuperative vigor of multiples: "One of my colleagues refers to their healing prowess as the power of positive thinking—several times over."

That hadn't been answer enough for Cheever. "What happened to you?" he asked Helen.

"I changed," she said.

At first Cheever had thought Helen's answer an understatement. Now he realized just how complete it was.

"You want to listen to the radio?" Cheever asked.

"Sure," she said.

"What kind of music do you like?"

"It doesn't matter."

That's right, thought Cheever. You don't need to change the station. All you have to do is find a personality that likes whatever's playing. He started searching the stations, not sure of what he wanted to hear. It was clear Dr. Stern hadn't approved of Cheever's playing chauffeur to Helen, but that's how it had played out. The shrink had said she needed to make some notes, and Helen had said she needed to make tracks. Dr. Stern was suspicious of him. She was right, Cheever thought, to have those suspicions.

Cheever gave up on his radio search. Nothing sounded right tonight. He turned to his silent passenger and wondered what she was thinking about. Should he offer her a penny for her thoughts? In her case it might end up costing him closer to a quarter.

"So," he said, attempting a casual voice, "What did you do last night?"

She shrugged. "I was out of it."

"Out of it where?"

"Who knows? I had a brief awakening around last call."

"Where was that?"

She hesitated before answering: "Sibyl's."

Ironic, he thought. "Sybil" was argumentatively the most famous multiple of all time, while Sibyl's Down Under was a club on Fifth Avenue in downtown San Diego.

"You don't sound certain."

"*They* were out. Not me."

"They?"

"I think Eris. And the Maenads. When they're doing heavy clubbing, I always feel it the day after."

Cheever remembered that the Romans had referred to the Maenads as Bacchanites, women who were frenzied with wine. There was a fierce ecstasy associated with them.

"Do you remember what time you arrived at Sibyl's?"

"No."

"Did you go anywhere from there?"

"I don't think so."

"You don't remember anything?"

She shook her head. "It's almost like sleepwalking, I guess. I just don't remember."

"And when did you hear about Bonnie Gill's death?"

The silence (Pandora again?) answered. Cheever didn't say anything for a minute or two, hoping that she would grow tired of the quiet, but she didn't. His weariness was deep. He opened a window, let the air play on him. He pretended it was water rushing over him, and closed his eyes for a moment.

"Where are we?"

The voice woke him up, shook him even. It was a little girl's voice. Not an adult playing at being a little girl, but the real thing. He knew. He remembered.

"We're traveling along Fourth Avenue," he said, "heading toward downtown San Diego."

Silence.

"In California. In the United States of America."

"You're silly, Daddy."

She was applying the knife now, and she didn't even know it.

"I'm hungry, Daddy."

"We'll stop and get something," he heard himself saying.

Cheever knew there wasn't anything open on Fourth Avenue that was appropriate for a little girl, so he detoured, driving east along University Avenue. He passed a number of fast food sites, rejecting them for one reason or another, and finally wondered what the hell he was doing. It wasn't like he was really driving a little girl around. He turned right on 29th Street and pulled into the Jack in the Box on Dale and Upas.

"What do you want?" he asked, hesitating for a moment before adding, "Caitlin."

"I want a hamburger, and french fries, and a milkshake."

"What flavor?"

"Choc-o-late," she said loudly.

He repeated her order into the speaker, without quite so much emphasis on the milkshake flavor, then drove to the window for the pickup. "Remember the ketchup, Daddy," she said.

The fast-food attendant heard her request, tossed some ketchup into their sack, and also tossed a questioning look. Helen was young enough to be Cheever's daughter, but far too old to be talking like a five-year-old.

Cheever handed her the bag of food, which proved to be a mistake. Her intentions were good, but she wasn't very neat. As Hygeia, she had bled on his seat; as Caitlin, she bled ketchup. She tried to be fastidious, but the ketchup packets seemed to be beyond her.

She ate contentedly. There are times when children have their own world and are serenely complacent in themselves. He watched her in that self-contained mode, wanting to see some adult giveaways, wanting to be able to say that she was acting and that her persona was a fraud, but he couldn't. She rang true. She was a little girl.

"Is it good?"

A barely perceptible nod in the dark, and back to eating. A minute later and he heard loud sucking on a chocolate shake. Then he heard other sounds, and tried to place them.

"Don't blow bubbles," he said. The noises stopped.

As Cheever neared headquarters, he began to worry about the situation. He couldn't just let her get behind the wheel of her car in this condition, could he? It would be like child endangerment.

He wasn't the only one worrying. "You didn't eat anything, Daddy."

"I wasn't hungry, honey."

His answer, and everything in it, the soft tones, the endearment, came out without thinking. He should have challenged her "Daddy" from the first, should have distanced himself from her manipulation.

"Are you tired from work?"

"Yes." He stopped himself from adding "sweetie."

"Poor Daddy."

Her words hurt too much. He changed the subject. "What did you do today, Caitlin?"

"Nothing."

Cheever remembered that catchall answer from the past. "Did you play?"

"Yes."

"With friends?"

"With Dolly."

"Who's Dolly?"

Accusingly: "You know who Dolly is."

Probably a doll, thought Cheever, but he couldn't help but wonder if Helen had an imaginary playmate or two. As an adult, she certainly had them. How far did her memories go back, he pondered, and in what personalities were they present?

"Caitlin," he asked, "do you know a woman named Bonnie? Bonnie Gill?"

Her breathing changed; he could hear that. Cheever could almost feel someone—something—else emerge. A head turned and regarded him. The wide eyes of Caitlin, her innocence and trusting, were gone. Her departure left him feeling flat, as if something precious had been stolen from him once again.

The woman next to him stretched out like a lissome cat. Her lip curled in mock amusement, and a knowing smile came over her features. The expression wasn't quite evil, but it was a long ways from Rebecca of Sunnybrook Farm. She stretched out a hand to Cheever's leg, felt along his thigh, massaging as she went. He felt a trail of heat work its way up to his crotch. Then he pulled away from her.

"Hey," she said, her tone equal parts mocking and sensual, "don't you want to come out and play?"

"Eris?" he asked.

She laughed. "The one and only," she announced, then reached for Cheever, tickled the back of his hair. "You're cute," she said, "for a cop."

He turned the Taurus west onto Broadway. "You've had dealings with the police?"

"Here and there. They like to shine lights and speak big."

Her hand moved from Cheever's hair down his arm, her fingernails lightly scratching. She reached across his chest, and her hand felt the bulge of his holstered gun.

"Hey," she said, "is that a pistol in your pocket or are you just glad to see me?"

A goddess quoting Mae West.

Cheever took her wandering hand and firmly placed it next to her side, but that only amused her. "Let's play good cop, bad cop," she said. "I'll be the bad cop, and you'll get good oral cop."

She reached for his zipper, laughed when he slapped her hand, then gave Cheever a look that said there was no worse sin than being a party-pooper. Her attitude suggested she was the one in control, and he was the passenger along for the ride. She was more right than wrong. The woman was distracting. And intoxicating. There was a part of Cheever that wanted to be swept up in her madness, to damn the consequences and let go. He tried not to show that, but he sensed she knew it anyway.

"Where'd you park?" he asked.

"*She* parked on the next street. Make a right."

"What kind of car?"

"VW Bug," she said dismissively. "I'd want something with more horses under my legs."

She had a way of saying things that grabbed attention. It wasn't only the promise of sex; cops were used to seeing that flashed all too often. In her eyes, and words, and movements were the promissory notes of an unforgettable experience, with delivery only a hot breath away.

Cheever pulled up behind the car. His headlights illuminated the bumper sticker: HUMPTY DUMPTY WAS PUSHED. He wondered which personality had applied the sticker on the Bug. In a way, it was appropriate for all of them. They were collectively Humpty Dumpty after the fall. He didn't envy Dr. Stern. She was trying to do what all the king's horses and all the king's men couldn't do: put Helen back together again.

"Are you going to be all right?" he asked.

"Yes," she said. "The question is, will you be?"

She kissed two of her fingers, then reached over and touched Cheever's lips with them. She manipulated the fingers slowly around his mouth, softly touching him. Her movements grew faster and harder, her fingers starting to press and twist into his lips. Cheever couldn't be sure whether he opened his mouth to her fingers, or whether she pushed them past his lips. She made small, appreciative sounds, then pulled her hand away and opened the door.

"I'd like to go multiple with you sometime," she said, exiting his car in one lithe movement, shutting the door behind her with a push of her backside.

She walked over to her car with the kind of fuck-me step that streetwalkers try to mimic, but forever parade in a sad parody of the real thing. She was licentiousness with an attitude, insouciant and incorrect, and she reveled in it.

Her VW started with a loud roar. It pulled away from the curb quickly, brazenly.

Cheever's head was spinning. He wondered about hers.

Six

Home to Orpheus. Cheever could tell the shrink had been curious about his knowledge of mythology, though she'd never inquired. She probably figured that by asking him an intimate question he was entitled to the same. The two of them, he thought, had a strange chess game going on.

Where Cheever lived in Leucadia most of the streets were named after mythological characters. After traveling the roads for a few years he had become curious and started exploring the mythology behind the names. In time the streets became a little more than streets.

The fog had settled along the coast, clustered thickly in some patches. Cheever passed by the streets of myths and gods, his way taking him by Athena, Vulcan, Diana, Jason, and Hermes, until he twisted around Glaucus, and descended down, down, just like Orpheus had done.

Cheever had always thought it unfair that Orpheus Avenue didn't intersect with Eurydice. The planners should have thought of that, should have made sure there was a Eurydice Street so that the star-crossed lovers could have at last had an earthly convergence. But there was no street named after her. Orpheus stood alone.

"You look for portents," Cheever whispered into the fog, "and you find them."

He turned on the wipers. The mist was thick. He thought about Orpheus and Eurydice, and about himself, remembering love gone wrong, and love lost, and the failure of love to conquer all. It was the eve of the twenty-first century, and Cheever was still mulling over myths.

Orpheus and Eurydice were in the first bloom of newly-wed love when a snake bit her on the foot and killed her. Orpheus put his grief into music and both gods and mortals cried rivers, and even the wild animals lamented.

Sorrow transports people to different places. Orpheus took his grief to Hades, his love and his lyre's petition allowing him passage to a place where mortals dared not go. The dead are not allowed to leave the underworld. It was the law, and the law was as immutable as death, but Orpheus sang his case to the dark lord Pluto, and, in the end, even the king of the underworld relented. Eurydice was delivered to Orpheus on one condition: that he not look at her, or speak with her, until he was free of Hades.

The ascent out of that dark place is long and difficult; very few have ever been delivered from there. Orpheus and Eurydice almost made it out. When he saw the lights of the upper world, Orpheus turned to shout the good news, and it was then that Eurydice was dragged back down to Hades by unseen hands. Orpheus could not forgive himself. Love had almost conquered death, but not quite. Death wishes are granted more easily than most. In a matter of days Orpheus died, and was only then reunited with Eurydice.

"And they died happily ever after," said Cheever, staring into the darkness.

He turned on his brights, knowing even as he did so that

it was a futile measure against fog. It illuminated the shroud around him, but not the road ahead. Light wasn't always the answer.

Was Sappho's Leucadia different than his own? The fog, Cheever decided, was obscuring reality, blurring time and events and taking away his footing. When he and his wife had split up twenty years past, Cheever hadn't had any idea where to go, only knew that he wanted to move away from her and their La Mesa house, away from all the memories. He had ended up renting a place in Leucadia from a cop who'd gotten the home as an inheritance. After a few years of renting, Cheever had noticed a FOR SALE sign on a nearby street. There had been very little to move.

All roads lead to Rome. Cheever wondered if the Romans had stolen the saying from the Greeks, just as they had stolen their gods and just about everything else. He could hear Interstate 5, but not see it. The proximity of the freeway had made his house affordable. Creeping along, aiming for the center of Orpheus, Cheever finally made it home. He drove up his uneven driveway. The roots of his eucalyptus and avocado trees had broken through the asphalt and were turning the drive into an obstacle course. Rather than attack the roots, Cheever had been thinking about getting a four-wheel-drive.

He had bought the two-bedroom bungalow in the seventies as a fixer and had never done too much to change its status. His home improvements were always out of necessity, work done to keep the place standing. The bungalow had been built in the thirties; most of its contemporaries had been bulldozed, replaced by more expansive, and expensive, houses. Cheever liked it that the house was older than he was. So few things in southern California were. It was a man's house because no woman had ever lived in it for more than a night. Over the years the female guests had always emphasized the "charm" of the house, and its potential. The general consensus must have been that the house had more possibilities than Cheever, as none of the women had ever stayed in his life very long.

He didn't blame them. He figured most self-help books were probably written for people like him, the same audience that didn't buy them. One of Cheever's few friends had told him he needed to learn how to build bridges. "That's how you connect with people," the friend had preached. But bridges were for those who wanted to get to the other side.

Cheever was more outgoing on the job. You made cases by opening your mouth and getting others to do the same. Nothing was more important for a homicide dick than getting people to talk. His peers especially liked his confessor routine, with Cheever looking and acting like Father Flannery, speaking softly and tiredly to the suspects, pretending he cared about their mortal souls. Time had improved the fit, giving him mostly white hair, deep wrinkles, and sad eyes. The suspects were ready for tough, but not their parish priest. They didn't want to disappoint him with more lies, but they discovered that the truth didn't set them free. It got them convicted, not shrived. When they confessed their guilt, Cheever walked away. He didn't think of that as a betrayal, but only as a part of his job. But sometimes it wasn't as easy to separate work from life and just walk away.

He didn't like working on cases that involved the deaths of little children, but the team counted on him. They expected him to go into the interview room and do his act. He remembered one time he had been sent in to talk with two parents who had battered their child to death but weren't owning up to it. He had offered the suspects smokes and Cokes and told them how he had four kids of his own and that he knew how necessary discipline was, and that the problem with society was that too many children didn't get hit when they should, and that he could understand they had only done what was necessary, but that they should tell him about it. And they had. He had nod-ded and listened, had never dropped his avuncular act, but he had kept his hands hidden under the table, hands clenched so hard that by the time all the talking was done, he couldn't even pick up a pencil for hours.

Cheever thought about Caitlin. The shrink had said she was five years old. To him, that was a cruel irony. Cheever had hoped Caitlin was the one personality he wouldn't run into. Even before she emerged, he knew how vulnerable he was to her. Their first meeting had gone worse than he could have imagined. After she had called him "Daddy," most of his brain had shut down.

Cheever remembered how he and his wife Karen and their daughter Diane had checked into a hotel in another city to see yet another specialist. Diane had lost her hair by then. Sometimes she wore scarves. When she wasn't so sick and tired she still cared how she looked. The desk clerk had asked how old she was, and Cheever had said five, and the clerk had said, "She's free then," and Diane had very indignantly said, "I'm five, not three," not understanding that children six and under were free.

Diane had died a few months later. She had been sick for two years with leukemia. Cheever had never thought she was going to die. There was always some promising drug or a remission just around the corner. His little girl never got better, but she never got bitter either. She had remained his little angel until the end. Sometimes he still imagined she was alive and five. He would replay their conversations in his mind word for word. "Daddy, why did the man throw a clock out the window? Because he wanted to see time fly." That was one of the curses of his memory. There was this part of him always repeating the past no matter how many clocks he threw out the window.

Time heals all wounds. He repeated the cliché like a mantra and tried to compartmentalize his grief. If there was a just law in the universe it should have been that parents could never outlive their children. He remembered the day he had broken down reading the epitaph of another little girl who had died too young, too soon. On her tombstone her father had chosen these engraved words: SO SOON DONE FOR, WHAT WERE YOU BEGUN FOR? That was a question Cheever had asked himself for so long. Where was the redemption? It used to tear him up inside when he'd hear other parents yelling out the name "Diane" to their little girls. That didn't happen very often now.

When his Diane was young it was a popular name. He remembered at her nursery school there had been two other Dianes. But now the name wasn't in vogue. It was going the way of Barbara and Betty and Martha, names that had been popular when he was a boy. The fashionable names these days sounded like cosmetic counter offerings. When he drove by elementary schools he heard girls calling out names like Ashley and Taylor and Tiffany and Brianna and Lauren. And, he considered, Caitlin.

Odd, how Helen had chosen that name so long ago. It wouldn't have been popular back then, would have been quite unusual. Cheever wondered how she had selected that name. An Irish folktale? An ancestral name? Maybe the shrink knew why.

Cheever walked up the path to his house, knew the way well enough so that he didn't have to use his foot like a tapping cane. A plaintive wail came from the house. It wasn't like the cat didn't have a cat door and enough dry food to last her for days, but she still wanted to complain.

The cat demanded to be fed first. Cheever flipped a poptop for her, then one for himself. As he dropped her can he noticed its label: 9 Lives. He took a long gulp of beer, reached for a second can, then made his way to the living room where he lay down on the worn sofa, fitting into its hollow perfectly. Like Cinderella's slipper, he thought. Too many times lately he had fallen asleep on the sofa and paid the price the next morning with a stiff back. A sign of age.

Who said that with age came wisdom? Aches, that's what came with it.

It didn't take long for the cat to work her way over to him. Sometimes Cheever still referred to Gumshoe as "he." The first time Cheever had taken her to the vet, he had explained, "He's got this rash."

"She," said the vet, who had only given the cat one perfunctory glance.

"What?"

"She," he insisted.

"How do you know?"

"She's a tricolor. I've yet to meet a male calico, although statistically I suppose it's possible."

The vet was in his sixties, had no doubt seen his share of calico cats. He picked up Gumshoe, did some looking that Cheever had never attempted, then said definitively, "She."

She. It still didn't sound quite right.

Gumshoe jumped up on the sofa. She was one of the original heat-seeking missiles. "You know," said Cheever, not for the first time, "I'm a dog person.

"Male dog," he added.

His revelation spurred the cat to nestle a little closer and purr a little louder. "I got a waif instead of a wife, didn't I?" Cheever said, using his index finger to scratch Gumshoe under the chin. Her redoubled purrs told him he still had the touch.

The murderer had never confessed, but they had reconstructed what had happened. He had killed the dogs first, two pugs, had used a club on them. His original intent had been to just burgle the house. But that had changed. When the mother had arrived home they struggled, and when their altercation ended, the burglar was a murderer. The daughter came home shortly after that and became the last victim. The murderer had tried to cover up what he had done by setting the house afire. Gumshoe had smelled like smoke for weeks.

The team was used to calling animal control to take pets of homicide victims, but the cat slipped through the cracks. Cheever first noticed the cat at the homicide scene the day after the fire. She had kept nosing around the ashes, kept looking for her home that wasn't there.

His work had brought him to the crime scene a third day, and the cat was still hanging around. She didn't seem quite so wary as she had before. At first she just watched Cheever while he worked, then she gradually approached, and finally she rubbed up against him. He remembered a tuna fish sandwich he had in the car. That day the cat ate most of it.

Cheever's intention was to make a call and have the cat picked up, but he knew there wasn't much of a call for middle-aged neutered (Cheever didn't see any balls and was already calling the feline "he") cats. They were considered about as cute and cuddly and desirable as middle-aged cops. He had hoped one of the neighbors would weaken and take in the animal, but by the fourth day that hadn't happened. Cheever was the one who weakened. He learned the cat was named "Gummy Bear." Cheever figured he did the animal a favor by renaming her Gumshoe.

He scratched her in that special spot just behind her left ear. So intense was Gumshoe's pleasure she started kneading him with her paws, her sharp nails moving in and out. Cheever gently removed her from him, placing the cat at his side so she could rend the sofa instead of his chest. Gumshoe's pleasure was voiceless. Her evocative wordlessness reminded Cheever of another one of Helen's personalities. By her silence, Pandora had made herself heard.

"Pandora was the first woman," Cheever told the cat. "Her name translates to the all-gifted, because the gods provided her with everything. Looks and wisdom and curiosity. Especially that. So imagine what happened when they entrusted a special box to her, one they told her never to open. You know something about curiosity, cat?"

She did. Cheever reached for a nearby paper bag and opened it. Gumshoe became alert. It was a favorite game of hers. She hopped down from the sofa to be nearer to the bag.

"Human nature was established early," Cheever said. He started rattling the end of the bag slightly, using a hanger. He'd learned not to use his own fingers.

"Pandora couldn't resist the temptation of the box," he said, "and when she opened it, all the ills of the world emerged. Hate and disease and discord flew out, along with greed, sloth, envy, jealousy, and everything terrible."

Gumshoe's body was tensed and poised. With each crinkle of the bag, with each movement, she readied herself for the attack.

Cheever talked softly while poking the bag. "Pandora shut the cursed box, but too late. All the evils were out, and never to be contained again. But there was one voice left in the box that asked to be set free. Pandora was afraid, but relented and released the last prisoner inside, and out emerged Hope with a palliative for all the evils that had been released."

He tapped the bag. "What do you hear, cat? Is that hope calling from inside of here? Or some gremlin?"

Gumshoe charged the bag. Even though Cheever was expecting the attack, he was always surprised at the quickness and ferocity of her lunge. When the cat emerged from the sack, it was slightly the worse for wear. But she came out proudly, having once again vanquished the dragons.

Cheever looked inside the sack. Like Pandora's box, it was empty. Maybe, just maybe, hope had escaped again.

SEVEN

Into the night with only one rule: boredom is death. She had the controls now. Not the wimp. Not the kid. Not that hopeless romantic. Not any of them. Just her.

Holly had popped out earlier and stopped to shower and change and take care of the mutt, but now it was her time. Jumping into the VW Bug, she turned on the engine and announced to an audience she knew only too well, "This is Captain Eris speaking. We are currently flying not nearly high enough, and traveling not nearly fast enough, but all of that will be remedied."

The vibes were right, she decided, for the Dead Club in Ocean Beach, a place where most of the living didn't fit in. It was the alternative to alternative clubs, a hangout for nightly gatherings of punkers, grungers, metal heads, ravers, zine-sceners, artists, hip-hoppers, bikers, exhibitionists, and the leather and S&M crowd.

It only took her thirteen minutes to get from downtown to Ocean Beach. San Diego's freeways weren't like L.A.'s, not yet at least. O.B. still felt like home to her. She had lived there for three years, had reluctantly moved when faced with ever smaller work spaces and ever greater rent. The artists in her didn't like bonsai art, didn't like to have their work limited by their living space. Eris couldn't care less about art; she just liked having room enough to play.

Parking was always tight in O.B. She was lucky to find a spot in an alleyway just two blocks away from the club. Even from there, she could hear and feel the beat of the music. Cultural Perversity was playing, and the walls couldn't contain their metal sounds. There was a line outside, but not everybody was waiting to get in. Show and tell was going on. The cover charge was five dollars, but it was Nipple Piercing Night; anyone flashing pierced nips got in for free. For those who wanted to beat the cover charge, and come away with a mutilated body part to boot, there was a booth set up inside for the piercing. It cost fifty bucks, but participants got to keep the nipple ring and had the pleasure of hundreds of people watching their pain. A few even looked at their tits.

Some in the line shouted to her, calling out different names. Here she was accepted. Here was where people tried to be different. She didn't have to try, and that made her a club star. There were those who attempted to copy her, who regularly changed their names, looks, and behavior just like she did, but they were a zircon set that couldn't quite cut it, glass or otherwise.

She walked by the bouncers. They didn't call out for her to get in line, or to pay the cover. Even they were in her thrall, trying to catch her eye, to have her recognize their steroided existence, but she was above them, above everyone. There was that saying, "To err is human, but to forgive is divine." She liked the abbreviation: To Eris Divine.

It was still too early for things to be really happening, so Eris high-stepped over to the bar. She had the kind of walk, the kind of *juice*, that opened up a space for her at the bar. A bartender with a dark goatee and long ponytail made his fastest approach of the night, ignoring all the others trying to call out their drink orders.

"Haven't seen you lately," he said.

Eris ignored his pleasantry. "I need some rocket juice," she said. "You got a special drink?"

The Dead Club wasn't the type of place where barkeeps labored over specialty drinks. "I make a margarita that's got a kick to it like a nuclear bomb," he said.

"I could use some meltdown," she said.

He free-poured a six count of Cuervo Gold, added Cointreau, Triple Sec, some Grand Marnier, and a dash of Midori, then hand-squeezed some lime juice and shook the concoction.

"Salt or no salt?"

"Who can turn down spice?" she asked.

The bartender grabbed a glass, flipped it in the air, kissed its lip along the salt, filled it with ice, and with a strainer poured out the drink. He dropped a napkin from shoulder level, waited for it to find the counter, then placed the margarita atop it.

After watching her take a long gulp of the drink, he asked, "What do you think?"

In answer, Eris tilted the glass back a second time and finished what was there. "I think," she said, "it's a good start."

"Another?"

"Is that a rhetorical question?"

He cleared her glass, quickly prepared her refill, then served it up with a flourish. Raising it up, she took a healthy gulp and said, *"La chaim."*

"You Jewish?" he asked.

She shook her head. "Early Greek Orthodox."

Several men drifted over, as they always did, and her drinks were paid for, as they always were. Voices got louder, the men wanting her attention. They acted like a troop of chimps, vying with each other to get her look, her smile, her nod, any token of her approval. She accepted their worship. Each of them thought they were clever asking for her telephone number when the others weren't noticing. She gave all three the number of an S.O.B. who owed her for some art. She hoped they would call him in the middle of the night drunk and horny, and then call again thinking they had misdialed. "I want Eris," they would say, and he would hear their longing. He'd wonder who was haunting them, and do some vicarious longing of his own. The bastard better pay up, she thought, or I'll give out his address next. I'll have them howling on his steps.

One of her rules was never to announce when she was leaving, but to just disappear. This time the music called to her, and took her, as music should. She walked away from the bar, only pausing once on her way to the dance floor. "You," she said, tapping on a shoulder. She continued to the dance floor, knowing he would follow. Eris took her rightful place at the center of the floor, the way opening for her. Her chosen consort had to fight and struggle to get through.

It wasn't only the music that moved her. The strobe lights offered a pace, a rhythm. She followed the sunbursts, imagined herself a plant unrooted, stretching for the light, reaching greedily, not worried about gravity or sunburn. The pulses came faster, in short machine-gun bursts, washing her in paparazzi flashes. For a time there was only the music and the lights, and when she awakened it was to her partner asking if she wanted a drink. He was perspiring heavily and panting. How long had they been out there? His hair was dyed black, and he was wearing too much eye makeup, but that was the point.

"Wine, lots of wine," she said.

The followers of Bacchus always wanted wine. They

could, and did, drink bottles of the stuff whenever they were given the chance. Eris never cared what she drank, so long as it gave her a buzz, but the other personalities were more particular. When everything was popping, so were the personalities. Every minute she'd be different. The bartenders never knew whether she wanted wine, beer, vodka, bourbon, the nightly drink special, or apple juice. They drew the line at grape Kool-Aid, Caitlin's drink of choice. When Caitlin popped out she usually had to settle for a Shirley Temple or Roy Rogers, but it was rare that she emerged during a clubbing, which was good, because the strange characters usually scared her into running off. The kid showed unusually good sense.

Mixing drinks never made her sick. It was as if all the alcohol went into different bodies. If one of her personalities was drinking heavily, then only that personality got drunk. Either Pandora or Eurydice always drove home. They were teetotalers.

Her dance partner brought a liter of wine, and with it out popped the Maenads. She grabbed the container and said, "Wine." Three gulps later she said, "Fine." Then another voice announced, "All mine," and finished the wine. Her dance date looked on with amazement.

The wine charged up the Maenads. She pulled her thirsty partner onto the dance floor, but he wasn't enough for her women. She stepped into the crowd and reached with her hands for two more men, running her nails up and down their shirts before leading them forward. "Toy boys," she announced, lining her drones up. Then the music grabbed her, and the Maenads screeched, and howled, and took over the floor. Everyone crowded to take in her show. Though her toy boys tried, they couldn't keep up with her, with them. She licked their sweat and cried the sound of the hunt in their ears, corralling them into her madness. She hopped from one to another and they desperately tried to follow her rhythm. Almost, this was enough, the music, the twirling, the frenzy, but there was something pulling at her, something more than her collective parts. The moment wasn't enough.

The art was calling. Damn it. The Maenads tried to overcome its urge, tried to dance through it, but they knew the hook was too deep. The muse pulled persistently, slowly gaining the advantage in the tug-of-war contest. Maybe that's why she'd only had her ears pierced thus far (seven in one ear, six in the other). Rings were for yanking.

The switch stopped her in midstep. Pandora backed away from the three men, the three strangers. She ducked under arms and slid between bodies, moving off the dance floor. Behind her she could hear the men yelling. She felt like Cinderella on a pumpkin-time deadline.

She ran to her car, popped the clutch, and then took off. Pandora raced through O.B. and Point Loma, picked up the Pacific Coast Highway, then sailed into downtown San Diego.

Her loft was supposed to be work space, not a living area, but she wasn't the only one who violated that rule, even if she was the only one with a dog. Though she parked a block away from the loft, she could still hear Cerberus barking for her. Which was louder, the Bug's failing muffler or his bark? Another switch, and it was Holly running to her building. She unlocked the doorway and raced up the three flights of stairs. By the time she opened the door, Cerberus was threatening to rip it off the hinges. He greeted her effusively, and his affection was returned, if not quite lick for lick. The rottweiler didn't have three heads like his namesake, but he understood better than anyone the different people inhabiting her body. Cerberus had his own ways of responding to the personalities; some he avoided, others he was lukewarm to, most he adored. The mythical Cerberus had protected the entryway to Hades. Depending on whether she had cleaned or not, her fourth-story loft could have been mistaken for that underworld.

She grabbed his walking equipment, a leash, a sandbox shovel, and a plastic bag, and before she could even say, "Let's go for a walk," Cerberus raced by her in a mad dash for the stairs, his nails clicking loudly on the old wooden floors. He moved up and down the flights, running forward, then back to her, hurrying her along. She felt guilty for not having spent much time with the dog lately, but he had been out of her mind.

Once she had forgotten about him for three days. He hadn't condemned her, had greeted her return with a tired, if persistent, thumping of his tail, but she had been beside herself. It was bad enough that she couldn't take care of herself, but she felt it was criminal to fail her animal. But instead of giving him away, she had enlisted others to watch out for him. Her loft neighbor had a key and he was supposed to check on the dog whenever he noticed she wasn't around. One time she had walked in and found them eating ice cream together. The solution might not have been perfect, but she had refused to run away from the problem. She knew that multiple personalities were wonderful escapists. With Dr. Stern's help, she was trying to change that behavior, to clean up after herself.

And even after her dog, she thought, scooping up Cerberus's droppings. His crap wouldn't have been out of place on the street, would have fit in with the emptied bottles of booze, and fast-food wrappers, and cigarette packages, but she felt better for having picked up after him.

She made the walk a short one. Tomorrow, she thought, she would do better by Cerberus. She would take him to Fiesta Island, to Dog Beach. It was late to be walking on the streets of downtown San Diego, even with hell's watchdog at her side. Besides, the pulling was getting more intense, the compulsion to get to her art. It was the one constant in her life. Everything else could be falling apart, but she always had her art. She wasn't sure whether that was a saving grace, or an anchor that pulled her down.

Cerberus stayed by her side. He had never been obedience trained, but was always right next to her if he sensed any uneasiness on her part, or detected some potential danger. Maybe there was a homeless person lying in the shadows, or maybe she was upset and didn't know it.

They walked upstairs. She quickly fed him, dropped him a rawhide bone for dessert, then changed into some old, comfortable clothes. A tingling touched her, almost electrical in nature. She was ready to create, even if she was unsure what form the expression would take. As might have been expected, she was an artist with many voices. Her first love had been painting, and she'd gone through more styles in ten years than most artists do in a lifetime. A few years back she had started designing jewelry, and still dabbled in it. Her sculpting had been her latest passion, starting with what she called "death masks," and then progressing into full figures. She couldn't afford marble, so she used whatever was available, had managed to sculpt with everything from papier-mâché to treated vegetables to synthetics. She was skilled at molding and trimming and sanding and applying enough layers of lacquer and paint to give a finish that looked like fine stone.

Though there were several pieces of statuary she was working on, that wasn't what had summoned her that night. She grabbed for her sketch pad. Her hand started moving, unconsciously drawing what had to be drawn. She called this Ouija board time, when the designs apparently came from somewhere outside herself. The spirit compelled her to do the background first, a building. It was night, so she shrouded the edifice in shadows. But the darkness didn't mean that all was gloomy. There was a warm feeling to the backdrop that came through even in pencil, something tropical about the setting. It wasn't exactly

South Seas exotic, not Gauguin's Eden, but it was clement and welcoming, with flowers popping up everywhere.

Mostly carnations, she realized.

Her pencil started working on another image. A figure emerged, materializing with his back turned to her. He looked to be walking rapidly away from the building down the pathway to the street. Or was that a woman hurrying off? She still wasn't sure. The figure had a trench coat on, and gloves, which didn't quite make sense in a setting with so many tropical flowers, but it wasn't her place to question what appeared on the paper. At times like this she didn't think of herself as the artist. She was only the vessel from which art flowed.

Her pencil gradually slowed. The artist examined her sketch critically, looking it over very carefully. It felt almost right, but something was missing. Her hand went back to the drawing, hovered over it, then found the detail that was missing.

She erased the figure's right arm, then drew it again so that it curved up around the small of the back.

There was one necessary addition. Within the gloved hand she drew a knife.

EIGHT

Cheever waited for his appointment on the stoop of the gallery. Someone who didn't know better might have thought he had stopped to smell the flowers. Sandy Ego Expressions was beginning to look like a shrine, with mounds of carnation bouquet tributes piled up along its entryway. Some of the bouquets had Bonnie Gill's picture taped to their cellophane wrappings, the same picture that had run in that morning's *Union-Tribune*. The paper had sprung for four-color but the print had somehow bled Bonnie's red hair into the next column.

The article made Bonnie out to be a saint, with a lot of corroborating quotes. There was a sidebar piece on the "Carnation Fund" that told how Bonnie's friends had already collected $50,000 in reward money for information leading to the arrest of her killer. "We want justice," Reuben Martinez was quoted as saying, "and we're willing to pay for it." From what Cheever had seen, those behind the fund were very organized. During his morning's canvassing, he'd seen that they already had bounty posters up all over the downtown area.

He looked at his watch. It was a little past ten-thirty and he wondered if his appointment was going to show. He'd give her a few more minutes. The day already felt long. His interviews had been mostly redundant, going back to places and people he had already seen. While walking the neighborhood, Cheever had kept smelling fresh-baked tortillas from a nearby tortilleria. He knew that in his mind Bonnie Gill would forever be associated with carnations and the scent of a Mexican bakery. It was a better way to remember the dead than most.

A woman in her mid-thirties walked slowly up the pathway to the gallery. She was cautious and tense, and her body language said she was just looking for an excuse to run away. Despite it being sunny and warm, she was holding her sweater close to her as if she were cold. Cheever had seen her kind of upset too many times before. Her mostly red outfit went well with her bottle-blond hair.

"Good morning," he said. "I'm Detective Cheever."

"Gretchen Stoeffer," she said, her caution replaced by relief. She shook his hand and started talking nervously. "My husband didn't want me to come in today, or ever again. He figures if I'd been working the shop instead of Bonnie, I'd be dead."

Cheever let her talk. Gretchen lived in Del Cerro, had two kids and an engineer husband, and it showed. Life was PTA, some sporadic drawing, and her part-time job at the gallery.

Together, they approached the gallery's door and all of the flowers. In a setting other than yellow crime scene tape the carnations would have been a pleasant sight. Cheever cleared a path for them.

" 'Think carnations,' " said Gretchen. "That's what Bonnie used to always say. 'If you give an area an identity, it will become special.' "

"Did anyone resent Bonnie's dreams?"

She shook her head. "Everyone seemed to think she was

the best thing that ever happened to this neighborhood. Bonnie's philosophy was to improve things. She believed in reincarnation and thought it only made sense for her to make the world better, because she wanted to return to a better place."

"Bonnie was a Hindu?"

"Not in the practicing sense. She was just sure she had lived other lives before, and not all of them in human form. She was at her happiest when she was nurturing, helping something to grow. That's why she loved the garden so much."

Cheever lifted up the crime scene tape, and then opened the door. As Gretchen stepped inside, her nervous chatter ran dry. Bonnie Gill's body was long removed, but the gallery hadn't yet been sanitized. The evidence tech had powdered everywhere, and the black dust was only the first reminder of what had happened here. Cheever knew that as they proceeded further into the gallery it would be even worse. He slowed their pace and tried to talk Gretchen through her initial shock, his voice calm and settling. "As far as we've been able to determine," he said, "neither Bonnie's pocketbook nor the store receipts were touched by her assailant. But we need you to look around to see if anything's missing, or different."

He stressed his words, forced her to look into his eyes. "You mean like missing art?" she asked.

"Anything," he said.

"Because," she said, upset, "it's not as if there are any Picassos here."

As gently as he could, Cheever said, "We're just curious about your impressions, Gretchen. May I call you Gretchen?"

She nodded.

"We want to see if you notice anything out of the ordinary, Gretchen, anything at all."

"Okay," she said, but her voice said it was anything but that.

"We're also curious about what you can tell us about a certain painting," he said. "It's a beach scene."

Cheever showed her a photograph of the painting. It was hard to tell from the picture that the painting had been splattered with blood, which was just as well.

"I think that's one of Keith Aubell's," she said. "I can check on that."

"Please do," he said.

She took a deep breath, as if preparing to dive underwater, and then walked toward the gallery's west wall. She stopped at a spot, and for Cheever's benefit pointed to what wasn't there. If you knew what you were looking for, you could see that there was a blank space along the wall big enough for a three-foot by three-foot painting to hang.

"That's where the painting was hanging," Gretchen said. "It's Keith's."

"Do you have his telephone number and address?"

She nodded, opened her mouth, then thought better of it and went off to get the information. It was clear she wanted to ask "why," but didn't find the nerve to broach the question until she returned with the artist's address and telephone number. Handing Cheever the piece of paper, she said, "I'm curious . . ."

"The painting was found by Bonnie's body," Cheever said. "It might be evidence."

He didn't amplify beyond that, didn't tell her that the painting had been used as a shield. It was presumed that whomever had stabbed Bonnie Gill hadn't wanted to get sprayed by her blood.

Cheever looked at Gretchen expectantly. Prodded, she began a tentative tour of the gallery. He trailed behind her, saying nothing, but his presence seemed to make her nervous. It was the nature of the beast, he knew. Cops made people, even law-abiding people, sweat. He decided to give her some room.

"I think I might head out to the garden," he said, "give you some breathing room to look around here."

The path to the back of the gallery was hardly a scenic tour. Bonnie Gill's trail of blood was easily discernible to the eye. And what couldn't be seen had been studied. The evidence tech had spent long hours analyzing the blood splatter. Her conclusion had been that Bonnie Gill's killer was an adept butcher, not to mention a fastidious one.

At the entryway to the garden was the sign announcing the Garden of Stone exhibit, and the suggestion that visitors pick up a brochure. Cheever backtracked a few steps to an information rack. Most of the pamphlets in the stand detailed the gallery's arts and crafts courses, with folders on glassblowing, pottery making, ceramics, and drawing. Behind those could be found a few Garden of Stone flyers.

Cheever picked one up and began his tour. Even in daylight the statues were disconcerting, their Mona Lisa eyes following him, their clothing playing with his peripheral vision. Again and again, he found himself turning, expecting to see a person.

He stopped walking and tried concentrating on the brochure. There was a picture of Holly Troy at work and brief descriptions of her creations. Cheever counted the statues, and then the descriptions in the pamphlet. By his calculations, only two of her statues had been sold.

Helen had titled all of her works. Cheever compared her names with the remaining figures. It was apparent that most of the statues were classically influenced, even if Cheever didn't know the stories behind them. With Helen, he thought, there were hidden meanings everywhere. Even in her titles. She liked to use wordplay and double entendres. One of her statues showed a man, presumably Anthor, pierced by a spear. Her title: *Death Called, He Anthored*. A boar being hunted was identified as *Pentheus*

Boarn Again, and the statue of a woman turning into a tree was called *Dryope as Sap*. A beautiful youth lying on the ground was described as *Hyacinthusis*, and a woman in the midst of great grief, tears running down her face, was named *Niobe on Mother's Day*. Not all of the statues were named, at least not directly. The identity of the knife-wielding priest and his victim remained a mystery, but perhaps their names could be discerned in her title of *Achilles as a Heel*.

Even in Helen's seemingly innocent statues Cheever sensed something lurking, some unseen beast. One piece showed two little girls playing, apparently happily. The brochure cataloged them as *Jason's Offspring*. Still, there was something about the girls that was far removed from Norman Rockwell, just as there was in the statue of the little girl who was afraid and crying, a piece entitled *Growing Up*.

Gretchen quietly entered the garden. Cheever turned, confirmed she wasn't a statue. He could tell without asking, but had to make the pro forma inquiry: "How's it going?"

She shook her head, a depressed motion that offered despair on several fronts. "I'm afraid I didn't notice anything out of the ordinary."

"Nothing at all?"

"Nothing if you don't count the . . ."

She didn't know how to say it, or didn't want to face up to saying it.

"Crime scene," Cheever offered.

She nodded, then asked, "Why wasn't everything cleaned up?"

"We had to do tests," Cheever said, "and we wanted you to look around first. The cleaning always has to wait until we're finished with the crime scene. We're done now."

"Will you be cleaning today, then?"

"I'm afraid that's not something we do."

"But . . ."

She looked like she might get sick, was probably picturing herself taking a mop and pail and trying to wipe up after her deceased friend.

"It's usually best to have a cleaning firm do it," Cheever said. "I'd be glad to give you some names and numbers. They can generally come out right away."

"Yes," she said distractedly, "I suppose I better get someone here."

He wrote down several numbers on his card and handed it to her. Gretchen accepted his written recommendations reluctantly, wasn't yet ready to face up to that responsibility.

"You never think about these kind of things," she said.

Cheever agreed, even though he thought about them all the time.

They stood looking at the statues together. Given the alternatives, Cheever thought, maybe they weren't so bad after all. Still, they were annoying. "What's with their clothes?" he asked.

"The sculptor liked to dress them," she said.

"Holly Troy?" he asked, using her brochure name.

She nodded. "You know Holly?"

It was his turn to nod. "Were clothes always a part of her statues?"

"No. Holly started dressing them a few days after the display opened. She said the clothes were a way to keep the exhibit fresh. Bonnie let her do it, but more to humor her than anything else. She started referring to the statues as Holly's Barbie Dolls. 'You can dress them up,' she told her, 'but I don't see anyone taking them out.'"

"They weren't selling?"

"Not very well. We only sold one or two. Bonnie told Holly she thought they were too serious and macabre, and said if she didn't lighten up on her statuary, she'd only be creating for herself."

"How did Holly take that?"

"About as well as most people take personal criticism. She said she wasn't going to pander to common tastes and that if Bonnie wanted her garden known as the bird bath emporium that was fine with her."

"Did Bonnie have an answer to that?"

"Something to the effect that 'birdshit sometimes pays the bills,' and that Holly could learn from that."

"Sounds like there wasn't any love lost between them."

Gretchen's head disagreed. "Bonnie understood that Holly needed space to fly, but she also knew when to yank her string. Bonnie wanted Holly to be more centered, to concentrate on one art form instead of jumping around. She thought Holly should stick to painting."

"Painting?"

Nodding, "We have a few of her paintings inside."

"I'd appreciate seeing them," he said.

Cheever followed her back inside the gallery. Though Gretchen didn't say anything, Cheever noticed that she detoured around the dried blood without looking directly at it. They ended up in the southeast side of the gallery, in what Cheever suspected were the bleacher seats for artwork. "There," said Gretchen, pointing. "Those three."

The paintings were hanging next to one another. Cheever glanced from one to another, and doubted whether even an art expert could have determined they had been drawn by the same hand, as the colors and styles and subjects were very different.

"Proximity seems to be the only thing they have in common," he said.

"Holly is diverse," she said.

That, Cheever knew, was an understatement. "Doesn't do fruit bowls, does she?" he said.

The first painting showed a woman of indeterminate age almost passed out from too much booze. Somehow she was still managing to hold on tightly to her broken bottle of vodka. The title emphasized the woman's straits: *Russian Roulette*.

"I think I'll make that phone call," Gretchen said.

Cheever gave a preoccupied nod while continuing to study the paintings. The second drawing was framed and set up to look like a billboard. He found himself not breathing when confronted by a familiar face. Surrounded by clouds was a smiling Graciela Fernandez. There was a special illumination around her face, a glow that came from within instead of from the billboard lights. The painting had been named *Now Playing*. There was something of a Hollywood feel to it, one of those feel-good movie billboards. Or maybe Helen was saying that Graciela was playing somewhere else, somewhere better, and was happy in her new playground.

In the background, Cheever could hear Gretchen talking. Her voice was high-pitched, nervous: "If someone could come out today, I would really appreciate it."

The third painting was called *The Cast*. There was a stage, but the emphasis was on the front row of mostly female patrons. The women were very different, both in person and how they were responding to the play. Judging by their expressions, they were all witnessing a different performance. One woman was uproariously laughing, another piteously crying. There was boredom and a glimpse of cruelty on one beautiful woman's face, shock on another. One of the figures was falling asleep, another was mesmerized. There was a red-haired little girl who was too frightened to look, covering her eyes with her hands, and in the shadows was a male figure, his eyes luminescent and intense. Predator's eyes. While one woman knitted, not bothering to watch the show, another was extravagantly gesturing. Cheever suddenly realized that what he was seeing was a self-portrait of Helen in all her guises.

"Yes, I have a major credit card," said Gretchen. "Let me give that number to you."

We're all multifaceted, he thought. We're all many people. But most of us aren't different people. To be laughing and crying at the same time, to be transfixed and scared and bored simultaneously, had to be a frightening existence. Helen was a woman out of control, and she not only knew it, sometimes she could see it.

Gretchen joined him again, and looked a little more at ease having made the cleaning arrangements. "Something about Holly's work," Gretchen said, "stays with you."

"Yes," Cheever said. "She opens doors." Doors that most would prefer were left closed, he thought.

Cheever bent down and examined the signatures on Helen's paintings; even they were dissimilar. The only thing consistent about Helen were her differences.

"What's going to happen to the gallery?" he asked.

"I suppose it will close. I don't know anyone besides Bonnie who could make a go of it."

"Bonnie owned this lot, didn't she?"

A small smile. "She liked to say she owned one percent of it, and the bank ninety-nine percent. She didn't want to go into some safe mall, or have one of those boutique galleries in La Jolla, or Del Mar, or Rancho Santa Fe. She wanted art to transform a community. That's why she liked this spot so much. The garden was important to her. It was like the business was a garden too, and that things were going to grow from it."

"Speaking of the garden," Cheever said, remembering his promise to Flamingo, "someone's going to have to water the plants."

"Yes. That can't really wait, can it? I'll take care of that tomorrow. I'll call some of the artists and get them to come out and help me. Tomorrow we can tend to tasks and remember Bonnie informally. Many hands will make light work, right?"

She wasn't looking for an answer; she was talking to reassure herself. It wasn't helping. Gretchen started playing with her hair. She had something to ask but was unsure how to say it. "I was wondering," she said, "if you wouldn't mind walking me to my car. That is, when you're ready to leave.

"I'm not in any rush, mind you," she added. "I can keep myself busy . . ."

"Let's go," Cheever said.

"I really don't want to take you away . . ."

"I'm finished," he said.

She had probably made the same walk by herself a thousand times, but now everything was changed. As they walked out the entrance they had to once again contend with the bouquets of carnations. Cheever edged the flowers aside with his feet. He was gentle, but couldn't help but trample some of the petals.

Gretchen led the way, and Cheever stayed at her side. They were silent as they walked. Gretchen didn't break the silence until she reached her car. She looked around her, saw all the grime and despair that had somehow been hidden from her before, and shook her head.

"This wasn't the right place for a garden," she said.

NINE

Flamingo was standing on the corner of 10th and J, looking like he was keeping some vigil. Funny, thought Cheever, how you never saw him walking around. He just suddenly appeared doing his one-legged sentry act. Maybe he flew from street corner to street corner. When Flamingo noticed Cheever, he waved for him to come over.

"Flowers looking worse, Captain," Flamingo reported.

"So am I," Cheever said. "It's autumn. It's almost winter. Maybe their time is past."

Flamingo didn't say anything, just gave him a troubled look. It made Cheever feel like a bully. "Don't worry," he said, "help's on the way. I've been told they'll get a watering tomorrow."

"That's good, Captain. Don't like to see neglect. Don't like to see it at all."

Flamingo offered the words without irony. He wasn't trying to be noble, wasn't speaking in metaphors describing his own situation, was just trying to get a drink for his friends.

"We got something to talk about besides crocuses, Flamingo?"

He nodded. "You heard about Doc-tah Denton, Captain?"

Cheever debated answering "Who?" or "What?" but instead said, "No."

"Word is the doc-tah's saying he's gonna get a Cadillac. He's got lotsa plans for that reward money."

"You mean the Carnation Fund reward?"

Flamingo nodded. "The doc-tah say he seen something the night the Flower Mama got kilt. He called that number and told them all about it. If they catch that lady, he says he's gonna get fifty thousand dollars."

"What lady?"

"The one he seen. The one in the garden."

"What'd he see?"

"Don't know. Some lady, that's all he say. I think the doc-tah's afraid someone might be trying to get his reward money."

"Tell me about this Dr. Denton."

Perched on one leg, Flamingo did just that.

The doctor, said Flamingo, was a man who liked to move around. His "rounds" included soup lines and shelters, Horton Plaza, the detox center, some of the canyons in Balboa Park, and a half-dozen vacant lots in the downtown area. Occasionally Dr. Denton gave plasma on 8th Street. He was known to panhandle from Harbor Drive to Fifth Avenue, and when he had money the doctor went looking for his pain prescriptions in liquor stores. He usually bedded down on 10th and K Street, but there were a number of other spots where he dropped his bindle.

The doctor covered a lot of territory for a man on foot. In a way, Cheever thought, that was his job. Cheever debated the best way to track him down. The doctor didn't keep office hours, didn't have a job, a home, or a phone.

But there were reasons, fifty thousand of them, for the doctor to have made his whereabouts known to the Carnation Fund organization. Cheever dialed their number and tested his five-figure hypothesis. A woman who identified herself as Madeline took his call. Cheever explained who he was, and who he wanted to talk with.

"Dr. Who?" asked Madeline.

"Denton. But that's not his real name."

"What is his real name?"

"I'm not sure. Dr. Denton's a nickname. His street name. He apparently likes to wear real long pants that hang down over his shoes. They look like Doctor Dentons."

"But that's not his real name?"

"No."

"I'm afraid no Dr. Denton has called today," she said.

"Did he call yesterday?"

"I'm afraid I wouldn't know. I wasn't working."

Cheever tried to ask a question that Madeline couldn't preface with "I'm afraid."

"Who can help me?"

"Mr. Adams."

"Rollo Adams?"

"Yes."

"Is he available?"

"I'm afraid not. But he does call in for messages."

"Frequently?"

"Every few hours."

"Can he be paged?"

"I'm afraid he is not available to be paged today."

Cheever was *afraid* he might lose his temper. "What happens if someone calls you, Madeline, and says they know who the killer is?"

"I'm afraid I'm not supposed to give out any information over the phone."

"You mean you don't have orders to call the police?"

"I'm af . . ."

Cheever interrupted her apology with a telephone number. "That's Sergeant Falconi's direct extension. Tell Mr. Adams it's urgent."

Madeline repeated the number, got it right, and Cheever thanked her. He hung up the phone and then called Falconi himself. When the sergeant came on the line, Cheever said, "God save us from amateurs."

Falconi asked: "What's up?"

"A potential witness supposedly called the Carnation Fund. He had some story about seeing a woman at the scene of the murder. My version is thirdhand. I called the operator working their phones today. She didn't know anything about the witness, or anything about anything. She's a professional apologist who answers phones and takes messages. I gave her your name and number and a priority of urgent. Rollo Adams is supposed to call you back. The receptionist said that Rollo's the answer man. If that's the case, I got a question for him: Why the hell didn't he call us with the witness story?"

"Still applying to the diplomatic corps, Cheever?"

"Shouldn't we be part of the fifty-thousand-dollar equation?"

"I'll make that clear to Mr. Adams. And at the same time I'll remind you that without the offer of a reward this potential witness might not have come forward."

"I'll let you be grateful for both of us. In the meantime I'll be looking for Dr. Denton."

"What do we have?"

"Black male, thirties, five-seven, weighs one-forty. And he wears pants that come down to his shoes. The doc's lived in the downtown area on and off for a few years. I'm sure some of the uniforms know him."

"I'll get a few assigned to your search party," Falconi said.

"Great minds think alike."

* * *

Doctors are usually easier to find on a golf course than in a hospital, but it was more coincidence than not that the two uniforms found Dr. Denton on a golf course. It was a different kind of golf course to be sure, but then he was a different kind of doctor. At Morley Field near Balboa Park, San Diegans play Frisbee golf. The doctor looked quite at home sprawled out on the expansive lawn. He was far enough away from the nearest "hoop"—the cylinder through which Frisbees were tossed—that he didn't have to worry about too many errant discs. It was a pleasant setting, unhurried and quiet, a good place to do some California dreaming about fifty thousand dollars.

The doctor acted as if he were expecting Cheever. In his right hand was the ubiquitous brown paper bag that made a mockery of camouflage. Waving his bottle, he asked, "Find that lady?"

He showed Cheever a lot of happy teeth, minus one. The doctor was missing a front tooth, a lateral incisor, which gave him a shifty look, whether or not it was merited. He stayed reclined, his show of independence. He was having his liquid picnic and didn't feel like being discommoded by a cop.

"We'll get to that in a minute," Cheever said, his voice neutral. "My name is Detective Cheever. What's yours?"

"Hell, you found me, you know my name. I'm the doctor."

Cheever's tone changed, took on an edge. "Your real name."

"Calvin."

"Calvin what?"

"Calvin Jackson."

"When were you born?"

"What'd, you come to wish me a happy birthday?"

Cheever looked at him. That's all it took.

"November the twentieth, 1966."

Every year they were younger, thought Cheever. "Ever been arrested before, Calvin?"

"Whatcha asking that for?"

Another look.

"Yeah," he said, "I was brought up on a coupla jackshit charges."

"Ever do time?"

"Coupla months here and there."

"Where and why?"

"Why's a good question. Why ya hassling me?"

"Where and why?" asked Cheever again. "And what for?"

Calvin sighed, and then started giving out particulars. He'd been up for a B&E, assault, and possession of a deadly weapon . . .

Cheever interrupted: "What kind of weapon?"

"A shank."

"A knife?"

The doctor gave him a sideways glance. "Shit, you're cold, man."

"I just want to know who I'm talking to, Calvin."

"I know how that lady died. What you be doing is looking for a convenient nigger to place when and where she got sliced."

"You know better than that, Calvin."

"It was a white girl that was there, man. That's who you should be looking for. But it's always easier to go after a brother, isn't it?"

"Tell me about that white girl."

Calvin shook his head, let out a persecuted sigh. "If I tells what I seen, the next thing I know you try to put me in the picture."

"I don't have any agenda, Calvin. I'm just trying to learn what happened."

"Thass what I hear now, but what about later?"

"Nothing changes, Calvin . . ."

"Doctor."

"Doctor," Cheever agreed. "I just want you to tell me what you saw."

"Already called up the reward people, you know. Anyone else says they seen the same thing is a liar 'cuz I was the only one there. My story's worth fifty big ones."

"Your story's not worth a damn thing unless we catch the murderer."

The doctor mulled that one over and then decided to talk. "It was around ten, I figure. I was walking down Tenth and I stopped to take some refreshment in front of that art garden."

"What were you drinking?"

"Some Colt. Had it in a bag. Figured I better finish it before making camp."

"Where was camp for the night?"

"K Street."

A block away from the gallery. "Go on."

"I was resting against that fence, doing some sipping. Feeling fine, you know. There was a light or two on in that outdoors area and enough moon so's that I could see pretty good. Wasn't looking for nothing, though, just sort of taking it easy. I'd seen them statues before, so I was just eyeballing 'em, you know, while I was hanging.

"Almost shit my pants when I seen one of them move."

"One of the statues?"

He nodded. "Thought that's what it was at first, leastways. She looked like one, I swear. It was like she was coming to life in slow motion. Spooky, man. Her arm dropping slow, man, and then her head starting to move. I almost run off. But then she started walking around regular and I could see she was no statue. What she was was a crazy woman."

"What do you mean?"

"Her face got all ugly and she started yelling."

"What was she yelling?"

"Couldn't make out most of the words. But she was pissed. Sounded like she was drunk, and looked like it too. She kept shouting 'no.' Heard her cussing, too. Then she fell down and started yelling, 'Oh, my God' over and over."

"Did you see anyone else there?"

"No. But that lady did."

"I don't understand."

"She kept talking to other people, but I didn't see none of them. You ever see that invisible man movie? And how he's there but nobody can see him and he's making everybody crazy by doing stuff? I kept looking for that invisible man she was so pissed at."

"Why was she pissed?"

"Who knows? But she was lunging at him. And it was like there were other invisible people around her. She kept shouting for them to get behind her."

"Them?"

Head nod: "She said 'girls' a coupla times."

"Describe your woman."

"Red hair. Hard to tell how old. Twenty. Thirty. Maybe even forty. White like a ghost. That's why she looked like a statue. Tall as me, maybe taller."

"Any distinguishing features?"

The doctor thought a moment before saying "No."

"What was she wearing?"

"One of those spy coats."

"Trench coat?"

"Yeah."

"What color?"

"Dark."

"What was her build?"

"Couldn't really tell with that coat. But her face was skinny, hard."

A flying shadow briefly crossed by. And then another. Cheever looked up to see an invasion of the flying discs. The golfers were laughing, enjoying themselves among the palms and the grass. He ignored them.

"What happened after she collapsed?"

"She kept bawling and groaning and her body got the shakes. Then after a few minutes of that she just shut up sudden like someone pulled the plug."

"What then?"

"She stopped to pick up a bag, then walked away."

"A bag?"

"Yeah?"

"What kind of bag? A purse?"

"Bigger. Like a suitcase."

"A duffel bag?"

"Something like that. A bag about so big." He motioned to something that was about three feet by two.

"What did the woman do then?"

"Guess she just left. I didn't see her no more."

"How'd she walk?"

"Whatcha mean?"

"How'd she walk?"

Confused: "Fine."

"You said she sounded and acted like she was drunk. Was she that way when she left?"

The doctor thought on that. "She wasn't making no more noise," he said, "and she seemed to be walking fine."

"Was she walking fast?"

"Yeah."

"Like she wanted to get away?"

A nod.

"Did you see her on the street?"

He shook his head.

"Then what did you do?"

"Finished my drink."

"What then?"

"Went to sleep."

"Where?"

"K Street. But a little later I saw the commotion going on all around there. It didn't look like a good night for sleep, so I picked up and moved."

"To where?"

"Back of that lighting store on Twelfth."

"Is that the only reason you moved? To get sleep?"

He shrugged. "Open your mouth around The Man and it's usually trouble."

"So no one from the police interviewed you that night?"

"Tha's right."

"When did you hear about the murder?"

"Yesterday morning."

"Did you know the woman who got killed?"

The doctor shook his head. "Not really."

"Not really, what?"

"Seen her around."

"You ever talk with her?"

"Coupla words maybe. She had parties at her place, and whenever there was extra food she always give it away."

"You resent her for tossing you scraps?"

The doctor was phlegmatic. "Everybody eatin' off somebody's plate."

"Are you sure the woman you saw in the garden couldn't have been Bonnie Gill?"

"Uh-huh."

"How were they different?"

"The art lady was smaller and rounder. And she had shinier red hair."

"How red was this woman's hair?"

"Pretty deep red. Like one of them roses."

"How long?"

"To her shoulders."

"When did you call the Carnation Fund with your information?"

"Yesterday."

"What time?"

"In the afternoon."

"Who'd you talk to?"

"Some lady. Then she got some man."

"You remember their names?"

"Mostly. He was Yallow Adam, or somethin' like that."

"Rollo Adams?"

"That's him. And I made sure he got my name. Before I told him anything, I asked about the money. He said he'd tape my conversation to make it official, then play it back for me if I wanted, seeing's I don't have no address."

"And did he tape your conversation?"

"Uh-huh. Played back some to show me."

"I'd like to take you to headquarters. Go over what you saw."

"Shee-it."

"We'll throw in lunch. We can stop and pick up some burgers and fries along the way."

"Not in the mood for burgers and fries, man."

"What is it you're in the mood for?"

"A plate of ribs, and a baked patatah with everything, and some corn with lots of melted butter on top, and a hunk of pecan pie. I get those and maybe I'll be in the mood to talk some. Maybe I talk your ears off."

The doctor smiled at Cheever. He'd been around long enough to know the score. And to know that house calls didn't come cheap.

TEN

"I had another nightmare," said Helen.

"Tell me about it."

"I dreamt that I was in a hole, a deep hole. And that no one could hear me. The more I cried, the more frustrated I became. I tried to crawl out, but I couldn't. And it kept getting darker. I woke up in a sweat."

"We've discussed," Dr. Stern said, "how dreams often symbolize real events, and also how the mind disguises the content of dreams, setting up buffers to protect us. The cost of those buffers is often immense. Whenever we keep bad memories bottled up, we tie ourselves down. It is a weight we have to carry. Do you understand that?"

Helen offered an unconvinced nod.

"You said there was a hole," said Dr. Stern. "What does that hole remind you of?"

She struggled with the idea. "I don't know . . ."

"Think."

Her hands clenched and unclenched. Her eyes fluttered and her head dropped. When she opened her eyes she no longer looked tense, even appeared to be enjoying herself.

"The hole symbolizes a vagina, Doctor. A love canal. A man-trap. It's a slash, a gash, a cunt . . ."

"I didn't call for you, Eris."

"The other one was afraid."

"But you're not?"

Disdainfully: "Of you?"

"I wish to discuss this matter with Helen."

"You always want to talk with her. She and the little snot are your favorites."

"I won't play your game of divide and conquer."

In sing-song response: "I can answer your question."

"The hole in your dream is not a vagina."

"I know that."

"What is it?"

"It's the place where dreams die. It's the grav-y, bab-y. It's childhood's end. It's tripping into darkness."

"In your dream it was getting darker. What do you think that means?"

"Death."

So serious, so deep was the word, that it hung in the air like a last note.

"Whose?"

"I'm the one in the hole, aren't I?"

"I don't know. Are you?"

"I suppose. You think I'm down there trying to avoid skin cancer?"

"You tell me."

"Don't have a clue."

"That's odd. The dream offers nothing but clues."

"What do you mean?"

"No one could hear you. That made you frustrated. Your silence stymies you. There are things that need to be said, life and death matters perhaps, and yet you are silent."

"Silence is golden—apples," Eris said, laughing.

Dr. Stern recognized Eris's mythological allusion to herself. There had once been a grand wedding that all the gods and goddesses had been invited to, all except for Eris, who was inadvertently forgotten. Eris wasn't the kind of goddess who could forgive being overlooked. She acted on the slight, making her absence known. Without being seen by anyone, she tossed a beautiful golden apple into the middle of the wedding hall. The inscription on the apple read: For The Fairest.

Three goddesses, Hera, Aphrodite, and Athena, claimed the golden apple as their rightful prize. Paris was given the unenviable task of judging the most difficult beauty contest of all time. The goddesses all offered him bribes. Hera said he could have power and riches; Athena tried to seduce him with glory and fame in war; Aphrodite promised him the fairest of all women for his wife. It was beauty that won over Paris. There was a problem, though. The most beautiful woman in the world was Helen, who was already betrothed to Menelaus. That didn't stop Paris from claiming his prize, which resulted in the Trojan War.

Eris enjoyed nothing more than throwing those golden apples into Helen's life. She sat there gloating.

"Of late," Rachel said, "Pandora is the one who has embodied silence as being golden. I would like to talk with her now."

There was something of the Cheshire cat in the way that Eris's grin continued to hang in the air, even as she disappeared. Helen's eyes closed for a long moment and when she opened them the brazen assuredness was gone. Dr. Stern welcomed the new personality.

"I'm glad you could join me, Pandora," she said.

The personality identified as Pandora said nothing, but her eyes were as open as her mouth was closed.

"I'm not going to ask you to speak," she said, "unless you feel so moved, but I would like you to listen to what I have been thinking.

"Is that all right with you?"

A tentative nod.

"I see your silence," said Rachel, "as a form of resistance. Whether it is a conscious decision or an unconscious one, you don't want to talk about some things you have seen. You prefer keeping those memories locked away because you don't want to deal with them. You think it is easier to put this pain away than to face it. But we both know that you won't get better that way. Keeping secrets from yourself, and secrets from me, will only hurt you more in the long run. Your secret lives in the dark hole of your dream. To see, you will need to let light in. Truth will free you from that hole. Do you understand?"

Another nod.

"Would you like to talk? About anything?"

An adamant shake of the head. Rachel didn't show her frustration. Therapists try to get their patients to do most of the talking, but this session hadn't gone that way.

"We could discuss anything you want. We could talk about movies, or your art, or dancing."

Still no.

"That's all right," Rachel said. "But please remember this: If you don't cry out when you hurt, the pain goes somewhere else, somewhere deep. If you try to cover up a limp, it will appear elsewhere, maybe as a stutter, or a twitch, or the kind of limp only you know about. Even without a voice, your pain is showing itself in different ways. We know it is emerging in your dreams. And I suspect it is displaying itself with your other personalities. Your mouth might be shut, but your wound is open. Do you understand that?"

An almost imperceptible nod.

The doctor offered a pen and notepad. "Since you don't want to talk, Pandora, perhaps you'd prefer to write?"

She shook her head.

"How about drawing me a picture then?"

The ultimate carrot. Most of Helen's personalities loved

to draw, but today even that wasn't enticement enough. Pandora shook her head again. Rachel backed off, but even while retreating she tried to forge an opening.

"None of the others have heard from you either, Pandora. That's bothering them. They know that something's wrong. I'd like you to talk to the others in the next day or two. Will you try and do that?"

Sometimes therapy was the ultimate game of chess, minds struggling mightily to get the smallest advantage. Rachel knew that Pandora might be less resistant talking to the other personalities than to her. If she could just get her talking, Rachel knew she might be able to facilitate a dialogue through the third parties. Such negotiations were often as labyrinthian as a Middle East peace process. The time frame Rachel had offered Pandora was elastic but not indefinite. It was presented to try and get a commitment out of Pandora without making her too fearful. If she felt too confined, she would run away without answering. For several seconds Pandora didn't react to the doctor's words. Then, hesitantly, she offered the slightest affirmation.

"Thank you, Pandora. I'd like to talk with Helen now."

Rachel had seen the transformation thousands of times, but she was still fascinated by it. There was that moment when Helen's face went slack, that Protean instant of transformation from one personality to another. In a glance, the doctor could see that Helen was back.

"I discussed your dream with Eris and Pandora," she said.

Helen didn't look pleased. She had come to accept the personalities, but she didn't know them, or want to know them. There were times when she still bitterly referred to them as "the body snatchers," but those condemnations were less frequent now.

"I thought you told me Pandora was doing her mute act," Helen said.

"She is. Which speaks volumes in itself."

"Then maybe I should just shut up."

"Is that what you want to do?"

"Do you think I know what I want to do?"

"Yes, Helen, I do."

"That makes one of us. Or did you poll the others, and they agreed?"

"I don't operate a democracy here."

"You're telling me."

"You seem tired, Helen."

"I was up working all night."

"Only working?"

"*They* went clubbing again. I didn't start drawing until very late."

"What are you working on?"

"A painting. Paintings."

The sketch had only been a preliminary idea. She had rejected it as being too one-dimensional. It needed more. For some reason she had kept thinking about Van Gogh's sunflowers, how they had appeared in so many of his paintings and in so many forms. The importance of flowers began to dominate her thoughts. Carnations.

Helen didn't discuss the flowers. The doctor was bad enough when it came to probing her dreams, but her art was even more personal. It was hers. She was in control of that world, could make it turn out just as she wanted. Just that morning she had decided to change the perspective on the painting's solitary figure. Instead of only showing a back, she had decided to offer up a side view. As the painting progressed, Helen knew the face would become more and more defined for her, and for the canvas as well.

She had made one other major change. She had decided to take the knife away from the retreating figure. The weapon diluted what she wanted to say. Instead, the hand was going to be holding a huge carnation, the focal carnation in the painting.

The giant flower would be red. Blood red. With a trail of its petals behind it. Petals that had dropped. Or been pulled, like little wings.

She loves me, thought Helen, she loves me not.

ELEVEN

Cheever watched the monitor. What was on the tube was the Kid talking with Dr. Denton. There were obvious surveillance cameras in both interview rooms but few people ever noticed them. Unless asked, the detectives never volunteered that taping was going on during the questioning. The doctor hadn't asked, at least about that. The only thing he had asked for was a second piece of pecan pie. Cheever had talked with Dr. Denton for an hour while the Kid had watched from the monitor room, and then they had reversed positions. Before long Cheever had to decide whether to book the doctor. If he did charge him, it wouldn't be for homicide, but for vagrancy, or trespassing, or whatever reason was most convenient to hold him. At the moment, Cheever's inclination was to let him go, even though a C.Y.A. mentality would have dictated otherwise. The doctor had a criminal record, one that documented use of a knife. But Cheever doubted he'd had anything to do with Bonnie Gill's death. He was being helpful, excessively so. Not that he didn't have his vested reasons. The doctor wasn't shy about revealing his grandiose fantasies à la the reward money. That, as much as prison bars, would keep him around.

"Why don't you tell me again," the Kid asked, "about how this statue went about turning into a woman?"

The doctor sighed. He'd been asked the question five, six times already. Cheever only partly listened to his retelling. What he was mostly hearing were the echoes from another conversation. Helen was buzzing in his ear. She had said to him: "Trouble always occurs when statues come to life." It looked like she was right about that. He remembered how she had stood in front of him, bleeding, emphatically saying, "It would have been better had Galatea just slept and never awakened."

Cheever had assumed Helen was talking about a mythical character, but it was hard telling where her fables ended and her reality began. It was the same with her personalities.

Galatea. He said the name out loud. Curious, he left the monitoring room, walked down the hall, and retrieved a battered dictionary from one of the desks. Without much hope he opened up to the G's, and was surprised to find an entry for Galatea: "a statue brought to life by Aphrodite in answer to the pleas of the sculptor, Pygmalion, who had fallen in love with his creation." Sort of like the Pinocchio story, he thought. But whenever Pinocchio lied, his nose always grew. It wasn't that way with criminals. Often when they lied only their smiles grew. Cheever returned the dictionary to the desk, then went back to the tape room where the Kid was still playing center stage with his grand interrogator act.

"You sure there was no one else out in the garden?" the Kid asked.

"No one I could see," said Dr. Denton.

"But this woman was seeing someone, or something?"

The doctor nodded. "Thass what I already told you. Hey, man, I need a drink."

"Coca-Cola?"

"A real drink."

"I'll get you a Coke and a smoke. How's that?"

The Kid didn't give Dr. Denton a chance to answer. He left the interview room. Cheever watched the doctor from his monitor. He sat quietly, expectantly, even appeared a little pleased with himself. Getting cops to jump for him seemed to be to his liking.

Cheever checked on the tape, saw that it was running low, and reached for a new one. While he was replacing it, the Kid opened the door to the room.

"Any place you want me to be taking this?" he asked.

"Keep him talking about the woman," Cheever said.

The Kid nodded and left. A minute later Cheever watched as he reappeared on the monitor carrying a cigarette and soda into the interview room. The doctor accepted the smoke, stuck the cigarette in his mouth, and looked like he expected it to be lit for him. The Kid tossed some matches his way.

"So did this redhead remind you of anyone?" the Kid asked. "Some actress, or somebody you know?"

The doctor inhaled thoughtfully, held the smoke for a while, then simply said, "No."

"You said she had straight hair, shoulder length."

"Yeah."

"Describe the color."

"I told you—red."

"Orange red? Flame red? Purple red? Blondish red?"

"Blood red." Dr. Denton tossed out the description almost as a challenge.

"Was the hair natural? Or was it dyed?"

"I guess only her hairdresser know for sure."

Cheever thought of a question he wanted to hear asked. Could she have been wearing a wig? It wasn't the question the Kid asked.

"You said she was standing among the statues. Do you think you could draw . . ."

The door opened and Mary Beth Carey walked inside. She made the small room that much smaller. Mary Beth was a big woman, weighed around two hundred pounds. She had unruly brown hair, and wore the thickest glasses Cheever had ever seen. Her eyesight was never an issue, though. If there was something to be found, Mary Beth was the criminalist who could find it. She was always anxious to help, actually seeking out the detectives to see if they needed her assistance rather than the other way around.

"How's it going?" she asked.

Cheever shrugged. His thoughts were elsewhere, but he still offered some desultory details. When his words stalled, Mary Beth turned to watch the show. The Kid was trying to get Dr. Denton to choreograph the red-headed woman's movements. Cheever kept thinking about something else. Like if he had screwed up. Like if he had neglected to do something. Thinking about wigs had him second-guessing himself. He remembered how Helen looked so different when she put on that black wig. What if she had a red one as well?

"Want to do a background check for a fellow Irishman?" he asked.

Mary Beth enjoyed playing with computers as much as Cheever disliked doing the same. Everyone on the team thought it was funny that Cheever always tried to get someone else, usually Mary Beth, to do his computer work. He was proficient enough, but preferred spending his time in the field or making calls. Or that rarity of rarities, thinking about a case, really thinking. Cheever had announced more than once that his teammates would rather be playing with computers than playing with themselves.

Acting on-line hard to get, Mary Beth said, "And I suppose if I was Bulgarian you'd be claiming that nationality as well?"

"I could only hope to somehow be related to you, Mary Beth."

"With that kind of blarney you've got to be Irish. What's the name?"

"Helen Olympia Troy," he said. "That's Helen Troy as in Tom Ray Orville Yogi."

"Is this on the level?"

"Yes."

"Any aliases?"

Cheever almost laughed. Helen's whole life was an alias. "Why don't you try Holly Troy as well?"

"Got a birth date, or social security number, or anything that will make the search easier?"

"She's around twenty-five, a local, stands five foot eight and weighs around one-fifteen."

"And now she's a missing person, right? Last seen on a hijacked Love Boat heading for Troy?"

"If you get a Bingo on her," said Cheever, "I'd appreciate your telling me ASAP."

"Sure you don't want me to run a search on Cleopatra while I'm at it?"

Cheever resisted joining in her badinage. "How soon can you do the background?"

"In just a little Nile," she said.

The computer terminals weren't more than twenty steps away. Mary Beth marched out of the tape room with alacrity. Sergeant Falconi caught the door before it closed. Both their timing was good. Cheever wasn't sure if the room could have held the three of them.

"Anything?" Falconi asked.

"Same old," Cheever said. "I'm thinking of letting Jackson go before he puts in his dinner order and bankrupts the city."

The sergeant didn't offer any second-guesses, just nodded. "Circle five o'clock on your desk calendar," he said.

"For what?"

"For Rollo Adams. I just got off the phone with him. He's coming to visit us. Wants to make sure we're all operating on the same wavelength. And rowing in the same direction. Those are his quotes."

"I figured as much."

"He wants an *interface* between the Carnation Fund and our investigation."

"His word?"

"Yep," Falconi said. "And your assignment."

The sergeant left the room before Cheever could tell him what he thought of that. Before he could offer his own word. It wouldn't have been *interface*.

Cheever went back to monitor watching. The Kid was trying to get Dr. Denton to remember everything the mystery lady had said. "You said she acted like she was drunk," he said. "Talked and walked like she was under the influence. What made you think that?"

"Been around lots of drunks. Guess you can say I'm an expert witness . . ."

The Kid stepped on his comedy act. "Tell me what she said and how she said it."

"Kept shouting, 'No.' Said something like, 'Stop it, you bastard.' Said 'son of a bitch' coupla times. Most the time it looked like she was waving around a sword."

"A sword?"

"The make-believe kind. Like the people around her. She kept lunging, you know. Fell down a few times."

Cheever listened with half an ear. He wished he'd run Helen through the computer earlier. As Eris, she had referred to the police in a familiar, if not exactly fond, manner. If the feeling was mutual . . .

"You said after the woman fell down she acted hysterical."

Dr. Denton nodded. "She was crying and screaming."

"What was she saying?"

"Kept yelling stuff like, 'No, oh my God, no.' Things like that."

"Did she sound like she was drunk then?"

"Sounded like she was damn sorry about something."

"Tell me about when she became silent."

"Not much to say. One moment she be carrying on, down on her knees, hitting the ground and crying and stuff, and then all of a sudden she's quiet as death. Not a sound."

"What then?"

"Got up like there was nothing wrong and then walked away."

"You said something about a bag."

"Already told you. She picked up a bag before leaving."

Cheever thought about Helen Troy, and how she had been carrying a bag when they first met. Mary Beth's sudden entrance added to his gnawing suspicions. She walked into the tape room, threw down a printout in front of Cheever, and announced, "Trojan War, part two.

"And," she added, handing him a folder, "anticipating your request, I also dug out the crime and arrest reports."

He waved his appreciation. Computers usually only tell half a story. They don't have the notations by the officers, or the names of witnesses, or addresses of the next of kin. Whenever possible, Cheever liked the *real* paperwork in front of him.

Helen Troy's arrest sheet showed she wasn't a stranger to SDPD. There were no wants or warrants on her at the moment, but that looked more the exception than the rule. There were three pages to her criminal *curriculum vitae*. She had a string of arrests over the last seven years, had been booked mostly for disturbing the peace, and being drunk and disorderly, but there had been other more serious charges, including soliciting, assault, possession of narcotics, and carrying a concealed weapon. Besides spending time in the drunk tank, she had been able to plea her way out of jail time, her felony arrests either getting dropped or kicked down to misdemeanors. Her most recent citation had been for indecent exposure. That had happened less than three months ago.

Cheever wondered if Helen's so-called multiple personalities were a great front, a wonderful way for excusing her behavior. Maybe she had decided they allowed her to murder with impunity.

He walked back to his desk, his anger growing with every step. Mostly he was mad at himself, but the shrink's deliberate misdirection in his investigation had him seeing red. The shrink could have told him about Helen's criminal history in a noncondemning way, could have said, Oh, by the way, Helen has an arrest record that runs about as long as *The Iliad*, but what Rachel Stern had chosen to do instead was to lie by omission.

Cheever called her at home, got her machine, gave up on that, then dialed her office. A receptionist who was running interference told him *the doctor* was with a patient, but Cheever interrupted her rote speech to say this was police business. The hold music was classical, but it didn't make the wait any shorter or improve his temper. When the receptionist finally came back on the line she sounded apologetic, and also sounded like she figured he'd chew her head off.

"Detective Cheever," she said, "Dr. Stern regrets that she can't talk with you now, but says that if you give me your number she will call you back in fifteen minutes. Or, if that's not convenient, I'd be glad to take a message."

He swallowed back several messages, decided it wasn't fair to behead the messenger, and managed to give her his number without saying anything else.

Rather than just wait for the doctor's return call, and getting more frustrated by the minute doing so, Cheever went back to looking at Helen's paperwork. There were others besides the doctor who knew Helen, people without agendas. One of them was Paul Rodriguez, the officer who'd had the latest run-in with Helen Troy. Over the phone, he remembered her well.

"Strange lady," Rodriguez said, but was quick to add, "hell of a figure, though," as if that excused everything.

"A nearby business owner said his employees were wasting too much time catching this naked babe's act, and he wanted us to do something about it. We checked it out, and there she was, up in this window buck naked. Thing was, you couldn't be sure she wasn't a mannequin, 'specially with all these other statues around her.

"My partner had some binocs, so we took us a close look. Sure enough, she was blinking every so often. That's the only thing that gave her away.

"She was up on the third, fourth floor. We got a tenant to let us in, walked up some stairs, and knocked on the door to her loft, which set off this dog that sounded meaner than hell. From inside we hear her calming the dog and saying she'll be out in just a minute.

"When she answers the door she's tied the dog up and thrown some clothes on and acts like she's all prim and proper. We tell her that we're going to have to cite her for indecent exposure, and she gets indignant. There's no way she'd parade around naked, she says. My partner gets a little wise, says he can describe her moles in detail if she wants. Then she gets all quiet, and acts embarrassed, looks like she wishes she was wearing winter clothes. We didn't take her in, just passed her some paper and warned her that if she got a hankering for walking around without clothes that she should do it with the shades drawn.

"Funny," said Rodriguez, taking a moment to think. "She acted like she got caught with her pants down. Which she did. But it was like she didn't know it."

"Thanks," said Cheever.

"She been doing her mooning act anywhere else lately?"

"Not that I'm aware."

"It's a show worth seeing," said Rodriguez.

Cheever hung up the phone. Now he had a precedent for Helen making like a statue. For doing her Galatea thing. According to her paperwork, she'd done worse, had been arrested for soliciting at the Cha Cha Club, a strip joint on El Cajon Blvd. Cheever was reading that arrest report when his phone rang. He picked up the receiver, identified himself.

"This is Dr. Stern returning your call."

Returning frostbite by the sound of it. Cheever didn't thank her for calling back. "Helen Troy's not a vestal virgin, is she?"

"That's not one of her personalities, and not one of my claims."

"Are you aware of her criminal record?"

"Of course."

"But telling me about it slipped your mind?"

"I thought there were more important things to tell you in the short time we had."

"Does she still strip, and hook, and do drugs?"

"I don't like the tone of that question."

"I don't like having to ask it a day late."

"Helen works at her art full time. She has never taken money for sex, your zealous police department assertations notwithstanding, but she has worked as an exotic dancer to support herself. At this time, the primary drug she abuses is alcohol. She's given up speed and cocaine, but she still takes Ecstasy, especially during raves. Is that all, because . . ."

"No. You said some of her personalities scare you . . ."

"I didn't use the word *scare*. I did, however, imply a certain volatility . . ."

"Volatile enough to kill?"

"I make it a rule not to answer such hypothetical questions."

"You seem to have a lot of rules," said Cheever.

"I also have another patient whose session is due to begin."

"I'd like to talk more about a patient named Helen."

"Now isn't a good time."

"When is?"

"Any time after six-thirty."

"All right. Six-thirty-one. Your office?"

"Yes."

He hung up, then dialed Helen's telephone number. There was no answer, not even a machine to talk to. Maybe she was making like a statue again and didn't hear the ringing. He considered driving over to her place, but feared it would be a waste of time. Not for the first time Cheever wished he could be two places at the same time. That wasn't possible. But could you be two people, or more, inhabiting the same body?

Cheever's jury was still out on that question. As for Helen Troy, supposedly she had enough personalities to be both judge and jury.

And, he considered, executioner.

TWELVE

"Mr. Troy?"

"Given a choice of titles," the man said, "I prefer Professor Troy. But I've been known to answer to almost anything. Detective Cheever, I presume."

The professor offered his hand and a weak grip. He was around five foot eight and plump. His cheeks were red and his eyes were blue, giving him an elfin appearance. He had dark hair and didn't show enough gray for a man who was supposed to be in his late sixties. Grecian Formula, thought Cheever. Or maybe it was the Grecian gods.

He motioned for Cheever to come inside and led him to the living room. Bookshelves filled with leather-bound volumes lined two of the long walls. The room was decorated with replicas of antiquities: classical vases and urns, marble busts of emperors and poets, reproductions of paintings with mythological scenes and characters, and miniatures of such landmarks as the Acropolis and the Colosseum.

"Rome sweet Rome," said Cheever.

The professor rubbed his hands and laughed. "I like

that," he said, "even if it's not geographically complete. Let's get comfortable, shall we? May I get you something to drink?"

Cheever shook his head and sat down on a sofa. Professor Jason Troy chose a love seat, crossed his legs, and faced Cheever with pert attention. Mary Beth had come up with the professor's address out of records. Cheever had called him, figuring that Jason Troy might be able to provide answers about Helen. The professor had been extremely amenable, had even suggested that Cheever visit.

"As I mentioned on the phone, Professor, your daughter might or might not have been at the scene of a very heinous crime. In questioning her, I've found her answers to be—cryptic."

"Cryptic? I like your choice of words very much, very much indeed. Cryptic originally came from the Greek word *kruptos*, to hide. Maybe you should be thankful for Helen's responses, Detective, for cryptic answers are sometimes the most revealing. Oracles knew to give cryptic responses. They were aware that we needed our enigmas to truly think."

"But aren't answers from oracles always suspect?" Cheever asked. "Aren't their replies invariably ambiguous?"

"There is that," the professor said, "but I daresay the blame is mostly human, with the questions asked not specific enough, and the interpretation not skilled enough.

"The Sibyl was the greatest of all oracles, and she well knew the need to be specific. When Apollo wanted to press his love upon her, she demanded a wish, asking that all the granules of sand she held in her hand be the years of her life. Apollo granted her that, but not her youth. Her body soon wasted, leaving only her voice, and her prophecies."

The professor enjoyed talking in the affected manner some academics assume, was enamored with theatrics and dramatic mannerisms. He liked to use his eyes, opening them wide and closing them slowly, and conducted his speech with operatic hands and exclamatory voice.

"Before blaming the oracles, Detective, be suspicious of the interpreters. Priests and priestesses translated from birds and rustling leaves. They divined from babbling humans at the Oracle of Delphi. To be certain of the message, I fear you'll have to learn the tongue of the gods."

"But who gods the gods?" Cheever asked.

Jason Troy gave him a delighted look. "A classical pun," he said, amazed. "You surprise me, Detective. I am reminded of what Dr. Johnson said of a dog's walking on his hind legs: 'It is not done well, but you are surprised to find it done at all.'"

"Wouldn't a dog say the same thing if he saw a human walking around on all fours?"

Troy laughed again. "Please don't take umbrage," he said, "but it's just that the constabulary that Helen's youthful antics brought into my life were uninspired sorts, bureaucrats really, with the sensibilities of troglodytes. You're older and wiser. I sense your philosophy is not based in its entirety on the funny pages."

"Not entirely. Sometimes I read the sports too."

"You're being modest."

"No, I'm attempting humor."

"Tell me about yourself."

"I came here to learn about your daughter."

"Alas," Jason said, "conversation seems to be a forgotten art, with pedestrian interests always elbowing aside true discourse. Though I suppose it is your job . . ."

It was difficult for Cheever to determine where the professor's academia concluded and his dissembling began. "You were saying about Helen."

Sighing, "The apple didn't fall far from the tree, I fear."

"Meaning?"

"Meaning Helen takes after my deceased wife. Delores was not very stable. She tried to medicate herself through a liquor store prescription. It didn't work. She was institutionalized a number of times, and ultimately committed suicide."

"How old was Helen when that happened?"

"Seven or eight."

"You're aware that Helen has been diagnosed as having multiple personality disorder?"

The professor clucked a little, then held his hands up to show both his helplessness and his skepticism. "Over the years a slew of analysts have pronounced their weighty diagnoses. She, like her mother before her, has been called, among other things, a borderline personality, a dissociative hysteric, and a pathological overreactor. I've been told she suffers from delusions and hallucinations. The mental health people said many of the same things about her mother."

"Her therapist believes her disorder occurred before the age of eight, and began as early as when she was five."

"You mean her current therapist. Who knows what her next one will conjecture."

"Most of Helen's personalities appear to be linked to characters out of Greek myths. It surprised me that such a young girl could identify with mythology."

"That, at least," Troy said, "is a natural enough offshoot. I read Helen myths from the time she was very young. We didn't have any Dr. Seuss around. We had Ovid and Homer and Bulfinch and Edith Hamilton and myths aplenty. Helen always wanted more. She was a sponge."

"How did you select what you read to her?"

"I didn't, really. I just pulled books down from the library and started reading. Sometimes I would simplify words for her."

"But," said Cheever, "some of the myths are very graphic."

Cheever knew they weren't exactly family entertainment, not with sons killing fathers, daughters arranging the murder of mothers, sons sleeping with mothers, and mothers serving their own children up for dinner.

"Have you ever watched Saturday cartoons?" laughed the professor.

Cheever didn't join in his mirth. He sensed the professor was being far too facile. "How long did Helen retain her interest in mythology?"

"It continues to this day, as far as I know."

"But you're not sure?"

"Helen essentially left home when she was sixteen and we have had very little contact in the years since."

"She left home very young."

The professor nodded.

"Why?"

"She wanted her independence."

Cheever thought about that. It certainly wasn't unique. "Since you taught Helen her mythology, Professor, I was hoping that we could discuss her personalities on both a mythological and personal level. I'd like to just throw out names and get your responses to them."

"That sounds like fun," he said.

"Cronos?"

Jason Troy nodded happily. "Born of Earth and Sky. His father, Earth, hated him, hated all his children. Those patriarchal gods were always afraid of being supplanted, you see? But Cronos's mother helped him get revenge on his father by making him a great metal sickle. When Earth came to lay with her, Cronos emasculated him. Of course, the sins of the father continued with the son. Cronos hated his own children enough that he started eating them. He swallowed them whole. Helen was always fascinated by that painting—Who was the artist?—Goya?—of Cronos gorging on his children. The painting was in one of my books and I'd always catch her staring at it."

"Eris?"

"Her brother was the god of war. The goddess of discord came by her ways honestly. She liked to make pots boil. Helen liked Loki too, I remember. The tricksters always appealed to her. She liked their wiles."

"Eurydice?"

"Ah, love that goes beyond the grave. Helen was always after me to tell that story. I must confess to being very fond of it myself. Imagine Orpheus descending into the underworld, driven by his love to get Eurydice back. But, oh, the sadness that Orpheus and Eurydice never achieved their earthly reunion."

"Hygeia?"

"Yes," he said, nodding his head while remembering. "I think Helen was interested in the goddess of health because her mother was never well. Where else would a little one turn for healing?"

"How did your wife commit suicide?"

"The Roman way. She opened some veins in a warm bathtub."

"Who discovered her?"

"I did."

"Did Helen see her in that state?"

"Thankfully, no."

Cheever returned to the myths that made up Helen. "The Maenads?"

"There is something attractive about the wild—don't you think so, Detective? Most of the time we like to forget that we are animals. The Maenads are our vital side, our bestial side. Give them wine, red wine, and they revel in orgiastic pleasure. They also hunted down animals as a troop, frenzied women overcoming beasts, tearing at their flesh, lapping at their spilt blood. Occasionally they tore apart humans, too."

"The Moirae?"

"Those crones are always turning up in one form or another throughout mythology. Little ones are attracted to witches and Helen was no different. She always wanted to hear about those eldritch women dispensing their lots."

"Nemesis?"

"Over time, the one lesson we all learn repeatedly is that life is not fair. How many times on your job, Detective, have you seen something particularly grisly and said, 'There but for the sake of providence go I?' The young don't understand that. I think that's why they love their superheroes, beings who can make things right. Nemesis was Helen's superhero. She drew crayon pictures of her flying around in her chariot of griffins, going forth to bring justice to the world."

"Pandora?"

"There's an interesting case. Pandora has so many faces. In mythology she's both a femme fatale and an earth mother. The gods blessed her, but cursed her with curiosity. Because of Pandora opening a box she was told not to, humanity was denied a paradise, but she redeemed herself partially by allowing hope a place on this planet."

"Does the name Caitlin hold any significance for you?"

He shook his head. "It's not a name I'm familiar with."

"What about Holly?"

"It was my wife's middle name."

"What was her first name?"

"Delores."

Cheever sat in thought. For once, Jason Troy didn't prattle. "How did you and your wife meet?"

"At the university. I was an associate professor at the time, and some years her senior. Minor scandal, that, if you don't mind the double entendre. You're not supposed to date your students, and Delores was only a freshman. She was a bright flame, but then they say those burn out twice as fast."

"Did she show any signs of mental illness while you were dating her?"

"I suppose there were signs, but who notices those kind of things when passions are enflamed? She drank too much, certainly, but that seemed to be the thing to do back then."

"How long after you were married was Helen born?"

"Less than a year. But I wouldn't want you to think my courtship assumed Zeusian wiles."

Cheever's raised eyebrows asked the question. The professor smiled and pointed to one of the paintings on the wall. Several women, attended by maids, were disrobing. To the left of the painting was a naked youth with wings strumming the lyre. There was a large white bird flying away, and another goose or swan was pursuing a naked adolescent. The youth appeared unsure of the bird, was fending it off with her hand. In the center of the picture was a beautiful nude woman. Her eyes were closed, the pleasure on her face was apparent. She had her legs spread open. A large white bird with a very long neck was raising itself into her lap. The bird's neck extended from the woman's navel up to her chin, navigating upward between the curves of her breasts. There was something very phallic about the erect white neck, something very seductive and yet aggressive in the bird's posturing.

"Corregio," the professor said. "He entitled the painting, *Leda and the Swan*. You see, Helen of Troy was conceived in a manner that was rather unusual even for the gods. Zeus desired to have Leda, a mortal girl, for a lover, but he feared that Hera would find out about his infidelity, so he disguised himself as a swan. In the words of Yeats:

> *A sudden blow: the great wings beating still*
> *Above the staggering girl, her thighs caressed*
> *By the dark webs, her nape caught in his bill,*
> *He holds her helpless breast upon his breast.*

How can those terrified vague fingers push
The feathered glory from her loosening thighs?
And how can body, laid in that white rush,
But feel the strange heart beating where it lies?"

There was a power in Troy's voice that Cheever hadn't expected. His passion vented, the professor smiled.

"You make," Cheever said, "the feathers fly."

Troy bowed. "I miss the classroom. Ah, the lonely life of a professor emeritus. The students used to enjoy when I would bring the ancient tales to life. I would quote Milton, and all the pagan romantic poets, and, of course, Yeats. You don't need to be Stentor with the right kind of words. Yeats understood intensity and ardor."

"You don't teach anymore?"

"They throw me a bone now and again. I even said I'd teach ancient Greek and Latin, but the administration says there's not enough interest in those courses to warrant any classes. Of course there's not enough interest. How could there be if they don't offer the classes?"

"When was the last time you saw your daughter?"

"About a year ago. I used to see her more frequently when she needed money."

"I am told Helen doesn't remember several years of her early life."

The professor made a noncommittal motion of his hand. "It's possible, I suppose. I can remember as a young woman she told me she had tasted of the River Lethe."

He looked over to Cheever, repeated the word *Lethe*, then waited in the manner of an intimate, much as lovers do when reciting words to "their" song, or a shared poem. Much to his apparent regret, Cheever didn't know the reference.

"The river at which the souls of the dead sip," the professor said, "so as to forget everything."

Cheever refrained from saying that he knew a lot of the living who sipped from the same trough.

"You must have admired Helen of Troy to have given your daughter her name."

The professor shrugged. "Having a surname of Troy dictated the choice more than anything."

"It would seem Helen has ambivalent feelings about the name. She started calling herself Holly when she was a young girl, didn't she?"

"I suppose so."

"But you continued to call her Helen?"

"A rose by any other name . . ."

"Why did she choose another name?"

The professor shook his head. "I don't know."

"Any guesses?"

"Maybe she didn't want to be identified with the historical Helen."

Or maybe the modern one, Cheever thought.

"Was Helen always . . ." Cheever stretched for the right word.

"Different?" said the professor. "Unusual? Odd? Don't worry about offending, Detective. We can dispense with euphemisms. To paraphrase Emerson, she always marched to a different drummer."

"Even as a little girl?"

"Especially then. Retracing steps, are you?"

"Just wandering along a few paths."

"Then you should remember what Virgil said:

Facilis descensus Averni;
Nectes atque dies patet atri janua Ditis;
Sed revocare gradum, superasque evadere ad auras,
Hoc opus, hic labor est."

"If you want me to know what Virgil said, you'll have to translate."

"Oh? I would have suspected you of having a classical education."

"The public schools did offer some classical insights, but none into ancient languages."

"Virgil said, 'The descent of Avernus is easy; the gate of Pluto stands open night and day; but to retrace one's steps and return to the upper air—that is the toil, that is the difficulty.'"

"It's a one-way ticket to Hades," Cheever said.

"That has usually been the case."

THIRTEEN

Cheever had a headache that he figured had originated in the Mediterranean. Helen Troy, plural, kept invading his thoughts. The day before he'd felt sorry for her. He had been intrigued by her condition, had been hard-pressed to keep his usual impersonal distance. Now Helen interested him more professionally than she did personally. He considered her both a potential suspect and witness.

Assuming she wasn't the murderer, Cheever wondered if Helen could have had the presence of mind(s) to have realized what was happening to Bonnie, and then acted to save herself by posing as a statue. Cheever tried to visualize the scene, tried imagining Helen standing there unmoving as her friend's throat was being cut. It might not have been that calculated, he knew. He had encountered many trauma victims who had frozen when confronted by violence. There were usually three responses to a serious threat: flight, fight, or freeze. He supposed it wasn't inconceivable that Helen had stood there frozen for hours. This was a woman, after all, who supposedly cried blood and grew wounds. Her being a potential witness to Bonnie

119

Gill's murder might even explain her stigmatas. Cheever had originally thought Helen's mortification of flesh had occurred over a period of eight hours, with the time clock starting after he had shown her pictures of Bonnie's wounds. But if Helen had been at the gallery at the time of the murder, she would have had almost a full day to sprout her lesions.

Cheever remembered how she had come to him looking for forgiveness. The image made him think of something. He had never really considered the location of Helen's wounds. Cheever pondered the matter so intently he stopped breathing for several seconds. No, it wasn't just coincidence. The stigmata on Helen paralleled Bonnie's wounds, duplicating those on her neck and back. Bonnie's murder was written all over her—literally.

From his car phone Cheever again tried calling Helen. No damn answer, just like the last half-dozen times. Maybe she just wasn't answering the phone. He'd find out. He was close now, only ten blocks away, which in downtown San Diego blocks wasn't very far. The short distances between the streets, and the lack of any alleys in downtown San Diego, were the legacies of Alonzo Horton, the founding father of San Diego. In the late 1800s, Horton earned the nickname "Corner Lot Horton." The developer had early on learned he could get more for corner lots, reason enough for him to design the downtown area with short blocks. Like all cities, San Diego was built on greed, though its blueprint was a little more apparent than most.

Helen lived on Seventh Avenue, but no one would have mistaken her loft for the high-rent district. Her building was four stories of long-ago whitewashed brick that had needed a coat of paint for at least a decade. The brick itself dated the building. In earthquake-prone southern California, developers had long eschewed brick, knowing it was a material that sometimes didn't even stand up to minor tremblers. Maybe that's what the owner was hoping for, an act of God that would save the price of demolition.

The building was a converted warehouse. It had probably been constructed during the boom years of the Second World War, and to survive had gone through several metamorphoses. The first floor was commercial, with a print shop and a dry cleaner facing the street, while the second floor had been converted into office space. Even with the continuity of off-white shades and uniform fluorescent lighting, floor number two appeared more deserted than not. There was a sign hanging on the building that read INEXPENSIVE WORK LOFTS AVAILABLE. Someone had used a marker on the sign to add an upward-pointing arrow with the notation PETTING ZOO UPSTAIRS. The mishmash of draperies, blinds, sheets, and naked windows on the third and fourth floors advertised the location of the lofts.

The entrance to the building wasn't readily apparent. Cheever finally found a security door with an intercom around the corner from the dry cleaner. Helen's unit was 4B, but no one responded to Cheever's button pushing. He walked around the sides of the building, didn't see another means of egress besides the entry door or the fire escapes, then went back to the intercom and pushed it a few more times. This time there was an answer, a dog's barking, deep and loud enough to travel down four floors. Cheever walked out to the sidewalk, looked up. He wasn't the only one doing some looking. A big tan and black face was pressed against a fourth-floor glass window. The rottweiler barked at him once, the dog's version of a warning shot. Cheever took a few more steps into the street to get a better view. Though the loft was dark inside, Cheever could make out the shape of someone standing there. After a minute of looking, Cheever realized the figure belonged to a statue. At least he thought so.

The dog watched Cheever all the while he walked to his car. He was still watching him as he drove away. Cheever didn't wave. He made a slight detour on the way to headquarters, stopping at the downtown library on E Street and coming away with an armful of books. He was five minutes late for the meeting with Rollo Adams, but the developer was even later than that, arriving fifteen minutes after Cheever.

The three men met in the fourth-floor meeting room, where the decor could best be described as functional. It wasn't the kind of conference room Rollo Adams was used to. The room was small, and didn't come with padded chairs or a view. But for Rollo that didn't matter. The important thing was having an audience.

He looked like an older and heavier Jimmy Stewart still ready to go to Washington. Rollo was no longer the *wunderkind*, being almost fifty, but he had a youthful appearance and mannerisms. For years Rollo had been mentioned as a potential candidate for the city council, or Congress. He'd flirted with the notion, but hadn't entered the political ring. It was probably easier for him to buy candidates, or anoint them, than be one himself.

"Gentlemen," he said. He took a seat at the head of the table, a position he was obviously used to. Rollo made eye contact with Cheever and the sergeant. "Thank you for meeting with me."

Falconi returned his pleasantries.

Rollo announced the agenda: "We obviously have a mutual goal, gentlemen: finding the murderer of Bonnie Gill. From what you have said, Sergeant, we need more cohesion in our joint efforts."

Falconi nodded. Cheever continued to listen. Rollo had a winning voice. There was a soft twang to it. The media had portrayed him as a poor country boy made good, his roots just a step up from a log cabin, or a manger, depending on the publicist. He had grown up in Georgia on a small pig farm, said that construction projects were easy compared to his early days of "slopping and chopping." His speech was an odd mixture of business jargon, modern buzzwords, cliches, and down-home homilies. It was like *Reader's Digest* come to life.

"I am here to answer any questions you might have," Rollo said, "and am hoping you will extend that same courtesy to me."

"Naturally," Falconi said.

Cheever said, "Tell us about your reward."

Rollo tilted his head forward. "Gladly. We decided we couldn't wait for a Good Samaritan to come forward. It stands to reason that someone, somewhere, knows what happened to Bonnie Gill. To bring that someone forward, we have committed fifty thousand dollars to the Carnation Fund."

He looked around the table with a proud expression, as if he expected applause.

"How does the fund work?" Cheever asked.

"Like you would expect: give us information that convicts, or helps us convict, and we give you money."

"Why didn't you go through Crime Stoppers?" Cheever asked.

Crime Stoppers was a San Diego organization that solicited information from the public for unsolved crimes. They often facilitated investigative efforts of both police and friends and family of victims by circulating brochures advertising rewards and airing film reenactments of the crimes on television.

"We had horses raring to jump, and if you know anything about riding, you don't pull in your nag when it's ready to jump. Strike while the iron's hot, you see what I mean? We didn't want to wait. We needed to channel our anger into something constructive. But that doesn't mean we won't be working with those Crime Stopper people. We just wanted to get the ball moving on our own."

"Most reward systems ask that any information be directed to the police," Cheever said. "Not yours."

"That's right. I already had staff in place, so I volunteered them for handling the phone lines."

The sergeant interjected before Cheever could. "The problem with your setup," Falconi said, "is that it potentially impedes our investigative efforts. The police can't be the second or third to know. We need to be the first contact so that we can work on any new information immediately."

Rollo looked slightly embarrassed, as if he suddenly saw a flaw in one of his blueprints. "The plan was to pass on everything to you, of course."

"Unless you want to do the investigating for us," Cheever said.

Cheever's attention was on Rollo. He knew better than to be looking at Falconi, knew without seeing that the sergeant was giving him the evil eye, but the developer wasn't an amateur in that department either. "Our intent was to help," Rollo said, his voice rising in anger. "My daddy used to tell me that a diamond with a flaw is better than a common stone that's perfect. It's obvious we got a flaw or two in our operation, but that just means we'll retrofit the original plans."

"It would help," Falconi said, "if your operators immediately referred callers to the police."

"Sounds good to me," Rollo said. "We assumed that since we were administering the reward we should also take the calls, but I can see now that doesn't make sense. Like they say, takes a lot of things to prove you're smart, but only one thing to show you're a dummy."

"How did you know Bonnie Gill?" Cheever asked.

"We go back a few years," he said. "I worked on a couple committees with her, and I was on the Board of the ReinCarnation Foundation."

"So yours is a personal interest?"

"Yes," Rollo said. "That is mostly."

Cheever and Falconi waited for him to say more. "Bonnie's death," he said, "has made some investors wary. Chicken Little types, you see what I mean, who think the sky is falling unless you show 'em different. They need reassuring, especially now.

"There are always people who will give you reasons that you can't do something. Remember those that said Horton Plaza couldn't be developed, that it was a breeding ground for drunks and degenerates and could never be home to a world-class shopping center? Look at it now, one of the most successful malls in the country.

"Lot of the same people said that the Gaslamp Quarter was a pipe dream. They said that downtown San Diego was dead. I told 'em reports of that death were greatly exaggerated, and I was right.

"Bonnie Gill had a dream. She wasn't alone. She wanted the downtown renaissance to continue east. I shared that dream with her. I'm not going to let her down."

"You have ample holdings in that area, don't you?" Cheever asked.

"Yes." Rollo looked around. There were no cameras in the vicinity, no reporters he needed to grandstand in front of. He could afford to be honest. "And Bonnie's death," he said, "was not good for business."

FOURTEEN

"What's good for General Motors is good for the country." Businesspeople were always saying things like that, but whenever Cheever heard them, he figured something was being whitewashed. It wasn't altruism spurring on Rollo Adams, though he clearly didn't mind wearing the good guy's white hat. The murder of a prominent citizen made bankers shaky, and made it that much harder for him to get financing for his downtown building projects.

The talk with Adams had taken less than an hour, but Cheever again found himself hurrying to make it to his last appointment of the day. He was tired, and the idea of more conversation made him feel more tired.

Cheever arrived at Rachel Stern's office at exactly six-thirty, but she kept him waiting in the anteroom for several minutes. Classic power play, he was sure. Cheever had come prepared, though, and didn't have to resort to thumbing through the kind of magazines that are offered at doctors' offices. He read from one of the books he had picked up at the library, and when Rachel came out to the outer office he held the book in front of him so that she couldn't possibly miss seeing that it was a text on multiple personality disorder. As they walked into her office she commented, "That book is over ten years out of date."

"So you're saying all psychiatrists are now in agreement about multiple personality disorder?"

"There is currently more agreement," she said, "and less skepticism."

"Gee, I imagine in another thousand years there might be some sort of consensus."

She sat down behind her desk, didn't respond unless you counted the two white patches on her cheeks. "When you called, Detective, you said you wanted to talk about Helen Troy."

He nodded, but didn't directly proceed to that subject. "From what I understand about therapy, and it's not first-hand mind you, I'm told that when you talk with patients part of your job is to listen for what's not being said."

Rachel sensed a trap, but answered anyway. "That's true," she said. "Freud said that an analyst had to be in three places at once: listening to the patient, listening to yourself, and keeping track of what was going on between the patient and yourself."

"Three places at once. I guess that makes you a multiple personality."

She ignored his sarcasm, waited for what he had to say.

"If our positions were reversed," he said, "you would probably tell me that my not mentioning Helen's criminal record was a significant omission."

"I might. But I certainly didn't have time to spell out everything about Helen's past."

"You didn't stop to think that in a murder investigation her criminal record might be an important matter?"

"Why should it?"

"Because Helen Troy has a history of breaking the law. Because you yourself alluded that some of her personalities were capable of violence."

"You seem to have settled on those words, Detective. I would think that in your line of work, you, more than anyone, would know we are all capable of violence."

"Including multiple personalities."

"Is your implication that such a condition makes someone with a dissociative disorder, or anyone who has psychological problems, more of a suspect?"

"Only if yours is that it makes them less."

"That hasn't been one of my assertions. Historically we've seen that society has long assigned guilt to those who are different. I don't want Helen caught up in some witch hunt just because she's expedient."

"I'm the one who's trying to learn more about Helen," he said, "and you seem to be the one who's stonewalling me. How about letting me read her case file?"

Rachel looked incredulous, shaking her head and laughing without mirth. "No. I can't see how that would be germane to your investigation. We're talking about four years of confidential sessions, with paperwork longer than *War and Peace*."

"With more battles too?" Cheever asked.

The doctor didn't appear to be amused.

"How did she come to be your patient?" Cheever asked.

"Helen was initially referred to me for treatment of her anorexia-bulimia and her drug abuse. Over time I found that those were wonderful masks for her even larger problems. I first worked on her potentially deadly symptoms, and after gaining her trust I moved on to her core problems."

"I've been reading about other multiples," Cheever said. "I've got one book here on Billy Milligan. He was a diagnosed multiple that raped and robbed."

"He was also found not guilty of those crimes on the grounds of insanity," she said. "Have you read enough of that book to know about Billy's early life?"

"No. But I assume you have a box of tissues in your desk in case I need them."

She opened a drawer, found that box of tissues, and pushed it across the desk toward Cheever. "Billy's biological father committed suicide when he was three. By the time he was eight years old there had been three men in his life he was instructed to call 'Daddy.' His biological father was Jewish, and his second father was Catholic. His third father, an evangelical, thought he had to purge those religions out of Billy. According to Billy, his stepfather abused him in a number of ways, including raping him, beating him savagely, and locking him in cupboards for days at a time. One of his more frequent threats was that he was going to bury Billy alive.

"Not surprisingly, Billy withdrew from reality. He started slipping into trances both at home and at school. Other personalities started appearing, each apparently suited to some task. All of the personalities were male except for one, a lesbian.

"When Billy preyed on the women around Ohio State University he was not mentally competent. His personality that he identified as the 'keeper of hate' attacked the women, and then the lesbian personality took over while the rape was being committed . . ."

"Wait a second," said Cheever, raising both hands up to protest. "You're saying his raping brought the woman out in him? Isn't it a little hard to explain the mental dynamics of that, let alone the physical ones?"

"Very hard," she said, not backing down from his theatrics. "*Laymen* have an extremely difficult time understanding."

"So, apparently, do the professionals. Does the name Kenneth Bianchi mean anything to you?"

"Yes."

"Then you know that as the Hillside Strangler he murdered at least nine people in the Los Angeles area. Since Bianchi couldn't successfully challenge the evidence, and he couldn't break out of prison, he tried using a new dodge: multiple personality disorder.

"The defense brought in one of the shining lights in your field, *this* psychiatrist who's supposedly an expert on multiple personalities, and lo and behold, Kenneth Bianchi is diagnosed as being a multiple. What a sham. What a circus act. Later, Bianchi confessed he faked the whole thing."

"I'm familiar with the story. Is there a point to it?"

"Just that your field isn't all-knowing."

"I hope I have not given you that impression, either personally or professionally. On the other hand, it would only be prudent to state that a little knowledge is a dangerous thing."

She looked pointedly to the book Cheever was holding. If anything, he made it more visible.

"You think," he said, "the state of mind of Billy Milligan mattered to the women who were violated?"

"I wouldn't think so, Detective."

"When all was said and done, Billy Milligan was still a rapist."

"Which means what?"

"Which means my job is to apprehend criminals. Cause and effect don't enter my equation. I'm not going to argue that Helen Troy isn't a multiple. She's certainly strange enough to be just that. The question I have to ask is whether she murdered Bonnie Gill and is now trying to cover up that crime by using her so-called disorder as a smoke screen."

"That's ridiculous."

"Is it?"

"It would be impossible."

"Is that Dr. Stern talking, or the caretaker of Helen?"

"Both."

"Why would you rule her out as a suspect?"

"What would have been her motive?"

"Bonnie Gill was an authority figure. Judging by her arrest record, Helen's had trouble with those. Bonnie was interfering in Helen's art, undermining her with negative comments. Helen could have flipped out. Assuming Helen is a bona fide multiple, maybe Bonnie said something that brought Cronos out, or Nemesis. Helen could have murdered, and from what you say, not even know it. Pandora is the only one that might be aware of what happened, and she's not talking. It's possible she's protecting herself, or, to be more accurate, her selves."

"You're jumping to wild conclusions, Detective."

"I'm examining possibilities, Doctor. It helps to have as much information as possible to do that."

"You're looking for a conspiracy."

"Helen Troy seems to be a conspiracy all by herself."

"Trauma," Rachel said, "is what is preventing Pandora from speaking. Time will bring her voice back."

"How much time? You don't seem to have had much luck opening that clam, Doctor. Pandora's still holding out part of Helen's youth on you, her long fugue period. There are two years of question marks, if I remember correctly."

He looked to her for corroboration. "Your memory is not the matter in question here, Detective."

"You're right. The matter in question is that I don't have all the time in the world to wait for a breakthrough."

"This is a profession that often heals by inches. Patience is necessary. Therapists know that waiting for a break is a part of the process. We live by a rule: When in doubt, do nothing. I have doubts."

"So do I. But I don't have your rule."

She rubbed her eyes, let her erect figure hunch slightly. Rachel was tired, and hungry, and she hurt. She could understand the impetuousness of this man, could almost admire it. How many cops would go so far as to check out a book on a mental disorder to better understand it? But he was out of his league and a potential danger to her patient.

"If you only knew," she said, "how far Helen has come. She arrived on my doorstep with a death wish. Now, she wants to live. We are working toward integration, toward eliminating the Greek Chorus and integrating all of the personalities into one, into Helen."

"I don't want to interfere with your treatment, Doctor, and I don't want to set it back. But I do have questions. Some of them you can answer."

His implicit threat was that if Rachel didn't cooperate he would go to Helen and make matters that much tougher on her. Dr. Stern nodded to signal her, if not willingness, at least capitulation.

"From my limited reading on the subject," Cheever said, "the common denominator for multiples seems to be that they were sexually abused as children."

"In almost all cases that's true."

"Do you think Helen was sexually abused?"

"It is my strong belief that she was, even though that has not specifically come out in our sessions. She fits the classic profile of someone turning to drugs to chemically dissociate from the pain of hurtful memories. As for her anorexia-bulimia, I believe it was Helen's way of asserting control over her body."

"In what way?"

"For once, someone else wasn't dictating to her body. She was. Helen could change how she looked. She could even punish herself, make her body reflect the unhealthy condition of her psyche."

"Any guesses who abused her?"

"It could have been more than one person. Usually it's a family member, be it the father, or mother, or both, but that's not to say in Helen's case it couldn't have been a neighbor, or an uncle, or a friend of the family. There's often collaboration going on, with one of the parents pretending not to know what is occurring. In most instances the abuse has been frequent, which allows little chance for the child to recover between the incidence of molestation."

"The book that I was reading said that most multiples were abused when they were very young."

"That's still all too true," she said. "The abuse happens before the child's defenses have formed. Personalities emerge as a form of protection. 'I' am not getting hurt—'she' is. It is one of the few ways a young child can escape the double bind being forced on them. The adult or adults who are supposed to nurture are usually the ones doing the hurting. A child learns from the parents. If one parent is abusing, and the other is ignoring that abuse, what kind of message is the child receiving? And what can a child do but dissociate? Helen certainly learned about dissociation from her mother, who was an alcoholic."

"I know."

Rachel questioned Cheever with her eyes.

"I met with her father this afternoon," he said. "He was quick to point out his wife's drinking problem."

"Why did you meet with her father?"

"To get answers. Helen wasn't around."

"Helen shouldn't be one of your suspects. And by going behind her back and talking with her father, you're playing with her mind."

"Seems to me she's doing a good enough job of that by herself."

Dr. Stern shook her head. The detective didn't understand, or wouldn't. She took a deep breath and tried to corral her anger. The sooner he finished with his interrogation, the sooner he would be gone. "Do you have any other questions, Detective?"

"As a matter of fact, I do. Professor Troy and I discussed the myths behind Helen's personalities. I was curious as to where all of her personalities live. Do they share her downtown loft?"

"No. They live in Olympus."

"Nice digs."

"Try paying the price."

"Is that what she'd write down on an IRS form?" Cheever asked. "Under address she'd just note Mount Olympus?"

"Her personalities would let Helen answer those kind of questions, and she would know to write down her conventional address."

"Tell me about Helen's Olympus."

"It is far from the madding world. It's not heaven, but it is a long ways from earth. At its entrance are clouds, great billowing clouds, she says. There is never any rain or snow. There are rolling fields, and expansive forests, and picturesque lakes. The gods make wonderful company, and there are always enormous flagons of ambrosia and nectar to quench any thirst. Musicians play, witty conversations abound, and there are diversions and games available to all."

"Can you book me passage?" Cheever asked.

Rachel offered her first smile that he could remember. "Me first." Cheever remembered his own retreat after his daughter had died. It had taken him deep inside of a bottle, a view that hadn't been nearly so pleasant as Mount Olympus. "All her personalities live there?"

"Except for Helen and Holly and Caitlin."

"They're stuck with us mere mortals?"

"Afraid so."

"Helen Troy keeps getting more and more—exotic."

"Her behavior is consistent with that of many multiple personalities. If you are going to escape, doesn't it make sense to choose a place you want to go? Remember, these are masters of avoidance. Most multiples live in a Shangri-

La where it's beautiful. The brooks run gently, the trees offer shade, and the weather is perfect."

"Why would they ever want to leave?"

"Many of them don't. Some of the personalities conspire against integration. They think of it as murder."

"Since you're working toward Helen's integration, aren't you worried that her personalities might respond violently to your trying to bring that about?"

She shook her head. "It's common for patients to have ambivalent feelings toward their analyst, and certainly not unique to patients with DID. The job of any therapist is to do psychic surgery. We often ask a patient to dredge up painful memories, memories that have been purposefully and methodically suppressed. No one enjoys being forced to reexperience terrible traumas. For many, reliving the past is something to be avoided at all costs."

Cheever knew that all too well. He looked at her, and no longer saw the doctor with a huge chip on her shoulder. She appeared to be as tired as he was. Cheever was almost tempted to ask her out for some coffee, or a drink. That was the kind of thing two professionals did, wasn't it? But he couldn't quite bring himself to do that. Instead, he asked her a question that had been nagging at him.

"Helen, or perhaps I should say Hygeia, referred to you as Antiope," he said. "What did she mean by that?"

Rachel wondered whether she was blushing. On those rare moments when her emotions superseded her intellect she didn't flush red, but instead showed white patches on her cheeks, what her former husband had called "frostbite imprints."

She considered telling a half-truth, but then heard herself telling the real story. "There is a part of Helen that is amazingly intuitive. I've seen this gift revealed too many times to discount it.

"Antiope was the Queen of the Amazons. I'd like to be

135

able to argue that I am a woman warrior, but that is not why Helen has linked me with Antiope. My connection with Amazons is apparently a physical one. Statues and paintings of Amazons often show them without a right breast. The Greeks interpreted the word *Amazon* to mean 'without breast.' According to legend, the offending right bosom was removed because it was considered a hindrance in battle; it inhibited their archery skills.

"Very few people know that I had breast cancer. It is not something I discuss casually. Five years ago I had a modified radical mastectomy on my right breast. There is no way Helen could have known this, but somehow she does."

Rachel didn't like how she sounded. Her speech lacked the professional timbre she was known for. Maybe he thought she was looking for pity. "Funny," she said in a much too cheery voice, "I never even took up archery."

"Thank you," said Cheever.

He stood up, nodded to her, then began to walk out of the room. "Wait a second," she said. "I have something for you."

She walked over to her bookshelves, picked out several books, and brought them over to him. "If you are really interested in dissociative identity disorder," she said, "you should read these."

"I appreciate it," he said, then stood there awkwardly. Cheever wanted to say something, but he wasn't sure what. He wanted to make things right between them, but didn't know how.

"I keep thinking about Trojan horses," he said, "and how they're inside all of us." He wanted to say more, but it was hard for him to get beyond that image, so he settled on repeating the words, "Trojan horses." Cheever raised his hands and opened his mouth, but no other words came out. Shrugging, he walked to the door, opened it, and quickly shut it behind him.

Rachel let out the air she had been holding back, and it

escaped in a long, tortured sigh. During the telling of her Amazon story she had noticed his eyes had never left hers, hadn't surreptitiously peeked at her right breast. He hadn't reduced her to a piece of anatomy, had, in fact, been far more considerate than she would have expected.

She walked back to her desk. Before leaving for the day she wanted to make notes of their conversation. That was the pattern, the routine she adhered to.

Rachel tried to summarize what had been said. Her focus wasn't sharp. She remembered the dream from the night before. There was a large banquet going on and she was the featured speaker. In the middle of her talk she opened her blouse, unclasped her bra, then exposed her right breast to everyone, swiveling it around for all to see. Her plastic surgeon had liked to talk up its advantages, how it was firmer than her left breast, and would defy gravity longer. He was proud of his handiwork, acted like his breast creation could pass muster in a showgirl's act, but she was still suspicious, still unsure of what was there. It made her feel like a fraud somehow.

She analyzed other people's dreams, but avoided her own. Rachel remembered what Cheever had said about Trojan horses, and how they were in everyone. He was right.

The doctor reached for the box of tissues on her desk. She allowed herself the luxury of pulling out a single one, then put the rest of the box away. A half-minute later she returned to her note-taking.

FIFTEEN

While driving away, Cheever realized he no longer thought of Rachel as the shrink, or the doctor. She had a name now, and that surprised him. Would that it were so easy to pin a single name on Helen, he thought. There were questions about her that he had meant to discuss with Rachel, but they would have to wait. To Cheever's thinking, that wasn't such a bad thing. That was a reason to call upon Rachel again, something he wanted to do. That surprised him, too.

He stopped on Market, picked up a gyros to go at a Greek hole in the wall. Cheever debated on calling Helen from his car, but decided he was close enough to chance a surprise visit. He took large bites of the gyros as he drove. Cheever had never learned how to eat slowly, and whether by chance or design, he usually ate by himself in his car. During his career he'd probably eaten more on the road than most truckers. Finishing a last bite, he parked on Seventh, but didn't immediately approach Helen's building. From across the street he took in the view of the converted lofts and picked out her window. The curtains were still open, but there was a light on now. The illumination afforded him a good view of the room's interior. This time he saw not one but two unmoving statues. Or was one of them Helen; posing again?

Cheever crossed the street and pushed on the intercom. When he pushed a second time a breathless woman was heard between the static: "Yes?"

"Ms. Troy?" he asked.

"Yes."

"This is Detective Cheever. I wonder if I could come up and talk with you."

The static seemed to last a long time. "Give me five minutes," she finally said. "I just took a sink bath."

"Fine."

Cheever passed the time by pacing, walking from one end of the block to the other. Cars passed, and allowed him only blurred glimpses of humanity. There was very little pedestrian traffic in that part of the downtown at night. With working hours over, the commuters had packed up and escaped to their bedroom communities.

"Detective."

Her voice drifted down to him. She was leaning out the window, her wet hair hanging down.

"Yes?"

"I can't buzz you in because the security door's on the fritz. You'll need this key to get in. Catch."

Cheever tried to follow the descent of a baseball cap through the semidarkness. It fell about ten yards from him, its landing marked by metallic clinking. He tracked down her hat parachute. The cap advertised her loyalty to the Twins. It figured.

The key worked on the door, and Cheever climbed the stairs. Halfway to the fourth floor the dog started barking. No one would have mistaken the sounds for a Chihuahua. Helen shouted, "Be quiet," and the dog obeyed, but not without a final bark to show his independence.

She stood at the door waiting, and motioned Cheever inside with one hand. With the other she held the dog. He was growling, and she said, "Shush, Cerberus." The rottweiler obeyed, but didn't take his eyes off of Cheever.

He handed her back the baseball cap. "Landlord promises the door will get fixed tomorrow morning," she said. "We'll see."

Her loft looked lived in, but not settled in. There was a futon bed, partially unrolled, some cinder block bookshelves, and a few plastic milk containers full of knickknacks. Her refrigerator was hotel-sized, and a ten-foot section of rope was stretched across a corner where some clothes were hanging. There were two unmatched chairs, and she waved for him to sit in one. He motioned back, indicating he preferred to stand.

"Would you like a peach?" she asked. "I got some at the Farmer's Market today. They're good and fresh."

"No, thanks," he said. "I already ate."

"I think there's a Diet Pepsi in the fridge."

He shook his head, remembered to smile to show he appreciated the offer. She was wearing jeans and a man's faded button-down shirt that was large enough to serve as a nightgown. Her hair was wet, the black and white strands matted together and not yet delineated. There was no hair dryer in sight. No bathroom either.

"It's down the hall," Helen said, as if reading Cheever's mind. "I share with the six other lofts on this floor. The bathroom doesn't have a shower, which I guess is a hint that we're not supposed to be living here."

"Do the other renters ignore that hint as well?"

"I'm the only one who calls this home sweet home on a permanent basis," she said, "but people are always crashing around here for one reason or another."

The loft had worn hardwood floors. There were some drop cloths thrown around, but no carpeting. Cheever started walking around, his footsteps setting off groans in the wood. Clicking nails followed him, stopping when he stopped. Cerberus was trailing him.

"He's friendly," she offered, "most of the time."

Cheever decided not to test her qualified endorsement. He stopped in front of a partially completed bust of two faces sharing a common head. The faces were looking in opposite directions. They shared very similar features, but they were somehow different.

"Janus," Helen said. "He was always portrayed with two faces, one for the rising sun and one for the sunset. One of his moods was light, and the other dark. He was a solar deity, associated with the beginning of things, and the ending of them."

The one face was happy and innocent, the other grim and foreboding. The amazing thing, Cheever thought, was that they were the same face, the only difference being a few lines and some coloring. But those were enough to make a world of difference—a difference of night and day.

"I stopped by the library today," Cheever said, "and checked out some books on mythology. Your statues at the gallery made me curious."

"Oh?"

"I wanted to know about the puns and hidden meanings. There was one of a woman being sacrificed by a priest entitled, *Achilles as a Heel.*"

"Read your classics, Detective. Polyexna was sacrificed to the already dead Achilles to satisfy the shade's clamoring. In death he still wanted her as a spoil of war."

"What about *Jason's Offspring?*"

"The innocent often suffer. Jason left his wife Medea and took up with Creusa. Medea took revenge on him by killing the children she had borne to Jason. She also sent a poisoned robe that killed his new wife."

"You created one statue of a woman crying . . ."

"*Niobe on Mother's Day.*"

"What caused her that kind of grief?"

"Niobe was proud, too proud. She tweaked the gods, and with their arrows, Apollo and Diana struck down her seven boys and seven girls."

"Cheery stories behind your statues," Cheever said.

"Don't blame the messenger," she said.

Cheever continued his walk. Near the window were two shrouded easels. "May I see the paintings?" he asked.

"Not without a warrant," she said.

He raised an eyebrow.

"I don't like showing unfinished paintings," she said. "It releases their magic early. As I work on them they change, take on lives of their own. If a painting's viewed too early, it undergoes a stillbirth."

He respected her privacy, but Cerberus wasn't quite as respectful of his own. The dog had started sniffing around his pant legs and worked his muzzle up to Cheever's groin. Cheever offered the dog his hand; a stub of a tail started twitching.

"Do you have a dog?" she asked.

"A cat," he said, "but I consider myself a dog person."

"I think I'm more of a cat person," she said.

"Consistent, aren't we?" said Cheever.

He finished his inspection of the room, ended at the chair that had been offered him originally, and this time sat down. Cerberus followed him, and put his big head on one of Cheever's knees.

"I ran your record through today."

The silence built between them, until she finally said, "You can't trust self-portraits."

"What's that mean?"

"I had problems. I was a kamikaze express. That's changing."

"You were cited just three months ago."

"*Eris* was."

"Is that splitting hairs, or splitting personalities?"

"In my case there might not be much of a difference."

"Why did Eris do her birthday suit pose?"

"To embarrass me. She likes it when I'm put on the defensive. She enjoys stirring the pot. I'm glad Dr. Stern was able to get her to agree not to do her Godiva Galatea thing anymore."

Myths and more myths. Could Helen distinguish between myth and reality? "I looked up Galatea in the dictionary today," he said. "It said she was one of Pygmalion's statues that came to life."

"Is that all it said?"

"Pretty much."

"That's the problem with definitions. They never tell the full story."

"What else should have been mentioned?"

"That Galatea caused a great deal of trouble before becoming inanimate again. Like some of my personalities."

"You have no memory of what your personalities do?"

Helen nodded.

"Do you resent them?"

She avoided directly answering. "I'm coming to understand them better."

"Why don't you tell me about your insights?"

Helen ran a hand through her wet hair. "From what I've been able to understand, the personalities often emerge to meet needs of mine."

"Such as?"

"When I need to reflect, Eurydice comes out. She is thoughtful and melancholy. Her opposite are the Maenads—sheer energy. Caitlin is the innocent girl in me, Cronos the harsh adult. Holly is more passive than Helen, wants to fit in more, and Eris is the firebrand. Hygeia wants to help, to heal, and Nemesis wants only revenge. The Fates are my intuitive selves, and allow me glimpses into my past, my present, and my future. And Pandora knows the good and evil in all of me."

"What about Helen?"

She shook her head, as if even she wasn't sure, but then said, "Helen is the mulligan stew."

"Heinz 57."

"Sometimes the mix isn't that complementary."

"You seem . . . normal . . . now."

"You haven't pushed the right buttons."

Give me a little time, thought Cheever. "I talked to your father this afternoon."

She didn't physically react, but Cheever sensed an alertness in her. "And how is he?" Helen asked.

"Seems fine."

He let her think, let her dictate where the conversation led. "And what did the two of you talk about?"

"Myths mostly. Your father recited some Latin and some poetry."

"That sounds like Father."

"He said you don't see him much."

"I don't."

"Why not?"

"Perhaps I tired of his Latin and poetry."

"Anything else?"

"What is this, therapy?"

"Think of it as humoring me."

"How can I," she said, "when the joke's on me?"

"What do you mean?"

"My father is a strange man. He lives in his mythological world most of the time."

"Like father like daughter."

She didn't respond.

"What do you remember about your mother?"

"She was never happy. Most of the time she had a drink, no, a bottle, in her hand."

"Did she love you?"

"I suppose so. But she loved booze more."

"What about your father?"

"Are you asking whether he loves me?"

"Yes."

"Same answer: I suppose so. But he loves the gods more."

"Does that have a bearing on your personalities? Your lives imitating the myths?"

"I have no idea."

"Can you control your personalities?"

"Dr. Stern has taught me self-hypnosis. That helps. She has also left several posthypnotic commands to assist in certain situations. And she tells me that I have an internal self-helper in the form of Pandora who has stopped some of the personalities from going too far."

"Give me an example."

She shrugged, tried to put on a bold face, but failed. Probably had too many to choose from, thought Cheever.

"Pandora's prevented me from self-destructing a few times," she said.

"From committing suicide?"

She nodded.

"What drove you to make such attempts?"

"A better question might be, 'What's kept me from doing it?' I had a boyfriend once I was afraid to be intimate with. He was too good of a lover. When we had sex, my personalities kept popping out with my orgasms. I tried to make a joke about it, called it popcorn sex, but he couldn't take it. How would you like to go to bed with a woman and have her keep changing on you, I mean really changing, every few minutes? I tried to tell him variety was the spice of life, but he told me chili powder and gun powder don't mix."

"He was one man."

"He said what I believed."

"How have you tried killing yourself?"

"Cutting my wrist, taking pills, the usual."

"And Pandora's thwarted you?"

"So I'm told."

"But she hasn't stopped you, or the other personalities, from hurting other people."

"You mean the assault charges?"

Cheever nodded.

"They deserved it."

"What happened?"

"Dr. Stern says I shouldn't dwell on the negative."

"Then tell me without dwelling on it."

She accepted his casuistry easily, as if she were well practiced in that art. "A couple years back this creep was laying into one of my girlfriends, really slapping her around. Or so I'm told. So I guess I retaliated."

"From what I read, he was her boyfriend and he was drunk."

"Are either one of those things supposed to be an excuse?" There was a sharp edge to her voice. Cerberus raised his head to look at his mistress for a moment, then back at Cheever. When it was clear no one was moving, he put his head back on Cheever's knee.

"You used a pool cue and a chair on him and sent him to the hospital."

"He was an asshole."

"Another time you used a razor and cut a woman's face."

"It was her razor," she said, "and she was coming at me with it. She was coked up."

"Do you know which personality came out during these incidents?"

"Dr. Stern tells me it was Nemesis."

The goddess of retribution, of punishment. It made sense. Or made as much sense as could be expected given the situation.

"Why did you put clothes on your statues?"

She pretended not to know. "They were cold?"

Cheever shook his head.

"To get attention, I suppose."

"Michelangelo didn't even give a fig leaf to David," Cheever said. "As the artist, I wouldn't think you'd want to cover up your work."

"What do you want me to say, Detective? I can't tell you why I dressed them. It's not something I remember doing. Maybe there's something significant in my covering them up. Maybe there's a reason why I undress myself and act like a statue. I don't know. Why don't you ask the personalities that do those things? They might know. And if they don't, Dr. Stern's probably your best bet."

"Which personality did the dressing?"

"I'm pretty sure Caitlin."

The little girl dressing up her dollies? Cheever considered that. Her question interrupted his muse. "Would you pose for me?"

"You mean model?" he laughed.

"I mean just be yourself for a while."

Cameras never bothered him. He was used to the media prowling around homicide sites. He'd seen himself on the eleven o'clock news too many times, a suit poking around in corners, to be self-conscious that way. But the idea of being under Helen's scrutiny, of being revealed in some form, was intimidating. Every painting is a caricature, he thought, with the artist's focus playing up different features. He wasn't anxious to see what his were.

"I'm not very good at sitting."

"You can stand."

"I don't think it's for me."

"You want to ask me more questions, don't you?"

The trap was being set. He nodded.

"Then that's how you'll pay. Otherwise you'll have to talk to some lawyer I pick out of the yellow pages. And I'll look for the biggest ad."

"Clothed," said Cheever.

"Of course," she said.

She went to get her sketch pad, came back, and immediately started scratching away with a pencil. Cheever felt as if he had made a deal with the devil and still wasn't sure how it had happened. Whenever he looked up he found her staring at him, peering at God knows what. Being subject to her scrutiny felt like a risky business. He might as well have agreed to pose nude. That's how exposed he felt. There were parts of him that he was sure were dead and buried, but she kept proving that wasn't so, kept showing him just how alive those nerve cells were, and how much they could hurt. He had visited Hawaii once and been told, "If you don't like the weather, just wait half an hour and it will change." With Helen you could almost say the same thing. She was volatile, far too volatile, but she was alive. For twenty years Cheever had insulated himself with the static weather pattern of gray skies. This young woman was the elements, was earth, and wind, and water, and fire. Oh yes, fire.

"You can breathe," she said, "even act human if you want."

"You might find me out then."

"Is that what you're worried about?"

She could draw and talk at the same time, which wasn't a good thing as far as he was concerned. "Who says I'm worried?"

"Your rigid neck, clenched fists, pursed lips, and frown lines."

"Sounds normal to me."

"Looks like rigor mortis to me."

It was better, far better he thought, to put her on the defensive. "Have you seen anyone in that state before?"

Helen didn't answer, though she continued to sketch. Was it that she didn't want to dignify his remark, or had silent Pandora stepped in?

"Were you at the gallery the night Bonnie Gill died?"

He wanted to connect her to the time and place of the murder. Her pencil stopped moving.

"Do you own a red wig?" he asked.

Her pencil slipped from her hand. He watched her face go slack, saw it reborn.

"Can you take me to the beach tomorrow, Daddy?"

Cheever felt the sting of her words. Play with fire and you get burned. Why hadn't Nemesis come out and attacked him for being an enemy? Or Eris—he had thought about Eris more times than he wanted to admit. But there was no better defense than the little girl, and somehow she must have known that.

Cheever and Cerberus had made a friendship of sorts, or at least an extended truce, with the detective scratching away behind the dog's ears, but now the animal was alert. He ran from Cheever to his mistress and tried to lick her face. When she said, "Good doggie," he trembled with delight. Then he awakened to his responsibilities, went on full alert, pressing his body between Cheever and Helen.

The dog growled at Cheever. No one was going to come near the little girl he had charge over. He showed his fangs, and another one of his faces, to the detective.

Cheever got up slowly, made soothing sounds, kept saying, "It's all right, Cerberus," while backing away. The dog didn't follow him, was uncertain of his own emotions, his hackles raised to the potential threat, his body wiggling at the touch of her hand.

"Promise you'll take me to the beach, Daddy."

The rational mind told him to refuse. The instinctual mind told him to hurry out of harm's way, to get away from the dog and not answer. The detective's mind was still figuring out the angles when his words came out: "We'll go tomorrow. I'll pick you up in the morning."

"Oh, thank you, Daddy."

He opened the door, closed it behind him, then started down the stairs. Why had he made such a promise?

Because, he decided, he had always been a sucker for his own little girl, especially when she called him Daddy.

SIXTEEN

Cheever read until very late, usually a form of escapism for him, but not tonight. He alternated his reading between Rachel's psychological texts and the books on mythology. Sometimes there wasn't much difference in the reading.

He delved into the mythology to better understand the themes Helen had selected for her statuary. Cheever thought it telling that she hadn't gone with classical choices, hadn't portrayed Hercules or Perseus or Theseus in some heroic contest, or picked beautiful gods such as Venus and Apollo to sculpt. Her choices centered around death and tragedy: Anthor being killed accidentally by a spear meant for another; Pentheus being turned into a boar; beautiful Hyacinthus dying after accidentally being struck by a quoit thrown by his friend Apollo; Dryope changing into a tree after inadvertently picking flowers that were the embodiment of the nymph Lotis.

Forbidden flowers, Cheever thought. He was reminded of carnations and Bonnie Gill, but perhaps he should have been thinking of hyacinths. Apollo was so grief struck at having caused Hyacinthus's death that he summoned a new and beautiful flower to arise from the earth, and on its petals were the letters *AI*, Greek for "woe." The sun god decreed that each springtime the flowers would bloom and forever mark the death of Hyacinthus.

"Woe," Cheever said aloud. "Woe."

The word spoke to the motif of Helen's statues. Death, or imminent death, was on display. Most of the deaths, he noticed, were the results of accidents. There was a sense of unfairness about them: death from a fluke, or ignorance, or as an object of some god's unjust wrath. Though the gods weren't on display, their emotions and responses were. Helen Troy's cosmos was a dangerous place. Pick the wrong flower, stand in the wrong spot, or offend the wrong god and you died, more often than not at the hand of a loved one.

Cheever had the feeling of reading ghost stories too late at night, the kind that keep you turning your head to shadows, or reacting to the sounds of the night. The sensation didn't pass when he put the mythology aside for Rachel's psychological tomes. The tales therein weren't so much ghost stories as people turned into horror stories. Minds didn't typically shatter into pieces without a lot of hammering.

He read about abuse, and torture, and traumatic experiences, and how they had translated into altered and twisted psyches. In some multiples there were personalities that were both right- and left-handed, had different politics and religion, were optimistic and pessimistic, had dissimilar handwriting, and held down two very different jobs. There were cases of one personality having a crush on another, and being devastated when learning that a face to face could never occur. And then there were personalities that hated one another with a pathological vehemence, that were more than willing to cut their nose to spite their face.

Not that all mental health professionals were comfortable with the quantifiable symptoms of dissociative identity disorder. There were researchers who said that the brain waves and just about everything else in multiple personalities were not demonstrably different from one personality to another. And there were contradictory studies about whether the personalities in a multiple displayed different physical, chemical, and psychological makeups. But it was hard not to believe, Cheever thought, when you read certain stories, like the multiple that had found herself pregnant. The host personality was convinced she was a virgin, certain she had never been with a man. But even that personality couldn't deny her pregnancy, couldn't wish away her burgeoning belly. When the baby came, the personality accepted the delivery as a blessed event, telling one and all it was a virgin birth.

Emperor's clothes, thought Cheever. We're all wearing them. But some of us have piled on more imaginary layers than others.

What Cheever enjoyed most about reading Rachel's books was getting the benefit of her many penciled notations. He invariably paid more attention to her jottings than to what the authors had to say. Her notes were written in a feather-light hand with small but neat handwriting that was feminine without being frilly. There was a touch of voyeurism in Cheever's scrutiny, an interest in wanting to undress Rachel's musings, a desire to see how she thought. His compulsion annoyed him, but he couldn't fight the urge to flip ahead through the pages to hurriedly see everything she had written.

It was late when Cheever lifted Gumshoe up and gently deposited her outside his room. Whenever an exit was forced upon her, she always acted like it was her idea. Cheever made a point of not looking at the clock in his room, didn't want to be dismayed by the hour. He settled into bed. As tired as he was, he still had the urge to read one more myth, and settled upon Hercules fighting the Hydra.

The Hydra lived in a swamp in the country of Argos. It had preyed on the nation, ravaging the citizens of Argos. The Hydra was a creature with nine heads, the middle one of which was immortal. Hercules battled the Hydra near the well of Amymone. Fighting well didn't help him, only seemed to make matters worse. For every one of the Hydra's heads Hercules decapitated, two grew back in its place. Driven back, facing defeat and death, Hercules was cued by his servant Iolaus to burn away the heads of the Hydra, and one by one did so.

The Hydra's ninth, and immortal, head could not be killed, but Hercules defeated it by another means. Lifting up a gigantic boulder, Hercules threw that last head under the great rock and buried it under its weight forever.

A Hydra can be defeated, Cheever thought, turning out the light. But tired as he was, he didn't get to sleep right away. There was that last head to think about, and wondering where it was buried.

Helen's encounter with Cheever had left her feeling out of sorts, angry. Her moods and personalities were often a chicken and egg question, with an uncertainty about which came first. In the midst of her confusion and discontent Eris assumed control.

Fuck the nosy detective, she thought, and fuck my humorless shrink too. She didn't need their aggravation and she didn't need them. Music was the ticket, loud and overwhelming enough to drive away any thoughts. She jumped into the Bug and drove to the Dead Club, expecting to find relief there. She thought she could outrun her demons, or better yet, outdemon them, but the club didn't provide the escape she wanted. The band was playing reggae music, and the musicians were too damn mellow. She drank heavily, but it didn't take away the edges, just added a few.

Grave diggers, she thought. A bunch of fucking grave diggers have entered my life. They keep poking and probing and hurting. Maybe I should get in some preemptive strikes, get them before they get me. The thought made her feel better, but it didn't sustain her. Eris needed action. She needed something happening. Things were too slow, sluggish. She felt claustrophobic, boxed in. On good nights the club's hanging layer of smoke sometimes reminded her of the clouds around Olympus. But tonight it felt heavy, like a shroud. She was glad when the lackluster band stopped playing to take a break, but not happy when the lights were turned up, the yellow glare adding to the oppressive air.

Eris walked up to a long-hair in a tank top. Tattoos ran along the length of his muscular back and down his arms, creatures that crept and slithered and crawled and hurt: a coiled rattlesnake with bared fangs, a black widow in a tangled web, a scorpion with a raised stinger. "The club's history," she whispered. "The deal was signed yesterday."

His muscles rippled, the creatures upset. "No."

"Yeah. A fast-food place is coming in."

The citizens of O.B. had once rallied against a proposed Winchell's Doughnuts coming to town with the kind of fervor that's usually reserved for toxic waste dumps. Starch and sugar and jimmies were fine, but not conformity, not in O.B.

Tattoo man's rumbling anger started reverberations all around him. Eris flew forward in front of the storm, landing in front of Corbin, another perfect patsy. He had wide, hopping eyes and cavernous dark circles, was a speed freak who dealt his product. "I just heard the cops are going to be coming in tonight," she told him. "They're planning a big bust."

Corbin was paranoid to begin with, but her words sent him to the next level. He bounced away from her, panicked, calling out. And Eris went on to her next mark, this one an androgyne of a sex no one could be certain.

"New management rules," she said. "No more unisexual bathrooms. It will be back to one for the little boys and one for the little girls, and they're going to enforce it."

An outraged shriek, and Eris moving on again, weaving, talking faster and faster, telling lies, agitating, provoking, pushing, pretending to be pushed, yelling, falling, expertly touching all the nerves around her that were just beneath the surface, spreading the tumult and anger that was in her.

Grabbing a surfer, she sobbed in his arms. "They're closing down the O.B. Pier for good. Gonna make an amusement park."

Around her the rumors met, escalated, and boiled. There was pushing and screaming and fistfights. In a giddy moment Eris felt like the Pied Piper of the disenfranchised. She knew how to play the notes of the dispossessed.

If the cops had been a little slower to appear, the temporary madness would have passed, but their arrival changed everything. Sirens blaring, two squad cars pulled up in front of the club. The ant hill, already agitated, spilled out, and the cops, ensconced in their squad cars, provided a target for unified anger. There was shouting, and jostling of the vehicles, prompting the police to put out calls for more backup. More black and whites arrived, the cavalry loud with their sirens. Amidst all the noise and confusion, Eris danced and laughed. Finally, something was happening.

The cops yelled for the crowds to disband, but that drew even more spectators. Siege mentality took over. It should have been a perfect forum for Eris, one of her "golden" opportunities for mischief making, but she was taken before she could further fan the flames. As she started slipping away, Eris had a fleeting vision of herself as the Wicked Witch of the West shrinking to nothing. She wanted to shout, "I'm melting," but couldn't make the announcement in time.

Eurydice emerged on the other side of Oz. She was able to walk away unnoticed; the light that was Eris was there no more. Eurydice's preoccupation made her invisible. She was thinking about a painting, and a world without love. She didn't hear the screaming going on around her, didn't notice the flashing red and white lights, just trudged to her Bug deep in thoughts and memories.

Cerberus welcomed her return, but with tempered enthusiasm. He knew this one tended to ignore him, offering few words and fewer pats. Still, she was responsive enough to recognize his needs. Grabbing his leash, she took him downstairs, opened the door, and said, "Go sniff. Go sniff."

Cerberus knew the euphemism, and did as bid. She stepped out to the sidewalk and waited for him. The other personalities usually walked with Cerberus, or at least watched his progress, but she was preoccupied. "Sniffing" was incidental to what she really wanted the dog to do, but this was one time he obeyed her instructions. Cerberus fell upon a scent that demanded to be followed. He went further afoot than usual, all the way down the street and then around the corner, his nose seducing him from his post.

Eurydice was good at waiting. She stood without moving, thinking about Detective Cheever and how he fit into the painting she was imagining, and how he fit into her world.

Something intruded into her dream world, something frightening. She jumped back, but not quite fast enough. She was running and screaming even before she felt the pain in her chest, but she didn't slow down to examine her wound.

Her cry awakened Cerberus. The hound of the underworld barked as he ran, and he ran as if he were racing to catch up to his hateful baying. He announced death, but when he came to her side there was only air at which to snap.

The presence of the dog gave her the courage to stop running and look around. There was nothing to be seen.

From around the corner she thought she heard an engine start, and a car drive away, but she couldn't be sure. She was in shock and her chest hurt. Eurydice reached for her heart, felt to see if it was broken anew, and came away with blood on her fingers. The dog sniffed around her, then started pushing her with his muzzle back toward the opened doorway.

"Good dog," she said, but Cerberus didn't acknowledge this one's rare praise.

He was too busy guarding the doorway to hell.

SEVENTEEN

"Last night's homicide has a lot of people on edge," Cheever said. "I'm thinking maybe you ought to come in."

Cheever was leaning back on his chair, talking into the phone. Five stories below him he watched as a man walked into the Edutek building, a student training for that new life.

"Why?" Dr. Denton asked.

"You're a witness. We want you safe."

"Slasher wouldn't want to mess with me. I'd give him a taste of his own medicine."

The Slasher. After the second knifing homicide in as many nights, the nickname was on everybody's lips. "Might be, but a vacation from the streets couldn't hurt."

"Like in jail?"

"No. A room somewhere."

"Catered, man?"

"We can set something up."

"I'll think about it."

"You going to call me back later?"

"The Man tells me to call him twice a day, I do what the Man says."

"Keep a low profile," Cheever said.

"There be any other kind?" the doctor asked.

Dr. Denton had called Cheever as he had promised. To try to ensure that line of communication, Cheever had handed him twenty dollars the day before, but even without the money he thought it likely the doctor would call. Rewards have a way of piquing interest. The doctor was listening mighty close to everything being said on the street about the murders. He was dreaming about that money.

The second homicide was boldly announced in that morning's *Union-Tribune*'s headline: SLASHER STRIKES AGAIN! Willie Lamont was a homeless man who had been found with a slashed throat two blocks away from where Bonnie Gill had been murdered. Even so, the headline presumed much. Though the police media representative had gone on record as saying there were "some similarities" between the deaths of Bonnie Gill and Willie Lamont, no one had determined they had died at the hands of the same killer. Except the headline writer.

Willie Lamont was fifteen years older than Bonnie Gill and had a well-documented fondness for alcohol. Cheever figured that someone with a knife might have relieved Willie of the bottle he usually went to bed with, or maybe some copycat killer had decided to look for a victim too out of it to fight back. The death of a Willie Lamont didn't sell newspapers, unless you happened to tie it in with a serial killing.

His phone rang again. "Detective Cheever."

"Detective, this is Rollo Adams."

First a call from the pauper, and then the prince. "Yes, Mr. Adams?"

"I'm hearing a lot of squawking from the hen house this morning, Detective. Business owners and concerned citizens got their feathers ruffled."

And what the hell was he supposed to do about that? Cheever wondered. But he did what any designated interface does. "I'm sorry to hear that."

"Some of these folks are talking up starting private patrols and taking back the streets."

"Historically," Cheever said, "there have been very few homicides in the downtown area."

He couldn't say the same thing about Barrio Logan, or East San Diego, but it was doubtful Adams had any building projects planned for those areas.

"You got a serial killer stalking the streets, Son. People don't give two hoots about historically."

"We don't know if it's a serial killer."

"You must know something."

"Not really. Another team is working the Willie Lamont homicide."

"That's not exactly the kind of thing I was looking to reassure the nervous Nellies with. You got a witness maybe, or a suspect?"

"Not that I've heard," Cheever said.

Rollo sighed in exasperation. "You're not giving me a polite way to say cow paddy, Detective."

Tough—cow paddy, Cheever thought. "You can tell everyone that we've increased patrols and will have a much more visible presence on the downtown streets."

"Mite late to be closing the barn doors."

Cheever wasn't in the mood for Rollo's country wisdom. "Is there anything else I can do for you, Mr. Adams?" He resisted speaking with a twang.

"I'd appreciate you bringing me up to speed if there are any developments," Rollo said. "I got some irons in the fire that have gotten pissed on pretty heavily lately. Any good news to mollify the natives would be welcome."

Rollo had that unique ability to use words like "pissed on" and "mollify" in the same breath. Cheever wondered if he had the talent to pull off the Ritz and the grits at the same time, decided he didn't, and concluded with a simple, "Will do."

Cheever spent most of the morning helping the Kid set up an undercover team. The Kid was in charge of planting an overt victim all but carrying a sign saying "Knife Me" in the area where Bonnie Gill and Willie Lamont had been murdered. Cheever had rehearsed the operation with the Kid and his recruits until he was satisfied, but his help hadn't ended there. Cheever also assisted Diaz and Hayes; they had been assigned to see if Gill and Lamont had known each other, or if their deaths could be connected in any way. From what could be determined, the answers were no and no.

The same answer, he realized, as to whether his helping the other detectives was necessary. What he was really doing was trying to avoid the personality of Caitlin. Though he had called Helen's loft twice that morning, each time he had only waited a few rings for her to answer. His promise from the day before had been hanging over him, clouding his day. He had been looking for any excuse to not visit her, had hoped something in the case would click so that he could avoid her. Besides, he told himself, she probably didn't even remember their agreement from the day before. Since Helen and Holly didn't share co-consciousness with the other personalities, Cheever tried to convince himself that he was justified in assuming their proposed beach trip was off. But when Cheever found himself ready to volunteer to help Falconi with some record checking, he reconsidered his behavior and knew he had to drive over to her place just to be sure. He needed to face up to her, and maybe his demons, at the same time.

Cheever signed himself out on the work board. Helen Troy's loft was less than a five-minute drive away. If she wasn't there, he'd catch lunch. Maybe he'd even call Rachel and see if she was free to talk and eat. He had questions to ask her, after all. Cheever drove down Broadway, turned north on Seventh Avenue, and then had to overcome his impulse to keep driving. There was a reason Helen hadn't answered his calls. She was out front waiting, embodying every parent's guilt of broken promises. Zinc oxide covered her nose. She had on a one-piece bathing suit that looked big on her, like all such suits look big on little children, and on her face was the classic expression of a child expectantly waiting; guileless, certain but slightly anxious.

She looked like she still believed that good always triumphed over evil, that Santa Claus made it to every house on earth, that parents always came through for their children. He might have been late, but she still believed he would come. With just one look he knew she would have waited for him all day. Cheever parked the car and started across the street toward her. She didn't see him at first, didn't spot him until he was halfway across the street.

"Daddy!"

"Stay there!" He stifled his urge to yell other advice: Don't run into traffic; watch out for the strangers walking by; there's no need to cry. I'm here.

She offered him a big hug, reaching up as children always do, even though there wasn't all that much difference in their heights.

"I waited a long time," she said, a slight accusation in her words.

"I was delayed."

"Can we go right now, Daddy?"

He nodded, picked up her small bag of possessions that he could see included a sand shovel and a change of clothes. She reached out a trusting hand, and he took it with the slightest hesitation. They crossed the street to his car, Caitlin chattering away. "Do you think the water will be warm? I went to the ocean once, but it was *sooo* cold. Do you see those birds? I can walk like that. They're happy, aren't they? Do you have any bread to give them, Daddy?" He enjoyed listening to her talk. She managed to bring a freshness even to pigeons and the tired streets.

Cheever debated on which beach to take her to, then decided on Coronado's North Beach. He wasn't thinking so much about scenery as safety. He wanted a wide, sandy beach, somewhere safe for Caitlin to play. San Diegans are very proud of their beaches. With 120 miles of ocean and bayfront in the county, it seems like every neighborhood has christened its stretch of water. Near to where Cheever lived were some nice beaches like Stonesteps and Moonlight and Boneyard and Swami's, but he rarely visited them, and when he did he rarely even wet his feet. Mea culpa, he thought, a blame he didn't extend only to beaches.

"Where are we going, Daddy?"

"Coronado Island."

Cheever thought about correcting himself, but didn't. Coronado wasn't quite an island, but that was how all San Diegans referred to it anyway. They took the Coronado bridge over, and when they descended to land, he played the tour guide a little, announcing that they were driving along Orange Avenue. Caitlin was quick to point out the street wasn't orange.

"You're right," Cheever said. "But there were orange trees here once."

Or that's what he had been told. The orange trees had been there before his time. For whatever reasons, they had been replaced by other varieties of trees. Now there were mostly palms and cypress and pines along the street. And stores. Plenty of those. Cheever turned northwest just before the Hotel del Coronado, one of San Diego's venerable landmarks, and found a place to park along the street.

November is San Diego's answer to the theory that God is dead. The days are balmy, and the nights are one-blanket cool. The tourists have gone into low profile and paradise isn't only something to be read about in Genesis. The slightest hint of fog remained along the coast, wisps that would give up the ghost within the half-hour. The sun was pleasantly warm, peaking out in the low seventies, and the wide beach was almost deserted, with no more than fifty people lounging in a half-mile radius. Cheever was glad for that, didn't want to deal with the curious stares drawn by a twenty-five-year-old woman acting like a child. Or a man old enough to be a grandpa trying to play the daddy.

She ran forward with coltish strides, a child in a woman's body, her feet kicking up sand. Her shrieks were high pitched, her laughter unrehearsed.

"*Come on*, Daddy," she said impatiently.

Cheever took off his shoes and rolled up his pant cuffs. He knew he should be questioning her, probing into the murder of Bonnie Gill, but it felt so good to just be with her. If he closed off a part of his mind, if he shaded his eyes, he could almost go back twenty years when his hair was dark and his little girl was alive.

He showed her how to look for the small holes in the sand, dug up sand crabs for her inspection, and dumped some into her hands. She shrieked with pleasure and with fear, then began to inexpertly dig her own holes. When that passion died, she took to running in and out of the waves. She pretended she was an airplane, her arms pushed back, her feet splashing along the white water. She chased birds, and played with dogs (the owners didn't notice her young girl's voice because they were so used to baby-talking their own animals), and built a sand castle that was long on imagination and short on structure. Cheever tried to help her, but she was critical of his assistance, so he let her do her own building. He hoped they'd be gone before the high tide collected her handiwork.

Naval planes passed overhead, taking off and landing at the nearby Naval Air Station North Island. Cheever suggested a walk to SEAL beach, and Caitlin enthusiastically agreed. They walked south toward the Naval Amphibious Base. He knew the beach was closed to the public, but sometimes from the civilian side you could still see the SEALs training. Cheever had watched a few of their intense workouts, groups of men being pressed to run and swim, being pushed to the breaking point, and he told Caitlin how at the SEAL training beach the men were often subjected to combat conditions, with live ordnance and barbed wire. When she heard that, when she learned that the SEALs he was referring to weren't the flippered type, were in fact human (though they liked to claim otherwise), she immediately wanted to go back to "their beach."

It was a good decision on her part. They both returned tired. When Cheever dropped to the sand, Caitlin was just behind him. She chose his lap as her resting spot. Her suit was wet and sandy, but he didn't deny her the seat she wanted, though at first he was embarrassed. Anyone walking by them would have thought he was a lecherous older man trying to make time with a young woman. And how could he explain anyway? Who would believe or understand that when she was with him, and talking like she was his little girl, it was as if he were traveling through time? For the moment, he was thirty-two and she was five, and the most natural thing in the world was that she should be sitting on his lap.

"Daddy?"

"Yes, Sweetie."

"What happens when you die?"

"You go to heaven." It was the only answer he could give her. Parents don't tell their little children about the possibility of a permanent death that means never seeing them again, or worse, of hell.

"Are you going to die?"

He thought about the actuarial tables for cops again, and told what was likely another white lie: "Someday. But not any time soon."

"Am I going to die?"

"Everybody eventually dies. But you won't die for a very, very long time."

She accepted his answers without demur. He watched her sitting there thinking. "What's all this talk of dying?" he asked.

"Don't know," said Caitlin, her answer traveling up the musical scale, followed by, "I'm hungry."

"What do you want to eat?"

"Pizza!"

They both took outdoor showers, changed in the rest rooms (Cheever having to convince Caitlin to go into the women's rest room and change by herself), then walked back to the car. Cheever had noticed an upscale pizza parlor nearby, the kind where cheese is called "fromage" and where getting tomato sauce is the exception rather than the rule. He debated about having Helen stay in the car and his going to get takeout, but even though she was twenty-five, Cheever still didn't feel right about leaving her by herself. He decided they should dine together, though he hoped they could get a table by themselves.

That proved to be wishful thinking. The restaurant was crowded and they were told there was an expected fifteen-minute wait. He suggested to Caitlin that they go elsewhere, but in a plaintive voice she said, "no," and Cheever accepted her wishes. A family came in behind them, a mother and father and two little children. Caitlin was shy of the kids at first, observing them from the corner of her eyes, but then she started playing with them. It reminded Cheever of the time he'd seen a young Great Dane frolicking with a puppy Pomeranian, kindred minds unmindful of their dimorphism.

"She loves kids," Cheever said. She is a kid, he thought.

They were finally seated in a booth where Caitlin was diverted by a mirror next to her. She made faces, gestured with her hands, and kept turning back to look at herself. What does she see, Cheever wondered?

"Let's play a game," he said.

"What game?"

"It's called, 'Describe Yourself,'" he said. "You have to look in the mirror and answer my questions. Okay?"

She offered a tentative "okay." The game didn't sound as fun as hide-and-go-seek.

"What color is your hair?"

"Red," she said.

"Do you have freckles?"

"Of course," she said.

Bonnie Gill's hair was red and she had freckles. "What color are your eyes?"

"Green."

Bonnie Gill's eyes had been brown. Cheever's momentary excitement subsided. "Do you have any scars?"

Her nose crinkled. "What's a scar?"

"It's where you've been hurt. After you get a wound your body tissue heals and leaves a scar. Here, I'll show you one."

Cheever started to roll up his shirt cuff, but then noticed she wasn't paying any attention. "Caitlin," he said.

She didn't respond, and the mirror held no more interest for her. "Pandora?" he asked.

She looked up at him, but didn't say anything. "It must be lonely," he said, "knowing things, but not being able to talk about them."

She still didn't say anything, but a tear rolled down her cheek.

Their pizza arrived. Not surprisingly, Pandora chewed with her mouth closed.

EIGHTEEN

"I think I was attacked last night," Helen said.

Dr. Stern didn't immediately respond to her words. Sometimes when Helen was feeling particularly needy she said things to get attention, but the timing of this announcement and the manner of her disclosure weren't consistent with her usual patterns of getting noticed. Their session was more than half over, and Helen's manipulations usually occurred at the beginning of their hour. It was common for multiples to have a sense of the dramatic. Therapists often gained their cooperation by allowing them their intrigues, and sometimes even encouraged them in their fantasies.

"Attacked?"

"I think someone tried to hurt me."

"When did this happen?"

"Last night. I woke up this morning in pain. And bandaged."

"Bandaged where?"

"Here." She pointed to her chest. "I think I was cut."

169

"Would you mind showing me?"

Helen answered by unbuttoning her shirt. She was used to the doctor examining both her mind and body. Given a choice, she would have taken the physical any time. Helen sometimes worked as an art model. One way or another she'd been taking off her clothes professionally for six years and had little modesty. She wasn't wearing a bra; atop her left breast was a bandage.

"I'll need to remove the dressing," said Rachel, but she was talking mostly to herself. When she'd been a medical intern she hadn't enjoyed tending to physical ailments. Part of her attraction to psychiatry was that the corporeal wasn't stressed. She much preferred dealing with the mental and biochemical. Rachel gently stripped away the bandage. It was clear the wrapping hadn't been professionally applied; the patches, cotton, and adhesive strips were piled on in a haphazard manner. Her stigmata had all vanished, only to be replaced by this new wound. The cut wasn't deep, but was about two inches long. The wound was healing nicely, though the scab made the cut look worse than it was.

"I'd like to take some pictures," Rachel said.

Helen consented with a shrug. The doctor was always snapping photos to document their therapy. She kept two cameras in her office: a Polaroid and a thirty-five millimeter. The doctor used both cameras and was methodical about taking the shots from several angles. She did some close-ups of the wound, and with a viewfinder perspective didn't see the change in her patient.

"Hey, Doc, how about taking a few cheesecake shots?"

Eris vamped for her, wet her lips, and did a few peek-a-boo poses. Rachel humored her by snapping several pictures, but as the poses became more outrageous she put the cameras down and assumed her professional persona. Pointing to the wound, she said, "I would recommend a tetanus shot."

"Looks like you're more worried about lockjaw," Eris said, "than I am."

Jealous over Pandora. Rachel didn't respond to the remark, knew only too well that Eris was always instigating internal battles. She opened a drawer, pulled out a first-aid kit, and said, "Please stand still while I dress your wound."

"You and your famous medicine chest."

Dr. Stern ignored her innuendo, just as Eris ignored her request. Reaching for some of the almost developed Polaroids, Eris looked at them critically, then said, "Good shots of my titties, wouldn't you say?"

Her smugness disappeared in sudden pain. "Hey!"

"I warned you about standing still."

"You should have warned me about your bedside manner. But then I could have guessed."

Rachel finished dressing the wound, her face expressing nothing. Eris frequently attacked her femininity and sexuality. As a doctor, she knew not to respond. As a woman, she couldn't help but feel.

"Were you clubbing last night?" Rachel asked.

"Yes, in-deed-y."

That explains how you got hurt, Rachel thought. The Maenads were probably jumping from table to table, or more likely, Eris was juggling daggers.

"Why don't you tell me about the cut?"

"Didn't happen on my shift."

Sometimes Eris "slept" while the other personalities came out. Her memory link was limited. "When did it happen?"

"After I checked out."

"Which was when?"

"A little past midnight."

"You retired early."

"It was involuntary."

"Who took over?"

"Eeyore."

That was one of Eris's nicer names for Eurydice. "Was there some problem?"

When Eris was too rambunctious, Eurydice often emerged. Eris didn't like that, didn't understand how a "weak sister" could gain control. "No real problem. I seem to remember there was some painting she was all anxious to get to. Like it couldn't wait."

That was probably why Eris had slept. She was one of the few personalities not interested in painting. Her palette, she said, was life.

"I went over our conversation yesterday . . ."

"Do you like to mentally masturbate, Doc?"

Rachel continued with her observation as if she hadn't heard: ". . . and was interested in several things that you said."

"I kind of think you get off that way, loving mind games the way you do. You probably think about some long-ago lover, and get hot and bothered by ancient memories of short strokes. You're so into your mind I doubt whether you even need a hand . . ."

"When you referred back to the dream you said that the hole was, and I quote, 'the place where dreams die.'"

". . . and you sure don't need a man, do you?"

"What did you mean by that?"

Eris regarded Dr. Stern with a smile. "Yesterday's news is yesterday's blues, lady. I'm not one to eat regurgitated meat."

"Which dreams died?"

"Hers."

"Whose?"

"Mine."

"Yours?"

"Ours."

"You as Eris, or you as Helen Troy? Or were you referring to someone else?"

"I need a cigarette."

Eris was the only alter that smoked. She knew the rule was no smoking in the doctor's office, but she also knew when to negotiate from strength.

"Go ahead."

She searched through her purse, found one lone, bent cigarette. "Bitch keeps throwing them out," she said, then lit up.

"We were discussing the death of dreams."

Eris took a long drag, blew out her answer with the smoke: "To be honest, Doc, I'm shooting from the hip. And I got kinda small hips."

"You're saying that you don't remember?"

"It's kinda hazy."

"What about when you said, 'It's childhood's end?' "

Eris didn't immediately respond, which was unusual for her. "You ever have trouble distinguishing between what's real and what isn't, Doc?"

The ten-dollar answer or the one-dollar answer? Rachel nodded her head.

For a moment the goddess of discord almost deviated from her character. She looked pensive and troubled before remembering who she was. "Then maybe you ought to get some professional help, Doctor."

Rachel didn't show her disappointment. "I'd like to speak to Eurydice please," she said.

"You know what they say: You can take the girl out of the underworld, but you can't take the underworld out of the girl." And then Eris was gone, with only her echo in the air.

"Good afternoon, Eurydice," said Dr. Stern.

Eurydice showed to what extent appearances were influenced by the personality. Eris considered herself alluring and vibrant and it showed. With Eurydice, the shades were drawn. There was a gravity to her, tragedy carried on her slumping shoulders.

"Hello," she said quietly, atonally.

"I was hoping you would tell me about your wound."

Eurydice never responded immediately. It was as if some censor put a time delay on her words. "Yes," she finally said. "Last night I took Cerberus outside. I remember thinking about the painting I wanted to get to. You know how preoccupied I can get, Doctor."

Rachel nodded.

"I wasn't paying attention. Then I got this feeling, this flash, that something was wrong. I turned and moved backward at the same time. And that's when I was stabbed."

"Your attacker tried to strike you from behind?"

"I believe so. A footstep or some noise must have alerted me."

"Did you see your attacker?"

She shook her head.

"No impressions whatsoever?"

Another shake of the head.

"Nothing was said?"

"I don't think so. I started screaming and running. And then Cerberus was barking. Everything was so confused it's hard to remember."

"If you had to guess," the doctor said, "was it a man or a woman who struck you?"

After a long consideration: "A man."

"Tall? Small? Dark? Light?"

"I couldn't tell you."

"Did he chase after you?"

"For a step or two, I think. With my screaming and Cerberus's barking, he gave up quickly."

"Your assailant ran away?"

174

"He must have."

"Did the dog chase after him?"

"No. Cerberus stayed by my side."

"Did you call the police?"

"No."

"Why not?"

"I wanted to get to my painting."

The answer would have been strange out of anyone else's mouth, but for Helen Troy and most of her personalities it made perfect sense to prioritize a painting ahead of personal safety, even an attempted murder. Her art superseded everything.

"It surprised me that I screamed," said Eurydice. "Death should not have frightened me."

Her voice was full of a familiar melancholy that was never very far from her. On those occasions when she emerged from her shell her conversations tended to be long, metaphysical ramblings. Rachel decided it was too late in the session for that. "I'd like to talk with Helen," she said.

Eurydice sighed, and was gone. Though Helen had no memory link with her personalities, she was always aware of her art, and considered herself the creator.

"Tell me about the painting you're working on, Helen."

"Paintings," she said. "I'm working on several."

As if that should surprise me, thought Rachel. "Which one were you working on last night?"

"I just started," she said, not hiding her annoyance. "It's only at the sketch stage."

"I know you don't like to talk about your unfinished paintings," said Rachel, "but I'd appreciate your giving me a little description."

An aggrieved breath, then, "I'm calling it *The Great Undertaking*. It shows Orpheus descending to the underworld. Around him there are other holes in the ground. It's not apparent whether someone was trying to tunnel down, or tunnel out. There is scattered dirt, a few bones, some debris, and a Georgia O'Keefe kind of cow skull."

"What was your inspiration for this painting?"

"I suppose the myth of Orpheus and Eurydice."

"Is Eurydice anywhere in the painting?"

A shake of her head.

"Does Orpheus look like anyone you know?"

Helen thought about it. "I guess he looks like Detective Cheever."

"Why do you think that is?"

"Because his face would have been on my mind. When he came over to my studio yesterday I asked him to pose for me. His weathered look made me want to paint him. He's got a face of the Old West, like he's walked through a lot of shit and breathed in a lot of trail dust."

"How did you get him to pose for you?"

"He didn't do it willingly. It's the price he has to pay for asking me questions. Maybe I should strike the same bargain with you."

"What is Orpheus's expression as he descends into the underworld?"

"He looks like he's been there before."

"Are you in that painting?"

"I suppose a part of me is in all of my works."

"Where?"

"Everywhere."

"Tell me about the holes and the bones."

Helen's head dropped to her chest. The room seemed to darken around her. She didn't raise her head, but kept it lowered. Then her hands started moving as if she were working at a spinning wheel. Rachel felt her throat tighten. She was in the presence of Clotho the spinner, one of the three Fates.

"So many lives," she said in her crone's voice. "So many tangled threads."

Was she talking about the personalities of Helen Troy, Rachel wondered, or other people as well? She cleared her throat to ask the question, but her voice failed.

"Paths are crossed; beginnings and endings are mixed." Clotho shook her head and continued spinning. "Ah, the common thread. Death and disease."

Rachel found herself trembling. The spinning wheel kept spinning.

"And enough pain to fill my skein." The discovery delighted Clotho. Her hands moved and she cackled.

Abruptly, the spinning stopped, replaced by hands that measured threads, stretching them out to appropriate lengths. It was time for Lachesis to dispense lots, to measure lives.

Her voice was gravel and tar: "The truth will set her free. The truth will destroy her. Death stalks her; death frees her. In her threads are carnation, incarnation, and reincarnation."

Lachesis raised her head, but somehow she was still shrouded. In the darkness surrounding her, it appeared that she had only one eye. She stared at Rachel, laughed, and said, *"Et tu, Brute?"*

Why, the doctor wondered, wasn't she responding to this pseudo-witchery? Why wasn't she just laughing and expressing her disdain? Rachel watched her life being measured.

"A frayed thread, afraid of zed. She works with minds from her ivory towers, but she's too high up to smell the flowers. Will Rapunzel let down her hair, so that he can climb her brunette stair?"

Lachesis finished her measuring.

"Three of me, three of thee. He steps on graves and searches for knaves, but how can he find truth when he can't even exorcise his own dark caves?"

She laughed. "Another common thread. The ties that bind. A family that bleeds together, needs together."

Her head slumped, as if felled, then the third Fate arose, Atropos, whose name means "inflexible." She didn't stop to talk, just went about her task of cutting, cutting, cutting. She snipped away at the threads of human life, severed a dozen or more.

Most of the threads, Rachel couldn't help but notice, were cut very short.

NINETEEN

Rollo Adams was being interviewed for a *Live at Five* spot on the news. He was trying to look pious, doing his best not to show how much he liked being in the spotlight. He talked about Bonnie Gill's death and her dreams. In his boutonniere he wore a very prominent carnation. It was a suddenly vogue symbol. Cheever had heard that several members of the city council had also worn carnations that day. If he was a betting man, he'd wager the whole damn council would be wearing them tomorrow. Bonnie Gill was becoming a cause célèbre.

"Turn that thing off," said Hayes. "Gives me gas having to listen to that much hot air."

A hand reached out and turned the television off. It was suddenly very quiet on the fourth floor. Team IV pretty much had the floor to itself. Though Adams had referred anyone with information on Bonnie Gill's death to call the police, the number that had flashed on the screen through-out his interview was that of the Carnation Fund. Cheever made a mental note of that. When Adams called with one complaint or another, and Cheever knew that would be sooner rather than later, he would have his own grievance to air.

Cheever's phone rang. "Cheever."

"This is Rachel," she said.

They had been playing phone tag all afternoon. Now Cheever was beginning to feel silly about having even called her. This was an investigation, not a forum for a schoolboy's crush. "There were a few questions I wanted to ask you . . ."

"Before we get into those," Rachel said, "you should know that Helen just left my office. She tells me someone stabbed her last night."

"Impossible."

"I saw her wound."

"I saw her in a bathing suit a few hours ago."

Instead of asking for an explanation, Rachel said, "If she was in a one-piece you probably wouldn't have noticed."

Cheever's silence corroborated her guess. "Which personality were you with?" Rachel asked.

He offered the name up reluctantly: "Caitlin."

"She probably didn't go swimming."

"She didn't."

"Did she mention having an 'owey' or a 'boo-boo'?"

"No," he said. The baby talk wasn't to his liking. It made Caitlin less of a person. Or was it that it made Rachel more of one? He hid his annoyance. "When did this supposed assault take place?"

"Around one A.M."

The ballpark time when Willie Lamont bought the farm. "If I come over now, are you available to talk?"

Available, she thought, but willing? She still wasn't certain. "I'll be here," she said.

Rachel and Cheever kept their eyes directed to her tape recorder while listening to that morning's session with Helen. It was easier than having to look at one another. Figuring out which of them was more uncomfortable would have been difficult. Listening to the tape, Cheever thought, was like having to witness someone possessed by demons. The unexplainable always bothered him, though he was sure he had managed to keep a poker face.

Rachel saw through his pose. "It was worse in person," she said.

"It usually is."

"I debated on the ethics of letting you listen. I know Helen gave me carte blanche to share with you, but it still goes against my training. I thought her being attacked, however, necessitated your hearing."

I let you listen, she thought, at the risk of exposing me to your ridicule. You heard Eris's jibes directed my way, and listened as she imagined my masturbation and described my mutilation. Her own exposure made Rachel feel terribly uneasy.

"May I see the pictures you took?"

She silently assented, handing him the small stack of Polaroids. Cheever looked at the pictures carefully. Or was that pruriently? she wondered. Did he like the way Eris was flashing for the camera?

"You have any idea," he asked, "how long it takes for a scab like this to form?"

"Not really. Why your curiosity?"

"I'm wondering when the cut could have been administered."

"You mean self-administered, don't you?"

"That's one possibility."

"And isn't another possibility that this slasher tried to kill Helen where and when she said?"

"Yes." He rubbed his jaw, and she listened to the sandpaper sounds. They were oddly lulling. "I guess both of us are trained to look beyond what's offered," he said.

Rachel recognized that what he said wasn't exactly a compliment. "What reason would Helen have for hurting herself?"

"By making herself a victim, she becomes a less obvious suspect in Bonnie Gill's murder."

"And did she then go out and murder that homeless man to further confuse the issue?"

Cheever didn't reply.

"My intention is not to belittle you, Detective. In four years of therapy I've found Helen's actions to be labyrinthian, but not Machiavellian. I have patients who would cut themselves, and derive pleasure from that. My practice has brought me clients who want to be punished and abused. Helen isn't like that. She wants to be well more than anything else."

"Even if that's true," Cheever said, "it doesn't tell me much. Why is it that Helen can talk about this attack? Isn't this the kind of thing Pandora insists on being mute about?"

"I am still trying to understand what makes Pandora silent."

Her voice sounded strained. It must be tough trying to be professional all the time, he thought. It wasn't an attitude to which he aspired. Cheever remembered Lachesis's words. He could almost imagine the doctor letting her hair down. Rapunzel and Rachel, names that started and finished the same way. He realized he had been staring at her longer than he should have, and looked away.

Still, he decided to let down a little hair of his own. "Pandora came out this afternoon when I was questioning Caitlin. We were talking about scars, and that's when her Quaker meeting began."

"Scars?"

"I was asking Caitlin to describe herself to me. We'd gone through hair and eyes and I wanted to know if she had any scars."

"Why scars?"

"I figured she was too young to have tattoos."

Rachel offered a very small, very fleeting, smile. It was enough for Cheever to continue. "I was curious as to how she saw herself."

"And did she have any identifying marks?"

"Freckles," he said.

Rachel nodded as if she had seen them herself. "In Helen's file I have a physical description chart of the different personalities as described by each of them. As you might imagine, none of the personalities look alike."

"What about their ages?"

"How do you put a chronology on the gods? Helen and Holly are the same age, twenty-five, and Caitlin is the perpetual child of five. The rest consider themselves ageless, although Cronos is the oldest."

"I wonder if you could get me a copy of their physical descriptions."

"Yes," she said, "but why?"

"It always helps to know how people see themselves." He hesitated before saying anything more. "I also found it interesting that both Bonnie Gill and Caitlin have red hair and freckles."

"Caitlin described herself as having those physical characteristics long before Bonnie Gill was murdered."

"I know," said Cheever. "But I'm still curious."

She nodded, made a note on a pad of paper for her administrative assistant to do a printout of the physical descriptions of Helen's personalities.

"Do the Fates," Cheever asked, "usually speak in rhymes?"

"Sometimes yes, sometimes no. When they do their rhyming, I often suspect that their speech has been rehearsed." That, or they *were* the voices of the fates, but she didn't tell him that. She barely admitted it to herself.

"You offered some revelations about yourself yesterday," Cheever said. "You said you didn't know how Helen divined your mastectomy. Somehow she seems to have picked up on my past as well. A long time ago I had a five-year-old daughter who died of leukemia."

Cheever had practiced those words thousands of times, though he had rarely uttered them. He wanted the statement to sound firm and final, like something that belonged in the distant past. But the Fates were right. It was a cave he didn't look into, that he did his best to avoid.

"I'm sorry," she said. "Do you have any other children?"

"No."

End of subject, he thought. Bringing up Diane always made him afraid, made him feel like he might lose it. Cheever was determined not to get off-track again, to be only the detective.

He lifted up a bag, physically changed the subject. "I brought your books back," he said. "Thank you for loaning them to me."

"Finished already?"

"Yes."

The door was open for him to make further comments, but he refrained. Cheever also handed Rachel back her Polaroids, though with a little more reluctance.

"May I have one of these?" he asked.

Rachel nodded. She offered them face-out to Cheever as if she were a magician asking him to select a card. He thumbed through his choices, picked out one, and placed it in his coat pocket. Rachel withdrew her deck, but before putting the pictures away, she looked at them once more.

"Strange how she keeps bleeding from the same spot."

"What do you mean?" Cheever asked.

"Well, if not the same spot, very close."

Cheever's face and hands still indicated he didn't understand.

"The other night," she said. "Her chest wound."

"There were two wounds," Cheever said. "One along the throat, the other in the back."

"Multiple wounds," said the doctor. "There was a stigma on her chest. The largest wound of them all. I thought you knew."

"You took pictures of it?"

She nodded.

"Show me," he said, reaching out an insistent hand.

At another time she might have taken umbrage at his demanding manner, but his intentness transcended etiquette. Rachel opened a drawer, and pulled out the photos. The day before, she hadn't seen the need to show him the frontal nudity shots. Rachel supposed she had been protecting Helen's privacy. Or had she withheld them because of her own insecurities?

Cheever stared at the photos for a long time. The third stigma was atop Helen's left breast, in much the same location as where she had been cut. It was a wound just above her heart.

Bonnie Gill hadn't been knifed there. So why had the empath picked up on such a wound? For whom was she bleeding?

"What the hell is going on?" Cheever asked.

TWENTY

Helen Troy pulled up to a stoplight. She looked into the Bug's rearview mirror and could see a woman clearly reflected in the red glow of her brake lights. The woman stood out because she was carrying on a vehement conversation with herself. Her head moved while she talked, bobbing up and down, and side to side. She wasn't singing along to music, or speaking into a cellular phone. She was having an internal dialogue, and an angry one by the looks of it. When the woman noticed Helen's scrutiny, she immediately shut her mouth and acted as if she had been caught doing something wrong. After the light changed she switched lanes to get away from the vantage point of Helen's rearview mirror. Maybe she was anxious to get back to her interrupted conversation.

Helen knew that soliloquies were acceptable on stage but not in public. Outlandish behavior was frowned upon also. She was often embarrassed to hear what she had said and done. Though Dr. Stern tried to ease Helen's self-consciousness about her condition, that didn't stop her from constantly feeling ashamed. It was her body that was on display doing crazy things even if she wasn't the one acting up. If only her public performances were limited to doing monologues. But no, she had roles enough for a full cast, and what made it worse was that she was rarely sure of her lines or the scene she was playing. They were hidden from her. Like right now. She didn't know why she was out driving, and she didn't have any idea where she was going. She had succumbed to a compulsion to get out and get on the road.

Helen had known better than to try and fight the urge. Had she done that, another more amenable personality would have just taken over. This way she was aware of what was occurring—or would be for a time, at least. In the past she had found herself in strange places with no recollection of how she'd arrived there. Helen remembered the time she had awakened in Las Vegas sitting at a Pai-Gow Poker table. She didn't even know how to pronounce the game, let alone play it. So how could she explain the huge pile of chips in front of her, chips she cashed in for almost two thousand dollars? Another time she had been in a fugue state for three days in Mexico, had emerged in a suite in Puerto Vallarta surrounded by a hundred red roses and a man named Carlos who said he loved her. She didn't even know the her he loved. It was scary losing time. Sometimes it was even more frightening regaining it.

Helen's head dropped, and then raised itself almost instantaneously. One by one the Greek Chorus emerged.

"They're trying to kill us," Eris said.

"They're trying to help us," said Eurydice.

Pandora was driving and saying nothing. She opened the window and the wind blew inside. The Maenads imitated the blustery sounds.

"We've got a good thing going," Eris said. "Better than the best of both worlds. We travel between Olympus and Earth. What could be better than that?"

"We're divided," said Eurydice. "We're confused."

187

The faces continued to change with the characters. Eris looked disdainful. "That's Helen's problem, but she's just one. We are many. Integration is another name for serial murder."

A frown appeared, and another voice emerged, higher than the others, but somehow more menacing. "The future is the future," Nemesis said. "Why are you getting so excited about tomorrow when we're not even certain about yesterday?"

"You can't change what is past," Eris said. "And besides, what's the point of looking back?"

"To be avenged," said Nemesis, in a voice that declared that should have been obvious to everyone. "*She* knows all that has gone on, yet *she* withholds it from us."

Eurydice rose to Pandora's defense. "She's explained why. Pandora holds memories like a dam holds water. She saves us from being washed away."

"Damn her dam," Nemesis said.

"We don't need her," Eris said. "There are other ways."

"What ways?" Nemesis asked.

"Strike at our enemies," Eris said. "Attack them first."

"Who?" asked Nemesis. She sounded eager.

"Does it matter? They're all against us. If the doctor succeeds, we die. And if the detective finds our missing pieces, we face an unknown we might not be able to control."

Nemesis's face contorted. "I am the goddess of retributive justice. My revenge is not random. It is just."

"And what if that revenge is against us?" argued Eris.

"So be it."

A new voice: "How do you know Nemesis hasn't already struck at us?"

"You're not welcome here, Pandora," Eris hissed. "Go back to your box."

"It is too dark in there," she said. "I have come out to whisper the word *hope*."

"Is that all you have to say to us?" Eris asked.

"Yes. That and I sense we approach the make-or-break time."

"Make," said some of the Maenads. "Break," said others. There was more discordance than rhyme in their voices.

"I don't have the gift of prophecy," Pandora said, "but in the darkness I offer a little light. Storms have swept through our body and left nothing aright. Our head has been displaced, and our heart hidden. We have been twisted inside so as to not resemble anything human. But now we must be brave and come to terms with ourselves. Ourself."

"You forget the dangers," Eris said. "Someone's trying to kill us. Isn't that right?"

"Half right," Pandora said. "We straddle the fence between sacrifice and victim. We are old enough to make choices now."

Eris raised her voice. "We can flee! All of us can escape! Go to a new city and start over. Leave the dangers, and the past, behind."

"You're afraid, Eris, that if we stay you won't survive either way."

"I'm not afraid only for me. What about the child?"

"Yes," Pandora said. "What about the child?"

The Greek Chorus died away. As the voices receded, Helen found herself driving the Bug up Lamont. The car strained to take the hill. Helen wished, not for the first time, that she took better care of the car. For too long it had endured neglect, performing better and more bravely than it should have.

The area was familiar to Helen. She had lived in Pacific Beach when she was young, her family renting a small house on Diamond Street less than a mile from Kate Sessions Park. Dusk was giving way to darkness when she pulled into the almost deserted park. The mothers had taken their children home, and the lovers had not yet arrived. There were a few dogs and dog owners, and Helen thought about Cerberus, and how she wished she had brought him along. I would have, she thought, if only I had known where I was going.

She stepped out of the Bug and began her stroll. Graffiti marred the rest area, the wall covered with Old English script and the square lettering of some tagger's signature. Helen never thought she would be nostalgic for "Fuck You," but at least that meaning was clear enough. There were several colorful but obscure drawings on the wall that looked like a series of rising suns, or perhaps they were blinking eyes.

Helen walked along the hillside, pausing to take in the San Diego skyline. It was a clear night, the lights of the city revealing familiar landmarks. Gradually her vision shortened, the shadows and contours of the park interesting her more than the distant glitter. Spread out beneath her was a grassy expanse. As a child, she had enjoyed rolling down the hill with her friends Jack-and-Jill style. Helen suddenly felt cold. She huddled her shoulders and grasped both of her arms close to her chest. Time to walk, she decided, time to warm up.

It was a cloudless night, and the warmth of the day was quickly dissipating into the open firmament. Helen moved away from the lights, headed north until the grass gave way to chaparral. She made her way along a canyon escarpment, following a wall of mostly chamise. The chaparral brush was thick and unwelcoming. Helen had walked the periphery of the canyon in the daylight before, and had seen a few dog paths that led into its interior, but even those didn't penetrate very far.

The canyon's many unlit acres looked like a blackout area in a war. Finding a truly dark place in most parts of San Diego wasn't easy, with street lights and humanity having filled the dark corners. Is that what attracted her to this place? she wondered. The darkness? The chaparral wasn't John Muir's wilderness, was just a vestige of what once was, a few acres of undisturbed land. Still, it held an unreasonable fear for her. There were no large predators in the canyon except for a coyote or two that lived off of rabbits, mice, and an occasional neighborhood pet. So why was it that she felt something deadly was out there? Helen stopped walking and listened. There wasn't much to be heard, just enough to tempt her to take a few steps into the shrubbery for a better sampling of sounds. Helen had found herself on the rim of the canyon before, but that was always as far as she went. She couldn't understand her trepidation to breach the canyon. It wasn't as if there was much of a drop down, just a gradual decline, but it was still a descent she was afraid of.

Maybe it wasn't that she liked the darkness, Helen thought, but that she was scared of it, and needed to confront her fears. She put her foot forward as if to test the waters.

Cold, she thought, so cold, and walked away.

TWENTY-ONE

"Think on that third wound any harder," she warned, "and I wouldn't be surprised if your own stigma formed."

Cheever and Rachel had occupied a booth at the City Delicatessen on University Avenue for two hours. The food wasn't the only thing that had kept them there. Cheever couldn't let the third stigma go. He could almost accept that Helen, or Hygeia, had taken Bonnie Gill's wounds onto her own person, but where had that third wound come from? It was like a wild card suddenly showing itself. Cheever kept playing with different possibilities, an old dog working at his bone.

He absentmindedly tapped at the black and white checkerboard tile on the wall. A lapsed Catholic, Cheever quoted St. Paul: "The invisible must be understood by the visible." Then he added his own muse: "And what's visible must be understood in terms of the invisible."

Rachel didn't know the source of his references, but did know he was talking about Helen. "The actions of her personalities make sense," she said, "even if we can't fathom their reasons. Helen is telling us things. The meanings are coming out in her dreams, in her art . . ."

Cheever interrupted: "In her wounds?"

"Perhaps."

"When I go to a crime scene," Cheever said, "I always look for what belongs or what doesn't belong. I'm not afraid to listen to my gut. I'll tell the evidence tech to go into a certain area even if I'm not sure why. I usually have a sense about what feels right and what doesn't. When I saw the third stigma . . ."

"Yes?"

"Something told me it didn't belong. Or maybe not so much that as . . ."

"Go on."

"As I was looking at this human tableau of two different crime scenes: Bonnie Gill's and somebody else's."

"Is there anything that leads you to believe that?"

"Nothing that makes sense to the head."

"I don't have a professional answer," she said, "but I do have a personal one: follow your instincts."

"If I did that, I'd be running the other way." He sounded serious, even if he did throw in a little smile.

The talk stopped for a few moments, but this time Cheever didn't panic. Earlier in the evening the lulls in their conversation had scared Cheever. He had figured silence would give Rachel an excuse to leave, and he had struggled to find interesting things to say. For Cheever, remembering how to converse in a social situation was like trying to speak a foreign language he'd let rest too long. He kept reaching for words, stretching for the right thing to say. At work he spoke in code much of the time. Victims weren't dead people—they were one-eighty-sevens, dispatch terminology for murder. And just as words were abbreviated, so were emotions. They worked with stiffs, not bodies. Most of the dead they investigated were scum and maggots. Everything was depersonalized.

"Tell me about the name Caitlin," he said.

"What do you mean?"

"All the other names have obvious connections. Holly was the middle name of Helen's mother, and we know about the Greek myths. But why Caitlin?"

"I wish I could tell you," Rachel said. "Helen says she doesn't know where the name originated."

"Could she have had a childhood friend named Caitlin?"

"Not unless she was a friend during her lost years."

"It wasn't a popular name twenty years ago," Cheever said. "It would have been uncommon. That's what makes it all the more curious."

"It might have just been a name she heard and liked. I don't think it's a name she's very familiar with, or at least not a name she knows well enough to spell correctly."

"Explain that."

"Several times I've had Helen write the name down on paper and she's ended up spelling it something like K-a-t-e-l-e-n, nothing even close to the traditional spelling. Even the personality of Caitlin usually misspells it. I know that very few five-year-olds can spell, but most of them at least know the spelling to their own name."

"How does she spell Caitlin?"

"Different ways. But she usually finishes the name with an l-e-n. I'm beginning to think we should just change the spelling."

Instead of changing the question, thought Cheever, you change the solution to the answer. Maybe that's what he needed to do.

Cheever waved down their waiter and ordered a cheesecake with two forks. Rachel tried to demur, said it wasn't part of her dietary regimen, but gave in. When they were down to licking their forks, Cheever asked, "You ever work with a multiple before?"

She shook her head. "And probably never again. I doubt I would have treated Helen as a patient if she hadn't already been seeing me for her other problems."

"Why?"

"Accepting a multiple as a client is akin to singlehandedly taking on an intensive-care patient. Not too many mental health professionals are willing to assume such major work for what amounts to pro bono wages. They don't want the hassles: the phone calls in the middle of the night, the excessive hours, and the potential for shortchanging their other patients."

What she didn't tell him was that many therapists were also afraid of being devoured by the beast itself. They didn't want to enter the multiple maze for fear of not getting out. Dealing with psyches is like treading around quicksand. The result was that psychiatrists have the highest suicide rate of all medical practitioners.

"The catch-twenty-two of being a therapist," she said, "is that you have to maintain a strong inner core that is yours, but at the same time understand the thought processes of patients. Sometimes to do that you have to assume their mindsets, even embrace their madness."

And sometimes to succeed with a patient you have to be willing to change yourself, Rachel thought, something she resisted doing. There had been times when she had seen how easy it would be to misstep, to let the borders merge between the real and the imagined.

"Does Helen have a red wig?"

His question drew Rachel back from her view of the brink. "Yes," she said after just a little thought. "Why?"

"We have a potential witness who saw a woman with red hair in the garden the night of the murder. The way he describes it, she was a statue come to life. That's a page out of Helen's book, that, or her becoming a statue."

Rachel didn't say anything.

"According to our witness, this Galatea behaved very strangely, even for a statue come to life. She appeared to be drunk, and at various times acted fearful, protective, and grief struck. She was staggering around, acting like Zorro, lunging at some demon or demons. Then she collapsed, and cried to God for forgiveness. A minute later she got up and walked away, showed no signs of being drunk. What's your take on that?"

"I'd need more information."

"Does it sound like Helen having a—what did you call it?—abreaction?"

"It would be irresponsible for me to speculate."

"How about speculating on the inanimate then? Her statues. Did you go to her opening exhibit, her Garden of Stone?"

"I did."

"Earlier you said Helen was telling us things in her art. What did you learn from her statues?"

Rachel shrugged, made him keep talking.

"You didn't notice that death was on display? Anthor dying, Pentheus about to be hunted down, Dryope being transformed, and Hyacinthus struck down?"

"You didn't mention Polyxena," Rachel said, "or Jason's children, just before their deaths."

Her response was a nice way of showing her powers of observation, Cheever thought, and a good way of chastening him at the same time.

"So what are we to assume from Helen's art?" Cheever asked. "A preoccupation with death?"

"To some degree. But she's also interested in what happens after death, the, if not resurrection, at least metamorphosis. Look at Hyacinthus. He isn't dead; he keeps returning as a flower. And Dryope was turned into a tree.' "

And Graciela Fernandez, Cheever thought, showing herself on a billboard.

"There was a statue of a little girl crying," Cheever said. "It seems that small girls keep popping up in her art. One of her paintings hanging at the gallery showed Graciela Fernandez with a beatific expression staring out from a billboard. Why do you think Helen identifies so with a little girl that was kidnapped and murdered?"

"Maybe she thinks of Graciela as a metaphor for her own childhood, consciously or unconsciously."

Cheever shook his head. The explanation wasn't enough. "The idea that Graciela is in heaven, and that she's now happy, seems very important to Helen."

"Yes it does," Rachel said. She looked at Cheever and wondered: Is that one of your demons as well? Do you need to know the same thing?

"You worked that case," she said.

"I'm still working it," he corrected.

"It's been . . . ?"

"Over two years."

"It means more to you than other cases?"

Cheever took a few seconds to answer. "When children are victims," he said, "we're all victims."

She nodded. "It's obvious that Helen identifies with Graciela," Rachel said, "but I don't think she consciously knows the reason for this identification."

"More than identifies," Cheever said, remembering her bloody tears. "She empathizes."

"Yes."

"In some ways I envy Helen," he said.

"Why?" she asked.

"She has multiple lives. Sometimes I'm not even sure I have one."

He was glad the waiter came along then, interrupting their talk. Their conversation was getting too personal. "Coffee?" the waiter asked.

Cheever put his hand over his coffee cup, and Rachel

shook her head. Their empty dessert plate was taken away, and the bill reappeared in front of them. Cheever drew it over to his side and Rachel didn't object.

"What motivates Hygeia to bleed?" he asked.

"Freud said that only two things motivate people," Rachel said. "Love and pain."

"What's the difference?" Cheever asked.

"Darned if I know," she said.

Both of them wondered at the same time whether they were flirting. They were too out of practice to know for sure.

Rachel always performed her breast examinations in front of a mirror. She didn't know why. Maybe it was because she could be the doctor, and the image could be the patient. Maybe she liked scrutinizing herself through a reflection. Or maybe she had foreseen a moment like this when she would need to look at herself in the mirror just to get a grip, to see a white, anguished face a breath away from a scream. The reflection shocked her. She wasn't that frenzied woman. She couldn't be.

Deep breath. Control and reevaluation. She told herself the lump wasn't really there, and that she didn't feel it. But the more she probed, the larger the mass seemed to get. It was the Princess and the Pea on a more personal level. It felt like there was a watermelon in her breast. No, a bomb that was ticking, ticking. A bomb that hadn't been there the day before.

It was probably just a cyst. Nothing to worry about. The vast majority disappeared on their own. And those that didn't were benign in most cases. Almost all.

Déjà vu. She remembered how much denial she had gone through five years earlier. She had kept repeating sweet medical truths, none of which eventually applied in her case. The reality of cancer had stripped away her

Pollyanna palliatives. In the end, she had survived, whereas every year more than thirty-five thousand American women don't. But Rachel had already played that troubled, horrible lottery. It wasn't fair that her number had been called again. She had already faced up to the disease once and given her right breast. And so much more.

The lump was in her left breast this time. The one that had been spared before. They checked me out just two months ago, Rachel thought, gave me a clean bill of health. Liars. They lulled me into complacency. They let me think I was better.

Do I hate myself so much? Is that what this is? Is that why my body has turned against me? The same angst, she remembered. You'd think over time I would have at least gotten more creative.

Rachel recalled a woman's grieving workshop she had conducted the year before. Many of the participants had found themselves in a loop, unable to get beyond their sorrow. Some mourned for their departed parents, or unborn children, or dead loved ones. Some were stuck over what they perceived as their own failed lives, and grieved for lost dreams. There was one woman who lamented over her lost breast. But it wasn't only her missing gland the woman mourned. The lost breast signified a loss of innocence, the symbol for all the vulnerability she was feeling. Things, she said, could never be the same.

It would have been a good time and place for Rachel to have talked about her own modified radical mastectomy, but she never said a word to the group. She offered advice to the woman, said it was necessary for her to think of herself as a person and not as a collection of parts, and suggested that she work on her inner scars. A healing from within, she said, was more important than any physical transformation. Rachel's words sounded so rich and full, so sage. How easy it was to advise someone else.

Physician heal thy own damn self.

The phone rang. Rachel's first impulse was to let the service get it, but she picked up the receiver anyway.

It had taken all of Cheever's nerve to call her. He was afraid to call, but more afraid of not connecting with her. He had practiced his first few sentences, and trusted to God for the rest.

Cheever said, "Hello, Rachel" (they were on a first-name basis now, or at least she had told him to call her by her first name, and he had told her to call him by his last). "I called to thank you for your time this evening."

When he had planned out his call he had liked that phrasing. It kept their meal on a professional basis.

"There were some other matters potentially pertinent to the case that we didn't get around to discussing," he said. "Maybe if you had time tomorrow we could go over them."

That was all he had practiced. There was no more to his script. He had hoped she would interject at that point and suggest they get together for lunch, or dinner, or drinks. Cheever listened to the silence on the other line.

Rachel felt so many things at once. She wanted to scream. She wanted to explain. She had this urge to laugh, and the inclination to cry. She wanted to tell him to come over, and hold her. She wanted to curse him for interrupting her introspection. She took a deep breath, and then managed to say, "You were right about Trojan horses."

"What?"

"What you said yesterday. How they're in all of us."

"Is something wrong, Rachel?"

"No matter how high you build your fort, and how secure you reinforce your walls, there are still those Trojan horses."

"What happened?"

"Tomorrow's not going to be good for me. Why don't you try me the day after tomorrow?"

By her tone, Cheever wondered if she wasn't really telling him to try her in another lifetime. Reluctantly, he said, "Okay."

TWENTY-TWO

Cheever threw away the retirement home information that had been left on his desk. Cops considered ball busting their fellow cops a part of the job. Balding officers could count on getting literature on follicle growth treatments, toupees, and hair implants; cops with guts got diet books, and whatever Jenny Craig, Weight Watchers, and Ultra Slim-Fast had to offer; older cops received the geriatric treatment. For his last birthday the team had enrolled Cheever in AARP. The support system was touching.

Team IV's work area was deserted. Most of the detectives had been working late on the victim stakeout and wouldn't be dragging themselves in for another hour or two. Cheever listened to his messages, and didn't hear anything that needed acting on. Falconi had left Bonnie Gill's autopsy report out, and Cheever thumbed through it. There wasn't anything that surprised him. She hadn't been sexually assaulted, and there were no other areas of bodily trauma besides the two knife wounds.

Cheever thought about the knife, and how it had been used. Knives were often the weapons of choice in crimes of passion. A knife wasn't anonymous like a gun. You had to get close to the victim. But there wasn't anything passionate about this murder. The body hadn't been riddled with entry wounds. There had even been a certain clinical proficiency to the killing. Perhaps the murderer had been worried about noise, but if that had been the overriding concern there were other ways to kill that wouldn't have been so—intimate.

Periodically, detectives from other teams drifted over and asked Cheever how the case was going. They didn't hear anything that kept them very long. Cheever made it clear he was preoccupied, his concentration directed to a yellow legal pad that he was filling with questions and observations. Under the heading THIRD STIGMA he noted: *It's almost like a scarlet letter in physical form. Check into Helen's romances.* A little further down the page he wrote: *Is there a mythological significance to the third wound?* And then, at the bottom of the page he scribbled: *Helen said, "If I accept their pain, she won't hurt anymore." By saying "their" she implied at least two people were hurting. Could that have something to do with the third wound?*

His phone rang, and he put aside the pad. "Detective Cheever, homicide."

"I like a man who's working early, 'specially when he's working for me."

"I aims to please," Cheever said.

"You any closer to getting me my money?" Dr. Denton asked.

"You got any hot new tips?"

"Nothing that's gonna help me. I heard the Slasher's one of them supernatural forces, a devil."

"Devil's always getting too much credit."

"Also heard that the beaners and slant eyes are nervous. Slasher's got a color thing going. He's got black and white in his mosaic, and now he's going for brown and red."

"Doubt it. Even the Slasher knows all blood's red."

"Thass the word on the street."

"Some imaginative minds out there, I'll give them that. Did you know Willie Lamont?"

"If I did, I didn't know it."

"I need another recap of what you saw."

"Shee-it."

"Not from the top. Tell me about the part where our mystery woman started acting like the protector."

Dr. Denton thought for a moment. "Yeah," he finally said. "She was yelling things, saying stuff like, 'son of a bitch,' then she shout, 'girls, get behind me.'"

"Girls? More than one?"

"Yeah."

"And how many times did she say that?"

"Coupla times."

Little girls again, thought Cheever. They kept entering the equation.

"You given any more consideration to being the city's guest for a few days?"

"Got a La Jolla mansion for me with a butler and cook?"

Cheever had an alliterative answer: "Motel and McDonald's in Mira Mesa, maybe."

"I can live without that. Got an investment to watch. And listen out for."

"Hope you hear more than vampire and rainbow murder theories."

"You want me to keep calling you?"

"You know it."

"Telephone change is getting low."

"How about we have a face to face this afternoon to remedy that?"

"Sound good to me."

"The art gallery at five?"

"You got it."

Cheever hung up the phone and returned to his thinking. He did a lot of looking off into space and remembering, tried to feel around for what was bothering him about the case, or not answered to his satisfaction. There was no shortage of either. In no particular order, Cheever continued with what he called his copping list, writing down inquiries that he wanted to pursue.

His pen had considerably slowed when Mary Beth Carey joined him. "Just the person I was looking for," Cheever said, leaning back in his chair.

"And looking very hard, I can see."

"Got time to do some checking for me?"

"What kind of checking?"

"I'd like you to run a history on any children who turned up missing, or were murdered, or just plain died in San Diego County from 1972 to 1982."

"Age parameters?"

"One year to ten years."

She nodded, observed him through her thick glasses, and saw his expression of wanting more. "What else?"

"Anything you can find on Delores Holly Troy. She would have died around 1976 or seven. And yes, she was Helen Troy's mother."

"It's going to take a while," she warned, "especially digging up the case histories.

"That is if there are any," Mary Beth added under her breath.

"I'd appreciate a printout of names," Cheever said. "I'm interested in newspaper articles, obits, anything."

"It'll take time," Mary Beth warned.

"'Time is but the stream we all go fishing in,'" Cheever said, remembering Thoreau.

"What are you fishing for?" she asked.

Answers, he thought. Truth. Clues. History. A hydra. No, before the hydra.

"The sum equaling up to the parts."

Mary Beth nodded, as if what he said made sense, then

walked away humming some tune. Cheever directed his attention back to his copping list. Several of the items on it could best be answered by Rachel. Cheever had been thinking about her on and off all morning. Last night he had almost called her back, certain there was something wrong. She had sounded disjointed and almost giddy, this from a woman who always appeared so self-contained.

Call her.

He heard the voice in his head. Maybe hearing things was contagious. He tried to ignore it.

Call her.

Cheever picked up the phone and dialed Rachel's office number. He expected to hear that the doctor was with a client, but instead was told, "Dr. Stern is not in today. Would you care to leave a message?"

He identified himself, then asked, "Where is she?"

"Dr. Stern is ill."

"The flu?"

"I don't know."

"Whatever it is must have come on all of a sudden. She seemed fine yesterday."

The receptionist didn't answer. She either didn't know anything or she was well trained.

"Will she be in tomorrow?" Cheever asked.

"As far as I know, yes. Would you like to leave a message?"

"No message, thank you."

Could her illness explain everything? Not really. It would have been a hell of a lot easier for Rachel to have just told him she was sick rather than announcing, "Tomorrow's not going to be good for me."

Cheever dialed her home number. After five rings her service picked up. Cheever didn't leave a message there either. Follow her advice, he told himself. Try her tomorrow. But the voice in his head wasn't as logical. Like an uninvited guest, it kept pushing Rachel's name at him.

He called Helen's number, didn't expect her to be home, but she surprised him by answering. "This is Cheever," he said. "I'm having trouble getting a hold of Dr. Stern."

"She's sick."

"Did you talk with her?"

"No. Her receptionist woke me up this morning and canceled our appointment."

"Maybe she took a mental health day," Cheever said, fishing for more. "That would be sort of ironic."

Helen didn't respond.

"I have some more questions for you," he said.

"Surprise, surprise," she said.

"How about I ask them over lunch?" Cheever asked.

"Lunch?"

"Is that a question or a yes?"

"I guess it was both. I was just trying to remember the last time I had eaten. Lunch would be good."

"How about Croce's at one o'clock?"

"I'll be there."

She could have just as easily said, Cheever thought, "We'll be there."

The rest of the team started drifting in. By nine o'clock everyone was working, most on four hours' sleep. Falconi, being the crime scene guy, was using both ears to listen to what everyone was doing. Mary Beth entered the suddenly busy work area and dropped a piece of paper on Cheever's desk. "You were lucky I could even dig that much up," she said.

Cheever examined the document. It dealt with the death of Delores Troy. The information was scant, but Mary Beth was right: it was as much as you could expect on a suicide pushing twenty years. Cheever decided it was time for an update.

Even before getting out of his car, Cheever had the feeling he was being watched. His antennae were apparently working. As he stepped on the walkway, Professor Jason Troy opened his front door and called a greeting. Cheever walked up the path, his strides purposeful. The professor appeared amused by that.

"All you would need is a lantern, Detective," he called, "and you would look like Diogenes on his quest for an honest man."

Cheever saved his answer until he reached the door. "I wouldn't waste my time," he said, "on such an elusive and ultimately fruitless search."

Troy laughed. "I fear Diogenes was not so quick on the uptake as you. Please come in, Detective. May I get you something to drink? Some coffee perhaps?"

Cheever shook his head. He followed Troy into the living room, but didn't immediately take a chair. Instead he examined the paintings that lined the walls, saw nymphs gamboling in the woods, Vulcan at work at his smith, and bare-breasted young muses surrounding Venus and Cupid. There was a print of a classical unicorn, and one of the waiting sphinx. And, of course, there was Leda and her swan.

The professor waited for Cheever to finish his inspection. "I'm curious," Cheever said, "as to where that painting is that Helen liked so much."

"Which . . . ?"

"Saturn eating his kids."

"Oh, yes. Goya. I'm afraid I don't have a print of that."

"Didn't you say it was in one of your books?"

"I suppose it must be. If you give me a few minutes, I'll try and remember which one."

"Saturn is the Roman name for Cronos, isn't that right?"

"Yes," he said. "It sounds like you've come here for another stroll through Elysian Fields, Detective."

"Not there, no," Cheever said. "I'd like to talk about the past, but without the mythology."

Both men seated themselves, taking up the same positions they had during his first visit. "We discussed your wife the other day," Cheever said. "I'm wondering if I could trouble you to see a photo of her."

"Certainly."

The professor left the room for half a minute and returned with a picture, which he handed to Cheever. Delores Troy was holding a baby in her arms.

"Is that Helen?"

"Yes."

"It hardly seems possible. Your wife looks like a child herself."

"She was twenty."

"Most middle school students look older."

"Delores was very youthful. Even when she started drinking, and having her psychotic episodes, she remained the picture of Dorian Gray young."

"Tiny hips? Very small bust? Thin legs?"

"All of the above. But why your anatomical interest?"

Cheever answered the question with one of his own: "Is that what attracted you to her in the first place?"

"I don't understand . . ."

"It was your pun. The last time we talked you said that your getting together with Delores was a 'minor scandal.' That's what she looked like, didn't she? A girl, a young woman who didn't even appear to have entered puberty."

"Your point still eludes me."

"You were over twenty years her senior. You were an associate professor and she was a freshman. It seems an odd match."

"Obviously you don't know much about academia," he said. "Those kinds of pairings are much more common than you would think."

"You still haven't said what drew you to her."

"Her mind, Detective."

"You sure it wasn't your mind?"

"What do you mean?"

209

"The last time we talked I knew virtually nothing about multiple personality disorder. Since then I've learned that almost all multiples were sexually abused as children. I thought that was something we should talk about."

The professor appeared perplexed. "I'm afraid that is a subject I know nothing about, Detective."

Cheever put on his concerned face, a face that had made so many want to confess, and need to confess. His voice changed, becoming avuncular, and concerned, and troubled. "People feel a lot better when they open up," he said.

"No one has ever accused me of being a clam. Quite the opposite . . ."

"You can help your daughter. This might be your one chance. She's not well now. By telling me about things, you could help make up for the past. This is your opportunity for redemption."

"Are you suggesting I abused her?"

"I think you want to talk to me. I think you want to let go of some bad memories inside of you. I think you should help Helen."

"This is ridiculous."

"No. What is ridiculous is what Helen had to become just to survive. And now she wants to go on, but there are these mountains she has to get through. She can't tunnel under them. She's tried. And she can't find the path over them. You can help her with that."

The professor didn't look quite so unflappable. His face was flushed and there was some evidence of perspiration around his lip. "I'm afraid I am not the right guide for your mountain metaphor. It would be the blind leading the blind. I am not to blame for Helen's mental illness. Her psychoses have an organic basis. Like mother, like daughter."

Cheever's expression changed, then his voice. He became harder, an adversary instead of a redeemer. "You seem to blame a lot of things on your wife. It's convenient that she's dead, isn't it?"

"I don't like your implication."

"I wasn't aware that I had implied anything."

But he was. Though Cheever's look dared the professor to pursue the topic, Troy chose not to.

"How long have you lived in this house?" Cheever asked.

"A long time. Going on twenty years."

"And where did you live before that?"

"In Pacific Beach."

"Where?"

"On Diamond Street. The number escapes me."

"You live anywhere else in San Diego?"

"Before I was married I lived in Allied Gardens."

"Why did you move here?"

"It was time to buy a house."

"Your wife committed suicide in this house, didn't she?"

"Yes."

"Things like that sometimes make people move."

"In some ways her death was a blessing."

"How so?"

"The last few years of her life were not pleasant. She had degenerated quite a bit."

"In what way?"

"She was almost never sober. And she was psychotic. She saw things, pink elephants and the like."

"I suppose she created fantastic tales?"

"Yes."

"Stories no one believed?"

"They were, as you said, fantastic."

"Did she try committing suicide more than once?"

"Yes."

"How many times?"

"Two other times of which I am aware."

"What were her methods?"

"She liked cutting herself. And she finally learned how to do it right."

"Where did she cut herself?"

"Her wrists."

"Each time?"

He nodded.

"What did she use to cut herself with?"

"Each occasion was different."

"Specifically?"

"Broken glass one time. A knife another. And a razor on the last occasion."

"She never plunged a knife into her chest? Or suffered any wounds in the area of her heart?"

"No." The professor's answer was high-pitched, annoyed. He didn't meet Cheever's gaze.

"I'm still curious about that Goya picture," Cheever said.

"Why, yes." Troy sounded happy to have something to do other than answer questions. He walked over to a wall of books, selected one, flipped through it, and then put the book back. The process was repeated a second time, but Cheever had the feeling it was all for show. He suspected Troy knew just where to find a picture of the painting.

The professor's third choice was an oversized book, one of those coffee table art books offering paeans to classical themes. After a brief search, Troy said, "Ah, here it is."

He handed Cheever the book and started prattling. "Did you know that *khronos* was the Greek word for time? Goya used Cronos as his allegory for time. He wanted to show how time devours us all."

That wasn't all he wanted to show, Cheever thought. The intellectual explanation was well and fine, but the horror was visceral. A monster was depicted in an unthinkable act of ruination. Goya defined a flesh and blood relationship in a horrible way. Cronos had wide, unfeeling eyes that were opened in an unseeing stare. In his gigantic hands the god held one of his naked children aloft. His maw was huge and distended. Cronos had chewed off the head and right arm of his own child.

There was much to see, and ponder, and be sickened by, in young Helen Troy's favorite painting. Cheever stared at the painting, then, pointedly, made the same study of Jason Troy. His scrutiny unnerved the man.

"What are you looking at?" the professor finally asked.

"Just trying to see," Cheever said, "if there's any resemblance."

TWENTY-THREE

Croce's had been a popular downtown restaurant and lounge for over a decade, which made it an institution in Southern California time. Jim Croce's widow, Ingrid, had opened and still operated the restaurant. There was some Croce memorabilia to be found in the restaurant, pictures and statements that marked the singer's life, but the reminders were subdued and in good taste. The restaurant wasn't selling memories, wasn't doing a Graceland thing, knew that tributes were well and good but the here and now of their business was serving good food.

Cheever was glad he had arrived early. All the tables were taken and he had to put his name on a waiting list. He was told a table would be available shortly, and that he was welcome to take a seat in the lounge. Cheever decided just to stand. It was mostly a business crowd, men and women wearing the suited vestments of lawyers and bankers and commercial real estate brokers. Cheever had on his worn blue blazer. He brushed it, but that didn't get out the wrinkles.

He tried to remember how Croce had died, and then

second-guessed himself for even having the thought. Was he that preoccupied with death? But recriminations didn't get in the way of his remembering. Croce had died in an airplane crash, he recalled, just when the singer's career was taking off. His music was the kind Cheever liked. There was a passion to many of his songs, a caring and wistfulness. He made his pain public, like Helen's Hygeia. His songs were operatic in that they didn't try to hide much, even if they weren't shouted and waved at you; like opera, the listeners were invited to experience some vicarious emotion-letting. You empathized as he tried to tell his anguish to an operator, or lamented about not being able to put time in a bottle.

"Hi."

Helen was underdressed too, but in an artistic way that made it acceptable. She was wearing her costume jewelry, a ten-gallon black hat that in the old days only the villains were supposed to wear, a colorfully embroidered vest over a white peasant blouse, and a black skirt. While he was nodding his approval there was an announcement for "Cheever, party of two."

"Good timing," he said.

They were seated at a small table that forced a closeness upon them, that even had their knees touching. Helen didn't seem to notice. She reached for one of the two menus that had been left and said, "I'm starving."

Cheever opened his own menu. It didn't take him long to decide on the angel-hair pasta salad with wild mushrooms, mixed greens, and strips of seasoned chicken.

"Everything looks good," Helen said. Instead of sounding pleased, there was a certain desperation to her tone.

"Good afternoon." A college-aged blond woman positioned herself next to their table. She had a pleasant smile and an expectant pen she liked to click. Her name tag read *Danni*. Cheever suspected she probably still drew hearts over the "i" in her name. She looked like a Danni, young, and athletic, and southern Californian to the bone. Stating the obvious, she said, "My name's Danni," but at least she didn't need to look at her name tag before making the pronouncement. "I'll be your server this afternoon. Is there anything I can get you from the lounge?"

Cheever looked at Helen, saw that she wasn't ready to answer, and said, "Just water."

Helen turned her head away from Danni, and mumbled some words. Cheever could see she wasn't talking to herself; she was talking with her selves.

The puzzled server said, "I didn't hear you, ma'am."

Helen turned around and faced her, then said, "Wine, wine." Her answer was offered from both sides of her mouth.

"What kind of wine . . ."

Cheever interjected: "A glass of the house red."

"And root beer." That, from Caitlin's mouth.

"We don't have root beer . . ."

"Any soft drink is fine," Cheever said.

"And I'd like some water as well, please," Helen said.

Danni nodded and wrote. She was about to leave when Helen's face twisted and then changed. "And rum."

"Excuse me?"

"Nothing," Cheever said.

"Rum," Eris said. "The drink of the devil." She offered a full smile.

Cheever shook his head to negate the order. Danni looked from one head to another. Cheever wondered how many heads she saw. Danni clicked her pen a few times, then walked off, backed off really, without saying anything. Eris wasn't as ready to leave. She encircled Cheever's legs in her own, then started pressing her thighs into them.

"Miss me?" she asked, then laughed.

"You can dress her up," he said, "but you can't take her out."

Her pressing became more rhythmic, more sensual. "You're a professional mind-fuck, aren't you?" Cheever asked.

She pretended to be a southern belle. "Why, Detective," she said dramatically, "such language." She didn't stop her thigh massage.

He picked up his menu again, held it so as to not have to look at her, but she just laughed. He thought about pulling his legs away from her, but figured he'd probably upset the table in the attempt. Eris would undoubtedly enjoy his making a scene. She was slightly slouched, but with her long legs, and the tablecloth, no one in the restaurant had any idea what was going on.

"I hope you're having fun," he said.

"Always."

The drinks arrived. All of them. Eris offered a pretend pout at not having any rum.

"I'd like to tell you about today's specials," Danni said. While clicking her pen, she proceeded to do so. Cheever wasn't dissuaded from his original choice, but Eris and the Greek Chorus were a more appreciative audience, commenting on everything she mentioned.

Danni finished reciting the selections on a weak note, her voice, and pen, trailing away at the end. "I'll be back for your orders in a minute," she said, not bothering to linger. Probably afraid to.

"What are you going to have?" Cheever asked, hoping to expedite the process.

"I was thinking of asking for the head of John the Baptist."

"Without even dancing for it?"

"And here I thought we were shimmying just fine." She offered him another pelvic thrust.

"You like men to lose their heads over you, don't you?"

"And they like to give them up."

"Tell me about your male friends."

"You mean my *lovers*?" Emphasis on the last word with both her mouth and legs.

He nodded.

"Long-term relationships have never exactly been my strong suit."

"No wonderful memories?"

"Many. But none worth reliving."

"What about the others?"

"*They're* notoriously bad about selecting men."

"What kind of men do they like?"

"Losers."

"For example."

"Art students. Activists on their way to being carny barkers. Idealists. Romantics. There was even a divinity graduate student, if you can believe it. He's probably studying exorcisms now because of me. He was Eurydice's choice. They'd probably still be sitting around drinking tea and talking deep, gloomy thoughts if I hadn't appeared on the scene every so often."

"Any married men?"

"There must have been. But no long-term affairs, if that's what you mean. Hey!"

She squeezed him particularly hard with her thighs. "What?" he asked.

"We're talking about sex and you're still managing to make this conversation boring."

"I'll try to do better," Cheever said. "Why don't you tell me about your first time? How old were you?"

"Why?" she asked. "Is that how you get off? You like stories of young tail? I can do better than that for you, you know. I could actually deliver you a little girl in just a wink of my eye. We could be in bed . . ."

"Shut up," Cheever said. He didn't hide the mean in his voice, or the threat that was there, but she kept talking anyway.

"We could be doing the in and out, and then she could come on the scene. She wouldn't know what's going on, but over her cries you could take her anyway. The younger the meat, the greater the treat, right? You could make the feathers fly . . ."

He felt his blood pounding, felt his own face hardening and changing. He reached out with his hands and grabbed her under the table, digging his fingers and his fury into her thighs. For several seconds she pretended to enjoy the pain, smiling as he pressed into her, but then her face changed, and her legs loosened from his. Cheever eased his grip.

"There are going to be bruises on my thighs tomorrow," a voice said. It was a voice of experience, but Cheever wasn't certain which personality it belonged to.

"I'm sorry," he said, removing his hands. And he was. For losing control. For being so angry. Now he felt spent and embarrassed.

As if cued by disaster, their server appeared. "Are you ready to order now?"

Going out to eat was a bad idea, Cheever thought. But he still didn't know how bad.

"I'll have the albacore melt," Helen said.

Then, in a voice Cheever hadn't heard before, "Give me a very rare New York steak."

Nemesis? he wondered.

A little girl announced, "I'd like a peanut butter and jelly samwich."

In a sad voice, as if Eurydice was the sacrificial lamb, she said, "I'll have the lamb salad."

"And for me," Eris said, "the chicken fajitas. And make it as spicy as hell."

Cheever wasn't hungry any longer. "Just bring me a coffee," he said.

The waitress repeated the orders in an uncertain voice. "The lady would like an albacore melt, a very rare New York steak, a peanut butter and jelly, a lamb salad, and the

219

chicken fajitas. And the gentleman wants coffee. Regular or decaf?"

Cheever savored her question for a moment, craving its normality. The choice was easy. He'd had enough excitement. "Unleaded," Cheever said.

He noticed Helen trying to catch his eye while motioning to the menu. She had her finger on a specialty pizza with feta cheese and artichoke hearts. Pandora had come out and wanted to put in her order as well.

Join the crowd, he thought. "And the artichoke heart pizza," Cheever said.

Danni's hand was trembling as she wrote down the last order. It was probably one of her first jobs and she had never had to deal with a woman speaking in tongues and ordering for a football team. "Shall I bring everything at the same time?" she asked.

Why not? Cheever thought. He nodded. "And bring lots of doggie bags," he said.

At least Cerberus wouldn't go hungry tonight.

TWENTY-FOUR

Round and round the mulberry bush . . .

Lunch with the damn detective and now everything was swirling, going round and round.

. . . the monkey chased the weasel . . .

She felt caught in the whirlpool, was being sucked down, down, down.

. . . round and round the mulberry bush . . .

Her art wasn't enough of an anchor. That fuck Cheever had started some heavy domino clicking in her mind.

. . . POP goes the weasel.

She kept switching. Personality parade. Who goes around, comes around. Everything and everyone changing. This was going to be a very intense episode. Her own personal earthquake was on the way and there was nothing on which she could hold. Heart racing, afraid, so afraid of the fall. On the threshold waiting to be kicked over, waiting out the desperate moments before a migraine, or serious cramping, or a seizure.

But the rainbow was also inevitable. She tried to hold on to that. It made everything worthwhile, that moment of intense clarity where she would see and touch all. The details didn't matter, just the kinship she felt. God opened up to her, and she felt close to this God. For an instant she would be Saul of Tarsus on the Road to Damascus, Buddha under the Bo Tree, Joan of Arc in all of her glory. But there was a price to pay for such visions.

It was coming closer. Soon she would lose herself to it, and the madness that would follow. Helen began to twitch uncontrollably, her muscles moving by themselves. Her personalities were taking their place at the start line; some wanted only to run; some, to run over bodies, to trample those in the way; and some only hoped to not be left too far behind.

Vigorous exercise sometimes helped her ride the storm. Helen walked to Broadway and then headed west. She had no known destination, felt momentarily panicked at that. Having a place to go always made things easier. There was a lot of car traffic, and for a time she kept pace with a Jeep traveling in the same direction. She kept being confronted by its bumper sticker: JUST BECAUSE YOU ARE PARANOID DOESN'T MEAN THEY AREN'T OUT TO GET YOU.

All of this was Cheever's fault. Their lunch conversation, and his words, kept following her.

"Tell me about your mother," Cheever had asked.

"Isn't that the kind of question some bearded shrink is supposed to ask?"

"Were you mad at her for committing suicide?"

"No."

Faster. She could walk faster. Already she had put the old and ornate U.S. Grant Hotel behind her. She could put everything behind her.

"You were a little girl. I would think it would be hard for someone so young to forgive. Mothers are supposed to nurture . . ."

"By dying she escaped her pain."

"She passed it on to you."

Maybe if she walked fast enough, maybe if she ran, she could outrun her thoughts. Her strides lengthened, quickened. Stores and buildings passed. But Cheever kept trying to herd her in. He had asked: *"Do you have a key to the art gallery?"*

"Yes."

"Why?"

"Since I was only a few blocks away sometimes I helped Bonnie out."

"What kind of things did you do?"

"Closed up some nights. Worked on graphics. Things like that."

"And dressed your statues."

Lights flashed in front of her, the present supplanting the past. The San Diego Trolley was moving along the tracks between Kettner Boulevard and the Pacific Coast Highway. The trolley was red like a fire truck, and clanging, probably at her. She slowed, let it pass, then kept running. Her breath was ragged and her sides ached. Helen wasn't dressed for running. Somewhere she had lost her hat. Her head.

"You looked nice in your black wig." That fucking detective wasn't one to give compliments. She should have known. *"But with your coloring you'd probably look even better in a red wig. Do you have one of those?"*

She had nodded.

"The night Bonnie Gill was murdered," he said, *"there was a woman with red hair out in the garden."*

She had reached for a piece of the pizza. You are what you eat. And he, Mr. Watchful, had backed off. His pale blue eyes didn't miss much. He had known the pizza was Pandora's choice. But when she went on to other food he had started in with his questions again.

"You wanted to call your exhibit 'What the Gorgon Saw,'" he had asked. *"Tell me about the Gorgon."*

Aloud, Helen repeated what she had told him in the

restaurant, but this time she did the telling on the street with strangers around her. "Medusa was once a beautiful maiden, but she was changed by a goddess into a gorgon. She became a frightful monster and whatever living thing she beheld turned into stone. Medusa is the one who is always portrayed as being so ugly, as having snakes for hair and fangs, but what about some of those she looked at? There is ugliness out there that should not be hidden, that should be turned to stone for everyone to see. A gorgon cannot say, 'Today I'll put on makeup.' The purpose of a gorgon is to turn beings to stone."

Those around her stared, not saying anything back, but stepping away as if she were some walking contagion. Through their silence Helen could still hear Cheever talking in her head: *"Was that your purpose?"*

She thought about closing her eyes. Maybe that would close her mind. Maybe Cheever would stop following her. And if she had her eyes closed she couldn't turn anyone into stone, could she? But it was too late for not seeing and changing things around her, in her.

"Did you hear about the second murder?"

She hadn't replied, but he had kept talking. *"A man was stabbed to death just two blocks away from where Bonnie Gill died. There's no apparent motive for his death either. Some people think a serial murderer is out there."*

Storm's coming, move faster, faster. She ran out of road at the end of Broadway, found herself confronted by Harbor Drive and San Diego Bay. Walk south or north? Or walk on water. Behind the commercial and naval and tourist enterprises she could see stretches of the bay. Directly in front of her was the Broadway Pier where boats were docked and docking, loading and unloading their mostly human cargo.

WHALE WATCHING.

That's what the sign said. November was the start of

San Diego's whale-watching season, the time of year when California gray whales migrated by San Diego on their way to their southern breeding grounds. The picture of a whale underneath the sign drew her to it. She could make out barnacles on the whale, little crustaceans. Hitchhikers. The whale image overwhelmed her senses, reverberating there. That's what she felt like, a whale that had sounded, that had gone deep to try to escape the hunters. She was at a depth where human probes could not venture, where the fathoms made everything murky. But there was still this pressure to breach, to breathe. That would leave her exposed. And those with the harpoons knew that.

The Bay Ferry's whistle made her jump. Gulls shrieked and called; their cries frightened her. Helen wasn't comfortable around birds. She felt the urge to escape, but was unsure which way to go. She spun round and round, ended up dizzily facing north. That was the direction.

For ten, twenty steps, Helen walked as if she were drunk before regaining her equilibrium. She made her way along at an uneven pace, slowing down whenever she was distracted, which was often. The signs of the times interested her. She could take a boat to Ensenada. Get lost in Mexico. Get one of those huge straw hats and lose herself under it.

She walked past the B Street Pier, slowing down as she approached the Maritime Museum. The Star of India captured her attention, a windjammer well over a century old. It was one of the legendary big ships that had once sailed the Seven Seas. The ship's high wooden masts stretched up to the sky and Helen had to tilt her head back to take in their expanse. To reach those heights would be a daunting climb . . .

She was no longer looking up, but looking out. Her epiphany arrived and carried her atop the mast. The day was clear, the waters calm. She saw with a clarity that was surreal. The world was so vivid, so alive, so full. The intricacy of how everything fit together didn't frustrate her like the putting together of some incredibly difficult puzzle, but instead gave her a sense of awe at the complexity of the mosaic. Even she fit into it, misshapen as she was. She belonged.

The overwhelming lucidity heightened her ecstasy, each sensation building on the last. There was so much to experience, to feel, but even that didn't matter. The storing of impressions seemed such a miserly and unnecessary act. To be truly alive, that was enough. There was this feeling of being on the edge of a wave that was pushing her forward, but she wasn't afraid. She was on the vanguard of the ineffable.

Under the weight of bliss she collapsed and dropped into the middle of the boardwalk. Half a dozen people ran over to help her. She was moaning, but not because of injuries. There was this feeling of abandonment, of paradise held and lost, of her having gone from all to nothing. She returned with the Greek Chorus out of control. People surrounded her, but she didn't notice them. They were just obstacles to her seeing.

She looked beyond the bystanders to the three berthed ships, and raised her hand and pointed in their direction: "The *Nina*, the *Pinta*, and the *Santa Maria*," she announced.

The onlookers laughed uneasily. One of her personalities joined in with the laughter, while another asked, "What's so funny?" A third alter wanted to say something to keep everyone laughing.

"Are you all right?" she was asked.

There were too many answers to that question. She didn't respond.

A man noticed her bracelet. "She's wearing one of those Medic-Alert things."

Nina, Pinta, Santa Maria. When Columbus had sailed, the maps of his time had warned, "Here there be dragons." True words, she thought, true words. There were dragons everywhere.

A hand reached down to her, grasping for her bracelet. The shifting of bodies allowed her to see the names of the ships. Her mistake, she realized. Columbus hadn't sailed on any of these. The biggest of the three ships was the *Star of India*. Next to it was an old ferry called *The Berkeley*. It took her a few moments to make out the name on the smallest vessel.

"It says to call a Dr. R. Stern," said the man holding her bracelet. He yelled out her telephone numbers, repeated them a second time to a woman writing them down on a piece of paper.

"No," Helen said, suddenly afraid. Not at the prospect of their calling Dr. Stern. But at the name of that third ship: *Medea*.

The portent caused her to uncontrollably shiver. Medea was not a sorceress to be regarded lightly. She was evil.

"Medea murdered her own children," she shouted. "Medea couldn't stand that Jason had chosen another woman to be his wife, so she murdered her, and then she murdered her own children because she had borne them to Jason.

"Flesh and blood didn't matter to Medea. Jason should have known this. She had her own brother murdered to help him. When Jason and his Argonauts captured the golden fleece, they had to flee from Medea's father, the king of Colchis. Just as the king's ship was overtaking them, Medea had her younger brother killed and his body parts thrown into the sea. It was with horror that the king saw the bobbing head of his son, and was confronted with his scattered limbs. He ordered the ship stopped so he could gather up the remains of his dismembered boy, and that allowed the Argonauts time to escape."

Everyone began to back away from this woman with flashing eyes and frenzied speech. Helen waved her hands around, then pointed out to the bay. "Look," she said, "behold the legacy of Medea. The scattered limbs are everywhere."

Fearful heads followed the direction of her finger. Her words, her fear, were persuasive. Eyes searched the waters, half expecting to see a bobbing head and human remains.

Helen swiveled her head around, her terrified expression causing a minor panic. Then her eyes alighted on a figure. At first she was confused, uncertain, but then she recognized who she was looking at and started screaming.

"Medea is here. Can't anyone see?"

The crowd moved further away, afraid of her irrationality, afraid of her stories. She believed what she was saying, and almost, so did they.

"Call Detective Cheever," she screamed, "and tell him not to stop for the body parts. They're only a diversion."

Then, riding a whale's back, she sounded, going deeper and deeper until no one could find her, not even herself.

TWENTY-FIVE

Rachel didn't bother to look at the faces of any of those sitting in the waiting room. She knew they weren't there for her. She was used to getting off airplanes and not being met by family or friends. At airports she just concentrated on getting where she needed to go. As Rachel walked, she employed the same mindset as when she traveled, focusing on getting to the garage where her car was parked. Gradually she became aware of a figure walking alongside her.

"Need a ride?" he asked.

She didn't say anything. She knew better than to try. She just kept walking.

"Or how about a drink?" he asked.

She didn't want her eyes to tear, damn it. But her pace slowed a little.

"An offer you can't refuse," he said. "A shoulder."

She finally stopped walking. "Shoulder," she said, then pressed herself into Cheever's chest. He held her to him, knew that if he didn't she would break their contact too soon. A wet spot grew in his shirt while she cried in silence.

"You know," he said, "I always think of you in terms of firsts. Like the time you first smiled. Getting that out of you was a lot of work. Or the time you told me to call you by your first name. Or now."

"What first does this qualify me for? The first time I made a fool of myself in public?"

"No," he said, and held her a little tighter, though he was careful not to press too hard.

"It doesn't hurt," she said, but it did, just a little, though it was the best hurt she had felt in a long time. "How did you know?"

"Hygeia," Cheever said, "and this voice in my own head. Maybe I'm becoming a multiple." Or maybe, he thought, he was opening up to possibilities.

"What did she say?"

"She popped out while we were having lunch and announced that Antiope was scared and in pain. She said she needed to find you and help you. I had to convince her that I was capable of doing that. And then I had to persuade her to let another alter come out before she started a healing session in the restaurant."

"I'm surprised you believed her."

"She spoke to my own doubts. I tried getting in touch with you this morning and I kept encountering walls."

"So how'd you find me?"

"Besides being a cop, I know something about hiding hurt."

"Antiope's trail," she said, slightly bitter.

"Let's go somewhere," he said. "For coffee, or whatever."

"There's really not much here besides the hospital cafeteria."

"Hospital food never sounded so good," he said.

They let go of one another, but stayed close enough so that their arms kept touching as she led him to the cafeteria. They talked very little. Even after they were seated, and he was sipping at his coffee, and she was playing with her apple juice, it was hard for them to speak to one another. He kept sneaking glances at her. She looked pale and pre-occupied, and he feared the worst. This thing was hanging over them, but he couldn't just attack it straight on.

"I hate hospitals," he said.

"Oh?"

"Diane," he said. "My daughter."

"Oh." Same answer but different emphasis, with an understanding and sympathy offered in her tone.

"I remember when she was born," he said. "For some reason I was given a doctor's scrubs. In those days men weren't automatically at their wife's side during the birthing. It was a long labor, and I went in and out of the delivery room several times. Nurses not involved with the labor kept calling me 'doctor.' And when I went to the cafeteria the servers also called me 'doctor.' Everyone saw me as this thing I wasn't. At first I explained, but then it just seemed easier not to say anything even though I felt like I was impersonating a physician."

"You probably looked dashing," she said, "and everyone wondered who the handsome new doctor was."

He sipped at his coffee. Was it bitter or was he? Cheever was hard-pressed to distinguish the difference. "I never thought she would die," he said. "I didn't prepare myself. There had been so many critical times before that I thought this was just one more.

"I was working. There was an hour where I could have seen her, but I decided to visit later. I'm still waiting to make that visit. It's been twenty years and I'm still waiting."

"What would you have said?"

"I would have told her how much I loved her."

"I'm sure you told her that many times."

"I failed her in the end."

"By not being there for one moment when you were there for so many others?"

"I worked the next day after she died, and the next. I didn't take any time off."

"We all deal with our grief in our own ways."

"My wife thought I was the coldest man that ever walked this planet. She probably still does, that is if she thinks about me at all. She remarried, had a few more kids, went on with her life."

"Why did she think you were so cold?"

"Because I didn't sit around the house bawling for days on end like she did."

"Did you cry?"

"A few times. In the bathroom. By myself."

"You're afraid of showing your emotions?"

"I'm a lifetime out of practice. Like you." He didn't offer the words as a challenge, but as an observation, and she didn't take umbrage, or at least not much.

"I'd prefer to think I'm only five or six years into being emotionally challenged," Rachel said, "but you might be right."

"Let's not be sphinxes to one another," he said. "Let's not have to figure out riddles. How are you?"

She thought a long time before answering. "If I hadn't gone through this before," she said, "I would say I was overreacting. But I did go through it."

It. Better to say *it*. Not cancer. Not losing a breast. Not sickness and helplessness and hurt. Just it.

"I should probably be jumping for joy," Rachel said. "In doctor talk, my mammogram was not suggestive of a malignancy."

"But?"

"But they just finished sticking a long needle into my breast. I had what's called a needle aspiration. They're performing a biopsy of the cyst, so I'll hold the champagne until I get the results."

"How long will that be?"

"I'm one of the privileged. When you're a doctor, and

you know how the system works, you can push a lot of buttons. I should hear by tomorrow afternoon."

"But until then, limbo."

"I'm used to it," she said, then contradicted herself by shaking her head. "No, you never get used to it. What I really am is angry. I'm tired of having a victim's mentality. I want to strike back, but it's hard to find another target to hit besides myself."

"Try a windmill."

"Your strategy?" she asked.

"I wish it was. But I do the same dumb thing you do. I beat myself up."

Rachel let out a long sigh. "When all this attention was being focused on my chest today, with all the lights, and cameras, and directions, it almost felt like I was being prompted for one of those pictorials in a men's magazine. I started thinking about their monthly pinups, and then I couldn't help but wonder how many of those foldout models ultimately got breast cancer. Was it Miss May 1982? Or Miss July 1996? One woman in eleven born in the United States develops breast cancer. Subscribe to one of those magazines for a year and you can do your own lottery. Which displayed woman succumbs? Pick a foldout, any foldout. Only problem is you can't airbrush breast cancer.

"With those kinds of numbers you'd think women would get mad, and organize, and rally for answers. But you see more magazine articles about how to avoid sagging and getting rid of stretch marks than you do about breast cancer.

"I had to confront the mortality statistics. I had to learn about my cancer. Did you know that the number one cause of death in American women between the ages of forty and forty-five is breast cancer?"

Cheever shook his head. "I didn't either," she said, "until five years ago when I was afraid I would become one of those statistics."

"You lived."

"A part of me did, but a whole other part was lost. My marriage broke up not long after I lost my breast. The losses seem interconnected."

"I am sure there were other factors."

"There were. But what I remember is my husband refusing to look at the scars. Refusing to look at me. Refusing to touch me. He wanted to remove himself from the pain."

"He was a fool."

"He's a doctor."

"Dr. Fool then."

Rachel smiled. "Maybe it was me. I remember feeling so besieged. At first they tried treating the tumor with radiation. They outlined the area with this special red ink that was all but indelible. It was like having this hateful tattoo. There's a reason for the red ink, of course. They want to irradiate as narrow an area as possible, bombard that exact same tissue every day. But I felt like it was my concentration camp tattoo. I couldn't dress or undress without seeing my cancer spotlighted. It almost glowed in the dark. As a preventive measure, my left breast was also irradiated. In my mind I began to think of one breast as Hiroshima, and the other as Nagasaki."

"No more bombs," Cheever said.

"What about a time bomb? When they reconstructed the breast they put in a silicone prosthesis. I'm thinking of having it removed and replacing it with a saline prosthesis, but I just don't want to go through the trouble. I don't want to face up to everything again. I try and teach my clients to break their avoidance patterns, and yet I'm the worst offender."

"Do as I say, not as I do."

"Amen."

Her pager went off, as if timed to her invocation. "Excuse me," she said, walking off to find a telephone. Her service was calling. Getting paged was a frequent occurrence, but there was another doctor on call. Rachel figured the service had either erred or it was a true emergency.

A minute later Rachel hurriedly returned to the table. "It's Helen," she said. "She needs us."

TWENTY-SIX

It wasn't difficult getting Helen released from County Mental Health's Psychiatric Hospital. Though Cheever's badge and Rachel's credentials certainly expedited the process, Cheever spoke for both of them when he said, "If we'd waited another fifteen minutes they probably would have released her anyway." Too many cutbacks had made CMH a revolving door.

Cheever found it hard not to stare at the Helen that had been handed over to them. It was almost as if someone had let the air out of her. She was a body without a personality, had gone from so many to none.

Helen wasn't talking, and it wasn't just a case of Pandora being quiet. She was completely mute. Even her body was expressionless. Her large blue eyes were open but unfocused. Though she stood without assistance, her shoulders were slumped and her body appeared to have sunken into itself.

"You ever see her like this before?" Cheever asked.

Rachel shook her head. She was holding one of Helen's hands, periodically rubbing it. Even though Helen wasn't responding, Rachel kept talking to her in a low, calm voice.

Where had everyone gone? Cheever wondered. What had caused the personalities to abandon ship?

Rachel caught his eye, brought him out of his own thoughts. "I live near here," she said.

"So?"

"I want to take Helen to my house."

"I don't think that's a good idea."

"You think it's better that I try and treat her in this parking lot?"

"I think it's better you treat her somewhere else. By taking her home, your professionalism gets questioned. You could get your . . ." He almost said, "tit in a wringer," but changed his wording in midsentence: ". . . self in trouble."

She didn't answer, not directly. "It seems to me I've kept turning my back," she said, "and now I'm having a hard time finding my front." Then Rachel didn't say anything, just took up Helen's right hand and motioned for him to take her left. Cheever reluctantly did so.

When Diane had been young, he and his wife had walked along with her between them like that. Every few steps they had raised their arms in unison and lifted Diane up. She had loved that. But this hand holding wasn't like that. There was no playing, no carefree waving of arms.

Helen was content to be led forward by them. Her expression never changed; her only facial movement was an occasional blink. Her chin rested on her chest, and though her eyes were opened they never raised themselves from the ground. Cheever was afraid he'd have to lift Helen to get her into the car, but she followed the prompts of their hands and was able to seat herself.

"Got time to follow me?" Rachel asked.

"I'll be the disapproving looks in your rearview mirror."

She gave Cheever her address just in case she lost him along the way, and waited until he pulled in behind her

Lexus before driving off. Their route took them along Rosecrans. The traffic was heavy but Cheever found the ride pleasant, perhaps because the long, white buildings of the Naval Training Center evoked memories of a former life that somehow seemed innocent. It was at NTC that Cheever was first introduced to San Diego. Even basic training hadn't soured him on the city. When Cheever was shipped out he'd made a MacArthuresque vow to return, and he had. Now NTC was scheduled to shut its doors, victim of a peacetime economy.

Rachel turned off Rosecrans on to Talbot and began to do some hill climbing. Cheever watched as she kept talking to Helen, could see her mouth move and her head turn. She kept up a steady patter of conversation, almost looked like a tour guide the way she pointed out things, but as far as Cheever could see, Helen remained unresponsive, her head rolling not to Rachel's words, but the motion of the car.

He followed her car up Gage and then Dupont. The higher they climbed, Cheever knew, the more expensive was the real estate, especially those homes with panoramic views of the bay and the city. Rachel turned on Via Flores, and judging by the colorful and lush landscaping, the street more than lived up to its Spanish name: Way of Flowers.

Rachel's house was the most unprepossessing on the street, a boxy, Frank Lloyd Wrightish structure that blended in well with the hillside. In one of the boxes was a three-car garage. Rachel motioned for Cheever to follow her in and park. He was amazed that the two free spaces were just that, empty berths instead of being loaded with junk.

They entered the house through the garage, leading Helen down some stairs to a den. Cheever's usefulness seemed to come to an end after helping Helen to the sofa. Rachel sat next to her and started talking, and Cheever drifted to the side of the room. After five minutes of one-way conversation Cheever saw little to suggest that Rachel was getting through to Helen. This, he figured, was going to take a long time. Sunken into the sofa, Helen looked like a human shell.

Wanting to do something more than gawk, Cheever used an imaginary thirst as an excuse to leave the room. Without interrupting the rhythm of her talking, Rachel told him there was juice and wine and sparkling water in the refrigerator. He took the circuitous route to her kitchen. Her home was immaculate, looked like it was ready for a photo shoot in one of those slick interior design magazines. There were names to her kind of furniture, not names he knew like sofa and chair and table, but names that belonged to Italian and French designers. Cheever thought of his own house. It could qualify as the "before" in a home improvement show where the expert went around pointing to all the things that needed to be done. For too long Cheever had viewed his place with eyes as oblivious as Helen's now were. Just as so many single people find it too much bother "cooking for one," he had found excuses living for one.

Cheever walked out onto the deck and took in the million-dollar-plus expanse. The deck was high above the backyard, giving it a catwalk feel. In less than two hours the sun would set and the view would be spectacular. Hell, it already was spectacular. He could see Tijuana and the Coronado Islands, could make out the tower at the University of San Diego, and the entire stretch of the point. Looking southeast to the bay he picked out some San Diego landmarks, and watched as airplanes took off and landed at Lindbergh Field. With this kind of vista Cheever thought it would be easy, perhaps too easy, to lead a vicarious existence. The world would always be flowing by with sights to see, and the pictures would continually be changing. Even the unmoving objects like office buildings and mothballed naval ships offered different looks, with the lighting and shadows acting much like clothes being thrown on and off.

Gradually he stopped looking afar and took in Rachel's backyard. Everything appeared to be in bloom—roses, bird of paradise, jasmine, hibiscus, wisteria, bougainvillea, and honeysuckle. It was November, but it was still San Diego. The days were getting shorter but the residents and the flora were still in a state of denial. Cheever remembered one of the most famous scenes from the *Iliad:* Ajax on the battlefield calling to Zeus for more light. The thought of death didn't bother Ajax, but if he had to die he wanted to do so in the light of day. More light, thought Cheever. It could have been San Diego's motto.

In Cheever's too many hours of solitude he had consumed books of all sorts, and remembered one story of a man overwhelmed by a woman's beauty. The man had invited her to his garden where he had said, "Come, I want my roses to see you." Cheever didn't remember the author, which was unusual for him. Maybe his memory was finally getting fuzzy. But he wished he could be that clever with Rachel. He wanted to take her out to the deck and point to her roses and say, "Come, I want the roses to see you."

It was madness to think like that. She had money and class and lots of certificates that said how educated she was, that said "call me Dr." The only thing they had in common was their loneliness. That wasn't exactly the foundation for a long-term relationship. What would happen when they tired of showing each other their scars?

Cheever's pager started to vibrate. Some of the detectives referred to their pagers as marital aids. He looked at the display, saw a telephone number he didn't recognize. In the kitchen he found a phone, and after dialing the number found Keith Aubell.

"You left a message on my machine," he said. "Something about my art."

"Yes," Cheever said. "I'm one of the detectives working the Bonnie Gill investigation."

"Oh." Aubell's disappointment was evident, the hoped—for potential customer vanishing.

"Mr. Aubell," Cheever said, "one of your paintings suffered damage during the commission of a crime. We've impounded that painting."

"What damage?" Aubell wanted to know.

Cheever's answer gave a new and grisly meaning to flesh tones. "Blood splatters."

Aubell didn't have to ask him what crime. His silence spoke for him. "I'm hoping you can meet with me at the gallery today at four-thirty," Cheever said. "There are some questions I'd like to ask you."

"Four-thirty," repeated Aubell, sounding as if he was working through his shock. "Today. Okay."

Cheever hung up the phone, and then walked across the kitchen to Rachel's refrigerator. It wasn't a Sears floor model. The refrigerator was built into the wall, a recessed stainless steel design usually only found in the kitchens of upscale restaurants. It was as pretty as a picture until you opened it. What was inside looked very healthy and very unappealing. He found brewer's yeast, whole grains, fruits and vegetables, wheat germ, soy products, tofu, dark breads, and juices that looked like they had more pulp than liquid. Cheever finally selected an imported sparkling water. The only imported water he usually drank came from the Colorado River via his pipes. Sometimes he remembered to use a cup.

He drank from the bottle, finished it, and put it on the counter. When he reentered the family room Rachel was still talking with Helen, even if it looked as if she were talking to herself. He didn't feel too guilty about interrupting the conversation.

"Duty calls," Cheever said.

"Thank you for all your help," Rachel said.

"How about if I drop by later and see how things are? I can bring some takeout. Chinese, Mexican, you name it."

"I can make dinner," she said.

He had seen her refrigerator. "Not necessary. Just tell me what you like."

"I love vegetarian chow mein. Or the Buddha's platter of fresh vegetables. Or even the shrimp moo goo gai pan."

Rachel said the last as if owning up to some serious confession. He nodded, her preferences remembered, and started to leave only to be stopped by another voice.

"Cerberus," Helen whispered. A ghost's murmur.

Helen still wasn't looking at them, still wasn't there, but something must have registered with her to announce that name. Cheever and Rachel exchanged glances. She motioned for him to be silent, and they waited to see if Helen had anything else to say. After a minute of silence Rachel began to question Helen, but was unable to coax any more words out of her.

The failure didn't appear to bother the therapist. She turned to Cheever and offered an explanation for the one word: "Helen has worked to accept more and more responsibility over her life. Taking care of Cerberus has been one of her own litmus tests. I think she's asking us for help."

Love me, love my dog. "Does opening your home extend to becoming a kennel?" he asked.

"If it comes to that, yes. But I believe Helen's condition will be short-lived."

"So we just need somebody," Cheever said, "to walk and feed the dog in the meantime."

There weren't too many choices for that "somebody." Cheever reluctantly reached for Helen's purse and dug out her keys.

"I'll try and be back by seven," he said, "that is, if Cerberus doesn't kill me."

"Thank you," said Rachel.

He was probably imagining it, but Cheever thought he saw Helen nod her head slightly as if to second that voicing of gratitude.

The bay was quite different close up, though there was something to be said for that distant view from Rachel's deck. From afar the water had looked pristine, but near the shore you could see the oil slicks, plastic, and debris floating insolently atop the water, and smell the brine and rot lingering like a bad conscience. But what couldn't be seen or felt from a distance was the vigor of the bay, the vitality that occurs when nautical and human currents mix together. Given a choice, Cheever liked the closer view, warts and all.

There was only one witness to Helen's breakdown still at the Maritime Museum, a docent. Sam Winans was costumed in an old-time sailor's cap, or at least someone's idea of one. His hat reminded Cheever of a shriner's fez.

Winans was around seventy, a short and heavy retired postal worker who seemed to regret not having run off to sea as a boy. Cheever led him away from the ships, and asked him to walk and talk through Helen's movements as he remembered them. Winans was delighted, had looked deliriously happy from the moment Cheever had flashed his badge and given him one of his business cards. They walked around the intersection of Ash and Market, Winans examining the boardwalk critically. At last he was satisfied.

"She dropped right here," he said, pointing to a spot.

"Was anyone around her?"

"Not that I saw, and I was one of the first to get to her."

"What did she say?"

"She said something about those three ships being the *Nina*, the *Pinta*, and the *Santa Maria*, then she started to act real crazy.

"I guess she read the name *Medea* off of our steam yacht over there. Most of the people didn't know what she was talking about, but then they don't lead tours here." Winans sounded proud of his insights.

"What did she say?"

"Talked about Medea and all her doings. Sometimes I tell those stories to groups. Course there's a story behind the naming of our *Medea*. Seems the original owners . . ."

"What else did she say?"

Winans didn't seem to mind having his tour interrupted. "Not much. She told 'em how Medea ordered the murder of her own brother, and how she had his body parts thrown into the sea to slow up the pursuit. Now I've heard that story, but it's not one I tell to paying customers. I figure they can go find gruesome on their own time. She had everyone looking out to the bay thinking they were going to see this dismembered guy. She was on drugs, wasn't she?"

Cheever didn't comment, but he still managed to let the docent think he had figured out the mystery of Helen's behavior. "Anything else stand out in your mind?"

Winans scratched under his hat. "She was really losing it at the end. She pointed to this one fellow and got all aggravated—was screaming and shaking. Said that Medea was here."

"What did the man look like?"

Winans thought about that. "Can't say I got a really good look of him. Everyone was watching her. And then he just sort of disappeared."

"Can you tell me what he was wearing?"

Winans shook his head, then shrugged his shoulders. "Coat, I think."

"How old was he?"

"Maybe forty. But I only caught a glimpse . . ."

"Anything else you remember about him? Height? Weight? Something unusual?"

"She was the show," he said. "You didn't want to take your eyes from her."

"What else comes to mind?"

"We were mostly just trying to calm her. She had one of those medical bracelets on. First we called her doctor's office, then we called you guys."

Winans bit his lip. He tried to think of something else that could help, but there didn't seem to be anything. He rubbed Cheever's card, looked at it, then snapped his fingers in triumph.

"Thought your name was familiar," he said. "She mentioned you."

"What did she say?"

Winans stretched out his moment of glory, trying to get her words just right. "She said to tell you to not stop for the body parts. She said they were just a diversion."

TWENTY-SEVEN

Keith Aubell didn't look as if he were in mourning.

"Hey," he said to Cheever. "I called my agent and told him what happened, and he told me that my painting had just increased in value about tenfold. I mean, don't get me wrong, I'm bummed about Bonnie, but . . ."

"Sure," Cheever said, cutting him short and opening the door to the gallery.

Aubell was about twenty-five, had long, curly blond hair, an earring in each ear, plum-colored and rectangularly lensed pince-nez glasses that did the sixties proud, and just enough facial hair to produce an inept mustache and beard.

"I'll get the lights," Cheever said.

He went and turned them on, and Aubell did an owl imitation, exaggerating his blinking. "My glasses aren't like a Hollywood thing, you know," he said. "I've got this thing about light, medical thing, you know. That's why light's so important in my pieces. Lighting's everything, you know."

Cheever didn't argue on behalf of darkness. He had just met Aubell but had already had about enough of him. "How long did you know Bonnie Gill?"

"About two years."

"Were you friends?"

"Bonnie was a Type A, you know. Not the kind of woman who was into being palsy-walsy."

"How did you meet her?"

"An artist I know introduced us. Bonnie took a look at some of my paintings and decided to take me on."

"Did she sell a lot of your paintings?"

"Five or six."

"How often did you see her?"

"Every other month or so."

"Were all of your meetings business-related?"

"One way or another they were. Bonnie was always having these gatherings, spaghetti dinners and stuff. She was big on recruiting for what she called 'artistic outreach.' Bonnie thought if the natives started finger painting, or whatever, they'd be better off."

"You didn't agree?"

Aubell shrugged. "Thing is, there are lots of talented artists out there that can't hardly make a living. I should know, I'm one of them. You think putting a brush in the hands of some street person is going to make a difference?"

"From what little I know, I understand the point of her program wasn't to discover a Rembrandt, or even a Grandma Moses. It was supposed to promote self-esteem."

Aubell reluctantly nodded. "Yeah, that's true enough, but it wasn't like Bonnie was only being a professional do-gooder."

"What do you mean?"

"Every year the gallery had its 'Voices of the Street' art show, and every year there was always lots of press and visitors. Bonnie was better than the Salvation Army at beating the drums."

"You sound as if you didn't approve of the project."

"It's not that, you know, but I wasn't the only artist to tell Bonnie that my works all but qualified for that exhibit."

"Were you resentful of her?"

"You got a gallery, the first order of business is supposed to be art. Sometimes Bonnie was too busy promoting her utopia to take care of business. But the road to hell, you know."

"No, I don't know."

"The road to hell's paved with good intentions."

"What do you mean?"

"Like, you know, Bonnie's ReinCarnation Foundation. It started out with the people from the neighborhood, but then she brought in a bunch of downtown suits."

"So what?"

"Beware of power lunches. Since when do art, and flowers, and street people fit into any development scheme? When it comes to the poor, it's always out with the old, in with the nou—veau riche."

"Any idea who purchased your paintings here?"

Aubell shook his head. "Privileged information, you know. Gallery owners never tell you that. They're afraid the artists will cut out the middleman. Why?"

"I'm wondering whether the killer could have bought one of your paintings in the past, and then told Bonnie he wanted another one."

"You think Bonnie knew the killer?"

"It's possible. Or maybe the murderer was just posing as a customer. Bonnie might have been walking to her desk to write up the sale when she was stabbed from behind. She didn't die right away. Bonnie made it out to the garden. The murderer followed her there, carrying your painting with him."

"Why'd he do that?" the artist asked.

"Judging from the crime scene, it was used to prevent the blood from splattering on him."

Aubell put his glasses back on and shook his head. "That's cold."

"But we haven't ruled out that there might have been

some other significant factor contributing to the murderer's selecting your painting."

"That's kind of a spooky thought, you know."

"This is kind of a spooky business. Maybe you have some theory on why your painting was utilized."

"It was probably just the right size, you know. I mean like, what do you want me to say? Keith Aubell's art is preferred by three out of four murderers?"

"Do any strange people collect your art?"

"Yeah, most of them former girlfriends, and most I've given the stuff to."

"Maybe there was something about your theme . . ."

"Dude picked my bubble gum piece, you know. Scenic San Diego beach. My contribution to the art world. Course my agent thinks this might be a breakthrough for me. Ghoul art sells, he says. You attach a murder or something sensational to a painting and people line up to buy. He even thinks I should splatter all my new paintings with red paint, make it my trademark."

Dr. Denton arrived at the gallery fifteen minutes late, and five minutes after Keith Aubell had left. Cheever had spent his time between the interviews watching the shadows grow larger and the darkness take over. When the doctor made his appearance the shadows had almost won.

They talked on the street for half an hour, Cheever grilling the doctor on everything he had seen. Cheever positioned himself to see as Dr. Denton had, stood where the doctor had done his watching and made him describe all that had occurred over and over. When he finished with the one vantage point, Cheever took Dr. Denton through the gallery then out to the garden and took up another. This time he stood where the murderer had slashed Bonnie Gill's throat.

Team IV had despaired of there being any witnesses. The murder had been committed just inside the garden in an area hidden away from passing eyes. Between the sidewalk and the murder scene was a wall of stacked pottery, and behind that a row of planters. But Cheever wasn't looking out to the street. His attention was directed to the Garden of Stone.

"Show me," Cheever told the doctor.

"Whattya talking about, man . . ."

"I need you to be the woman. Stand where she stood. Walk where she walked. Say what she said."

"Already told you everything a hundred fucking times . . ."

"It's important."

"Come on, man . . ."

"I need to see."

"This is ridiculous, man . . ."

"It's a matter of earning your expense money, Doctor."

"Awl-ready earned it."

"If you don't want the hundred bucks . . ."

"This is bullshit," Dr. Denton said, but he made his proclamation while walking out to the Garden of Stone. He hesitated, circled an area like a male dog debating the exact watering spot, and finally positioned himself. The doctor's chosen site was behind and to the right of the statue of Hyacinthus. On one side of him was the crying Niobe, and on the other Dryope was turning into a tree.

"Here," he said, sullenly.

"That's where she was standing when she started to come to life?"

None too pleased: "Yeah."

"Stay there a minute. Don't move."

Cheever tried to picture how everything had looked just prior to the murder. The evidence tech had removed some of the clothing from the statues as potential evidence. In his mind's eye Cheever envisioned what the statues had been wearing, and also thought about the red-haired woman in her dark trench coat. Most of the lights in the garden were directed toward the fence, leaving the Garden of Stone in a dark pocket of gray. The red-haired woman would have been further obscured by the other statues. In the absence of any close scrutiny, she could have easily been mistaken for a statue.

"Okay," Cheever said, "come to life."

"How many times I gots to say the same shit over and over . . ."

"Just do it."

Dr. Denton wasn't much of an actor, that, or he did his best to be bad. Like a director trying to get the scene just right, Cheever had the doctor repeat his performance half a dozen times. With each take, the actor became less enthusiastic, his gestures more wooden, and his speech, if possible, more monotone.

"Okay," Cheever finally said. He knew what had happened, knew what the woman had said, and when she had said it, and how and where she had tried to strike at the "invisible man."

But Cheever still had absolutely no idea what he had seen.

TWENTY-EIGHT

"That's a good dog. That's a good boy."

The praise of dogs by strangers is often commensurate to the threat they offer. Cerberus's barks and growls had Cheever going heavy on the platitudes. Neither dog nor human believed what he was saying, but Cheever was still trying to convince the animal of his good intentions.

For the dog's being such a splendid fellow, Cheever was amazingly slow to open the door. He continued to talk with Cerberus, letting him get used to the sound of his voice. The growling subsided, but didn't completely go away. Cheever decided to use a tactic other than sweet talking. That had never been his strong suit anyway.

"Sit, Cerberus, sit."

The dog cocked his head slightly. Cheever repeated the command, his voice even sterner. Cerberus circled around the door, and then much to Cheever's surprise he sat down.

Cheever inched the door open. He was glad Helen had taught the dog at least one command, and hoped that "attack" wasn't another one. "Good dog," he said.

The nub of a tail twitched. Cheever took that as a positive sign. The dog excused himself from sitting and cautiously took to sniffing at Cheever. The detective tried to act as unconcerned as possible, not an easy thing with an animal whose hackles were still up.

"You hungry?" Cheever asked, his voice a few octaves higher than usual.

The stub worked a little harder. Cheever walked slowly across the room, the dog with him every step, where he found a bag of meal and a jug of water. He poured a healthy portion of the kibble into an empty bowl, and refilled his water. Cerberus sniffed at the results, but it was apparent he was more interested in Cheever than the food.

"Ready to go for a walk?"

At the sound of those words Cerberus forgot his misgivings. He bounded toward the door, then back to Cheever. The detective picked up a leash, attached it to the dog's collar, then was dragged to the door. Cheever tried his luck on a second command, yelling, "Heel!" If anything, the word inspired the rottweiler to pull him down the stairs all the faster.

Cheever let Cerberus pick their route. The dog started out traveling south along Seventh Avenue. There were no other two- or four-legged animals out strolling. An occasional car passed, the nightly migration to escape the city. Over the years Cheever had considered moving downtown just for the convenience of being close to work, but had never gotten around to doing it. Very few cops lived in the downtown area. Most had families, and downtown wasn't very child-friendly. Redevelopment had brought plenty of upscale developments and urban attractions to San Diego, but little in the way of greenways or parks. Part of the ReinCarnation Foundation's stated goals was to see to the building of playgrounds and so-called friendly space, magnets for families. Build it, Bonnie Gill had said, and the children would come. It didn't look like her theory was going to be tested out any time soon.

Cheever pulled at Cerberus's leash, a signal to turn around. The dog didn't think it was time to go back, and they had a short battle of wills. The leash won, but barely. When they returned to the loft, Cerberus went directly to his food, leaving Cheever free to wander about. There were three shrouded paintings, one more than had been on display his previous visit. Cheever remembered how Helen had said works in progress had a life of their own, and hadn't wanted him to look at them as if it might jinx the final product. They were naturally the first things he decided to inspect.

He removed the coverings. None of the paintings were finished. The first painting was the least polished of the three, hadn't progressed much beyond the sketch stage. A man was descending into a pit of darkness. Slung over his shoulder was a lyre. The musical instrument was the giveaway, that, and the way to Hades. Cheever knew he was looking at Orpheus. Around the forbidding pit were other holes that gave the appearance that someone had been digging. A cow skull had been dug up, as well as the carcass of a bird and some bones. It wasn't until Cheever looked at Orpheus a second time that he noticed his own likeness.

I don't play the lyre, he thought, trying to distance himself from the figure in the painting. Cheever knew his response was silly, but he wasn't comfortable seeing his own face identified with a hero's. He wondered who was supposed to be his Eurydice, and decided it had to be someone already dead (but was that physically or literally?). He also wondered if Helen's drawing was an editorial of sorts announcing that his quest was already doomed to fail.

He turned his attention to the second painting. It reminded Cheever of one of those "paint by the number" sets, but with at least half the numbers missing. Part of a woman's face was painted. There was a nose, and a chin, and ears, and the outline of eyes, but even with all those facial elements there was still very little there. Lines needed to be connected, and colors added, and shadows drawn in, but most of all, a character needed to be included. The woman was still very incomplete.

The last painting showed a man leaving a building. The background was dark, and the streets surrounding the structure had an ominous feeling, but the uneasy images were softened by all the carnations popping up everywhere. The escaping figure looked to be in a hurry. He was wearing an overcoat over a business suit, and his hands were gloved. Behind his back he was holding a huge red carnation. The man didn't appear to be aware that his carnation was shedding. There was a trail of red petals that led back inside the building. Cheever followed the petals. They took him to a tiny figure looking out of the darkened window; the gloom all but hid the little girl. The only thing that distinguished her from the shadows was the outline of her red hair.

Cheever reached for the painting and brought it close to the floor lamp, wanting to get a better look at the faces of the figures, especially the man. "Damn it," he said aloud. The closer inspection didn't help. But at least some things were clear. He was able to make out the exterior of Sandy Ego Expressions, and recognized the surrounding neighborhood. Cheever also assumed he was seeing the murderer and the witness, even if their faces were obscured.

He searched through the loft, spent most of his time examining Helen's sketch books. Cheever took pains to study all of the sketched faces, but he couldn't find a match to the man leaving the gallery. Helen had done some preliminary sketches for the painting, but in none of them could the man's face be clearly seen.

Cheever wished he could say the same thing about his own face. In his short modeling session with Helen she had managed to capture half a dozen distinct expressions.

He looked like six different people, and that was disconcerting to him. Cheever wondered whether he was as many things as Helen seemed to think he was. But this was a woman, he consoled himself, who saw him as Orpheus.

Excluding Helen's art, there were very few personal items in her loft; no letters or diaries, no mementos or keepsakes. He rifled through two chests that held the bulk of Helen's eclectic wardrobe. Not even the sizes were consistent. Her collection of wigs was found in a large box, eight of them, including two shades of red. Most of her wigs rested on styrofoam heads, although one was draped over a model of a Cro-Magnon man's head, and another cloaked a small basketball. She used coffee cans and cigar boxes to store glasses, makeup, costume jewelry, and various personal knickknacks. There appeared to be enough accoutrements for all of her statues *and* personalities.

Cheever rummaged through a reinforced plastic dairy container and found a collection of masks. There didn't appear to be any consistency to them. The masks were made of wood and plastic and porcelain and cloth. Some were the kind of masks worn to costume parties; others were decorative; still others were art, ready to be hung on a wall.

He picked up one of the masks. It was hand carved and showed an African woman's face. Cheever brought it over to a chair with him and took his time examining it. His fingers traced the elaborate carving. There were bevels and beading and finely wrought design work. It wasn't quite like holding Cinderella's slipper, he decided; it was more like being left with one of Helen's heads. And unlike Cinderella's slipper, Cheever had the feeling that for Helen there was no perfect fit, just a mask for every occasion. And no fairy godmother either.

Cheever called in the order for Chinese food. As he hung

up the phone, another head dropped into his lap. Cerberus was looking for affection. The detective scratched behind the dog's ears and told him what a good dog he was, this time offering the words softly, and with a little meaning.

TWENTY-NINE

She opened the door, and Cheever, who was holding a large bag, said, "Beware of geeks who bear gifts."

Rachel inhaled deeply. "Right now I'd welcome anyone carrying such an aromatic calling card. I'm famished."

"That's two of us."

"Then let's eat." She hesitated a moment. "There's a table in the kitchen, or we could eat in the dining room . . ."

Cheever had seen the dining room. It was large and formal, the kind of setting appropriate for state dinners. "Kitchen's fine," he said.

She set the table with dishes that had painted floral designs on them, no two apparently alike. Cheever was happy to see his plate came with a lily instead of a carnation. The wine glasses were also hand-crafted. Cheever held his glass up to the light, interested in its imperfections. A trail of small bubbles ran through the heavy, blue-hued glass; it looked as if a miniature scuba diver had been swimming around inside.

Rachel appeared with a bottle of wine. "The house white?" she asked.

He put down his glass. "Thank you."

While she poured, Cheever started pulling out the cartons of food from the bag. "I ordered for Helen," he said. "That was probably wildly optimistic, but . . ."

"It was the right thing to do," Rachel said, "but I don't think she'll be sitting down with us. About an hour ago I fed her some chicken soup.

"Canned," she added regretfully. "She's sleeping now."

"Did she say anything?"

"No. But there are signs that she is . . ." Rachel searched for words: ". . . beginning to awaken."

"Where's Prince Charming when you need him?"

"What do you mean?"

"The damsel in distress in a deathlike sleep, and Prince Charming coming along and awakening her with a kiss."

"Is that the story where they all lived happily ever after?"

"Unless they've changed the ending."

Rachel took notice of all the cartons he had pulled from the bag. "You brought enough for an army."

"I got your vegetarian chow mein, and Buddha's platter, and shrimp moo goo gai pan."

"I only meant one dish . . ."

"I know. I thought we'd share. And then there's Helen's order."

"What did you get her?"

"The combination plate. What else?"

Rachel knew she shouldn't smile, but did anyway. Cheever handed her some wooden chopsticks, and they both started scooping out the food onto their plates, and then, a few moments later, into their mouths. Between bites, they kept talking.

"Has Helen ever withdrawn before?"

"Not like this," she said.

"What do you think brought it on?"

"It's likely she perceived some threat. I've heard of others with DID similarly withdrawing."

"Because of a threat?"

"Often because their worlds were changing. I'm wondering if Helen's response has something to do with her moving closer to integration."

"Is that event imminent?"

"I don't know. Every integration is different, even if in popular literature it seems more like spontaneous combustion than anything else. Integration often occurs in degrees. There usually has to be consensus among the alters before a successful integration can take place, that, or one personality becomes dominant over time."

"And subjugates the others?"

"And assumes the others, becomes them."

"How is an integration performed?"

"The treatment is predicated upon the patient. There is no one method. Integration occurs when the patient is ready and not before. That can be over time, or overnight, or never. It is usually the preparation which is the work, and not the integration itself."

"And how do you prepare a patient for such an event?"

"You discuss how life will go on after integration, how it will be a different life, but ultimately a better one. To get Helen ready, I have been posing an old Zen question to her: Show me the face you had before your mother and father were born."

Cheever thought about the meditative question. How flexible was the human mold? Maybe there was something literal in the expression "losing face." Maybe that's what happened to everyone over time. He also considered the unfinished painting in Helen's loft. Was she working on the painting of what she looked like before her parents were born?

"Has she come up with an answer yet?" Has she come up with a face, he wondered?

"She's working on it."

"And when she discovers her face, will she be ready for integration?"

"That's the hope. We're also discussing the aftermath of integration."

"Isn't that putting the cart before the horse?"

"In some ways. But Helen needs to understand not only what is happening, but what is going to happen. She needs to come to terms with being one person. When a multiple gets fused they often experience a great loneliness."

It must feel, Cheever thought, like the disintegration of a family. Like losing loved ones.

"Today at lunch," he said, "her personalities reminded me of children. None of them wanted to be overlooked. They all had to put an order in."

"Sometimes it's that way in therapy," Rachel said. "There is jealousy if one personality gets too much attention."

"By the end of the lunch it was a free-for-all. The personalities were out of control."

"Maybe they didn't like the questions you were asking. Their collective behavior might have been an escapist strategy. By becoming unglued, the Greek Chorus avoided having to deal with you."

"Not completely," Cheever said. "They kept doing their changing, and I kept doing my asking."

Cheever refilled her wine glass, and then his, killing the bottle. "There's another bottle chilling," she said, then quickly added, "that is if you want any more."

He could sense her nervousness. Probably part of her "escapist strategy," Cheever thought. He should know. "Let's let it chill a little longer," he said, his words calm and unhurried, even if that wasn't how he felt inside.

They kept eating, but more slowly now, the soft clicking of chopsticks staving off silence. For a time they studied the food too closely, and avoided looking at each other too obviously.

"Tonight I studied three of Helen's paintings in progress," Cheever said. "One of them shows the gallery where Bonnie Gill died. It also shows a man hurriedly leaving from there. You can't see his face in the painting, but you can make out a red-haired little girl staring at him from the window. When the painting's finished I'm willing to bet we're going to have another picture of a traumatized little girl."

Rachel nodded, not sure of where Cheever was going with his thoughts.

Cheever reached out with his hands, as if balancing two loads, as if weighing something. "Do you think Helen's most recent fugue state has some tie-in with her two-year childhood blackout?"

She offered a careful answer: "There was certainly a trauma or traumas in Helen's youth with which she has yet to come to terms, but whether her latest fugue state has any connection with the trauma from her past I don't yet know."

"Then and now," Cheever said, still weighing the scales with his hands, still trying to reconcile the gap of twenty years, wondering if there was some connection. "Could she be confusing the present with the past?"

"Yes. It's possible that whatever triggered her most recent fugue state made her recall her initial trauma."

"Brought it back to her? Blurred the lines?"

"Again, that's possible."

"Yesterday," he said, "Caitlin asked me about death."

"In what context?"

"She wanted to know what happened to people when they died."

"I can't say the question is significant in itself. Five is a normal age to ask those kinds of questions."

"You qualify everything." He sounded frustrated.

"Yes."

"At last, an unequivocal answer." Cheever offered a small smile with his tease.

"You don't like riddles?"

"Only if I can solve them. Today Helen was at the Maritime Museum when she noticed the name of one of the ships: *Medea*. You know the myth?"

"Yes."

"She screamed out a message for me there, said I should ignore the body parts. What do you make of that?"

Rachel considered whether Helen was talking in the past or the present. She tried to ignore the throbbing from her breast. She hadn't taken the pain medication, had figured the wine would be better than a pill.

"It sounds as if Helen was afraid someone was trying to divert you."

"With a body?" Cheever's question was to himself. It didn't make sense. Or did it? With the death of Willie Lamont everyone thought some slasher was loose. Could he have been a sacrifice to slow up the investigation?

Cheever awoke from his musing to see Rachel shifting around uncomfortably. She was pale and appeared to be in pain. Too late, he remembered her own wound and fears. "Are you all right?" he asked.

Rachel wondered if she was that transparent. "Fine."

"Any pain?"

She shook her head, but then realized she was giving a passive-aggressive response. Her body language said she was hurting. Between head and heart and breast she was giving conflicting messages. In the face of such mixed signals, he stood up. Rachel knew she had driven him away, knew he was going to say, "You've had a rough day," and then say he should be leaving. And then her script would be to reluctantly agree. She felt a mixture of regret and relief at his leaving. More mixed signals.

Cheever opened his mouth, but he didn't offer parting words. He didn't want to leave, not yet, so he offered a reason for his standing: "How about some more wine?"

She was prepared for the niceties of his departing, but not his question, and covered up with a moment's hesitation before saying, "Thank you."

He retrieved the bottle from the refrigerator, and then inexpertly worked on the cork. She didn't have a corkscrew, had one of those wine-pulls he had to figure out. Naturally, he didn't ask her advice.

"Why is it," Cheever said, finally finishing with the cork, "that Moses walked around the desert for forty years?"

"I don't know."

Cheever poured into her glass. "Because like most men he was too damn stubborn to ask for directions."

She tried to hide her smile behind the glass, but he saw it. He saw a lot of things.

They sipped their wine for a few minutes. "I can make some coffee," she said.

"Not necessary for me," he said.

He reached for the bag of takeout, shook it, then shook his head. "They forgot to include our fortune cookies."

"That's just as well," she said. "I've pretty much given up on processed foods."

"And I've pretty much given up on the future."

Rachel laughed, even if she wasn't sure where the line lay between his truth and his joke.

"Where'd she go?" Cheever asked.

They kept playing ping-pong between themselves and Helen, kept bouncing back and forth between them and her.

"Deep inside herself. She wants to hide. Helen once had

264

a psychosomatic blindness. She claimed someone had stolen her eye."

"Her eye?"

"You know how the three Fates are sometimes portrayed as having only one eye, and that for each of them to see they have to pass that eye back and forth?"

He nodded before asking, "What happened with Helen's blindness?"

"It only lasted a day or two. It was a period in her life where she didn't want to see. Things weren't going well."

"Sometimes her disorder is convenient for her."

"At times it is a magnification of the human condition."

"What do you mean?"

"We choose our blind spots. We put on one face, and then we put on another. We pretend we are one person, as if such a thing was possible. We say we should know ourself, as if there was this one being set in concrete. But to be human is to be multifaceted."

"We're all multiple personalities?"

"Not in a diagnostic sense. But you are, or have been, Cheever the father, Cheever the detective, Cheever the lover. You have played, and continue to play, different roles."

"Just as you do."

"I think women have to play even more roles than men. In relationships we're expected to go from madonna to whore in a blink of the eye."

"Do you know about Helen's masks?"

"Yes. There's a German word: *maskenfreiheit*. It translates to the freedom allowed by masks. Some of her alters allow her that freedom. Helen doesn't even need the masks. But consciously or unconsciously she collects them as a metaphor for herself."

"There's that part in all of us," he said, "that wishes we could be at a costume party and be totally anonymous, that wishes we could say and do things as someone else."

She nodded. Cheever felt like he was talking too much again, but with her he wanted to open up. "What's that word again?"

"*Maskenfreiheit.*"

"*Gesundheit.*"

She smiled. He made her forget her pain.

"Do patients try to hide things from you?"

"All the time."

"Do they succeed?"

"Not very often. I know how to look for love and a cough."

"Love and a cough?"

"Neither love nor a cough can be hid."

As if summoned, Cheever coughed. A piece of food must have caught somewhere in his throat. He coughed again, and she laughed, thinking he was doing it on purpose. Almost, he could pretend that he was.

"I'm in one of her paintings," Cheever told her.

"Yes. Helen mentioned she was up late painting, and told me about your modeling."

"She's cast me as Orpheus."

"Does that portrayal bother you?"

"No." And then a moment later, "Yes. To go to hell and back for a loved one, and then come up empty, strikes me as a terrible travesty. In some ways I feel I took that same journey for my daughter. And like Orpheus, I failed."

"Whom would you rather she portrayed you as?"

Cheever shrugged. "No one."

"Unacceptable answer."

"How about Odysseus then? All he wanted to do was get home again. For twenty years he tried. There was one trial after another for him, but he never gave up."

"It's a good thing no one told him you can never go home again."

"That was the only thing that sustained him."

She heard the pain in Cheever's voice, knew of his twenty years of wandering.

Cheever looked at her and felt all constricted inside. He wanted to touch her; he wanted to tell her things. "You bring out this cough in me," Cheever said.

But he didn't cough. He reached his hand out for hers, and she reached back. Then he leaned forward and kissed her.

This is madness, she thought, as their lips met. He kissed her a second time. This is irresponsible, she told herself. At their third kiss she was thinking, this is problematic, but her lips met his halfway. And she was the one who initiated their fourth kiss. Her cautionary voices were preaching to a disinterested audience.

You think a thing like this might happen sometime, Cheever thought, but you don't know. And sometimes at night you wonder if it ever really happened before, or if you just imagined it. And you think certain feelings are gone forever, and that the pilot light in your insides has gone out for good. But it was lit now. It was roaring.

They were kissing and groping, moving along like a pushmepullyou. "Bedroom," she gasped.

Somehow they made it there, zippers loosening and buttons coming undone along the way. They fell on her bed, and she disentangled herself. "Bathroom," she managed to say.

He didn't like it when she left his arms. With her next to him, he had been carried along. It was as if some river had taken him up. Now he felt dropped on a bank. He noticed the room for the first time. If she had still been there he wouldn't have seen it. The moonlight, coming in through opened curtains, illuminated the room. Another designer's showroom, he could see. Cheever wondered whether he should shut the curtains, then decided not to. The moonlight was the best part of the room. Cheever started to take off his clothes, then stopped. Did she want him waiting for her naked? Or would that be presumptuous? He compromised by leaving on his boxers.

As Rachel finished peeing she thought of Denise Jacobson, one of her patients. Denise had a theory about relationships. She said that in the beginning of a romance all western women went through a "constipation cycle."

"You're afraid to go to the bathroom in the same household early on in a relationship with a man," Denise said. "It's like you don't want to admit you have bodily functions. So the more time you spend with him, the more constipated you get. Luckily, the cycle usually passes before you blow up."

Rachel took off her clothes and looked at herself in the mirror. Her left breast had a bandage on it. Very sexy, she thought. And the right breast, the right breast she thought was more her doctor's than hers . . .

She hadn't been with a man since her husband. She was afraid. It wasn't too late to reconsider.

Her nightgown wasn't what you would call enticing. It had been so long since she had bought any lingerie that they didn't even send her catalogs anymore. She put on the nightgown anyway. Maybe he'd just ignore her breasts. Maybe they'd grope in the darkness. She could warn him away from touching her there, say how much her breast hurt, and maybe he wouldn't touch either one of them.

Rachel walked out of the bathroom into the moonlight. She went to close the draperies but he intercepted her, rising from the bed with opened arms.

They found each other, and discovered each other anew. They kissed and touched and felt and held. They offered each other sounds without words, and there was that wonderful amnesia of impressions without thoughts.

When her gown came off Rachel felt herself freeze. Reality had returned. She was that deer caught in the light. She tensed as he gently touched her bandaged breast. Then he kissed her left nipple, softly, not sensually, as if bestowing a healing.

He moved over to her other breast. His fingers traced its lines, and then he touched her nipple. She could feel it harden. She knew it didn't look quite right, and didn't respond in the way it used to. She had the need to say something, anything.

"What's that expression," she said. "You take from Paul and give to Peter? I used to have very large nipples, but when they reconstructed they took from my left and gave to my right . . ."

"Shhhh," he said. He pressed his reassuring lips to hers, and then he went back to her breast. He kissed her right nipple differently than he had the left, working his tongue and fingers and lips around it and her. She felt his passion, and responded to it. Instead of being inhibited, she felt a freedom denied to her for so long. Then she heard him say, "You're beautiful," and they weren't words meant to make her feel better, but words offered in wonderment, as if he couldn't believe his good fortune. And then he coughed, and she thought what a wonderful sound that was, and she found herself crying silent tears because everything felt so good.

Because it was all so good.

THIRTY

Cheever whistled as he took the elevator up to his workplace. Life had been routine for so long he had forgotten it could be anything else. He was happy even though he didn't want to admit it, because that would be tempting fate and he knew only too well the ephemeral nature of happiness. Though he hadn't been celibate over the years, intimacy hadn't made him content, not like this. He thought about Rachel and hoped she was facing the morning with as many smiles as he was.

It's not right to feel this good with only two hours' sleep, Cheever thought, but it was a good tired, a happy reminder of the hours he and Rachel had spent exploring, and talking, and holding one another. He had arisen before dawn so that he could drive home before going to work, and she had seen him to the door. She had offered him some herbal tea for the road, but he drank from her lips instead, a long and passionate kiss that he knew would sustain him more than any herbal tea.

Rachel had made arrangements for a nurse to watch Helen at her house for the day. The plan was for Cheever to

270

relieve the nurse at five o'clock, with Rachel making it home by eight ("if I'm lucky," she had warned him). Unexpectedly missing a day, she told him, always resulted in "serious payback," with her working from very early until very late to make up for her canceled appointments.

There were signs that everyone from Team IV had already made it in to work, but Cheever was glad no one was sitting at their desks. He pulled open the yellow pages, found a 24-hour florist, and dialed the number. Speaking softly, so that none of the detectives in the nearby cubicles could hear, he asked that a dozen long-stem red roses be sent out that morning. He gave Rachel's name and work address, and then was asked for his credit card number, and what message he'd like to accompany the flowers. Cheever had to think for a few moments on what he wanted to say.

"Just write, 'For the doctor of my cough.' And sign it from Cheever."

His message was repeated back to him, and Cheever gave his okay, but after hanging up the phone he spent a full minute second-guessing himself. He hoped he wasn't scaring Rachel off with the roses and talk of his "cough." It wasn't like him to be so impetuous, and he was afraid he might be coming off like a lovesick teenager. But what was done, Cheever decided, was done. Besides, it had been so long, so very long since he had felt the desire to send a woman roses, that he didn't want to stifle the impulse.

The pile of paperwork on Cheever's desk was a deterrent to any more introspection. Mary Beth had come through in her usual diligent fashion. She had attached a sticky atop her handiwork that read: "To Over A. Cheever: Only was able to get you '74 through '79. Will try to get to other requested years today. M.B." Mary Beth was known for her stickies. She had one of the great sticky collections of the Western world. Her stickies were never just plain stickies. They always had some saying or pithy phrase.

This one read: "This Is a Nice Place to Visit But I Wouldn't Want to Work Here."

Mary Beth had sorted by year, had filled each folder with paperwork. Cheever opened one of the folders, saw that it consisted mostly of newspaper articles. And obituaries. Reading about missing and hurt and dead children wasn't something Cheever was looking forward to doing, but it was a theme Helen Troy was particularly taken with. She had cried tears of blood for Graciela Hernandez even though she had never met the girl, and over the years her art had featured little girls in pain and terror and death. Helen's pain had a public quality. Cheever had wondered whether there was more than a psychological trail to her tortured psyche. A grievous injury, or a murder, or the disappearance of a child weren't things easily hidden, and if such had contributed to Helen's mental state it was possible they had been documented. The articles were another way for Cheever to look back, another haystack for him to search through when he had the time.

Cheever heard Falconi and Diaz before he saw them. They were discussing whether another set of late-night interviews near the gallery was needed. Trailing behind them was Hayes carrying a cup of coffee and reading a newspaper.

"Hey, Cheever, you notice Neil Morgan's column this morning on the Gill kill?" Hayes asked.

Cheever shook his head. It was usually his routine to arrive at the office early and read the newspaper. "I haven't read the paper yet," he said.

Hayes pulled at his walrus mustache and looked at Cheever with feigned surprise. "Hasn't read the newspaper, and he was the last to get in this morning. Don't tell me you're getting a life, Cheever."

"Yeah, I'll be joining you real soon at your NRA and Birch Society meetings."

Hayes labeled himself as a conservative. Even by typically conservative law enforcement standards, most on the force considered him far right.

"That would do you some good. Clear the liberal cobwebs out of your head."

"Hayes," said Diaz, pointing to her head, "all you have in your *cabeza* is cobwebs."

"No *comprende* your foreign talk," he said. "That's the problem with this country. It coddles to all the immigrants. They think they don't even have to learn English."

"You're the immigrants in this part of the globe," she said.

Cheever could see that Hayes was warming up for the argument, so he pulled the paper from his hand and scanned the column for the Bonnie Gill piece.

Where have all the flowers gone? Television crews from tabloid TV have invaded San Diego covering the "Carnation Killing" of Bonnie Gill . . . Speaking of carnations, they're popping up everywhere, especially at City Hall. The fashion trend started when one council member wore a carnation in his boutonniere earlier this week. That prompted fellow politicos to do the same. And now Her Honor the Mayor has been seen sporting a large carnation corsage . . . Flower Power? Posthumous recognition for Gill is just around the block(s). Word is that redevelopment plans are now referring to the area from Eighth to Twelfth Avenues as the Carnation District . . .

Cheever tossed the newspaper over to Hayes's desk. He and Jacoba were just starting in on affirmative action. That was usually good for fifteen minutes.

"You talk with that artist?" Falconi asked Cheever.

"Yeah. I don't think our murderer was making any art statement other than he didn't want to get splattered, but as a possible tie-in I'm going to check the gallery records to see if I can find out who bought Aubell's other paintings."

Falconi nodded, but didn't look hopeful. "How's Helen of Troy?"

Cheever shook his head. "She's a long ways from the witness stand. She had a breakdown of sorts yesterday."

"Wonderful." The sergeant's frustration showed in the one word.

"Is the mayor really wearing a carnation?" Cheever asked.

"Don't know," Falconi said. "But I do know if I see the chief wearing one it's time to start worrying."

Reuben Martinez was banging away on a fender. His muscular right arm lifted and lowered itself in strong rhythm. The sound of metal on metal reverberated around the small shop. Part of Cheever's thoughts were still on a mythological track. He mused about Vulcan hammering at his forge.

Martinez neither saw nor heard Cheever's approach. When he did notice him he offered a nod but continued with his work for another half-minute before putting down his hammer and extending his hand.

"Afternoon," he said. "Got us a killer yet?"

"Not yet," Cheever said. "I just got tired of sitting in the office. It was too quiet."

"You came to the right place to get away from that."

"You work the shop by yourself?"

"I got two part-time guys when I need 'em. But business hasn't exactly been hopping lately."

"Wish I could say the same thing," Cheever said.

He looked around the shop and his eyes rested for a moment on the old coffee can that used to hold carnations. The flowers had been removed. At least Martinez wasn't doing the politically correct thing.

"Your name came up today," Cheever said. "I was talking with a Detective Lincoln who's also working the case. He's been looking into the ReinCarnation Foundation and tells me you're on the board."

"Yeah, the B-O-R-E-D."

"He said you were one of the old-timers, told me you were there from the beginning."

"Yeah, I tried to tell Bonnie I wasn't the kind of guy who sat on a board, but she had her own ideas."

"Are you friendly with the other board members?"

"I know 'em, but it's not like we're drinking buddies."

"What do you think of the way the board's changed over the years?"

"What do you mean?"

"I hear it's gone establishment. Ties instead of tie-dyed."

Martinez didn't seem convinced. "The faces might have changed, and there might be more suits now, but it always remained Bonnie's show."

"There's a saying that power corrupts."

Martinez laughed without much mirth. "There's also a saying that poverty sucks."

"Did Bonnie like being wined and dined by the money set?"

"My grandfather used to tell me that to meet the nanny you kiss the child." With his large hands Martinez pantomimed rocking a baby, then opened up the gesture to include a very feminine body.

"What's your grandfather's saying got to do with Bonnie?"

"You play the game if you want the sweets. Bonnie knew what she wanted, but she wasn't a sell-out."

"What did she want?"

"She wanted artsy-fartsy shit, but more than that she wanted a neighborhood with hope. I remember one meeting she said she didn't want no reservation thing happening."

"Reservation?"

"Yeah. She said the ReinCarnation Foundation was supposed to be working for the neighborhood, not thinking it should bulldoze it and push everyone off to a reservation somewhere."

"She said that in a board meeting?"

Martinez nodded his head.

"What was the reaction of the rest of the board members?"

"They all agreed with her."

"You remember any bitter arguments during your time on the board, any enmity?"

Martinez shook his head. "Nothing like that," he said.

In the silence that followed Martinez picked up his hammer, started maneuvering it in his hands. He looked over to Cheever to see if he had any other questions. Cheever shook his head to indicate he didn't.

Martinez walked back to the car he had been working on and stood over its fender. "I worked late last night," he said. "I was sort of hoping the slasher might pay me a call."

He raised the hammer and then started pounding again. Cheever wondered if all the muscle work was necessary. Power tools had supplanted much of his John Henry kind of work a long time ago. But a look at Martinez's face made Cheever decide his hammering was necessary.

It was almost three o'clock when Cheever returned to his desk. Mary Beth had left two new stickies atop his paperwork. One showed a phone in the heavenly clouds. The heading said: "Things to Do." The first item on the list was *Call Dial-A-Prayer*. Beneath that Mary Beth had written: *Was given some rush jobs this morning. There's not a prayer of a chance I can get the job finished today.*

The second sticky looked like a recent addition. The top border read, "Everything's Coming Up Roses," while at the bottom it concluded, "But I Planted Violets." Mary Beth had crossed out *Violets* and written in *Carnations*. As if that wasn't humor enough for one sticky, she had also added: *To Under A. Cheever: You do intend to justify my efforts by reading all of this some day, don't you?*

To avoid the possibility of any more sticky sermons,

Cheever picked up the folder marked 1979 and started his reading. Mary Beth had made most of her copies from microfiche but left it to Cheever to discern which article or obit was meant for him. That typically meant he had to scan the entire copied page from the newspaper.

What struck Cheever was that yesterday's news looked all too current. San Diego's climate had remained consistently good over the years, and its professional sporting teams consistently bad. There had been talk about building a new San Diego airport back then, just as there currently was. Politicians had railed about the need for better border sewage treatment in the seventies, and were making the same arguments about shit in the nineties.

But the timelessness, Cheever knew, was really an illusion. He kept being surprised by the passage of years, kept asking himself whether it was possible that the stories he was reviewing could have really happened so long ago. The articles took him back. Some of the memories he would just as soon not have dredged up, like the Monday when sixteen-year-old Brenda Spencer shot and murdered a principal and a custodian, and wounded eight elementary school students and a San Diego police officer. The murderer wasn't much more than a girl herself, and had justified her sniper attack by saying, "I don't like Mondays."

Cheever finished with 1979 and started in on 1978, but the stories weren't any better. He kept reading, kept pushing back the years, finished with '77 and '76 and '75. The further back he went, the more the time capsules made him remember another life. For most of 1974 he had still been chasing brownie points, had been working robbery figuring that was the best route to career advancement. He'd had hopes of ending up as a looey, or even a captain some day, had planned to finish the classes necessary to get his degree in law enforcement, but then everything had changed. Water under the bridge, he tried to tell himself. Polluted water.

Amidst all the history, Cheever didn't expect his own past to surface so emphatically. He caught his breath while scanning the copy of August 11th's obituary page. Her birthday he remembered: May 16. Every year since Diane's death he had approached that day with a certain trepidation. The day meant more to him than the more recognized birthdays, like Lincoln's and Washington's and King's. Probably even Christ's. But he had never tried to memorialize the day Diane had died, must have blanked it out on purpose.

It was a short obituary, as obituaries go. What could you expect for a five-year-old? There was no banner headline saying: SHE LIKED MONDAYS. But she had. She liked all days, and she would have liked to have had more of them. The obituary didn't say that Diane's favorite color was blue, or that she loved chocolate ice cream, or that she had never met a dog she didn't want to bring home. It didn't mention much more than her cause of death and where the memorial service was being held and where the family requested donations be sent. There was no picture of Diane. Cheever counted up the words. Her life had been summed up in sixty-eight words.

Name that tune, he thought.

Cheever read her obituary a second time. He was listed as one of the survivors. Maybe that was something he needed to remind himself. "She is survived," her obituary read, "by her parents, San Diego Police Officer Orson Cheever and his wife Karen." Minutes passed and Cheever still couldn't bring himself to continue with his reading.

How was it, he wondered, that he and Helen and Rachel continued to be stuck in a limbo of the past, and that whenever they tried to get sprung they were somehow pulled back? Cheever didn't ascribe much to the supernatural, but there seemed to be this synchronicity between the three of them, this loop of past and present. Even his investigation was intertwined: Was he looking into the murder of Bonnie Gill, or the disintegration of Helen Troy, or examining the threads of his own existence?

For an hour Cheever sat there, the obituary of his daughter held in his hands. The other team members came and went. He heard himself answering their questions, and talking with them, even if he really wasn't aware of what he was saying. Some part of him continued to work the investigation with the team, even if most of him was working through his feelings of twenty years past.

He finally put the obituary aside and went on with the reading, but he didn't escape very far. Kathy Dwyer had turned up missing right after his own daughter had died. She was a six-year-old who had vanished from her Pacific Beach house. Cheever remembered very little about Kathy's disappearance, but he had been in a fog for weeks after Diane's death, able to work and function, but just barely.

Kathy's disappearance was front-page news for a week. The search for her had continued long after the newspapers stopped printing their stories. As the months and years passed, Kathy became a ghost, surfacing only when there was a tragedy of a missing child. Mary Beth had included all the Kathy Dwyer articles over the years, not just those in '74. There was lots of rehashing and speculative ink, but not much else.

Her disappearance nagged at Cheever even as he tried to finish up 1974. He assumed Kathy's history clung to him because she was close to Diane's age. Or maybe it was just that she was a missing little girl like Graciela Fernandez. But at least Graciela's body had been found, even if her murderer hadn't. Assuming Kathy was long dead, that meant another murderer had gotten away with killing a little girl. That pushed his buttons. There were nights Cheever still stayed up thinking about Graciela. He hadn't given up on her case and he never would. Maybe that's why he wasn't ready to retire. Somebody needed to remember.

There was something about Kathy Dwyer that also stirred up memories of his own daughter. He wasn't sure of the connection, save that Diane had died and Kathy turned up missing at about the same time. The girls were close in age, but physically they didn't look at all alike. Diane's hair had been a light brown, and she had her mother's olive complexion. Kathy was a redhead, very fair and freckled.

Red hair and freckles. Like Bonnie Gill. And Caitlin.

Cheever went back into the pile of copies and carefully reread all of the Kathy Dwyer articles. Kathy's mother had told police that at the time of Katie's disappearance she was wearing a yellow dress with red polka dots. The image played on Cheever's mind. Somewhere he remembered seeing an outfit just like that. And then it came to him. He had seen that dress on the statue of the crying little girl at the gallery.

He started scribbling furiously on a pad, connecting his words with lines: *Caitlin—Statues—Dress—Little Girls—Murder(s)?* He turned the page and started working on another chart, but didn't get very far. He had only jotted down the words *Gallery* and *Pacific Beach* when he remembered how Jason Troy had said his family had lived in Pacific Beach. Cheever took a long breath. His hands were wet. An electrical charge seemed to run along his spine and then emptied into him. It was hard enough working one jigsaw puzzle. But now he had the feeling he'd been working several with all the pieces mixed up. Getting that first match, he knew, was often the hardest. Sometimes the rest of the puzzle followed from there.

It was too late in the day to get the investigative reports on Kathy Dwyer's disappearance. Everyone in Records was gone, and besides, the twenty-year-old files would have been shunted off to some storeroom in the hinterlands. He hoped the paperwork still existed. Though SDPD purged most of its files after seven years, missing persons that remained missing were supposed to be treated like unsolved homicides, with the cases never officially closed.

Cheever began writing down a new copping list. He needed to get the names of the detectives that had worked the case. He wanted their reports and observations. He wanted their suspicions, the kind of things they wouldn't have written down. But it was already four-thirty, and he had promised he would take over the care of Helen at five o'clock.

Still, he couldn't resist making one phone call. Professor Troy wasn't happy to hear from him. "I have nothing to say to you, Detective. For whatever reason—How do they say it?—you seem to have it in for me."

"Two questions . . ."

"I'm leaving . . ."

"Did Helen know a girl named Kathy Dwyer?"

There was a long moment of silence. Cheever feared Troy had hung up. But then he said, "Kathy Dwyer?"

"She was around Helen's age. She was the little girl that turned up missing twenty years ago."

"Kathy Dwyer," he said again.

"She lived on Diamond Street. The same street where you lived."

"Ohhh," he said, as if remembering. "Katie."

Katie. When said aloud, Cheever thought of Caitlin. "You knew her?"

"Not really. But I remember the search . . ."

"Did Helen know her?"

"They were acquainted."

"How near were you to the Dwyer house?"

"It was three or four doors down from us."

"What do you remember about her?"

"You have far surpassed your two questions, Detective."

"It's important that I hear your recollections of Katie Dwyer."

"That's ancient history, Detective Cheever. Now please don't bother me anymore."

Cheever listened to a click, then was forced to speak to a dial tone.

"Odd," he said. "I thought a professor of classics would be interested in ancient history."

THIRTY-ONE

The nurse was an older black woman who carried herself with the authority of someone who had put in a lifetime of nursing service. She wore a white uniform, crisp almost to the point of cracking, both cleanliness and starch apparently being next to godliness. Cheever had seen nuns' habits that looked less intimidating.

"I'm your relief," Cheever said.

The woman nodded, then turned her thick glasses to her watch, and looked at it in silent reproof. Cheever was four minutes late. Her bag was packed and ready. She draped it over her arm, but before giving up her post she passed on the news of her watch.

"Not a word out of her," the nurse said, pointing in the direction of the living room. "Mind you, I'm not complaining.

"Her appetite's just fine. She ate some cereal this morning, and had a cheese and tomato sandwich for lunch. Had some fruit too, an orange and a banana."

"Did you have to feed her?" he asked.

"No need. You put the spoon or the food in her hand and she takes over from there."

"What about going to the toilet?"

"You take her there and sit her down. She knows her business."

The nurse sensed his apprehension. "She went about a half-hour ago. You're safe for a while."

Until Rachel got home, Cheever hoped. "Sounds like she listened to you," he said.

She shook her head. "It wasn't a matter of listening. Nature was doing the talking. But she can hear well enough. We went outside for a time and sat. Might still be out there 'cept she didn't like it when those big parrots came around and started making all sorts of noise."

"Parrots?"

"That's what they looked like. All sorts of colors they were, and big as hawks."

Cheever figured it was time for the nurse to get a new prescription for her glasses. "She didn't like those birds?"

"Not at all. I could tell she was all bothered by them, so we came on in."

"How'd you get her to go with you?"

"Just took her by the hand. She'll follow you like Mary's little lamb if you just take her by the hand."

The nurse demonstrated on Cheever, taking his hand and then patting it. "Don't worry, child," she said, "you'll do just fine."

The starched uniform had fooled him, he thought. As the nurse left, Cheever tried to think how long it had been since anyone had called him "child." He felt like she had given him a shot of Ponce de Leon tonic and bestowed a blessing at the same time. The nurse's absence accentuated the quiet. In the silence of the house, Cheever trepidatiously made his way out to the living room. Helen didn't turn at his approach, or acknowledge him in any way. She took up very little space on the sofa, had huddled into herself. Her eyes were open, but unmoving. She was looking off somewhere into the distance.

"Hello," he said.

She didn't respond to his greeting, just continued to stare out the large bay window. Cheever remembered how Rachel had seated herself next to Helen and started talking. His idea of a conversation was to ask questions and get answers. Apparently he'd have to find a new way of communicating. It was time he learned anyway.

"I'll join you if you don't mind," he said.

If Helen did, she didn't say anything. Feeling stupid, Cheever sat down on the sofa. It wasn't as if Helen was going to pat a pillow and motion for him to join her. He really didn't even know what he was doing. He wasn't Rachel, for Christ's sake. For a few minutes he joined Helen in just staring out the window, then, hesitantly, unsure of what to say or how to say it, he started talking aloud. It was like speaking to God, Cheever thought, something he had only tried a few times in the last twenty years. The problem he'd had with addressing God was that he could never be sure if he was talking to himself, or if he was making some grand connection. Like now.

"I don't know where you are, Helen, but I hope it's somewhere safe. I can understand your seeking a refuge. I'm beginning to understand a lot of things about you. If I had lived your life, I'd sure as hell be on Olympus, or wherever you are.

"There are a few earthly worries you needn't concern yourself with, like Cerberus. Earlier this afternoon I fed and walked him and I can tell you that he misses you. It was clear I wasn't much of a substitute for you. He let me pet him, and tell him what a fine dog he is, but he knew it wasn't the real thing."

Cheever exhaled a lot of air. It wasn't so difficult talking about animals. Talking about Helen—talking about himself—wouldn't be so easy.

"I should tell you that Cerberus wasn't the only reason for my going to your loft. Cops are terrible snoops, you see. I hope you don't mind, but last night and today I spent time looking at your paintings and statues. You told me about that statue Pygmalion made, how he called her Galatea, and how she miraculously came to life. Well, the more I look at your art, the more it's been coming alive. You might not be talking, but it is. Your art speaks for you, all of you. It does your storytelling, and reveals some of your history, and does your weeping.

"I remember the first time I saw your statues at the gallery. They pissed me off. I have this antiquated view that art should be uplifting. But I can understand how it would be hard to do Disney when you're in the middle of Hades. That's the landscape you've had to work from, isn't it?

"I still don't understand everything, Helen. I'm hoping you're going to fill in the blanks for me real soon. The more of your art I look at, the clearer everything becomes. And the more horrible.

"I think I admire you more than any person I've ever known, Helen. You're like this boxer who keeps getting up. You've been battered and bruised. You've taken more punishment than anyone should ever have to, and you're still not through. Somehow you keep answering the bell."

In his own life Cheever wished he had been as valiant. Rachel had said that multiples often avoided reality because reality offered them only pain and hurt. They compartmentalized feelings and responses to survive. He had done the same, only not to the extent that she had.

"I've been doing a lot of thinking on things you've tried to tell me, not only the art but everything. One time you said, 'If I accept their pain, she won't hurt anymore.' I didn't pick up on that then, but now I understand that you were telling me you had seen more than one person being hurt. By taking on *their* pain you were paying a penance of sort. Your three stigmata should have shown me that. Two of the wounds were for Bonnie Gill, and I think the third was for a little girl named Katie Dwyer. She was red-headed like Bonnie, and had freckles, and I think Caitlin saw someone do something terrible to her, maybe something like what happened to Bonnie Gill. Hygeia wasn't only taking on the wounds of the dead, she was taking on the psychic scars of a personality. The pain that a little girl couldn't handle was accepted by another better equipped for that kind of hurt."

Cheever targeted his own heart, smacking his chest, and though Helen still didn't say anything, Cheever sensed a turbulence inside of her, had this sense that water was on the verge of boiling.

"You also told me that, 'You don't raise the dead without paying a great price and making yourself a target for mighty enemies.' I've wondered about that, Helen. It was easy to dismiss the statement at the time because I thought you were talking about being the daughter of a healing god, but I should have been more perceptive. I need to know about your mighty enemies. I want to help you vanquish them."

His plea was met with silence. Was it his imagination, or was her entire body slightly vibrating? Was her world(s) being shaken up?

"You know, I keep thinking about those little girls. There's young Helen who went through a long fugue state, and when she emerged she wanted to be called Holly. Helen was gone. And then there's Katie Dwyer. And finally there is Caitlin.

"It took me a long time to figure out that Caitlin is an awful lot like both Helen and Katie. She has reddish hair, but it's a light red, somewhere between Helen's blond and Katie's red.

"I don't think Caitlin's name is any coincidence. I talked with Dr. Stern just a little while ago and I told her about Kathleen Dwyer. I told her about the dress on your little girl statue being the same dress that Katie was last seen wearing, and then Dr. Stern came up with an interesting theory. She pointed out how the name Caitlin is a combination of the names of two girls: Katie's first syllable and Helen's last. Kate and Len. Caitlin. You weren't misspelling that name all these years. You were revealing what only you knew.

"When Katie disappeared Helen could no longer go on being what she was. That was when Caitlin emerged. She was the only child that could continue to live because the others were lost, lost forever."

Cheever stopped talking. He wondered if Rachel should have been with him when he revealed these things. But he wondered even more if Helen had heard. Or God. He felt drained. Words, as usual, had failed him. He took his hand, put it atop Helen's, and joined her in looking out the window.

The sleeper was difficult to awake. She had hidden her soul. Helen had read of others who had done that, put their souls at the top of mountains, or in the middle of a tall tree, or in the back of some hidden cave. By doing that it made them impervious to harm. Their physical bodies could be touched, but not their essence.

But this one's words had found her hidden soul. She had positioned her spirit, thinking that nothing could touch it, and yet he had. His words (or were they incantations?) had traveled through her thousand-and-one defenses. The first time she had seen him she had wondered if he was the one the gods had chosen to lead her out of darkness. She had looked at him and thought of Orpheus who had tried to reclaim the dead. But Orpheus had failed. He had looked back.

Damn his words. They had found her even though she was deep, so deep, in depths beyond human understanding. It was possible that she could keep going, submerge to a place where other voices could never reach her, but she knew his words had already hooked her and that his line would follow her. She could try to free herself, but the hook was deep. Even now she could feel him working her, pulling her line. He was this old man of the sea who wouldn't give up. No matter how tangled their lines were, he held on.

It was time for air. She had sounded long enough and deep enough and now her lungs needed filling again. How inconvenient it was to be a mammal. To have to take in bothersome air. To have to expose herself time and again to the harpoons of the world.

The surface. She pushed for it. She sensed some barrier, and knew that to break free she'd have to rid herself of encumbrances, of baggage. She didn't want to just escape. She wanted to be alive. The breach was closer, closer. There was no going back now.

Her scream awoke Cheever from his reverie. Then she was crying, and trying to talk, and shaking, and he found himself holding her and telling her over and over, "It's all right. It's all right." And while he was consoling her, words from his past kept slipping out. Her surfacing had startled him, and he still wasn't completely awakened from that place he had been, which is why he kept saying, "It's okay, Daddy's here."

And somewhere in her mind she knew that Orpheus had looked back, but it was all right, because they still had each other.

THIRTY-TWO

A little girl was born.

She didn't come into the world easily, but children rarely do. She came into the world crying, and for a time had trouble getting her breath, as if her lungs weren't used to the atmosphere around her. When her breathing stabilized, and her crying stopped, she said, "It hurts."

"What hurts?" Cheever asked.

She shook her head and said, "Everything," then started looking around, moving not just her eyes but swiveling her head in the manner of a curious child, her trauma seemingly forgotten. "This is a big house," she said.

Her voice didn't sound like Caitlin's. It was different somehow. And her mannerisms were distinctive, not Caitlin's. She acted like a young girl, but not the young girl Cheever had come to know. Her change made him nervous. Was this another personality? He thought he had met the whole lot except for Cronos.

"Who are you?" he asked.

She smiled at him, a child's smile that recognized an adult game: "I'm Diane, silly Daddy!"

She had called him Daddy before, but that was as Caitlin. Now it was different, even more personal. Diane. Cheever was sure he had never said his daughter's name in her presence, and wondered where she could have heard it. But he didn't ask her that question. He stood there immobile and silent as she walked around the living room.

"I can see water out there, Daddy," she said. Her face was close to the window, and as she spoke condensation formed on the glass. She blew some more, and started drawing figures into the mist.

"Look what happens when I blow, Daddy," she said.

"I see," he said.

"Come and do it," she said. "It's fun."

He walked across the room, and then they both took turns blowing on the glass. Cheever made a sun for her, and she made a flower for him. He drew some waves, and then she drew a three-sided figure that he identified as a triangle, and she disdainfully corrected him, saying, "It's a pyramid."

Cheever tried telling himself that he was too surprised at the turn of events to have his wits about him. But that wasn't it. He accepted the charade because he didn't want to deny what she offered him. And as they played and talked he could almost convince himself that each of them gave the other something they needed, and that there were enough positives in their behavior to outweigh the negatives.

Though he kept resolving to step out of his role, and tell her very firmly that his daughter was twenty years dead, she kept doing or saying things that immobilized his intentions, or so he kept rationalizing. He wanted to protect her, and have time stand still. She was the picture of innocence, and trust, and love, and he needed all three, but most of all he needed the redemption of a living daughter to tell him that he hadn't failed her. Their relationship was clearly symbiotic. She was dependent on him to be the loving father who would let her be five, and who would never violate her young trust. But Cheever knew they were both feeding each other's weaknesses. They weren't getting ahead; they were reverting. They weren't going on with their histories; they were rewriting them, even if their casting wasn't right. For a time, and a price, they were willing to try to do the impossible and forget twenty years.

"What's for dinner?" she asked.

"Are you hungry?"

She held her stomach dramatically: "I'm starving."

"I can make some spaghetti."

"Yummy."

They walked out to the kitchen and she sat at the table, playing with the salt and pepper shakers. He rummaged around, didn't find any spaghetti sauce in a jar, but didn't expect to either. There were cloves of garlic, and some fresh oregano and basil. Rachel's prejudice against cans didn't extend as far as tomato sauce and tomato paste and stewed tomatoes, so he set to opening, and mixing, and stirring. There were enough ingredients for him to make a complete mess, and something he hoped resembled spaghetti sauce.

"When's Mommy coming home?"

"She said around eight."

Mommy, he thought. How easy it was to fall back into old patterns, patterns that should have been forgotten. She was asking about Mommy. Yeah, they were a regular nuclear family, fallout and all.

He found some mushrooms, and cut them up along with a clove of garlic and an onion. Rachel didn't have any butter or margarine, so he used extra virgin olive oil to sauté everything. It worked except for sound effects. The sizzle wasn't quite the same.

"That smells good, Daddy."

"Bene, mi amore, bene."

292

She giggled and said, "Daddy, you're crazy," then went back to work.

So did he. Cheever wished he could put a tap on her brain and listen to her mental dialogues. She seemed so much like Diane in all that she said and did, or was he putting that interpretation on her every action? He thought about closure, one of those in-vogue and overused psychological words, jargon he usually eschewed, but he knew there had never been any closure with the death of his daughter. He had just put the event on a shelf somewhere, hoping there would be an expiration date on emotions. Good only until a certain time.

"So, Princess, what's your favorite meal in the world?"

"Pasghetti," she said.

Hadn't Diane mispronounced the word the same way? Was that a universal among children, or was he grasping for straws?

"Really?"

"And chocolate cake," she said.

"That's a dessert."

"And I can eat a million pancakes."

Diane had loved pancakes too. Usually his wife had done the cooking, but he remembered one day when he had pulled out the flour and eggs and buttermilk and salt and made some pancakes from scratch. That day Diane had eaten more pancakes than the adults. How she put away so many in her little stomach he never knew. She couldn't have been more than three then, just before her disease first surfaced. "More," she kept saying, pronouncing the word like "mower." And she had smiled at the announcement, as if it were a wonderful private joke, as if she knew she was doing something astounding. And each time he had repeated in disbelief, "More?" And she had giggled and said, "Mower."

"Can we play 'Go Fish,' Daddy?"

"Maybe later, Honey. We'll have to see if Mommy has any playing cards."

Cheever wondered if his relationship with Rachel was similarly based on fantasy. Had he imagined her as something she wasn't? They had certainly fulfilled needs for one another, but he hoped they hadn't only been dancing to tunes from the past.

"Pasghetti coming up," he said.

He had remembered that children weren't as big on spices, had created a sauce especially for her that was more tomato than not. Rachel apparently didn't believe in processed Parmesan cheese. He found a wedge of the real thing, and a grater.

"I gotta some cheese-a, if you a please-a," he said in a bad Italian accent.

She laughed, and asked for some, but he suspected it was more to get a show than her desire for cheese. He did the grating anyway, and judging by her reaction he didn't even need the monkey and the organ. Little kids are wonderful for failed comics.

He served himself, and was just about to start eating when she announced, "I'm thirsty."

"What do you want to drink?" he asked, remembering too late that offering options to children can be a lengthy process.

"Chocolate milk."

"We don't have any. And we don't have milk either. I'll get you some juice."

He filled a glass, brought it to her, then sat down again. She took a gulp of her drink, made a little face, then vigorously started in on her spaghetti, unmindful of her precariously placed drink. Her elbow toppled her glass, not breaking it, but spilling juice all over the table.

"I'm sorry," she said, and looked very contrite, even afraid.

"It's okay," he said, using Rachel's cloth napkins to sop

the liquid up. "Just be more careful next time." What had his mother used to tell visitors when he was young? "We have the smoothest table in the world." And when they looked at the scarred old table she always explained, "Table's gotten milk baths for years. I don't know how it couldn't have the smoothest finish in the world."

Cheever finally started eating. The pasta wasn't half bad, even if it was some imported whole-wheat stuff. At least it was suckable. That's what she was doing with it, sucking in long strands and getting the sauce on her chin in the process. It was what kids did with spaghetti. For them, food could be fun. He pictured her that way: a little girl at play. Funny how you stop looking at people, he thought, as soon as you put an image in your mind. She talked and acted like a five-year-old girl, his little girl, and that was good enough for him. The only time he saw a twenty-five-year-old woman was when he forced himself to truly look at her, and that wasn't very often.

He cleared her plate and tried without success to interest her in some fresh fruit for dessert, but she had a project and wasn't about to be bothered for anything less than chocolate cake. He found her some colored markers. Judging by her critical face, they weren't as good as crayons, but they apparently sufficed. While he did the dishes she worked on a drawing. Between his scrubbing and rinsing he listened to her humming some tune. It was catchy enough that he whistled it while he washed.

"Daddy?"

"Yes?"

"Here." Shy but proud, she extended the drawing. "It's for you."

Smiling, he said, "Thank you, Sweetie," and then he looked at her drawing. After a moment's scrutiny he said, "It's great, Honey," then gave her a gentle hug.

In truth, he liked it more than any of her adult paintings. It wasn't that the drawing was exceptional; it was

295

what you would expect from a talented five-year-old, somewhat recognizable figures and objects. But what Cheever liked most was its cheery tone. There were three figures—a mommy, a daddy, and a daughter—and they were all smiling. There was a green lawn and a yellow sun and a blue house. It didn't take much of a stretch of imagination to include your own white picket fence.

The little girl in the picture was blond. The drawing showed she didn't know his Diane had been a brunette. Or maybe she was finally putting herself in her pictures, finding that face of what she really looked like before her mother and father were born. Cheever wondered if Caitlin was gone for good, and also wondered where the other personalities were. He had considered calling Rachel and telling her about the developments, but was reluctant to interrupt her at work. There were other patients who needed her attention. And besides, he would have had to explain his own behavior, and he wasn't sure he wanted to do that.

"I love it so much, Sweetie," Cheever said, "that I'm going to hang it on the refrigerator."

"I need to sign it," she said.

Once an artist, he thought, always an artist. He handed the drawing back to her and she returned to the table. "How do you spell Diane, Daddy?"

He repeated the letters for her slowly, and watched as she struggled with each one. She struggled almost as much writing the letters as he did saying them. When she finally finished he found some tape and hung the drawing from the designer refrigerator.

Rachel's showpiece home was suddenly showing signs of being lived in. Children leave trails, and she was no exception. Shoes and papers and pillows, and whatever had occupied her for a moment or more, marked her path out to the living room.

"Let's play a game, Daddy!"

"What game?"

"Something fun."

She didn't know how to play Tic Tac Toe, so he taught her. At first he let her win, but he soon didn't have to give her any advantages. For half an hour they staked out their X's and O's, and when they finished, a sheaf of papers was left in their wake.

"Who wants cocoa?" he asked.

"I do!" she shouted.

Rachel's kitchen closet had few indulgences, cocoa being about the most decadent item Cheever had discovered. He mixed the hot water and cocoa together, then carried the cups on a tray out to the family room where they did their sipping in front of the TV. They watched a documentary on the migration of birds, but neither of them was particularly interested in the show. A migration did occur, though. She moved across the sofa onto Cheever's lap.

"Tell me a story, Daddy," she said.

Her eyes were heavy, but still expectant. He took her mug from her hands, and cradled her close to him, deliberating on what story to tell. He wished there were some children's books on Rachel's bookshelves. It would have been easier just to pick and choose that way, to not have to think, to read some words and just hold her. Myths kept popping into his mind, but those were stories he wanted to distance her from. And he didn't want to tell any stories with witches, or goblins, or miraculous events. He wanted something wholesome and decent and honest. Mythology of another kind, he thought cynically.

His ultimate decision was colored. He picked what had been one of Diane's favorite stories. "Let me tell you about the little engine that could," he said.

He told her about the brave little engine, and the big mountain that needed to be traversed, and all those who were depending on the train's getting through. As its struggles mounted, as the little engine kept pushing forward, they repeated in unison, "I think I can, I think I can." The three of them labored together, she and Cheever and the little engine, going painfully along, and for each obstacle they had their mantra: "I think I can, I think I can."

The story didn't end with a wild flourish. You'd think in a train story there would have been bells and whistles and heavy smokestacks at the finish, and then more whistles. Maybe that's why Cheever liked the ending so much. It wasn't braggadocio, wasn't some wild exclamation of steam, but just an assertion of quiet pride. And like all good heroes the little engine hadn't lingered, had just disappeared into the sunset, content in a job well done. His words changed, but not his tone. In the end he echoed to himself, "I thought I could, I thought I could." And that's what she and Cheever said as they passed over their own rails. She repeated the words until her own steam ran out. And then, with a last valiant effort, she kissed him on his cheek. He watched her eyes give up the struggle and close. Gradually her breathing became slow and regular.

He held her in his arms, lost somewhere in time, awakening with the one thought of getting his girl to her bed. Rising to his feet while holding her was almost more than Cheever could manage. His struggle intruded on the fantasy of his carrying his little girl. He remembered her as being as light as an angel.

Straining, he made it to the guest bedroom, and there pulled the covers back, and tucked her in, and then kissed her good night. As he left the room he heard her murmur, "I thought I could."

THIRTY-THREE

With a surreptitious glance, Rachel saw that it was quarter of eight. Five more minutes, she thought.

Mr. Kooper continued to drone on. "You know, I always figured if I had the job I've got I'd be happy. I thought that the money and power that came with it . . ."

This was only Mr. Kooper's third session with her. He was having a mid-life crisis that a recent affair and a new four-wheel-drive vehicle hadn't helped. For a moment Rachel felt guilty about not listening more closely, but for once she allowed herself some latitude.

Rachel breathed deeply through her nose. It wasn't even necessary to turn and look at them. The roses had a magnificent fragrance. She had left them out in the open, left them for all her patients to see. Red roses. They had been her contact with Cheever throughout the day. Their busy schedules had allowed them only one brief phone conversation. Cheever had told her about Kathy Dwyer, and she had speculated on the origins of Caitlin's name. The call hadn't only been professional, though. Rachel had thanked Cheever for the roses, and, with a certain intonation that she hadn't even known she was capable of, Rachel had told him she knew just the thing for his cough. "Whatever you say, Doctor," he had said.

She tuned in to Mr. Kooper for a minute. "You ever hear that saying about how kids suck the mother when they're young, and suck the father when they're older? Well, I don't feel like I got put on this planet just to grow tits for my kids . . ."

Rachel thought about her own breasts. She had wrongly assumed that anticipating the biopsy results would consume her thoughts. It wasn't that she had been nonchalant about the impending news, it was just that she had felt too alive to be obsessed. Not that her heart hadn't surged, and all of her suppressed fears hadn't come to the fore, when her doctor had finally called with the news. Her cyst, he told her, was benign.

". . . so what I think is," said Mr. Kooper, "I've got to start looking out for number one. There are things I want to do. I'm thinking it would be nice to get my pilot's license. I've already got one of those leather jackets . . ."

The nights were getting a little cooler now. San Diego's so-called fall was her favorite time of year. There was a hint of the change of seasons, or what passed for the change of seasons, with the November evenings now getting down to the fifties. Maybe that would be excuse enough for her and Cheever to put a log on the fireplace.

The minute hand on her clock edged forward just enough. At last, she thought, though what she said was, "Alas, Mr. Kooper, our time is just about up."

She finished up their session quickly, offering Mr. Kooper some observations (fudged, she had to admit), and matters to think about (more fudge), before showing him to the door.

Rachel was tempted to forgo her notes on Mr. Kooper's session, but her habits were too ingrained. Early in her career one of her mentors had faulted her painstaking approach. "Rachel," he had said, "the mental health industry isn't too different from a fast food operation. Most of the time you're looking for an analysis to go. These are not six-course meals to be thought about, and slowly digested. Sometimes you're lucky if you have time to throw in the fries."

Of necessity, Rachel had become more expeditious with her note taking, but she never viewed her profession the way her mentor had.

Narcissist, she wrote down. She wondered if Mr. Kooper had heard of the myth of Narcissus and Echo. One benefit Rachel had gained from treating Helen was that it had forced her to delve into mythology. Scratch a myth, she had found, and usually there was a human truth. The pioneers of psychotherapy had known that all too well. They had understood that many myths were more than stories, and had used myths to describe symptomatology and give names to conditions.

She remembered how the mythological Narcissus had embodied self-love, and how his demise had resulted from his falling in love with his own reflection. It had taken Rachel months before she became conversant enough in mythology to follow Helen's stories without needing a mythological road map. Cheever hadn't had that problem. She thought about Cheever while scribbling notes on Mr. Kooper's session, entries she knew were far beneath her standards, but that she had no intention of elaborating upon or improving. The sound of a male voice coming from the intercom surprised her.

"Dr. Stern?"

She looked around the room, wondered if Mr. Kooper had left something, but didn't see anything, then spoke into the intercom: "Yes?"

"It's Cheever."

"What . . . ?" Why his formality? And who was looking after Helen? But Rachel didn't ask her questions. She didn't want to talk through a box. Maybe he had Helen with him. She buzzed him in. Rachel rose, thought to greet Cheever at the entryway to the anteroom, but never made it to the outer room. The door was flung open, striking her arm and shoulder. She caught a glimpse of someone who was definitely not Cheever, a man in a mask. Scream, she thought, but even as her mouth opened a gloved hand grabbed her by the hair. She was pulled forward, then thrown backward onto her desk. The collision made her cry out in pain, but her cries were suddenly stifled when a knife was pressed up against her throat. With it came the single admonition of, "Shhhhh," a warning she obeyed.

Standing over her was a man wearing a red and white ski mask. Rachel looked into his dispassionate blue eyes. "Can we go with that thought, Doctor?" the man asked.

The knife raised itself from her throat, but only slightly. "If you scream, I'll kill you. Understand?"

Rachel decided not to chance speech. She nodded.

He motioned for her to get up, then pointed to her chair and said, "Why don't you take your seat, Doctor?"

She rose on uncertain legs, then walked around her desk and sat down in her chair. He watched her every movement, and made sure she was watching him as he cut the phone and intercom lines. He looked all too comfortable handling the knife. It sliced through the cables easily. Behind his mask she could see he was smiling. Rachel had a feeling the smile was for her benefit.

"It's tough getting a session with you, Doc. You're a damn popular woman."

Rachel didn't say anything.

"Are you that good, Doctor?"

There was something invasive in his voice. It wasn't only his innuendo. It was his callousness. He didn't care about her one way or another, but he did enjoy being clever.

302

"My problems," he said, "probably stem from an inadequate toilet training. But yours, Doc, yours are a result of something quite different."

She said nothing, just continued to watch him. Her not participating annoyed him. The game wasn't as fun without her in it. He took his knife and started carving into her desk.

"You ever dig a heart out?" he asked, then after a pointed pause added, "on a desk, I mean."

He was asserting his power to do terrible things, implying, no, more than that, stating that he had already done such deeds. In a deceptively calm voice she said, "No."

The tip of his blade cut into the wood. He carved out the shape of a heart. "You never put your initials with someone else's? R.S. and whoever?"

"I don't remember doing that."

"You must have been a lot of fun in school, Darling."

He finished his carving. By this time he figured she would have been begging, but she was a real ice queen. Not that it mattered.

"You want to know where your problems started?" he asked.

"I am sure you are going to tell me," she said.

"You have a patient named Holly Troy. She was taken away by the men in white coats yesterday. I need to know where she is."

"I'm afraid I don't . . ."

"Don't fuck with me, lady. I'm not asking you. I'm telling you."

He pulled a nylon from his coat pocket. "It's up to you whether I conduct an operation, Doctor. I can gag you, and then start carving. You'll tell me what I want to know either way. But I'd prefer being civilized about all of this."

She could tell that being civilized was the farthest thing from his mind. Psychopath, she thought. It wasn't an officially sanctioned word anymore, but just because the mental health field had purged it from their diagnostic vocabulary didn't make this man any less dangerous. She was convinced he could act with complete emotional detachment, could kill without compunction or remorse. Rachel had worked with several patients like that. They were their own universe; everything existed for them. Though they didn't feel, they knew how to fake feelings. Like birds that mimic, they learned how to take on the sounds of others. Some psychopaths even succeeded in getting ahead. Ostensibly they were reasonable people. They could laugh, and talk, and interact, and most of all they could manipulate. Killing her wouldn't bother him. He would only be concerned about the ramifications of how it might affect him.

"Holly," she said, using the name he had used to identify Helen, "is very disturbed right now. She has withdrawn into herself and isn't communicating. She had to be isolated."

"Where?" he asked.

"We're not sure," Rachel said, "if she will ever talk again. In many ways she evidences symptoms of posttraumatic stress syndrome. She is like a combat victim who has seen and experienced too much."

"That's fascinating, Doc. Maybe we could have a long tête-à-tête sometime. But right now I'd like to talk to her, not about her."

He impatiently tapped his knife on the desk. Rachel tried not to look at it, tried to think of some way to gain control of the situation.

"Holly shouldn't be disturbed," she said. "She's heavily sedated. She's . . ."

The knife slammed into her desk, penetrating a good half-inch into the hard wood. He stood up and wrenched it free, leaving a gaping wound in the desk. Knife in hand, he leaned over the desk. Despite her best intentions, Rachel cringed.

"Where?" he asked.

"The Torrey Pines Center in La Jolla," she said. "It's a private convalescent facility."

"What's the address?"

"I have it here somewhere."

He motioned with his knife for her to get it, then slightly straightened while Rachel rummaged around her desk. She flipped open her Rolodex, turned over some cards, and looked frustrated. Then she reached down and opened her desk drawer, pulled out a stapler and a tape dispenser, thumbed through some papers, and finally announced, "Here it is." He leaned down toward her and stuck out a gloved hand. Into it she pressed her stun gun and pulled its trigger. Both of them screamed at the contact, she from fright, and he at the contact. The knife fell to the ground and she dropped the stun gun. Rachel grabbed her purse and started running, but her assailant wasn't as incapacitated as she had hoped. He came at her, moving to cut off her escape. His eyes, so distant before, were more expressive now. They were angry. It was those eyes she aimed for.

The pepper spray squirted at his face. His mask partially helped him, and partially hindered. It absorbed some of the spray, shielding his eyes, but the fumes from the liquid blinded him. Rachel tried running by him, but even with his eyes on fire, and his right arm hanging limp, he lunged at her. His fingers caught and tore her blouse, but Rachel was able to pull out of his grasp. He fell to the floor yelling curses at her. He wanted to cut her throat more than anything. To silence her. But he was half blind. And she had hurt him. The bitch had fried his arm. As she pulled open the door and ran out of the office he picked up the fallen knife with his left hand. His right hand, his right arm, was useless. It felt like someone had taken a hammer to it, and he couldn't shake the numbness. But he was going to catch her and make her pay. He took off after her, tried opening the door with his right hand, cursed her and himself for not being able to manage that. Sticking the knife between his teeth, he grabbed the doorknob with his left hand and wrenched it open.

The bitch was really screaming now. She was running for the stairwell, was almost there. He knew just how to quiet her. He'd do her like he had Bonnie Gill. She'd been trying to get away, too. At the time he had thought she was calling out, "Help me." But he had misinterpreted. He knew now that she had been saying, "Holly." Bonnie had wanted to alert Holly Troy.

"Got a dream I want you to analyze, Doc," he shouted.

He was coming. He wanted her to know he was coming. The garage, he knew, was all but deserted. Some of the doctors probably left their extra cars there. He was tempted to take off his mask. His eyes hurt like hell, and the fumes from that fucking spray were making him tear, but he couldn't chance shucking the ski mask. Someone driving out of the garage might see him. He'd make the bitch hurt for what she had done.

If only the Gill thing had gone better. He had scouted the gallery, walked around to make sure no one was inside except for Bonnie. And when he had made his entrance he had said, "Where are all the customers?" And Bonnie had replied, "One finally walked in." How was he to know that weirdo sculptor was in the garden dressing her statues?

He crashed into the stairwell door. His numb arm had thrown off his equilibrium. Bitch. He yanked the door open. She was two flights down. Her screams were loud in the enclosed space. They pumped him up.

"Time for surgery, Doctor," he yelled.

Rachel knew she was running for her life, and knew that he was gaining. It was hard for her to think straight. She threw out prayers to a God she didn't think she believed in. She was gasping. Her screams sounded fainter, were muted for lack of breath. Someone be there, she hoped.

Keep running, running. Somebody hear me, she prayed. Don't stop now. He's closer. He's so close.

He leaped down the stairs three at a time, using his body to bounce off the stair rail. Fucking arm, he thought, and fucking eyes. He couldn't trust either. He kept stumbling, but still he was gaining on her.

Rachel threw open the door to the garage. For a moment she panicked, afraid that she had run out to the wrong floor. She was glad her reserved space didn't identify her by name. Please don't have sabotaged my car, she thought. Please, God, please.

She kept running, turned a corner. Sobbing in relief, she saw her car.

The door didn't have time to close behind her. He was that close. He put his shoulder into it, and then burst out into the garage. She only had about twenty steps on him now.

Rachel reached into her purse and desperately fumbled around. She didn't want to look down, didn't have the time. Her eyes were on the prize of her Lexus. Where was the damn remote? Her hand kept grasping. There! A moment of hope before she realized she was holding her cosmetics case. Brush, lipstick, checkbook. Oh, God, where was it? Then her fingers closed on it. She threw her purse back at the pursuing steps that sounded so close, then pushed the button. It didn't work. She pushed again, desperate. The salesman told her it was good from fifty feet away. She must be closer than fifty feet. Maybe the batteries had run out. He was closer. She could hear him. It sounded as if he were right behind her. Sobbing, she pressed the remote again, and then again.

He was gasping as hard as she was. He could barely see. His eyes had almost shut. But he could see well enough to make out the blur in front of him. He'd catch her. Just a few more steps.

Please, she thought. Please. She was pushing at the remote, pressing time and time again. Panic clouded her thoughts. The salesman lied, she thought. Never believe what anyone tells you. Work, damn you, work.

She was less than fifteen feet away when the remote activated, turning on the car's lights and unlocking the doors. Rachel reached for the door handle, pulled it open, then threw herself into the driver's seat and activated the locks. It felt like it took her an hour to put the key into the ignition, even if it was only an instant. But in that time he had reached the car door. He punched at the window with his gloved hand and it cracked. With trembling hands Rachel turned the key, started the car, and threw it into reverse, but not before he threw a second punch. This time the window gave way. Pebbled glass fell all over her head and lap. She pumped at the gas, then had to brake sharply to avoid careening into one of the stanchions. As she put the car into drive he caught up with her again. With one hand he grabbed for the steering wheel, and with the other he tried to reach for the key. She was lucky his right hand was still too numb for him to grasp very well. Rachel fought for control of the steering wheel, and at the same time slammed her foot on the gas pedal. As the car accelerated the fight for control continued. Only when a crash appeared imminent did he let go of the wheel, dropping to the garage floor. Rachel regained control of the car just in time to miss ramming into the support column, but she didn't slow down. She rocketed toward the garage's exit as if death were right behind her. When she reached the street, Rachel still didn't slow down. Rachel ran red lights and stop signs, pushing her car to its limits. Only when she reached the haven of her garage, when the door closed behind her, did she feel she could stop running. But she still couldn't bring her fingers to turn off the ignition. She was shaking too much.

That's how Cheever found her, huddled over the wheel of her car, the engine running, her entire body uncontrollably shaking. He reached inside the car and turned the ignition off.

"Hold me," she tried to say, "hold me," but she couldn't manage the words. Everything was gibberish. She could only make sounds. And the harder she tried the more insensible were her words.

But Cheever didn't need to hear words. He lifted her from the car, then draped his arms around her and wouldn't let go, not for anything. He held her all the while Rachel made her mewling sounds and shook, held her until at last she stopped shaking, and her words were finally intelligible, but still she kept saying, "Hold me, hold me, hold me, hold me, hold me, hold me, hold me . . ."

And he kept repeating, "I'll never let go, I'll never let go, I'll never let go, I'll never let go . . ."

THIRTY-FOUR

A cop's world usually allows room for a policeman to distance himself from a victim. Sometimes, though, a case gets personal and the lines get blurred, but Cheever did his best to not let that occur, tried to remain a cop and only a cop while he interviewed Rachel. She wasn't sure she liked that side of him, much preferring the man who had held her and said he wouldn't let go.

Cheever acted even more dispassionately than the young uniformed officer who sat with them in the den taking notes. The officer looked and performed like a Marine, had short hair and was full of, "Yes, sir," and "Yes, ma'ams." His chest was broad even without the extra bulk of his kevlar vest. Though he was ostensibly in charge, it was clear it was Cheever's show.

From her easy chair Rachel sipped a cup of tea that Cheever had made. Tea-making was apparently not one of his talents. He had used a strainer, but must have secured it improperly. The tea had steeped only long enough for some of the tea leaves to escape, but not long enough to release much flavor. Rachel looked at the floating leaves, and momentarily wondered if she should try and read them.

"Let's start at the beginning again," he said. "At the intercom."

She didn't let her impatience show; instead she took another sip of his brew. Though she did her best to leave any sediment in the cup, a few dregs found their way into her mouth. She picked at them with her thumb and forefinger.

"He asked for me by name."

"He said, 'Dr. Stern?' "

"Yes. And then he said, 'It's Cheever.' "

"He didn't say, 'Detective Cheever,' or 'Orson Cheever?' "

Rachel was feeling well enough to smile. She never thought of him as having a first name. He was a one-name sort of person. "No, *Orson*," she said. "He identified himself by saying, 'It's Cheever.' "

He didn't respond to her teasing. "You'd still gauge him at six foot and two hundred pounds?"

"More or less."

"Blue eyes?"

"Cold blue eyes. Pale."

"No facial hair?"

"None that I could see."

"How old do you think he was?"

She shrugged. "Maybe forty."

"Any general impressions of the man?"

"People in my field are trained not to say this, but I will anyway: he's evil."

"What else?"

She started to take another sip of her tea, reconsidered, and put the cup aside. "He's smart and good at planning. He enjoys being in control. And he's sure he is smarter than everyone else."

"He used the name 'Holly.' "

"Yes."

"And he knew about her breakdown."

His was more of a muse than a question, so she didn't answer.

"You said she was at the Torrey Pines Center. Does such an establishment really exist?"

"No. I gave him a fictitious name."

Cheever digested her answers. The uniformed officer used the lull in the conversation to ask, "Will you be needing me for anything else, sir?"

Preoccupied, Cheever shook his head. It was Rachel who walked the officer to the door. When she returned to the den, Cheever was still in a contemplative state. Still the cop, she thought.

"Anyone home?" she asked.

"He was there," Cheever said, "when Helen had her breakdown. She was wearing her Medic-Alert bracelet. That's where your name was announced. And mine. I think Helen saw the killer and recognized him. It probably put her on overload."

Cheever pulled at his chin, still thinking. "But that still doesn't explain how he knew to identify me as 'Cheever.' "

"He obviously did some research on both of us."

Cheever nodded, but didn't look convinced. "He called her 'Holly.' "

"That's what most people call her."

"Does that mean he knows her?"

"At the least," she said, "it presumes some current knowledge of her."

Saying Holly's name aloud made Cheever only too aware that he hadn't yet told Rachel about her newfound voice. Rather trepidatiously, he said: "She's—better now, you know."

"No, I didn't know."

Rachel looked at him closely. There was something

furtive in the way he had broached the subject. Even now he wasn't meeting her eyes.

"Tell me what happened," Rachel said.

Cheever found himself reluctant to say too much about Helen's recuperation. He didn't want to tell her about Diane. "She just sort of awakened," he said.

He wasn't acting like the cop now, she thought. He was acting more like the criminal. "Sort of?"

"Did. She talked. We ate. I put her to bed."

There had been too many other things going on, Cheever thought, *were* too many other things going on, to tell her about Diane. When things weren't so hectic they could deal with Diane. It was possible that Rachel wouldn't encounter her in the next few days. It was even possible that Diane would only come out for him.

"When did this awakening occur?"

"Not too long after I took over for the nurse. Maybe six o'clock."

"And Helen just started talking then?"

"Not exactly," he said. "I talked to her for a while, kind of like you did last night."

"When she . . ."

"That's not important now," he said, interrupting her. "What is important is how the murder of Bonnie Gill ties in with the assaults on both Helen and you. That's what we should be concentrating on."

"Is it your usual habit to decide what's important for everyone and what's not?"

He tried to be self-righteous, but wasn't sure if he pulled it off, wondered if his voice sounded as false to her as it did to him: "It is when I'm on a case."

"You're not the only one working a case."

"This is a murder investigation, Rachel. This is what I do."

"And treating Helen is what I do."

Ferreting out avoidance was also a part of her job, but she didn't tell him that. She didn't have to.

"I'm sorry," he said, backing down. "For the moment, though, I think it makes sense that this investigation take precedence over Helen's treatment."

Rachel didn't answer, just continued to look at him with unconvinced eyes.

"We'll talk about Helen a little later," he said.

"All right," she said, not completely reassured, wondering what was going on.

Cheever picked up his cellular phone and called Falconi. The sergeant was supervising the crime scene at Rachel's medical building. Not bothering to identify himself, Cheever asked, "What do you got?"

"Not a hell of a lot. No mask, no gloves, no witnesses. There are some signs of a struggle in the doctor's office, and we've got a tech going through there for trace evidence, but don't hold your breath. We picked up the doctor's purse in the garage. Her wallet was there, and so was her checkbook. They look complete, but that doesn't mean he couldn't have taken down her address."

Or already know where she lives, Cheever thought. "I have that end covered for tonight," he said.

"Oh?"

Cheever didn't elaborate, and Falconi didn't press for details. "You sure you don't want me to come down to the scene? I'm up for a while."

"No need. We're just waiting on the tech, and I don't think she'll be much longer."

"You sure?"

"Positive."

Disappointed, Cheever finished the conversation. He had wanted to get out of the house, had wanted to run away, even if not very far.

"They have your purse, and wallet, and checkbook," he told Rachel. "It doesn't look like they've been touched."

"I suppose I should be grateful for that."

"There's still the possibility that he knows where you live," Cheever said. "Even with your alarm system you're going to have to be cautious. The more lights and vigilance the better."

She kept rubbing her hands. "Times like these make me reconsider my stand on handgun control," she said.

"Being attacked brings out the conservative in all of us. If you don't mind, I'd like to stay here tonight."

"I thought that was the plan anyway."

Her remark flustered him. "It was. It is. I just wasn't sure with everything that happened whether you were up for company."

"I understand."

The tone of her voice was softer, less confrontational. It made him want to talk, or, if not that, at least make things better between them.

"Little girl came out tonight," he said. "I'm not good when that happens. She stayed the evening."

"It's all right," Rachel said.

For telling a half-truth, he didn't feel half-better, felt worse if anything. He hadn't defined which little girl, had implied it was Caitlin. But the rest of what he said was true. Rachel reached for him, and Cheever gratefully went to her arms. This time he was the one who needed the holding. For a minute they held one another, saying nothing. He finally broke the silence.

"Earlier, I put a bottle of wine in the refrigerator," he said, "and I cut up some cheese and carrots and apples and celery. Combine all that with one of your boxes of no-salt no-fat crackers and you almost have something edible. How about I bring everything out here?"

"Let me do it."

"No. Lie down on the sofa and relax."

Rachel didn't want to argue, so she didn't. He was back in less than two minutes, filled tray in hand.

"For dinner I made spaghetti," he said. "There's some extra . . ."

"No. This is dinner."

"This?" he asked, not hiding his doubts.

"It's how I usually eat."

He poured the wine, helped her pick at some of the food. Cheever looked especially suspicious of the cheese.

"It's a French cheese," she said.

"Does that explain its smell?"

"It hasn't been processed and isn't full of preservatives like the cheese you're used to. This is much more nutritious, and I daresay healthy."

"Healthy is having a cellophane wrapper attached to every piece."

"You are kidding, aren't you?"

He was—mostly, but didn't admit it. Being reminded about Rachel's special diet suddenly jarred his memory. "Your biopsy," he said. "I thought about it on and off all day. I . . ."

"It's all right," she said. "It was negative."

"I feel bad that . . ."

"Don't."

She said the word with an adamancy that stopped the conversation. Both of them sipped at their wine, and avoided each other's eyes. They each excelled at retreating.

"It's just that I feel like I've dwelt on it for too long already," she finally said. "For too many years."

He nodded. They continued to eat and drink in silence. It was easier that way. They could avoid all the subjects they didn't want to talk about. Rachel noticed Cheever's expression gradually changing, taking on the cop look again. Murder, she decided, was their safest subject. She purposely didn't analyze what that said about them.

"Let's talk about the case," she said.

He didn't need to be convinced. "Bonnie Gill didn't die a random death," he said. "To make her murder look random, Willie Lamont was killed. The murderer wanted the public to think there was a mad slasher out there. You remember how Helen warned me about that. She told me not to stop for the body parts.

"I just wish she'd given me more advice. What she's done most is to muddy the water, not purposely, but because her demons past and her demons present were so hard for her to sort out. When Bonnie died in front of her, Katie died a second time."

Rachel nodded. "Pandora's box was already full when Helen saw the second murder," she said. "She tried to stuff in all the additional horror, but couldn't. There was just too much pain to tuck away. Helen knows she'll never heal, never integrate, with so many memories suppressed."

"All the evils bottled up," said Cheever.

"And hope, too."

Cheever looked troubled. "Would it be so terrible for her if total integration was never achieved?" he whispered.

She could hear he wanted to say more. Rachel also knew he wasn't really asking a question. Cheever knew the answer, but for some reason he edged around the issue as if it were some hurtful truth.

"Understanding myths is one thing," she said. "Living them is quite another."

"But the personalities serve purposes. They help her cope. They do things she can't. They protect. They predict. They feel."

"Helen will be able to do all of those things. Helen. Not the Greek Chorus."

"Have there been cases where a full integration hasn't taken place? Where one or two personalities have remained, while the rest have integrated?"

"Yes. But that's not the treatment we're working toward."

"Show me the face you had before your mother and father were born," Cheever said.

"Yes."

Cheever thought about Helen's masks. And maybe he considered a few of his own. Then he thought about the mask of the killer.

"When you sprayed your assailant in the face with the pepper spray, where'd you get him?"

"All over his ski mask."

"But he never took it off?"

"No."

The hoot of a nearby owl made Rachel jump. It also made her move that much closer to Cheever. He put an arm around her. She sighed, let herself nestle into his chest.

"I must be edgy," she said.

The owl hooted again.

"He comes around every so often," she said, "and seems to like the pine tree out back, probably because of its high vantage point."

"Regular aviary around here," Cheever said. "The nurse said some 'really big parrots' were bothering Helen and drove her inside."

"Must have been the macaws."

"What?"

"There's a flock of five or six that live around here. They're quite colorful. And loud."

Disbelieving: "Macaws?"

"Two came from the O.B. Pet Store fire a few years ago. They were released from their cages and flew to safety. One or two others are escapees from homes, and the rest are offspring. The macaws haven't had any problems adapting to San Diego. They're regulars in my backyard. They like the citrus and nut trees."

"Macaws," said Cheever again. He had discounted the nurse's story, because he was sure parrots and their ilk weren't the kind of birds seen freely flying around San Diego. When you don't expect something to be in the picture, he considered, it's that much harder to see it when it's actually there.

Rachel's closeness gave him a chance to kiss her on the head and run his hand through her hair. All day that had been what he wanted to do. To hold her. But there had been so many obstacles in the way of their coming together. And there were still all the unsaid things that needed discussing. But not now, he told himself. Not now.

"Let's go to bed," she whispered.

In each other's arms, they walked to Rachel's bedroom. Neither of them noticed the huddled figure sitting just outside the guest room.

Holly had been close enough to hear everything that they had said. She watched them enter the bedroom, saw the door close behind them. It was as if the wall had been erected especially for her.

She got to her feet, then silently opened the door to her bedroom. Why was she being quiet? They were the ones who had ignored her, who hadn't even checked on her. She could be dead as far as they were concerned. They pretended they were all interested in her, but what they had done was betray her. She started to slam the door, wanted to make enough noise to bother them, to stop their lovey-dovey ways, but another personality popped out and stayed her hand.

Gently, she shut the door.

THIRTY-FIVE

Rachel had put a night light in Helen's room, a "glow worm" so she wouldn't be scared of the dark. A shrouded female figure sat in the shadows of the room just outside the illumination of the small light. Her movements and sounds made it appear as if she were working at a spinning wheel. Or at a web.

In the darkness Clotho's mouth moved, announcing, "Some spin designs, others spin stories, some cast lines, others seek glories."

A second voice, that of Lachesis, answered: "What are we making for Helen Troy? What are we spinning, what kind of toy?"

With a raven's voice, Atropos answered them: "While the two of you prattle, I brandish death's rattle."

Softly, Clotho taunted: "You have competition."

The head turned, and offered a rebuking stare. "I have many subordinatesss," Atropos hissed.

Clotho's chin set: "I am not one of them."

"Sisters," said Lachesis.

An arm moved, probing the darkness, reaching in and

out of the shadows. A snipping was heard. "His cutting hand," Atropos rasped, "has all along been a part of my plan. To everything, and everyone, a time and a place, with one snip hell, with the other grace."

The snipping stopped. Other hands took over, diligently spinning. "I wonder," Clotho said, "who strings whom. He tried to kill the doctor today."

"So what?" spat Atropos. "All mortals are puppets, and all puppets have strings, one way or other angels get wings."

"And devils?" asked Clotho.

"They earn the fate of their revels."

"Sissss-terssss!" Lachesis, the middle sister, looked to her right and to her left. She always sat between the creator and the cutter. She measured. She was measuring now. Her hands moved back and forth, testing a particularly tangled thread. At last, she seemed to be satisfied.

"I have a plan," Lachesis said.

In the darkness, there were movements, the sounds of bodies coming together to huddle.

"It has always been my place to measure lots. I determine the length of the thread. I hand over the measure to be cut. In my hands I hold our three joined threads. I think it is time I passed them over to Atropos."

There was the sound of thread being wildly pulled, of fishing line being pulled by a leviathan. Clotho said, "What you propose . . ."

The snapping of shears filled the room. Atropos said, "Is for us . . ."

The background noises quieted. But there was another chorus, one note loud, the other low: ". . . to be dead."

"Yessss," said Lachesis.

"Why?" Clotho asked.

"For Helen, for us."

Atropos mocked, "For us to be dust?"

"Yes."

"But we are the ones," said Clotho, "who know what was, and what is, and what will be."

"If we truly know the last," said Lachesis, "then surely you can see."

Clotho shook her head: "She needs us to guide her."

"Sister is right," rasped Atropos. "She needs us inside of her."

"No," said Lachesis, "she doesn't."

Her hands reached out, a ballet of motion. The disposer of lots ran her fingers along their existence. There was a certain melancholy to her tracing, but there was enough light from the glow worm to show her resigned face.

"We have run our course," Lachesis said.

There was a sharp intake of breath, and then the sound of line being drawn out. Or was that in? "But we are the Daughters of Night," Clotho said.

"It is our time to make way for the dawn, then," said Lachesis.

"We can escape," said Clotho. "We can run and hide."

Lachesis shook her head. "Part of what we'd be running from is us. That is a race we could not win."

"Talk to her, Atropos," said Clotho. "Tell her that she is wrong."

In the room, the sound of scissors was heard. Cutting, cutting. Atropos was there, but she didn't say anything. She couldn't argue. Then the room grew silent. Even the cutting stopped. The Sisters of Night faced their own destiny.

Slowly, painstakingly, another thread was pulled from the loom. Clotho whispered, "There's something to be said about taking the time to reason."

"Your suggestion," said Lachesis, "is treason."

"Against the state?" asked Clotho.

"Against that which is called a state of reason. We have already had our season."

"But why do we have to die?" asked Clotho, her voice shrill.

"For Helen."

"Are you sure that this will help her?"

"It will force her from this shelter," said Lachesis. "And it will embolden her to what will be. We can leave her with that prophecy." Atropos laughed. It sounded like a rusty gate opening and closing. "Scant consolation that."

"No. She will know we loved her more than we loved ourselves. We are her teachers."

Clotho offered her final argument: "But we are the Fates."

"Fated to show her the way. Are we agreed?"

Of the three voices, not one answered. There was only heavy breathing. But then arms started to move, and fingers twisted. Three strings were twined as one, and then that string was measured. A single word found its way out of three voices: "Yes."

The voices raised themselves, almost to a scream, only to be silenced by the final snipping. Cords were cut. Vocal. Umbilical. Gordian knots. All was quiet.

A breeze blew in through an opened window and rattled some papers. It was a good breeze, the kind that takes kites aflight, some never to be seen again.

Thirty-six

They lay in the aftermath of good sex, bodies glowing, weights seemingly lifted from them. Naked, their hands kept taking the measure of the other, touching hair and arms and faces and curves, and then finding the other's hand and holding it, only to ultimately disentangle and start the tactile process again.

Had she been too loud? Rachel wondered. Sex and guilt, she thought, an inevitable link. We program ourselves not to feel that good, not to let go. She felt a certain pride, though. Her passions were still there, still strong. They'd just been asleep for a time, just been waiting for the right kiss to wake them and her.

Her untethered mind drifted until it found something else to be guilty about. Helen. Maybe she had heard their love-making. Or maybe she needed something. Rachel chided herself for not having looked in on her before going to bed.

She started to get up, explained, "I'm going to check on Helen," but Cheever reached over and put a light but insistent hand on her shoulder that stayed her leaving.

"Wait," he said.

She looked at him expectantly. He considered what to say, and knew that every second he delayed speaking condemned him that much more. But there was no easy beginning.

"You should know something," he said.

Another delay.

"When Helen's consciousness came back tonight, she returned with a new personality."

Rachel knew that some multiples had hundreds of alters. She was acquainted with therapists who encountered new personalities weekly, and had read about alters that appeared for a short time, and then disappeared for years, or forever. Helen's "troop" had been amazingly consistent compared to most of those with dissociative identity disorder. The emergence of a new personality didn't trouble Rachel nearly as much as Cheever's tentativeness.

"I thought you were with Caitlin . . ."

He shook his head. "Another five-year-old," he said. "I think Caitlin's gone now."

"Tell me from the beginning," she said. It didn't matter that she was naked and had just made love with this man. Her voice was firm, professional. It was her own cop voice.

"After I relieved the nurse," he said, "I talked to Helen for a long time. I sort of babbled, said anything that came to mind. I told her how she was a fighter, and how I admired her for having never given up. I told her that I'd looked at her paintings and statues, and how they had told me things that she hadn't, or couldn't. I told her how we had discussed the name of Caitlin, and let her hear our guesswork at its origins. At first she didn't react. I thought my words had fallen on deaf ears. For a few minutes I just sat next to her on the sofa, saying nothing, just thinking. Then, suddenly, she screamed.

"I tried to comfort her. It took her a while to calm down. Then she started speaking in a little girl's voice, but it wasn't Caitlin's. She told me her name was Diane."

Rachel she worked on keeping her breathing steady and her face expressionless. "Diane?" she asked.

"My daughter."

"What did you do?"

"I spent the evening with her."

"Doing what?"

"We ate dinner. We played games. We talked."

"And you were Daddy, and she was Diane?"

Though she asked the question in a neutral voice, he responded defiantly: "Yes."

It explained a lot. His behavior that night. His questions. "I see."

Rachel wished she were behind her desk, wished she had her glasses on, and her Evan Picone suit. She wished the sudden pain in her stomach didn't hurt her so much.

"What the hell do you see?"

"At the moment," she said, "I see misdirected anger."

She was right, Cheever realized. He took a deep breath, and then tried to explain what he knew he couldn't. "You think that what we did is wrong," he said. "You don't see any good in it."

"You're right."

"But it's like a miracle. It's as if I've been given back my little girl."

"Go on."

"She sounds just like Diane. She acts just like her. I can close my eyes and swear she's alive again. I know what you're thinking. You think that what we have is wrong. But what's so terrible about loving a little girl? My little girl. It could be good for her. Nurturing. And good for me, too. I've needed her in my life. There was this void there. It was so large I wasn't sure if there was any me or if it was all void. And then this resurrection happened. That's what it feels like to me. Diane's alive again. It doesn't feel wrong."

Her eyes were soft and understanding, but she didn't allow that luxury with her words: "I've heard pedophiles say the same thing."

Cheever looked shocked. He moved his head away from her as if she had slapped him.

"What we have couldn't be further from that," he said. "You make it sound ugly. It's not."

She offered more hard love: "That's another remark popular with pedophiles."

Cheever's hands beseeched. "You don't understand . . ."

"I'm trying to."

"If I hadn't experienced it, I wouldn't have believed it either. But I'm telling you, Diane's come back. I don't know how. I know it doesn't make sense. But she's just like her. She is her."

"Cheever," she said, her tone pleading, "Helen is a twenty-five-year-old woman."

"Not when she's Diane."

"Diane's been dead," she whispered, "for twenty years."

His loud voice contrasted with her soft: "Don't you think I know that?"

"I'm not sure if you do," Rachel said.

"I've lived with her death . . ."

A hurried interjection: "But have you really ever let her go?"

". . . for all this time."

"In your head," Rachel said, reaching for his head, but not quite touching it, "you know that what you're doing is wrong. Very wrong."

Cheever shook that head. "I never believed in the supernatural," he said. "I've experienced enough terrible things on the job to not count on any happy endings in life. But when I was given this gift . . ."

"Gift?"

". . . this miracle, I accepted it."

"Did you believe," asked Rachel, "in the miracle of

Graciela Fernandez's spirit appearing on the billboard?"

"No."

"Why not?"

"When they pulled the plug on the spotlights, Little Grace's image disappeared. That doesn't sound like any miracle to me."

"Helen still believed. And so did many others."

"What's your point?"

"They wanted to believe."

"Do you believe in miracles?" he asked.

"I believe in working toward the miraculous," she said.

"That's a clever way of saying *no*. I guess I've never been a believer either, but this thing with Helen, and you, and me, seems more than coincidence. My Diane died just before Katie Dwyer. And the little girl that was Helen somehow died in childhood. There are people who believe in wandering souls resting and nesting again. Maybe they know something we don't."

"Maybe," she said. "But short of that metaphysical answer, Cheever, we have to look at what we do know. Helen has dissociative identity disorder. You've witnessed some of its manifestations, and understood they were a part of her illness. But you never actually believed Helen became a Greek god when one of those alters emerged, did you?"

"Of course not."

She willed her eyes to remain dry, but the waver in Rachel's voice gave her away. "So why is it that you're willing to believe your long dead daughter is somehow now embodied in Helen?"

"There was this . . . connection. It overwhelmed me. After a time I didn't even see Helen's body."

Rachel didn't comment. She knew how persuasive Helen's personalities could be. Sometimes even she, with all of her years of training, was briefly seduced by the personas of Helen's alters.

328

Cheever looked down at the bed covers. As a cop, he was sure he had seen and heard everything. You go out in the field, he thought, and you see more aberrant behavior in a month than the average psych major studies in four years of college. But now he was the one acting as if his deck were a few cards short. Like maybe fifty-one.

"I didn't ask for this to happen, you know," he said. "This wasn't what I was looking for."

"I know," she said, her voice as sad as his.

"She never got to be a little girl," Cheever said.

Rachel wondered whether he was talking about Helen, or about Diane, or both of them.

"So what do I do?" he asked, his voice desperate.

"The next time she emerges you tell her that your daughter is dead. You say that you want to speak with Helen."

"Simple, huh?"

"No," she said, shaking her head. "But necessary."

"If you asked anyone who knows me," he said, "if you had asked me this afternoon, I would have told you that I couldn't have acted that way."

"I believe you."

"I hope you do. I'm stronger than that."

"What occurred doesn't have anything to do with strength."

"But I'm willing to bet it makes you wonder what kind of a man I am. How I could have done that."

"No."

"I didn't know how far I would go for a single yesterday," he said. "Now I do."

"You won't do it again."

He didn't answer directly, just repeated his words, "For a single yesterday," then said, "I think about that a lot, you know. I'd give anything to go back to the day she died and tell her that I loved her. I'd be there in the end."

Rachel didn't say anything. Platitudes would have been

inadequate; analysis would have been inappropriate. Her silence frightened him.

"I haven't scared you away, have I?"

She shook her head, then offered her hand. For several seconds they squeezed each other's hand.

"One of these days," he said, "we're going to run out of wounds to show each other."

"Probably not any time soon," she said.

His laughter sounded a little less strained.

"I'm going to check on Helen now," she said.

At least this time he didn't have to call her back to explain. Cheever wasn't sure if he felt better for having talked with Rachel, but he was glad that there were no more secrets between them.

"Cheever!"

The alarm in her voice brought him running. Cheever didn't even stop to grab his gun. Rachel was at the front door. She was trying, unsuccessfully, not to tremble. "Helen's gone," she said, then pointed to the alarm box. "And the alarm's been turned off. Do you think that he . . . ?"

Cheever examined the front door. It was still locked, but the dead bolt was no longer in place. "Activate the alarm again," he said, "and stay here."

Picking up his department-issue Ruger, Cheever conducted his own search of the house. He examined sliding glass doors and windows, making his way around the house until he returned to the front door.

"No sign of entry," Cheever said, "forced or otherwise. I suspect Helen turned off the alarm."

"But why?" Rachel asked, "and where did she go?"

"I'll call the police," he said.

I am the police, he thought. But that wasn't what it felt like at the moment. Before making that call, Cheever analyzed his motives and behavior. He wanted to be sure he was doing the right thing. He needed to know he wasn't acting like a hysterical father afraid for his missing little girl.

THIRTY-SEVEN

She knew there were fewer voices to her Greek Chorus, but kept having trouble remembering why that was so. The Fates had vanished, and so had Caitlin. She felt scared. It was as if she were leaking life essence. Vying thoughts and impulses kept pulling at her, each trying to direct her to a different purpose. She tried to hold onto one or two things while this civil war raged, but everything kept slipping away from her.

Instinct kept her walking. In a moment of clarity she wondered whether she would end up like a man she had once seen walking along a highway. He had been leaning over a shopping cart, looked as if he were attached to its frame. He moved forward like an empty-eyed automaton. It was clear he didn't know where he was going. He was just moving. That's what she was doing.

The image vanished, replaced by another and then another, a kaleidoscopic offering of the past and present. She couldn't be sure what was real and what wasn't. At times she felt she was floating instead of walking along the residential streets. The way was dark, clouds getting in the way of the mostly full moon. She noticed lights approaching. A car, she initially thought, but as it came closer she saw it was a truck. Headlights picked her out, then the brights were turned on her. She stopped walking, couldn't move, felt like a blinded deer. The pickup slowed down, then came to a stop.

A window opened. Over a rumbling engine a voice asked, "You need help?"

She was blinded, and couldn't see who was doing the asking. There was only his voice. It sounded friendly.

He spoke again: "You need a ride?"

"Yes," she said, suddenly decided.

"Where you going?"

"Downtown," she said, not pausing to think.

"Hop in."

He kept his brights on. She shielded her eyes while walking in front of the pickup. The truck was jacked up, riding high enough on oversized tires that she had to step up on a running board, then pull herself up to the passenger seat. The driver offered her a hand and a smile, but Helen accepted neither. She closed the door behind her, then tried to make herself as small as possible huddling next to the door. That amused the driver. She could see his white teeth flashing. The truck pulled away from the side of the road, its big wheels crunching the gravel.

"Name's Travis," he said.

She could smell the alcohol on his breath. Though he wasn't in uniform, it was clear he was military, probably Navy. He had the short hair and trimmed mustache and attitude of enlisted men she knew.

"You got a name?"

"Lots of 'em," she said.

He laughed. She could feel his eyes on her, but she didn't look at him, just stayed huddled next to the door.

"Here I'm driving the back roads hoping to not run into the cops," he said, "and I run into you. Not that I'm wanted or anything. It's just that I had a little to drink. Last thing I expected to see on the road was someone like you."

She didn't respond, didn't tell him anything. But he figured he knew her type even without her talking. A John had probably just kicked her out of his car. But not damn likely before she had provided a service.

"So what were you doing out here?"

"Walking," she said.

He laughed again. "Funny one, aren't you?"

She didn't answer. That's a first, he thought. Hooker playing hard to get. "I thought you was a ghost at first. Then I figured I was really shitfaced. But you're real enough, aren't you?"

His hand reached out to her, touched her shoulder, lingered a moment.

"Oh, yeah, you're real enough."

He reached inside his pocket, pulled out a cigarette, lit it, then took a deep puff. "You a professional?" he asked, his question punctuated by smoke.

"Professional what?"

He laughed again, the easy laugh of someone drunk, and shook his head. "Oh, you'll do," he said. "Yeah, you'll do."

They approached an intersection. Travis looked around, turned onto a sleepy road.

"This isn't the way," she said.

"Thought we could find ourselves a quiet spot to talk," he said. "I saw you walking along and I said, 'Here comes manna from heaven.' Or is that womanna?"

"I don't want to stop."

"I got money, honey," he said, as if that decided everything.

He pulled the truck over, parked near two large eucalyptus trees. The nearest house was a hundred yards off and could barely be seen through the trees and the darkness.

She reached for the door handle, but he grabbed her hand. "You're not being very friendly," he said.

"Let go."

"Relax, sister. You don't need to run off. We haven't even had the chance to get to know one another yet."

"Let go." Her voice was louder and deeper this time. More demanding.

"Just calm down, honey," he said. "I'll drive you downtown in a bit. This is just our little detour. Time for games."

"Let go."

He was too drunk to notice how her voice had kept changing. Had he been more aware, he would have heard the threat. With her free hand, she gouged her thumb into his right eye. He raised both hands to defend himself, but her nails were already raking his face, and her teeth already snapping at him. He grabbed one of her hands, but she was much stronger than he ever would have expected. She pulled away, and with the flat of her palm smashed his nose. He tried to cover up, but her hands kept finding vulnerable spots, kept hurting him. What really scared him, though, was her voice.

"We'll play my game," she said, in a bass voice, a man's voice. Or a demon's. "Do you like my game?"

For a moment she backed off, but it was a tactical maneuver. She swung one of her legs up and into his ribs. He heard a cracking, and a moment later felt the pain. He grabbed at her leg, but that didn't stop her attack. She kneed him, and kept coming at him with her hands and teeth. And words.

"You like my game?"

He reached for the door handle. This time she was the one who tried to stop him. Travis suddenly felt very sober and very scared. He pushed with his weight against the door and fell to the ground. Still, she kept coming at him, jumping down from the truck atop him.

Rolling on the ground, he managed to get to his feet and

then he started running. "Help!" he screamed. "Help."

He had picked a spot to park where no one could easily hear them. Now he regretted his choice.

Cronos decided not to run after him. His response wasn't merciful. He wanted to hurt the man, felt like his punishment had only started, but there were others who needed his disciplining even more.

Free at last, Cronos thought. He had been bottled up for so long. They only allowed him out when the weakling was in danger, and then only for a short time. But not anymore. There were fewer of them now. They couldn't dictate to him any longer. He was the ruler. And there were so many things he needed to do without delay.

He got in the pickup, turned on the engine, and drove off. There were still dangers out there, he thought. Challengers. Obstacles to be removed. His impulse was just to attack. That's what he was best at doing. Hurting and terrorizing. Most of the time he didn't have to think, or want to, but he needed to plan the night. She was good at things like that. The Trickster. Snakes have their purposes. He distrusted words. They were for weaklings. Fools yap. He didn't talk much, he just did. He reacted. She could do the talking. She'd like that.

Cronos parked in front of the loft. He got out of the truck, then decided to let her out. But he kept control, didn't relinquish his rule, although she pretended to act as if he weren't there, and as if she weren't afraid of him, but she was. He could sense how Eris thought she was smarter than everyone else. As if that mattered. Breaking necks and smashing bones. That mattered. That was all the clever you needed to be.

He didn't have keys, and would have broken down the security door, but she showed him another way. Mike was another artist living in the building who was currently using his loft as a living space, though he claimed it was only temporarily. She buzzed him, finally got a sleepy response, and said, "Hey, Mike, this is Holly-wood. Forgot my keys. Open Sesame, please."

They were buzzed inside. After climbing up the stairs another locked door faced them, but she retrieved the spare key under the fire extinguisher and opened the door to the loft. Cerberus greeted them at the door. As they entered, the dog looked unsure. He backed off, wagging his stub of a tail slightly. Cerberus sniffed the air from a distance. The scent he picked up didn't bring him any closer.

"Hey, flea face," she said.

The dog whined, came forward, and let her run her hand over his head, but then he backed away again. Eris wished she could get away that easily. She was also only too aware of the other presence. He was like this big shadow that didn't allow light. She felt him pressure her to make the calls. Eris acceded, but decided she'd do it her way.

She sat down next to the phone. *They* sat down. She dialed the number, then picked up some scratch paper and started sketching. Or someone started sketching. Eris usually didn't care about drawings, or paintings, but this was one time she felt compelled to doodle. Even before anyone answered, Eris felt as if she had dialed into a party line. He was there listening, hearing everything she said and heard and thought. Jason Troy picked up the phone, answered with the tone of someone disturbed from sweet dreams.

"Daddy?"

She used a little girl's voice.

"Yes, I know. I'm sorry it's so late."

Sorry. She wanted to laugh.

"It's just that I've been up thinking."

He responded to her words, suddenly didn't sound sleepy anymore.

"I've been remembering all these things . . ."

He sounded as if she had prodded him with something hurtful. And she had. The memories.

". . . and I didn't know whether I should call you, or the police."

Now she was pushing him. And he was afraid to push back.

"I know Detective Cheever would like to talk with me. The two of you have met, haven't you?"

Eris enjoyed the goading. She pretended sweetness while inserting the knife.

"I think he'd like to hear about these awful things I've been remembering . . ."

She was pleased with herself, enjoyed playing with him.

"Oh, it wasn't that long ago, Daddy. I remember it now. I remember it like it was . . ."

Was he sweating? she wondered. Was his face flushed?

"Tonight? Now? I don't know."

The old man talked very quickly.

"No, not your house, Daddy. Somewhere else. Why don't we meet at Kate Sessions Park, Daddy?"

He didn't want to go there. Eris pretended to waver, but she was only playing with him. That's what he always said, didn't he? Playing.

It was then that Cronos intervened, forcing Eris into saying his words. Into calling his tune.

"I'll be at Kate Sessions Park in half an hour, Daddy. You better be there, too."

Eris hung up the phone and tried to pretend she was independent of his commands, but he opened his mind up to her, just a little, enough so that she responded. She dialed the number, but all the while kept drawing as if she wasn't concerned. A woman answered.

"I saw something," Eris said.

The woman started asking questions, but Eris ignored her.

"I saw Bonnie Gill being murdered. I was there. I was hidden. But I've been afraid to come forward. I don't want any publicity. And I don't care about the reward . . ."

Eris sounded frightened. Troubled. The voice on the other line tried calming her, tried asking her questions.

"I don't want to give out my name," Eris said. "I just want to tell what I know and then disappear. I saw the murderer. I got a good look at him . . ."

The operator asked for a description, but Eris pretended to be hysterical.

"You're not listening!" she shrieked. "I can't be involved. Calling you was probably a mistake . . ."

The voice worked hard at assuring her that it wasn't a mistake.

"I've written everything down," said Eris. "It should answer all your questions. I've got it sitting here. I just want to get rid of the notebook so I won't have to think about this anymore."

Calm down, the woman said. Let's just talk . . .

"No more talk," Eris said. "I figure if I give you my notes then maybe I can sleep again. Live again. I'll be at Kate Sessions Park in an hour. Send somebody there."

The operator started protesting.

"In an hour. That's Kate Sessions Park in Pacific Beach. And I don't want cops or anyone like that. I'm not answering questions. I'm just there to hand something off. You got it?"

The operator did, but she tried to prolong the conversation. At his directive, Eris hung up the phone. She was a little slower to drop the pencil. Enough doodling, she thought. Enough of being someone else's mouthpiece.

Co-consciousness was the shits, she decided. Eris liked being in total control, didn't enjoy having to share sensibilities with a black hole. She whistled for Cerberus, and he reluctantly came to her. After putting a leash around his collar, she walked him downstairs to the truck. He hopped up into the bed of the truck, his nails scrabbling along the metal. She hoisted herself up into the bed as well, tied his leash to a hook, then lowered herself down.

Cronos didn't care about the dog. But he'd had enough of her. He let her start the engine, and then she started screaming.

Hurting the other man had whetted his appetite. Now it was her turn. She was one of the pretenders to his throne. He, and he alone, would have control. He would rule. First the girl had left, then the Fates. It was her turn to go now. He was Cronos. He had eaten his own children. He was used to dining on himself.

Eris tried to escape, but it was like seeking escape from herself. There was no appealing to him. There was only his blind consuming rage. It was like talking to a furnace. She tried to put barriers between them, but he tore them down. Oh, gods, he was eating her mind. That's what it felt like. She felt herself coming apart. Leaving . . .

In the bed of the moving truck, Cerberus howled, and then howled again.

THIRTY-EIGHT

When they passed the second patrol car, Cheever turned to Rachel and asked, "Had enough?"

His question broke a long silence between them. He was frustrated at their failed search. For half an hour they'd driven around Point Loma looking for Helen. With the police now out looking for her as well, it seemed as if the two of them were literally just spinning their wheels.

"I suppose."

Rachel could hear the passive-aggressive tone in her response. Neither one of them was in a good mood. She was worried about Helen and angry at herself. Rachel kept second-guessing what she had done. *I shouldn't have brought Helen to my house. I should have made sure she had round-the-clock help. And I never should have had a man over while Helen was in my home, especially someone she knew.* Rachel wondered which one of Helen's personalities was out. She hoped it was the Maenads. They usually only wanted to dance and party.

Cheever was doing his own self-recriminating while playing a similar guessing game. That was the major reason for the uneasy quiet that had grown between them. They both felt guilty about their thoughts. Cheever kept imagining Diane going out into the night. Would she be as helpless as she seemed? And what would have motivated her to leave the house, to leave him?

Even though they had supposedly agreed to end the search, Cheever kept driving along the residential streets, and both of them continued to look right and left.

"Helen could be anywhere," Rachel finally said. "She could be on this street hiding in the foliage and we'd never see her."

"She could certainly stay lost," he said, "if she had a mind to."

"Is that supposed to be funny?"

Cheever shook his head. "No, it was just an unfortunate choice of words."

He sounded dejected enough that Rachel regretted the sharpness of her response. "Or my unfortunate need to misinterpret," she said.

The tension between them eased. Both of them found it a little easier to breathe. "I keep thinking about where she could have gone," Cheever said. Or at least, he thought, that was one of the things he kept thinking about.

"She doesn't have any money," Rachel said. She had seen to that detail, though at the moment Rachel wasn't sure whether that was a good thing or not. "But she does have lots of friends, especially in Ocean Beach. If she hitchhiked, she could have hooked up with them already. Or she could have met up with them at one of her clubs."

Cheever checked the time. It was five minutes after two. Last call had already come and gone. "Too late to look for her in the clubs," he said. "They're all closed now."

Rachel had another idea. "What about her loft?"

"The motivation of home sweet home?"

"More than that. Her art's there."

The Taurus responded to Cheever's right foot, rapidly

picking up speed. Cheever sped through the deserted residential streets, cut over to Rosecrans, then turned onto Harbor Drive and didn't spare the gas heading into downtown San Diego. Cops can speed with impunity, but even without a badge he would have been safe that night. Only a handful of cars were on the road. The deserted streets reminded Cheever of too many other nights.

"Because of my job I get called out a lot in the middle of the night," he said. "Sometimes it seems like I'm the only person awake in the whole county. The whole world."

"How does that make you feel?"

"Alone. Jealous. I wonder why I'm up and everyone else is asleep. I have fantasies about being one of those people nestled in bed and oblivious to everything. A few times I've had to stifle this impulse to honk the horn and shout out Paul Revere kind of messages."

"The British are coming?"

"No. Something that would really wake people up, like, 'A tax increase is coming.'"

Rachel smiled, turning away to look out into the night. She took note of the empty streets and lifeless ports and said, "I'm not used to seeing everything look so deserted."

"You notice it even more on the freeways," he said. "I remember one Christmas Eve coming back from a homicide and everything was so absolutely still. Must be about a million people that live along the route that takes me home, but I was the only one out. I don't think I ever felt so alone as that night."

Cheever wondered what it was about her that kept bringing out his admissions. Drive and shut up, he thought. He pushed hard on the accelerator along Broadway, ignored the traffic lights, and turned on Seventh Avenue. As they pulled up to Helen's building, Cheever noticed something.

"There are lights on in her loft," he said.

They hurried out of the car. Cheever had Helen's keys,

courtesy of his dog-walking. Before opening the security door, Cheever pulled out his gun.

"Is something wrong?" Rachel asked.

"Just taking precautions," Cheever said, but he still made a point of preceding her up the stairs.

His ascent, Rachel noticed, was a very vigilant one. He motioned for her to stop at the top of the stairwell landing.

"You stay here," he whispered, "while I check out her loft."

"Why? And I don't need to hear an encore about 'taking precautions.'"

Cheever closed his mouth before opening it again, apparently swallowing the reply he had originally intended. "Cerberus isn't barking," he said. "He's too much of a watchdog to have let us get this far without sounding an alarm."

While Rachel considered his words, Cheever walked to the doorway, his footsteps slow and careful. Positioning himself to the right of the door, he reached out with his left hand to work on the locks, but that proved to be unnecessary. The door was unlocked. He inched it open, then surveyed the room with two quick bobs of his head before going inside. After less than a minute, he returned to the doorway and motioned for Rachel to approach.

"It appears that Helen was here," he said. "She must have taken the dog with her."

"Maybe they're only out for a walk."

Unconvinced: "Maybe."

Rachel followed him into the loft. She had attended several of Helen's exhibitions, but had never been inside any of her residences. While she walked around examining Helen's loft, Cheever turned his attention to a piece of paper. He was still looking at it a minute later when Rachel came up and stood at his side.

"What do you make of this?" he asked.

Helen had used the back of a large, white mailing envelope as scratch paper to draw on. There was a penciled sketch of a sickle, as well as a bulbous-looking knife. Both objects appeared to be bloodied. Faces lined the four corners of the envelope. Behind one of the faces were deep shadows; behind a profile of another was the sun. The face in darkness glowered; the one in light looked angelic. The two other faces weren't as easy to read; one looked determined, almost obsessed, while the other was watchful. In the middle of the sketch, encased between several boxes, were the numbers 7867.

"Helen's scribbles," Rachel said. "I often supply her with a pad during her sessions with me. She talks and scribbles at the same time. Sometimes I compare her messages. What she says on paper doesn't always match what she's telling me."

"What do you mean?"

"Her hand often conveys a different story than her mouth."

"Do you trust her sketches more than her answers?"

"I find it helpful to examine both."

"How fast could she have sketched something like this?"

"A minute or two."

Rachel went back to looking at the drawing. "I think all four faces are Helen's," she finally said. "I believe the face in darkness, the angry face, belongs to Cronos. If Cronos is loose, I would approach Helen very, very, carefully."

"You think she'd be out of control?"

Rachel shook her head. "I think she'd be dangerous. Cronos isn't like any of the other alters. It's not a case of Eris wanting to come out and cause mischief and trouble. Cronos exists to hurt. He comes out to lord over others, to dominate with force, to punish."

"What about the other faces?"

"I'm fairly certain that the one who looks grim and resolved is Nemesis. She's not as unpredictable as Cronos, but can be every bit as deadly. Nemesis is out for justice, or what she perceives to be justice. That often means she emerges to avenge, and pursue that cause with vigor. I think there's some ambivalence in Helen about these forces being unleashed. You can see that in Pandora, the third face. She's watching everything that's happening. Notice how her eyes are looking everywhere. She's worried. Judging by all the tremors and squiggles and lines and distortions in this sketch, it appears that Helen's world is coming apart and Pandora knows that only too well."

Cheever looked at the sketch again, took notice of the waves and twists for the first time. He had just assumed they were artistic doodads. Now he could see how they added tension to the sketch. There was this sense of an impending eruption. Cheever was reminded of one of those Van Gogh self-portraits where it looked as if there was so much turbulence going on inside him that his head appeared to be in danger of exploding.

"You didn't identify the last figure," he said.

"She's in profile. I can't be sure."

"Guess."

"It could be a partial portrait of the face Helen is looking to find, her *after* picture that's still not complete. You'll notice she's in the sun. No more darkness, nothing hidden."

That sounded and felt right to Cheever. The sun and Helen's profile were the only parts of the sketch that weren't somehow distorted.

"What significance do you think there is in her drawing the sickle and the funny-looking knife?"

"I could only hazard the vaguest . . ."

"Disclaimer accepted."

"Zeus emasculated Cronos with a sickle. It could symbolize that event."

"Or symbolize someone set to challenge a tyrant?"

"Possibly."

"Or even a father?"

"That, too."

Cheever picked up the phone, pulled Professor Troy's number from his memory, and dialed it. He waited for four impatient rings, then had to hear out a message before being able to speak loudly.

"Dr. Troy, this is Detective Cheever. Please pick up the phone. I'd like to talk with you about a potential emergency."

Cheever waited for several seconds, then started to deliver the same message again when the machine cut him off. He called back a second time, and spoke even more loudly, but still the professor didn't get on the line.

"Either he's a heavy sleeper," Cheever said, "or he's out, or . . ."

Cheever didn't finish the thought. "You have any idea about the numbers written in the boxes?" he asked.

"Multiple boxes," she said.

"Pandora's boxes?"

"Possibly. Or it could just be doodling, the kind of thing we all do. Make boxes and stars and the like."

"Do the numbers mean anything to you?"

"No."

"Was Helen in the habit of writing down numbers on her other sketches?"

She shook her head. "Not that I remember."

Cheever found himself shaking his own head. Still, there was something familiar about the numbers. 7867.

The numbers suddenly kicked in. Cheever picked up the telephone and started dialing.

THIRTY-NINE

"Stop. For the love of God, stop."

"Is this the place?"

"I don't know. How could I possibly know?"

"How could you possibly not?"

"It was twenty years ago," he said.

Cronos reached for his collar, ready to pull the old man through the chaparral again. Jason Troy was already bloodied from being dragged through the chamise and manzanita. The underbrush had opened cuts on his face and arms, had added to the beating he had already suffered.

"No," Troy begged. "I think it was further down the wash. It was just above two or three scrub oaks, if they're still around."

Cronos shoved him forward. Jason Troy stumbled, but didn't fall. It was better not to fall. He had learned that already.

The sky had cleared, but it was still difficult to navigate through the chaparral by moonlight. Roots clawed at feet, and branches pulled. It was as close to a jungle as could be found in southern California. They pushed through a stand of laurel sumac, were pinched by manzanita, and then came out to a small opening. The arroyo appeared as a crack through the chaparral defense, an opening of sand and worn fissures and exposed red rock. Above and to the side of the wash were two scrub oaks.

Jason Troy sobbed in relief. "Eureka," he said. "From the Greek. 'I have found it.' Archimedes . . ."

The slap in his face stopped his lecture. Tears welled up in his eyes.

"Dig."

"I have no shovel . . ."

"Dig."

Professor Troy didn't contradict that voice. It came from his daughter's mouth, but it didn't belong to his daughter. He made his way up the incline, went about ten yards past the oaks. He hoped they were the right oaks, but was afraid to voice any doubts. He had known better than to select an area anywhere too near the wash line, afraid of what the rains and erosion might expose. He looked around, made his best guess, then dropped to his knees and started his digging into the soil. His tears started falling, moistening the tough earth. He wiped sand and dirt out of his mouth. His shoulders shook, but he didn't sob aloud. He remembered how it hadn't been easy before, even with a shovel. Then, as now, they had seemed so far from civilization. But that was illusory. Sounds of the outside world sometimes carried into the elfin forest. An approaching car could be heard.

"Company," Cronos said.

For once, he sounded pleased.

FORTY

It wasn't until they were in Cheever's Taurus speeding along the downtown streets that Rachel asked her question: "Where are we going?"

"Kate Sessions Park," he said. "In Pacific Beach."

Cheever didn't volunteer any other information. His attention was on his driving, and whatever he was driving toward. The Taurus hit eighty miles an hour on the on-ramp to Interstate 5, and then the speedometer climbed even more when they gained the freeway itself. Cheever turned on his brights, warning off the vehicles ahead of them. Rachel remembered her drive away from death earlier in the evening and shivered. Cheever must have noticed.

"How are you feeling?" he asked.

"That's my question," she said.

"You're contagious," he said, but didn't make that sound like a bad thing.

"I'm wondering what we're racing toward. I'm trying not to be afraid."

"Macaws," Cheever said.

"Macaws?"

"When the nurse told me she'd seen those 'big parrots' outside of your house, I figured she needed glasses. I didn't expect macaws to be in your neighborhood. And when you're not looking for something, there is a good chance you won't see it, even if it's right under your nose. I should have seen it before."

He didn't elaborate on what "it" was, only reached for his radio and turned the frequency to Northern Division's dispatch. Cheever picked up the microphone, identified his unit number and name, and was acknowledged by the dispatcher and told to go ahead.

"This is a Code Three," Cheever said. "I'd like all available units to proceed to Kate Sessions Park in Pacific Beach. Repeat, this is a Code Three to Kate Sessions Park."

The dispatcher's voice was the only one to answer Cheever's call. "Do you want me to put out an all units call, Detective?" she asked. "Another Code Three just came in and has all available units tied up."

"That's not necessary," he said. "I'll be waiting at the entrance to the park unless the situation dictates otherwise. I'm driving an unmarked gray Taurus, license Two Sam Adam Victor Seven Four Zero."

After his transmission was acknowledged, Cheever turned the radio down low.

"What's a code three?" Rachel asked.

"It's a hot call. It gets priority. Cops give it an emergency status."

"Did the other units hear you?"

"They heard. And it's on their computer."

"But right now they've responded to another Code Three?"

He nodded, not taking his eyes from the road. She could only guess at their speed. The Taurus's speedometer only went to a hundred, and they were over that. The car was shaking.

"I still don't understand what all of this has to do with macaws," she said.

"Nothing, really. They're just sort of a symbol. The birds popped in my head when I realized what the numbers seven-eight-six-seven translated to."

"I'm still short that explanation also."

"They're the last four digits in the Carnation Fund's hot line. But most places they were just printed as S-T-O-P. Helen called the number and said she had information. She insisted upon the meeting that's about to happen."

"I'm still lost."

"Helen, or Cronos, or Nemesis, or whoever, wants to confront Bonnie Gill's murderer. She's called Rollo Adams out."

"The developer?"

Cheever nodded. "His paid operator finally admitted that he's the one on his way to Kate Sessions Park. Helen would have known that. She told the operator she could describe the murderer, but pretended she didn't know who he was. Rollo's had a busy day. He attacked you earlier tonight."

Rachel wanted to tell Cheever to slow down. If he was right, they were racing toward the man who had tried to kill her. That was the last direction she wanted to be headed. Rachel stifled the impulse to ask Cheever to drop her off along the way. They weren't driving along at breakneck speed to get to Adams, she remembered. It was Helen they were trying to reach. But still, she couldn't help but hope that police cars would be waiting for them at the park.

"When you told me your assailant left his mask on," Cheever said, "that bothered me. Why did he do that? From what you said the mask was saturated with pepper spray. It must have been stinging like hell. There was a reason the mask wasn't removed. Rollo was afraid someone might see him, recognize him."

Cheever slowed the Taurus down to seventy-five miles an hour, took the Grand exit with squealing tires.

"The Carnation Fund," he said with disgust. "The fox in charge of the hen house. I assumed the group was a bunch of amateur do-gooders. But Adams had his reasons for supplying the fund with their own telephone number, and paying for a twenty-four-hour hot line. From the beginning he made sure the police weren't the first referral, and that Crime Stoppers wasn't brought in. Adams wanted control of all the early information. It was his way of ensuring his safety. He was even privy to our investigation. That's how he knew to identify himself as Cheever over the intercom at your office. He had heard others call me that."

"But why did he kill Bonnie Gill?"

Cheever shook his head. "I don't know. Not yet. On the surface of things it doesn't make sense. But then neither did all those macaws flying around your backyard. Dig enough, and answers are found."

Answers, she thought, or bodies? Rachel didn't voice her fears. There was a red light at Garnet, but Cheever drove through it and headed west. Rachel tried not to look at the blur of storefronts along Garnet. Cheever braked hard just before Lamont, then turned right, the wheels of the Taurus squealing at the assault. The commercial district quickly turned to residential—or geological. They passed by the streets of stone, Felspar and Emerald and Diamond and Chalcedony and Beryl. Rachel noticed her clenched hands stood out like white patches in the darkness.

"Why'd she want to meet him here?" Cheever asked aloud. "It's not public. It's going to be dark. It's as if she wanted to put herself in danger."

Rachel's voice was calmer than she would have expected. "That's not how Cronos would think. He sees himself as stronger than anyone. I believe his personality evolved out of Helen's identification with an aggressor. Cronos thinks he's all-powerful. Cronos commands. He has no compassion, and has no qualms about inflicting pain upon others. It's significant that Cronos is the only male in Helen's repertoire. I suspect that when Helen becomes Cronos she in many ways becomes her abuser. But I also know that Cronos is more than that. He's this powerful but terrible father figure in Greek mythology. She becomes that myth."

"Myths die hard," Cheever said.

But not mortals, Rachel thought, as they drove through three stop signs. Cheever didn't even slow for them.

"If Cronos is out," Rachel said, "then we have more to be worried about than Rollo Adams. Cronos is the most volatile of all Helen's personalities."

Cheever nodded. "I'll be careful," he said.

"We should wait for backup."

She kept changing his "I" into "we." At another time Cheever would have welcomed that, but not now.

"If the police aren't already at the scene," he said, "you're going to have to stay in the car and wait for them."

"No."

"They'll need someone to explain what's going on. That only makes sense, Rachel. You know it does."

Her mouth was opened to say "no" again, but she didn't say anything.

The Taurus climbed up a hill that signaled the ascent to the park. There were no reassuring police beacons at its entryway. There was only darkness. Cheever pulled the car over just before the park entrance. He turned off the ignition and put his keys into Rachel's hand. For a moment he paused, squeezing her hand, then he released the hold.

"Keep the doors locked," he warned.

"Be careful."

He stepped out of the car, and moved off into the night. She tried to follow him with her eyes, but he quickly disappeared. It was as if he had been swallowed up by the underworld. Try as she might to surrender that image, she could not.

FORTY-ONE

In the distance Cheever could hear a dog barking. Cerberus? There was only one road in and out of the park. On both sides of the lane were greenbelts with vast stretches of lawn. Cheever decided to investigate the dog's baying. He walked the lower path, the trail taking him alongside a copse. It was a decidedly roundabout way to get to the park's eastern parking lot, but Cheever figured it was a route where no one would be able to see him.

The dog's increased frenzy made Cheever reconsider his indirect approach. Why was the animal so agitated? From a distance, Cheever could see that there were two vehicles in the parking lot, a pickup truck and a sedan. The lighting was too poor for him to make out anything else. Cheever decided to cut across the grass field and work his way up the slope. He stayed low, his back hunched down, his knees close to the ground. He knew it would make more sense to wait for backup, but he didn't slow down, didn't give in to the pain and strain put on his posture, or the temptation to rest. Helen could be in trouble.

He approached the rise, crawled the last few feet up.

The grass was wet enough that it soaked his shirt and pants. A shiver ran the length of his body. When it passed, Cheever raised his head above the crest of grass until he was eye level with the road. He had come out about fifty yards west of the two vehicles. They were parked side by side. Although there didn't appear to be anyone in them, or near them, the damn dog was still raising a ruckus. Someone or something was pushing the dog's buttons, but Cheever still couldn't see anything . . .

The attack came from his blind side. He heard something at the last instant, turned his head just as the foot caught him under his jaw. His neck whipped back and he fell backward. He tried to get up immediately, but had to fight both his assailant and the incline. Cheever was kicked a second time in the face, a blow that connected with his left eye. He tried reaching for his gun, and just managed to clear it from his holster when it was kicked out of his hand. He rolled on the ground, desperately patting the grass around him, but couldn't find the gun. His back was stomped, and his ribs kicked. Though gasping for air, he still fought back, turning over just as a leg was being swung at him again. He pushed up and kicked out, dropping his attacker, and then threw himself on the toppled form. He threw a punch, connected, and was throwing another when he realized who was beneath him.

"Helen," he said.

He was both right and wrong. His hesitation allowed Cronos to buck him off. Cheever tried to fight a defensive battle, and things went from bad to worse. The detective slipped on the wet grass, and Cronos made him pay, kicking him savagely. Cheever covered up, but not completely. Cronos saw his exposed collarbone and moved to stomp it, but the leg never came down . . .

Nemesis emerged, and slowly lowered her foot. This was not justice, she thought. The detective had only been trying to assist her host body.

From out of the darkness came a laugh. "Why stop now?" asked Rollo Adams.

Nemesis didn't hesitate. She went straight for him and he shot her twice. She fell near his feet. Her hand stretched toward him, clawing the grass. She tried to pull herself forward, but her body failed her. With vengeance too impossibly far away, Nemesis disappeared. And then a little girl started crying for all the pain she had suffered and all the hurt her body was carrying.

In the distance Cerberus howled, lamenting the terrible agonizing of his young mistress.

"Daddy," she cried. "Where are you? Daddy, I hurt so much."

"Here," Cheever said. "Right here."

He walked toward her, paying no attention to the gun. Nothing was going to stop him. He went to her, got down on his knees and took her hands so that he could be close to her.

"Daddy, I'm so cold."

His tears fell on her face. He hadn't cried for so long that he couldn't even remember what it felt like. A stream came out of him.

"I'm here to warm you," he said.

"Daddy, I can't move."

She tried to mute her whimpers, tried to be brave, and that made it all the harder for him.

"Yes, you can," he said. "All you have to do is think of where you want to go and you'll be there. Can you picture that place? Can you feel its sunshine and warmth?"

"Are you there with me?"

The gun was pointed at his face. There was enough light that he could see the smirk on Adams's face.

"Yes."

"I feel so strange, Daddy. I feel so light."

"I love you," he said, his voice choking.

She must have waited to hear those words for a long

time, as long as he had waited to say them, and yet they were words meant for that moment, meant for each other as much as for any ghosts of the past.

"I love you," she said. Her words were weak.

In the distance, Cerberus barked furiously, as if trying to keep something at bay, as if trying to protect her from something that was approaching. But then he howled, a cry full of pity and anguish, and howled again.

Helen Troy closed her eyes. She didn't move. To all appearances, her journey was over. Cheever took a deep breath, then exhaled more than he had taken in.

"I prefer a knife to a gun," Adams said, his tone conversational, as if he were discussing the weather. "I used to butcher pigs with a knife, knew how to stick 'em so that they couldn't even squeal. But I usually didn't do it that way. I liked to hear them squeal."

Cheever didn't say anything. He knew he should be planning something, stringing Adams along. Help would be there soon. But he felt too numb.

"It's just business," Adams said, referring to the trigger he was about to pull. "There was talk that I had put my money down on the wrong horses, that I had made some stupid investments downtown. I needed to show them I hadn't blown it. That's what everyone was whispering. The Carnation District's going to prove that I knew exactly what I was doing. We'll see who's snickering then. Nothing stands in the way of my business."

Or in the way of your pride, Cheever thought. He waited for death. He thought about trying to jump Adams, but he was so tired that even death didn't excite him. His marathon was run and he was out of strength. He thought about Rachel, hoped she'd be safe, and wished there was a way for her to know that he thought about her at the end.

Cheever never heard the approach. He became aware of the attack only when Adams screamed. When he looked up Cerberus was already ripping into his arm. The dog appeared to be myth incarnate, the watchdog from Hades with a mission. Pluto had a need for another soul. The dog's eyes were red, surreal, and his bared teeth were already awash in blood.

Adams fought desperately. He had lost his gun at Cerberus's first lunge, but tried to hold the dog off with his hands and feet and body.

"Get away! Get away!"

But neither Adams's words nor his blows deterred Cerberus. The dog kept springing at him, rending whatever flesh was available. He forced Adams back, lunging, feinting, biting, and finally dropping the man to his knees. His level. The dog pressed his advantage. Adams tried holding off the dog's jaws with his hands, but it was as if Cerberus really had three heads, all of them snapping.

"Help me!" he screamed at Cheever. "For the love of God, help me."

But Cheever didn't move to help him. His attention was on Helen, or most of it. The dog didn't have Adams's talent, didn't know how to "stick 'em" so his squeals couldn't be heard. The man squealed plenty while the dog sent him to hell.

It was Rachel who led the police to where they were. On one side of Helen was Cheever, and on the other was Cerberus. The dog licked her face while Cheever performed CPR. He kept breathing in and breathing out, refusing to give her up to death. Between breaths he gasped, "Don't let her pass through the gates, Cerberus. Don't let her in." And the dog would stop his licking to reply with a whimper.

Cheever didn't give up trying to breathe life into Helen until the paramedics took her away.

FORTY-TWO

Police had their hands full. Bodies kept turning up at Kate Sessions Park. The present and the past kept merging.

The presence of Jason Troy's sedan in the parking lot prompted the police to search the entire park for the professor. Just as day was breaking, they found Troy deep in the chaparral still busy at work. He was digging with a rock. His fingers and hands were bloodied, but he seemed unmindful of that. He had partially uncovered a small skeleton. Kathy Dwyer's. The police helped him finish the job. The professor said he'd talk, but asked that Cheever be the one to interview him.

They met a little after nine at the downtown station. Cheever had come from the hospital, had left Helen to talk with her father. The irony wasn't lost on him. Both men looked like they should have been in hospitals themselves.

"How is Helen?" Troy asked.

"She's survived one operation, but the doctors say they're going to have to go in again. They're waiting for her to stabilize before they do."

"I would be there with her," Troy said, "except that the

constabulary is insisting that I answer other questions first."

"Skeletons make us curious," Cheever said.

"The body is Kathy Dwyer's," he said. "I buried her twenty years ago."

"I'll need to read you your rights," Cheever said.

Troy waved him off. "I've already consented to speak with you freely, and of my own accord, and on the record," he said.

Cheever Mirandized him anyway, then asked, "Did you kill Kathy Dwyer?"

"No. Kathy's death was a tragic accident."

"Tell me about the accident."

"Katie and Helen were playing downstairs. I was with them. My wife awoke from a drunken stupor. She had been mixing pills and alcohol and awoke very disoriented. Her speech was slurred and her coordination was unbalanced. She was carrying a vodka bottle in her hand. For whatever reason, Delores became incensed. She broke the bottle, and then started waving the broken hilt around in a threatening manner. I suppose Delores slipped. Her makeshift weapon pierced poor Katie . . ."

"Where?" Cheever asked.

"In the chest. It must have caught a vein or artery near her heart. There was blood everywhere."

The third wound, Cheever thought. The one Hygeia wanted to take on. The one Helen showed to the world.

"Go on."

"My wife broke down when she saw what she had done. She tried to cut her own wrist, but I disarmed her. At the same time I tried to help Kathy, but it was clearly too late."

"What'd you do then?"

"I medicated my wife, and put her in bed. I debated calling the police, but I knew Delores had suffered too much already. I made the decision that I know in retrospect was very wrong. I buried Kathy Dwyer in Kate Sessions Park."

"When did you bury Kathy?"

"In the early evening. I went out driving. I pretended to be looking for Kathy. By that time the entire neighborhood was out searching for her."

"Was Helen with you?"

"Yes."

"Weren't you afraid Helen was going to tell someone what really happened?"

"That's why I kept her near to me. I didn't trust her to say the right thing."

"You mean the wrong thing."

"Over time I knew she would come to understand."

"How did you manage to keep her silent for so long?"

"I worked on her story over and over again. After a time, I think even Helen began to believe that Kathy never came over that day. Helen stayed home with us all week, but no one thought that was unusual. Most of the parents on the block also kept their children home."

"Did Helen ask you questions about what happened?"

"She tried to, but I kept telling her that she had had a nightmare, and that if she persisted in such foolish talk terrible things could happen to her mommy and me. I said that if she told anyone her stories we could end up being taken away and never see her again."

"How did Kathy Dwyer come to be at your house in the first place?"

"I suppose she just wandered over. The world was more innocent in those days. Children were freer to come and go."

"What set your wife off?"

"I'm told that with drugs and alcohol . . ."

"Did she catch you abusing the children?"

"No. It wasn't abuse. It was . . ."

The professor stopped speaking.

"It was what?"

"Nothing. Everything happened as I have already explained it to you."

"You were vague about how Kathy was stabbed."

"That's because it was all so confusing at the time."

"But surely you've had enough time to sort matters out by now."

"I've tried not to think about it. We're talking twenty years ago."

"Think about it now, then."

There wasn't any compromise in Cheever's voice. During the professor's telling, Cheever realized he had already heard another version of this story. Helen had unknowingly shown it to Dr. Denton in the garden where Bonnie Gill was murdered.

"But I've told you . . ."

"I want to hear what happened when your wife entered the room."

"She was walking downstairs. Delores broke her bottle on the banister . . ."

"Purposely?"

"Yes."

Another image came to Cheever: Helen's painting of the drunken women and the title *Russian Roulette*. "Then what?"

"She started saying all sorts of incoherent things."

"Give me a few examples."

Troy wouldn't meet Cheever's eyes, only said, "I don't remember."

"So what do you remember?"

"She started jabbing with the bottle, using it like a weapon. I kept yelling for her to calm down."

"Where were the girls?"

"Helen was behind her."

"How'd she get there?"

"Delores had grabbed her and pushed Helen behind her."

"And where was Kathy?"

"Katie was with me. I was trying to protect her."

That wasn't how Dr. Denton had heard it. Mrs. Troy had been yelling for the girls to get behind her. She'd been incensed at her husband. "Did Kathy need protection?"

"Delores was acting like a madwoman . . ."

"And yet she was also acting as a protector. She had put Helen behind her. That would suggest she was afraid of something. Or someone."

"She was probably seeing pink elephants . . ."

"No," Cheever said. "I think she was seeing you. I think she caught you doing something you don't want to talk about."

Cheever got up from his chair. The interview room was small. But it was large enough for Cheever to act out what had happened to young Helen Troy and her friend. The murder of Bonnie Gill had made Helen remember another death, confuse the two perhaps. In a state of shock, she had pantomimed the tragedy of what her mother had done. He played out what Dr. Denton, and Helen, had showed him.

"Your wife was screaming 'No,' and 'Stop it.'" Cheever's voice was loud in the small room. "She was weaving around the room, but it was you she was after, you she was trying to subdue." His arms flailed as if battling ghosts. "She tried to use her glass shard like a sword. I suspect she was trying to cut your exposed genitals."

Cheever lunged a last time, brought his hand close to the professor's body. Troy flinched and turned away. "That's preposterous," he said.

"Is it?"

Troy didn't answer.

"Your wife kept calling for the girls," Cheever said. "She got Helen safely behind her, but she was still concerned about Kathy. I think she also wanted to hurt you.

She was mad enough to want to kill you. But something happened, didn't it?"

"I told you, she slipped . . ."

"Professor Troy, you didn't call me here to tell more lies, did you?

I think you asked for me because you were finally ready to tell the truth. You buried that poor little girl, and you helped unearth her skeleton. It's time to let go of all the skeletons."

Troy started to shrink, first his shoulders, then his head. "When Delores burst into the room it was all so confusing. I had Kathy by the arm. Delores came at me, and I moved away. I didn't mean to pull Kathy. I forgot I was even holding on to her."

"But she ended up being your shield, didn't she?"

"Unwittingly. I certainly didn't mean . . . I never . . ."

"Why don't you tell me the whole story? You'll feel better."

The professor opened his mouth, but then he closed it and shook his head.

"Your wife caught you sexually abusing the girls, didn't she?"

"No. It wasn't really that. Maybe it looked like it, but it wasn't."

"Why would it have looked like it?"

"Because the three of us were playing a game."

"What game?"

"It was a classical game. Educational, really. I was Zeus, that is, Zeus in disguise."

"What disguise?"

"A bird. That was one of Zeus's favorite transformations. He . . ."

"Tell me what Zeus was wearing."

"Some feathers. And a mask."

Cheever remembered that Helen had been bothered by

the birds. He could understand why. "How were you able to wear feathers?"

"I had this fabric, very gossamer, very fine, with feathers glued to it, soft, downy . . ."

"Was this a game you had played before?"

"Yes."

"What did you call it?"

"Leda and the Swan," he said.

Cheever remembered the Correggio painting, the swan with the very phallic neck. He remembered the way Troy had recited the Yeats poem, recalled his fervor and excitement. After all these years, and all the misery, the man was still turned on by his perverse memories. Cheever took a deep breath, willed himself to be in control.

"Did you wear clothes during this game?"

The professor turned away from Cheever's stare. "Look at almost any classical painting. All of the frolics are natural . . ."

"You were naked, weren't you?"

"It was in keeping with the spirit of the classical era," he said. "We combined play and mythology. It was really very innocent, just a game . . ."

"Had Katie Dwyer ever played that game before?"

"No. When Helen brought her over I remember being slightly annoyed. I had told Helen we would be playing Leda and the Swan, and then Katie was suddenly there. But Katie said she wanted to play the game too."

"How far did the game go?"

"I don't . . ."

"Did you force sexual relations on the girls?"

"Please don't say those kinds of things. You don't understand . . ."

"You were aroused, weren't you?"

"It was necessary for the swan," he said, allowing his admission as if pointing out the obvious. "That was part of the game. The swan's neck, you see. But it wasn't perverse . . ."

"What was it?"

"They petted the swan. That's all they did. That's all we did. You should be able to understand. You know about the power of mythology."

Cheever had heard enough. He wondered if he had ever felt so tired and empty before.

"I don't know about the power of mythology," Cheever said. "I'm still working that out. But I do know about the power of prison. And you should know I'm going to work to put your bird in a cage for the rest of your life."

FORTY-THREE

Cheever still didn't like hospitals, but for the better part of a week he'd been spending all of his spare time at one. He walked into the ICU, and saw that his lunch date was already inside finishing up a yogurt. Rachel moved her index finger up to her lips and motioned for silence. Cheever nodded.

Helen was asleep on the bed. Tubes ran in and out of her body. The bullets had ricocheted around her organs, seriously damaging her liver, spleen, and one of her kidneys. But Helen was a survivor. Rachel joined Cheever. They kissed, more than a peck, less than a display; a promise for later.

"She's exhausted," Rachel said. "I had a cancellation, and got here early. Pandora's not being silent anymore. She had a lot to say to me."

There were fewer personalities now. More deaths had come out of that one night than had been reported. The media's body count hadn't included Nemesis and Cronos and Diane. Rollo Adams had been their emphasis, and still was. The lead story in that morning's *Union-Tribune* had been a patchwork piece on Adams's financial dealings and his dark side, with all the hindsight sages coming out of the woodwork.

Cheever and Rachel walked out of the ICU, and settled themselves into some chairs in the waiting area. He had brought a sandwich, fooled with its wrapping, but discovered he wasn't really hungry.

"Read the article today?" he asked.

She shook her head.

"It was about Adams, but I think it missed the point. It made it sound as if he was financially desperate, but that wasn't really the case. Sure, he was losing money on his downtown holdings, but Adams was rich enough to be able to afford that."

"So what's the answer, Detective?"

"I don't know, Doctor. If I was to voice my speculations, I'd be venturing into your territory."

"The mind is the biggest world of all," she said. "Feel free to enter."

"Adams could afford to lose money," he said, "but to his thinking what he couldn't afford to lose was face. He lived for being the Golden Boy, and Golden Boys don't make mistakes. Adams didn't want to be a part of some low-income housing feel-good plan. He wanted glass and chrome and headlines, and decided Bonnie Gill stood between him and that. He wanted a downtown coup where everyone would acknowledge the brilliance of Rollo Adams. He wanted to be the man who made things happen."

Rachel considered Cheever's points.

"Jonathan Swift once wrote of such a man," she said, "a description that might apply to our Mr. Adams as well: 'Untroubled by the knowledge that he was a devil, he could not bear the suggestion that he was a dunce.'"

"How'd you get to be so smart?" Cheever asked.

"Figuring out matters before and during the difficulties

is the tough part. It's a lot easier speculating afterward. But I daresay you're right: Rollo Adams had to protect his world of illusion."

"And Helen Troy had to lose hers."

Rachel wondered whether she heard any wistfulness in Cheever's tone. She didn't think so. Cheever had told her how he had lost Diane a second time, but it wasn't a tale of mourning. He was more at peace with himself now than she had ever seen him. He accepted that his daughter was gone, his ghosts laid to rest.

"There were matters," Rachel said, "that Pandora wanted me to discuss with you."

"I haven't exactly been a stranger here," he said. "What's stopping her from talking directly to me?"

"She's afraid of your reaction. She thinks you might want to arrest her."

"Why?"

"She blames herself for Kathy's death. Or at least Nemesis always did. Now that Nemesis is gone, she's still trying to punish herself, or find others to do that."

"I'm confused."

"Helen encouraged Kathy to come over to her home. She's still not sure whether she brought her over in the hopes that Kathy's being there would spare her from having to play her father's game, or whether she made a conscious decision of offering Kathy up to her father. In some ways Helen believes that Kathy died for her sins. But that didn't stop Nemesis from punishing her all these years for being evil."

He let out a long sigh. "Poor Helen sounds like a textbook case of being self-destructive."

"Or a textbook case of coping. The little girl that was Helen couldn't go on. She tried to make order out of a horrendous world. How else could she cope with murder, and mayhem, and sexual abuse? How could she make sense of all those conflicting images? She wanted to scream, and she was told to be silent. She was betrayed, and yet was convinced she had done the betraying. And she wanted to punish, and be punished."

Neither of them spoke for a minute. Both considered all of the prisons of Helen Troy.

"What should I say when I see her?" Cheever asked.

"How about what you told her the other night?"

For a moment Cheever wondered at what he had said, then he remembered. "Tell her that I love her?"

"All of the doctors were sure Helen would die and that her recovery is nothing short of miraculous. She remembers what you said, you know. I think your words entered her worlds, all of them. And I believe they carried her through."

"Love conquering death," Cheever said. "Orpheus would be proud."

His tone was disparaging, but Rachel wouldn't allow him his deprecation. "Yes, he would," she said.

Cheever drew a deep breath. For a moment he thought he'd lose it, feared that his breath might turn into a sob. Then he looked at Rachel and she looked back. "I'll go tell her that," he said. "I'll tell her those very words. But first, I'm going to say them to you."

FORTY-FOUR

Cheever remembered how a friend had once tried to offer him sympathy over the death of his daughter, telling him, "Time heals all wounds." In his bitterness, Cheever had replied, "No, time infects all wounds."

It had been a long infection, causing a fever that he could never shake. Until now. His journey was done, he thought, after twenty long years. After a terrible siege. Like Odysseus, he had finally found his way back.

Helen wasn't released from the hospital for a month. When Cheever and Rachel drove Helen home, Cerberus was there waiting for her. Helen wasn't very ambulatory at first, so Cheever accepted the duty of Cerberus walking. For months, the dog was the only one in the loft who ever offered him an enthusiastic greeting.

Helen was subdued, much quieter than she had been before. One day she explained her silences to Cheever by saying, "There's less of me now." She often asked Cheever to pose for her. Usually he just had to sit. He was no longer as afraid to see how she drew him.

Her art had changed just as she had. It was simpler, and

371

less disturbing. On her sketch pads she didn't keep conjuring up demons from her past. Even the mythology was played down.

"She's not so immersed in what she was," Rachel explained. "Right now she's convalescing. Her body's healing, and so is her mind. She's getting to the point where she can live for the present. In time she might even be able to ponder her future."

"It beats the Fates doing the same," Cheever had said. There were some of Helen's personalities he didn't miss at all.

She had been out of the hospital for two months when Cheever first noticed the covered painting. It was positioned near the window that had the best morning light, and was the only piece of art Helen chose to shroud. Cheever didn't ask her what she was working on, but he had his suspicions. She never referred to the work, though it was clear that she covered up the painting whenever he came to visit, and took up the paintbrush again after he left.

Helen worked on getting well, and she worked on her painting. She kept shedding things along the way, sutures and crutches and stitches and canes and dressings and pills. It was as if she were shedding her skin. Six months after being shot, Helen announced to Rachel that she was physically well.

It wasn't her only announcement. In the middle of her session she told Rachel that her self-portrait of what she looked like before her parents were born was almost finished, and then she said, "I think we'll be ready soon, too."

After making that declaration, Helen changed subjects. She knew Rachel had heard, and knew that she understood.

Three days later, while gathered for an early Sunday dinner, Helen announced to both Rachel and Cheever that her painting was finished. Then, in a small voice, she said to Rachel, "Tell me about my integration."

Cheever had heard vestiges of that voice before: When

Caitlin had asked him about heaven; when Diane was dying and wanted to know about that better place. How must it be, he wondered, to leave behind other worlds and people that sheltered and protected you? He had once told Helen she was the bravest person he had ever met, and he had never had any reason to reconsider that.

"I've given a great deal of thought to the appropriate ceremony," Rachel said. "I know just how we'll proceed."

She took Helen's hands in hers. "It's the right decision," Rachel said. "I'm absolutely convinced of it. I have no doubts whatsoever."

"When should we do it?" Helen asked.

"Whenever you're ready."

Helen didn't say, "now." Maybe she couldn't. She only said, "We'll need to stop by my loft."

Cheever drove. The reason for the loft visit became apparent when Helen returned to the car holding her painting. It was still shrouded. She kept looking at it as they drove, as if the cloth weren't there. Maybe she knew the painting so well she could see it even through the covering.

Rachel also had Cheever make a stop. She picked up some firewood. Without announcing where they were going, she directed Cheever along their route. They ended up at Torrey Pines Beach in Del Mar. Nearby were the cliffs of the Torrey Pines Reserve. Rachel led them along the sand. The beach was mostly deserted. It was cool by Southern California standards, chilly enough to keep spoiled San Diegans away. Rachel stopped at a fire pit, and carefully positioned the wood. The sea breeze was no deterrent. Within two minutes she had a fire blazing away. The fire appeared to take in the essence of the setting sun. A lane of red ran along the Pacific, a red carpet along the blue ocean that went straight to their fire. The flames kept reaching higher.

"Of all the myths," Rachel said, "I can think of none that has tantalized me more than the story of the phoenix.

This was a bird like no other. It consumed itself by its own fire, and then rose from its own ashes, renewed once again.

"You are that phoenix, Helen. This fire symbolizes your baptism of flame, your renewal into a unified you. It is up to you to become that phoenix, to rise from your ashes reborn. Like that fabled bird, you willingly die to be born again."

Helen stood close to the fire. She swayed with the flames. In the growing darkness, the reflection played off of her eyes. Cheever stood close to her, afraid that she might throw herself into the flames. But instead she unveiled her painting.

It was Helen, but it wasn't. Her expression was focused into the distance, looking ahead. It was a familiar face, but one Rachel and Cheever had never seen before. It was Helen in another life, or perhaps a future life. She looked serious, but her lips were slightly upturned. Her blue eyes were opened wide and were clear. It was a magnificent painting, the work of an inspired artist.

She threw it into the fire.

The phoenix burned. Helen emerged.